The Glass Façade

by

Richard Cameron

Author of Famous People Who Dropped Dead - Non-Fiction

RoseDog  **Books**

PITTSBURGH, PENNSYLVANIA 15222

RoseDog Books
701 Smithfield Street
Pittsburgh, PA 15222
Visit our website at *www.rosedogbookstore.com*

ISBN: 978-1-4349-0908-4
eISBN: 978-1-4349-5750-4

Dedication

For Gil Hausman, Norman and Sandy Lowy, Marty Katz, Anne Jonali, Rita McCauley, Bob Levy, Ray Jacobs, Sandy Goldsmith, Bernie and Al Moss, Olen Seidler, Joe Gsell for teaching H.S. photography, and to those "Candid Men" who lived the life!

11/20LI

To Judy & Stanley:

Thank you Both So much for being At My Book Launch.

Thanks For taking An Interest The Garbage I Write.

Richard Cameron.

Chapter One

Brooklyn, New York, Late 1950s

The couple stood under the *chuppah*, the rabbi was about to pronounce them married. It was a beautiful Sunday afternoon in June of 1958. It was a warm day, but not too hot or humid—a nice day to walk along the Coney Island boardwalk, or to take a stroll through Prospect Park. It would have been a great day to go see the Dodgers at Ebbets Field, but what are you going to do? No more Dodgers.

Of course, this was also a great day to be getting married. It was also a great day for an outdoor ceremony.

This temple in the Manhattan Beach section of Brooklyn was the loveliest in the borough at which to have an outdoor wedding. It was starting to get warm now, but the reception would be held inside, in the air conditioning. The world was coming into the space age. More and more homes had air conditioning now. To think that only a few years ago there were some who said television wouldn't last. Tell that to Lucy and Desi.

The wedding photographer stood poised before the couple, ready to capture the action. This was a great time to do this for a living. People were getting married. The war was over, Ike wasn't messing up the country too much, and the "commies" were going to take over, so hell, let's live it up! These days photographers were being hired to capture precious moments at Bar Mitzvahs. Girls were being called to the Torah for their Bat Mitzvah. It wasn't unusual to see a photographer at sweet sixteen parties. Folks planning anniversaries and confirmation dinners realized they needed to engage the services of a professional to record those events also.

The wedding photographer held on to his very large Speed Graphic camera like it was a gold bar. Today the camera was heavier than usual. This

Chapter Two

Brooklyn, New York, June 1991

The spoiled brat Bar Mitzvah boy was being lifted in the chair. The job was getting to the photographer. He always liked shooting in this beautiful Manhattan Beach Temple, but tonight his clients were giving him the fucking business.

The photographer remembered fondly, the first job he had photographed there. That was what, back in June of '58? Yeah, back in the old days the people he dealt with were people.

What an event—celebrities, politicians, a band, and a DJ, yet. The photographer had shot several affairs of this type, since his early days as a 'candid man.' However, he knew all this bullshit was a show in flashiness by the kid's parents; it had nothing to do with the solemnness of a Jewish boy's passage to manhood.

What was with these snotty little spoiled rich kids? The photographer could remember when kids were respectful to adults. True, some of the Bar Mitzvah boys and Bat Mitzvah girls were respectful, but not like the old days. Just last week at a Bar Mitzvah, while the photographer went to take a leak, some kids messed with his camera. He saw the friends of the Bar Mitzvah boy giggling when he picked up his camera. Then he saw the exposure dial was moved, and the f-stop setting was changed. *Those little dickheads!*

The photographer walked over to these little shits and chewed their asses out, but good. When asked, they told him they didn't open the back of the camera. The photographer had to reshoot several poses of family groups on that roll. There was no way he was going to take the word of those little fucks. There was only one way to tell if the film had been exposed. But when the proofs came back, it was too fucking late. The damage had already been done.

Those lousy little bastards were telling the truth. They didn't open the camera. Still, better to have duplicates, than not having shit.

The boy's older sister was up in the chair now; her party dress was flying up exposing her thighs. Then parents had their turn.

Nothing lasts forever.

This business is on its way out. The photographer knew rough times were ahead. On the way to a fancy wedding in Manhattan last week, the photographer griped to his assistant about the hard economic times. He had nothing better to do, because they took the Fifty-Ninth Street Bridge, and they sat in traffic for two hours.

"Everybody is lowering prices or going outta business. Why? 'Cause people ain't spending anymore. Look at what has been happening on Long Island at Grumman. A whole shitload of people are outta work. People just don't want to spend right now. The sad part is it ain't gonna get better. Now that the war is over, and we kicked ass, we're gonna have four more years of that fuckin' Bush."

"You don't think the Democrats can win?" his assistant asked.

"Nah, Kerry from Nebraska is going to be the nominee; against Bush, he doesn't have a leg to stand on."

"Funee!" replied his assistant. "Verrry funee!"

The affair was winding down. The job was really getting to the photographer now. Christ, if there was ever a week to retire, this was it.

Earlier in the evening when the photography and video crew were having a nosh at the smorgasbord table, they were approached by the guest of honor. "Are you supposed to eat?" the kid inquired. "You *fagin* me one cocktail frank?" Sid asked. *Fagin* is the Yiddish word for 'deny.' Sid was sure this kid did not understand one word of Yiddish.

Later on, when the photographer asked him if he wanted to take a picture with all of his friends, the kid replied, "I dunno, go ask my motherfucker."

"If my son ever spoke about his mother that way..." the photographer interjected.

"Your son would kick your ass; leave me alone, you old faggot." The Bar Mitzvah boy ran away.

Well, thought the photographer, *my son may want to kick my ass, but he hasn't done it yet.*

The DJ was playing a Madonna record.

The guests were getting into it. The photographer had a wedding to shoot tomorrow morning, so he just wanted to get the hell out of there. He had to drive back to Long Island, shower, and go to sleep.

A nice-looking redheaded woman was dancing in the center of a small group of men. With a swift motion, she pulled her blouse off. The men roared with approval. Then she pulled her bra off, revealing large breasts. She tossed the bra to the Bar Mitzvah boy. He caught it, and placed it around his neck.

"The panties next, baby," one of the male guests shouted, "throw the panties next!"

The woman was dancing wildly to the music, shaking her big tits. The men were dancing in front of her. They were gyrating like fucking Chippendales.

The photographer shot a few frames of 'Ms. Big Tits' dancing with the Bar Mitzvah boy. His video crew also recorded this. Right, now a shot with 'tit lady' kissing the boy. Okay, now her posing with her arm around the boy. Whew! What a bash!

How times do change. The boy's mother had told the photographer that, originally, she had planned to serve the guests steak with "Lahbstah, but the hall wouldn't allow it because, lahbstah isn't koshah."

Finally, thank God, it was over. The photographer got his check, and bid the host and the guest of honor, good night. Holding back his bile, the photographer told the boy's father that his son was a fine young man.

Now it was time for a pit stop and then the drive home.

In the men's room, the photographer's assistant asked his boss if he was going to put a picture of 'tit lady' in his front window.

"You kidding? I'd have all the *shvartzes* on the block thinking I was selling the white woman."

At that point, a young man staggered into the men's room. He walked over to the sink and started to snort some white powder.

"Hey, guys," he asked, "wanna snort a couple of lines with me?"

The photographer and assistant started to leave, when he placed his hand on the photographer's arm, getting the powder on his tux.

"C'mon, it's good stuff from Columbia, the best." The guy was stoned out of his head.

The photographer swung his right fist, cracking the doper across the right jaw, knocking him through the door of the toilet stall. Out cold, the schmuck laid with his head against the bowl. "That where shit belongs," he said, "in the toilet."

In the lobby, he told a custodian that a guest passed out in the men's room.

The photography and video crew gathered up their gear.

As they were leaving the hall, the Bar Mitzvah boy and his pals called out after them.

"You guys suck!" called out one boy.

"You guys take lousy pictures," called out another boy.

The photography and video crews did not look back; with all the dignity they could muster, they walked out of the hall.

The mother of the Bar Mitzvah boy ran over to the kids.

"What is the problem?" She screamed, "My God, stop it!"

"But Ma," the Bar Mitzvah boy explained, "that photographer was an asshole."

"I know he was," the mother shot back, "but still, you don't shout at people like that in a hall."

Well, the 'asshole' had to stay awake for the drive back home to Long Island. Tonight a little snot nose kid's Bar Mitzvah, tomorrow a wedding. Oh well, that's how it goes in life. Another fucking day, another fucking dollar.

Chapter Three

A wedding day is important to a lot of people. After all, there are a lot of people involved in planning a wedding. In Sid Weitz's mind, the only two parties involved with a wedding who really mattered were the bride and the photographer. Today, he was going to shoot a wedding.

The day started out beautifully. Sid awoke this Sunday morning exhausted because he photographed a rotten kid's Bar Mitzvah the night before. He didn't know what knocked him out. Was it the shoot itself, or that lousy kid? Jewish affairs on Saturday nights often run until one o'clock in the morning, sometimes beyond. He had the luxury of four hours sleep.

His brand new Chevrolet Caprice, which ran fine the day before, did not start. He borrowed his wife, Norma's, new Nissan Stanza, which he was not used to driving. At least there were no limousines to chase today. When Sid met his assistant at the Woodmere Reform Temple, the kid asked him what happened to the new Caprice.

"I wish I knew, probably the same thing that happened to the old Caprice."

Sid wondered if he should have bought the Nissan Maxima or that big fancy Volvo.

A wedding is a beautiful occasion that should take place on a beautiful day, in beautiful surroundings. Today, it was raining. The synagogue in which the wedding was to take place did indeed have beautiful surroundings, but in the rain, who could enjoy them.

The banquet room upstairs would have been just fine for the formal photographs, but the banquet manager informed Sid that because the serving staff was busy setting up, the room would be off limits to him. Sid did not press the issue. As experienced photographers know, you tread very lightly with caterers in the Five Towns of Long Island. They won't hesitate to throw a photographer out. One jerk hung a light from a ceiling at this temple, and he was thrown out in the middle of the reception. The poor bride! The guests had to finish taking the pictures.

"We have a large banquet hall downstairs on the basement level, which is ideal for pictures."

Ideal, the room was not.

The white vertical blinds would have been perfect to pose people in front of, but of course, they were broken, unevenly spaced, and hanging off their track. The only available background was a folding wall partition of a faded robin's egg blue, which could have used a spot of paint. There was a large track at the top of the partition for the wall to slide on. This would not have been a problem, if the bride and groom had been of average height. They were both very tall. Both sets of parents were very tall, as was the entire bridal party, which consisted of six. Even the flower girl, the bride's niece and age three, was tall for her age.

A similar situation with a shitty background happened to Sid in an American Legion hall last Friday night. The walls were decorated with memorials of war and photographs of past post commanders with large double chins, which were extensions of their bellies. When booking the hall, the clients didn't realize there wasn't any place to pose. Sid had to fight like hell for the only vacant spot to shoot as the band was setting up.

"I don't give a shit where the outlets are, this is where I'm taking the pictures; tough shit, you'll have to wait for us to finish the pictures."

"Holy shit!" Sid griped to his assistant, "This fuckin' place charges two hundred and eighty dollars a couple, and they don't even give you a place to take fuckin' pictures. Shit, I'm gonna be blamed for this, because the wall is shitty to begin with, and both of them are very tall. I'm gonna try like hell not to get that fuckin' track on top. But they're gonna end up saying the pictures suck, I just know it."

Sid lit a Viceroy, "Watch, watch, you watch," he continued, "I'm gonna be blamed because it's raining outside."

The video crew entered the room. They were from another studio, which was not what he needed. He needed the money he could make if those creeps used his own video production service. The bride's mother said she could get the video for less, the cheap bastards.

"How ya doin'?" the videographer asked.

"I'm doin' just great." And, it was only ten A.M.

Sid Weitz looked around the banquet room; it would have to do. The lighting was a mixture of fluorescent, incandescent, and natural, which came in through the large first floor windows. Technically, these lighting sources should all be taken into consideration. Unless you're an aging shooter, then you do it your way. This was a simple way to determine the exposure for all these light sources set the camera on f/8, set your main strobe on f/8, and your second strobe on f/11.

The double lighting method, which would be used today, was always used by Sid. Several photographers said the second light was a myth and didn't do anything. Those who use the second light know better.

This method served three purposes—to add more light and dimension to the image, and to justify a higher price by telling your client how vital the second light is.

"Oh, that other photographer uses one light, which causes shadows. The shadows make the pictures look flat. We double light everything, which adds dimension, gives a brighter look to the picture, buh, buh, buh…" The third purpose of using the second light is to make your studio look as professional as possible. A photographer and a lighting assistant looks a hell of a lot better than one photographer struggling.

Photographers tend to use double lighting for lavish Jewish and Gentile weddings, as opposed to the tacky, low budget Gentile weddings. As for Jewish people who don't want to spend on quality photography, tough shit!

The Jewish clientele is much more demanding than the Gentile crowd, which was alright with Sid Weitz, because he preferred doing Jewish affairs. The people don't get drunk on you. The Gentiles start boozing it up in the limousine en route to the reception hall from the church. On a Jewish job, there is no limousine chasing because everything is held under one roof. Most photographers of the Jewish persuasion secretly admit that their Jewish clients are much more intelligent. Jewish brides who are college educated and come from exclusive areas of Long Island, seldom use the expression, "Ya know what I'm sayin'?" as in, "I'm looking for a photographer, 'cause I'm getting married, but I don't want to spend a lot of money, ya know what I'm sayin'?"

Sid kept his light meter in the case. After so many years, he knew what exposure he would shoot at. The lighting factor in the temple wouldn't cause him any problems. He used Kodak VPS Versicolor film, rated at ISO 100. This was the most dominant film in the wedding industry. As a professional portrait film, it exposed for the true tone of the subject's flesh, not for the clothing. Clients were warned of this, in a note when the proofs were picked up at the studio. Although at times there were color shifts on clothing, nothing was ever strenuously objected to by clients.

Another good reason for the use of the Versicolor—it was known as a very 'forgiving' film—meaning the photographer could either shoot one stop over exposed, or one stop under exposed, and the processing lab would print the negative so that no one would know. This film could also be printed if, by chance, the photographer was off by two or three stops. Being human, photographers sometimes made mistakes on exposure. If the picture looks good and the client doesn't know, why tell them. It is important for a photographer to have a reliable professional processing lab, because many photographers don't always know what the hell they're doing. Fortunately, the people who work in the labs know what they're doing. What the photographer couldn't figure out, the lab could.

The bride getting married today never knew that Montclair Studios would be playing a smaller role in the production of her wedding pictures than she was led to believe. Sid would pose and photograph the subjects, as well as direct the placement of the second light. The processing lab would clean up all his mistakes in printing. The bindery, which Montclair Studios used for the past thirty years would mount and bind the pictures into a genuine leather book.

People who booked photographers to record their affairs seldom realized the high markup photographers had. Recently, they started to catch on. There were appearances of bridal centers with their package deals, discount video services, and the ever present part-time, sideline weekend hack, who worked from their homes and undercut studios. True, there were fine established professional photographers with studios in their homes. Several of them charged correct industry prices, based on their ability and clientele in their area. They paid sales tax, workman's compensation, and liability insurance. They also had more training and equipment available than the hacks. What would happen if a hack without liability insurance hurt someone, or had an equipment malfunction, or got sick and didn't show up? Those hacks didn't have any staff, for God's sake.

The cut-rate bridal centers have a staff alright. A staff which consists of inexperienced kids who have graduated from doing in-home baby pictures, weekend hacks, or burnt out seasoned professionals, who used to shoot for, or even owned, major studios at one time. Sid knew from experience, that using these bridal centers was a crapshoot at best. A bride may get someone who is very good, or someone who sucks.

The video production studio was another story. Many of those fellows never worked as still photographers, therefore, had absolutely no artistic skills. There were many fine videographers Sid knew and had respect for. They started out as photographers, and were able to apply their knowledge from shooting stills to video. Some of the old-timers in the video game used to shoot movies, until that type of coverage fell by the wayside. Many Orthodox Jews used movie coverage at this time. Some very religious families did not own television sets.

There are so many schmucks out there doing videos, who have never had any kind of photographic or videographic training. They have the equipment alright, but nothing else. Anyone who thinks that to be a videographer you don't need to know how to pose, set up groups, compose, or know how to use different types of lighting is wrong. They are usually very cheaply priced, but wrong.

When videotaping came into play, Sid took a course in videography. The course was given by a video production company. This was really to train people for their use, but with the price of the tuition, anybody could take the course. Being a very experienced still and movie photographer, he did very well. His partner Lenny Schecter, who ran their in-home baby photography service in the offices above the studio, didn't want any part of the new video craze.

"It's a goddamn waste of time and money. It ain't never gonna sell, believe me."

Sid didn't believe Lenny. He took another course in post-production video editing. He bought editing equipment with his own money and built an editing suite in his house. He was making good money editing videotapes for others. Some in the video business did take courses and learned their craft well, which was too bad for the studios that did both stills and video. Today, so many people book with video companies and not with photographers in order to save a buck. At least those videographers do give a damn about their work.

If the video company across the street charges four hundred dollars to shoot and you charge a grand, there is nothing wrong with that. As long as your work is different and of higher quality, you can justify your price.

Some people look for quality and are willing to pay for it. Then, there are the cheap fucks who don't care what they end up with, as long as it is cheap. If an unedited tape shot in a camcorder is all they can afford and are happy with, so be it.

All the trade associations to which Sid belonged—Professional Photographers of America, Professional Photographers of Greater New York, Professional Photographers Society of New York, and Wedding Photographers International—now accepted videographers. There was now an association on Long Island, dedicated to the knowledge of the trade. Uncomfortable about joining at first, because he was primarily a still man, he learned quite a bit. There were too many members who spent an hour at each meeting bashing photographers. Sid thought those guys were assholes.

On night one dumb ass retired cop was bitching off to Sid about photographers. Sid told the asshole, "Videographers evolved from us, not the other way around."

On another occasion, a retired high school teacher was complaining his ass off about people not being willing to pay his prices. Sid stood up and told the membership to open a store.

"You guys are pathetic. If you want to justify prices, open a store, get an overhead, pay rent, and pay taxes!"

Naturally the membership mumbled and grumbled. There were only about three full-time videographers there. They could be full time because a lot of their work was commercial and industrial.

"Yeah, that's right!" Sid lectured. "You scarf up all the profits, none of you have sales tax resale numbers, and your clients pay you in cash. The editing is not very expensive. If you do your own editing, you only pay for the tape. Get an overhead, then charge higher prices."

Later he told a Jewish colleague, he didn't know why he bothered wasting good advice on those *goyim*.

Besides, the real reason why there are a lot of schmucks charging very low prices is because they have debts up their asses. They need those jobs to pay off all the editing equipment, and all those brand new three-chip cameras.

In the funny business cycle of this industry, the folks were certainly getting their asses kicked by the weekend hacks who charged less. The quality of their work was bad, because amateur equipment was used. Some of them just set a camcorder up on a tripod in a corner, and that's it. To them, an editing system is two VCRs and a television set.

And now, what about these DJs and bands who were offering videotaping in a package deal? Why, God, why?

Sid looked at the videographer's setup. Good, at least he's professional. He had a Panasonic industrial three-chip, broadcast camera, along with a deck and color monitor mounted to a dolly cart, with an adequate light on top. Video lights on stands were set up in the reception room.

It was not raining any more, but this was hardly an improvement; now it was pouring. It was now a fact that the members of the Meltzer/Schiener wedding would not have any photographs taken outside, in the beautiful gardens of the Woodmere Reform Temple.

The rain beat against the large glass windows.

It was a nice day for an affair. It was a great day for guests to schlep in from the city or New Jersey.

Sid motioned his assistant over to a huge rolling table near the folding wall, on which his battered black metal equipment case rested.

"Let's start setting up. We're gonna have to move this desk. It's on rollers, so it should be easy."

They started to push that huge desk. It wasn't so easy.

The videographer called out, "Hey, youse fellas need any help?"

Ya wanna help me, pal, Sid thought silently to himself, *get on the Long Island Expressway, drive east to Suffolk County and get off at exit sixty-three in Centereach, climb up that big fuckin' water tower, and throw yourself off! That's how you can help me. Maybe you'll land on my son's redneck in-laws.*

"Nah," he answered, "we're fine, thanks."

Sid Weitz and his assistant Jeffery Glassman, a budding wedding photographer, pushed the desk away from the picture area. They began to set up the equipment. He opened the battered equipment case, which was the size of a lady's traveling makeup case. It contained the body of a Mamiya M645 1000S medium-format camera, a 55 mm wide-angle lens with a lens shade attached, and a metal matte box for special effects, which was now mostly used as an extra lens shade for his normal lens, a 70 mm. At this point, he left the special effects to the printers at the lab. The case also contained an extra flash unit, a portable Vivitar 283, and some white-topped straight pins for tacking down trains of bridal gowns outdoors. There were also two spare dry cell batteries to power the flash units, a battery charger that could recharge in one hour while working on location, extra synchronization cords, and a small video light, which could be 'Velcroed' onto the bracket of the main camera, to ease the focusing of table photographs in dark halls. Also, a small screwdriver, a penlight, four extra cassettes loaded with 220 film, two packs of Kodak VHS film, two white *yarmulkes*, an extra film advance crank for the camera, and pen and paper to note all the guest tables in the hall. The numbers of tables were marked off as each one was photographed.

On the right side of the case was a small metal box that contained slave units that plugged into the strobes. Sid used GVI radio slaves that were made by Quantum Instruments. They were triggered by a radio signal, not a burst of light. In the old days, any guest with a camera could set off your second light. The radio slave prevented the second light from firing without the photographer firing the main light. Still, it was good to have the old standby, photocell slaves. Some houses of worship had radio frequencies for their sound system that prevented these very expensive units from working. On top of the metal case, a small glass ashtray that had been swiped from a catering hall. Not many places had ashtrays anymore. Who the hell smokes in this day and age?

Sid Weitz still smoked. He had tried to quit for twenty years. His wife, Norma, quit twenty years ago. Their kids never smoked. He should quit. He breathed alright, he didn't cough, and his doctor told him, so far, there was no lung damage. Sid had cut down, out of fear for his own mortality; in addition, cigarette prices were getting too damned costly.

It was getting close to the time for the shoot. Sid began checking his main camera, which was a Mamiya M645 with a standard 70 mm lens. He screwed the matte box onto the lens, and loaded the camera with film. The camera was situated on a deluxe 'L' grip bracket made by Mamiya. The top part of the bracket was a customized metal arm, which enabled the strobe to be above the lens for horizontal shots, and swiveled forty-five degrees for vertical shots. The bracket had a plate for the transmitter part of the radio slave to be 'Velcroed' onto. There was also a plate on top of the arm for the small plastic box from Mamiya that contained a spare film cassette, which was always ready.

"Jeff, turn on the slave and your unit; I wanna test this."

The assistant complied with the photographer's request.

The 'slave' unit, which was carried by the assistant, was a Vivitar 283 portable strobe, customized with a Matador head. The old Matador heads were once one of the most powerful light sources in the wedding photography game. Being an old hand at the game, Sid Weitz still had plenty of Matador strobes. He didn't think the standard Vivitar head was powerful enough for large jobs, so he had a technician put the Matadors onto the top of the Vivitars. This procedure, while expensive, was worth it. Sid felt good about being one of the few photographers based on Long Island to light with a Matador. The strobe unit, along with the receiver part of the radio slave, was screwed to the top of a heavy monopod, which could extend ten feet. Years ago they carried an extra one for backup...now Sid only carried one. If the second light goes, he would just shoot the remainder of the job with a single light.

Sid was not using a Matador head today. On his bracket, he had an Armatar strobe, which was a customized Vivitar 283 with a round Norman silver reflector head. Round reflectors on strobe heads provided soft, even illumination, as opposed to a harsher burst from rectangular heads.

Sid pressed the unit's test button, and his main strobe fired, but the second unit did not.

The assistant shook his head, "Nothing."

"Ah, shit," said the photographer, "let's have a look."

The key to being a good photographer is handling emergencies well. It also helps to be a good camera repair person. On location, your technician will not be able to help you. It helps to be able to troubleshoot and repair.

"Shit, bitch, and shit," Sid muttered. "What the fuck is it with these over-priced slave units today?"

Sid Weitz was what one could call a 'maven' on equipment. Any kind of candid, portrait, motion picture, or video equipment used in his business for the last forty years, he owned it. Some of the purchases were out of desire, but most of the accumulation was just out of being in the business over thirty years.

It was a long time since Sid shot with a Speed Graphic and a flash gun with bulbs. Once in 1955, a flash bulb exploded on firing, and shattered into the grooms face. The groom was not hurt, and Sid was not fired by the studio. This never happens today. No more struggling with 4x5 sheet film holders or sheet film packs on weddings; large sheet film was only used by commercial photographers or high-priced portrait studios.

In the fifties, roll film holders were available for the Speed Graphic; this made life somewhat easier. Sid shifted back and forth with the Graphics and the more modern cameras throughout the sixties and seventies. But those old graphics looked so ancient today. They were also too heavy for an old fart like Sid to schlep around. Occasionally, he would use an old Graflex speed light. Those babies were wonderful for the second light.

Still, equipment did change through the years, although, not as radically as the video equipment. One terrible thing about the video end of the business, which caused Sid and a lot of other photographers-cum-videographers worry, was the constant upgrading of equipment. There is a saying in the video industry, "If you buy it on Wednesday, it's obsolete on Friday." How fucking true that was. *A hell of a cycle,* Sid mused, *the Jups are making money off of me; to break even, I have to make money off the J.A.P.s in South Merrick.*

Engineers try to keep the changes in still equipment to a minimum, which is why many photographers have shot with the same system for years. There are modifications, of course, sometimes for the better...sometimes, what the hell.

The last major changes were twenty years ago when flash units were manufactured with automatic modes, turning the light off at the proper exposure, eliminating exposure calculations.

In the mid-nineteen seventies, the 6x6.45 format camera was introduced. This camera enabled photographers to shoot vertically and horizontally. This 645 format, as it was known, produced an ideal 8x10 photograph, requiring a minimum amount of cropping on the negatives. There were some disadvantages too, however. This format could not produce an 8x8, or a 10x10 square photograph. However, Sid swore by the camera…it handled comfortably.

Before the 6x6.45 format appeared on the market, the 6x6 square format was the photographer's mainstay. They are still widely used today. Many studios insist on square format. Several photographers look on 645s with disdain. Sid owned a square format system. It was a twin lens reflex camera, which accommodated different lenses and prisms. He used this system throughout the 1960s and '70s. He also had a medium-format single lens reflex camera, which accommodated 6x7 size negative backs. They were fine for studio work, but the cameras were much too heavy to be carried about on location. Sid had photographed affairs with these camera years ago. There was a time when he would bring those large cameras on location, for portrait work at big affairs. Seldom did he bring those big cameras, along with studio lights and backdrops. He was just too old and that shit was just too heavy.

There was a time in the late'60s when Sid shot exclusively with a range finder 6x7 camera. It was a Koni Omega. The 6x7 was also an ideal negative, because of the minimum cropping needed for an 8x10 photograph. The Koni-Omegas were discontinued years ago. Sid kept them in the house; today, they are not seen around on location that much. A few of the old-timers in Brooklyn's Boro Park area still use them.

Two recent changes in still equipment that affected Sid's life in recent years, was the plastic version of his 645 camera and the radio controlled slave units. Sid bought one of the new plastic 645s on impulse, but seldom used it. He was used to the metal cameras, as the plastic did not feel right in his hands. It was not always so easy for a candid man to get used to the feel of new equipment. It took him two years to get used to the feel of the twin lens reflex after the Speed Graphics were retired to the attic.

The radio controlled slave…ah, now that was a good investment. The strobes on the assistant's monopod were now controlled by radio frequency. This prevented a guest's strobe unit from setting off your light. Photographers no longer had to ask guests to please not fire when they do. They no longer needed to worry about guests ruining the picture by setting off the second light, causing it not be ready when the photographer needed it, causing a subject to blink, or causing an exposure problem.

Thank God, still equipment doesn't change that much…not like all that expensive video equipment. Thank God for the fact that at his age, he could still piss without straining. Being able to piss like a man of twenty was one of the few things Sid was thankful for that day.

Sid's eighty-five year-old father, Burton Weitz, did not agree with his son's equipment investments.

"You're pissing away your money on shit," he had often told his son for the past forty years.

Sid's wife, Norma, a terrific lady if there ever was one, supported her husband of thirty-six years.

"Whatever he needs for the business, he should have; he's a very good photographer. He knows what he's doing."

Today, however, Sid's equipment valued more than his incoming jobs for the coming year. What are you going to do? Things are tough all over.

He rummaged through his case for a screwdriver to repair the damn radio slave. He looked over at the videographer. The guy was talking with his assistant. Sid lit a Viceroy.

The videographer's assistant was carrying the deck on his shoulder and wearing earphones to monitor the sound level. The deck was heavy to carry, but it would be brought into the dressing room for the signing of the marriage certificate. There wouldn't be any room for that huge cart. This guy knew that. An assistant, who carries the tape deck on his/her shoulder, enables the videographer to handhold the video camera without extra weight restricting his movements. There were jobs when Sid handheld his video camera and wore the deck on his shoulders. It was heavy. For this reason, Sid liked to do his handheld work with Super VHS camcorders. They were lighter, really good for that kind of work, although not as impressive as the big three-chip cameras.

Sid looked at the man's setup. He was in no mood to work with an asshole today; he hoped to hell that this guy wasn't an asshole.

Three-chip camera, good viewing monitor, proper camera light, and nice wireless microphones. *Their setup is the same as mine*, Sid observed, as he puffed on his Viceroy, wishing he was handling the video for these creeps. He noticed they were using Super VHS tapes. Most pros used Super VHS. The hacks just used plain old VHS. Super VHS was used to record events because it had a higher quality of resolution. Later the affair would be edited and transferred onto a VHS tape for the consumer. This practice won't be going on much longer, because VCRs that will accommodate Super VHS tapes will soon be available to consumers. New computers will soon allow people to shoot, as well as edit, their own tapes. As if things aren't hard enough in business.

Hi-8 videotapes were being used more and more now. Still, a lot of wedding pros were shying away from them. The equipment required Hi-8 editing decks. Some of the video cameras could dock with Hi-8 decks. This was still too new a format to trust. Who needs such aggravation? There were even some people who taped in the Beta format. Super VHS was easy for Sid, he liked the results, and his clients seemed happy with the results, too.

In the past thirteen years, Sid had gone from silicon tube, to single, now to three-chip equipment. The fucking upgrades in video were enough to send any sonofabitch to the poorhouse. The three-chip cameras were great for lowlight conditions, in houses of worship, or poorly-lit reception halls. But for a price tag of seven grand for a good one, a videographer had better have the bookings, before shelling out that kind of bread.

Pissed off at himself, Sid took the nine-volt battery out of its compartment of the receiver.

"Ah, fuck, I think this battery is dead, I don't have another one."

Yes, this day was off to a fine start.

Sid didn't have a spare battery because he carried a lot less than he used to. His other accessory case was like a satchel. It was a fact of life, in this business, the older you got, the less you carried, unless you were a perfectionist, a glutton for punishment, or maybe if people were still using you.

"Hey, I got a spare nine-volt battery," said the videographer

"What's your name?" Sid turned around, offering his hand.

"Vinny."

"I'm Sid. That's a nice setup you have there. Is it yours?"

"No, it belongs to the boss, Nick Tavella, Treasured Memories Video in Bellmore?"

"Oh, yeah," Sid stubbed the out his Viceroy, "I knew him years ago when we both shot stills for Garfine Photographers in Brooklyn, on Church Avenue."

"That must have been some time ago," Vinny smiled at the thought of how much older his boss was.

"Well, Benny Garfine has been dead for at least twenty years. Don't look surprised, Vinny," Sid went on, "Nicky is my age. Shit, I was doing video before he was. Nicky used to subcontract jobs out to me."

"How long you been doing video, Sidney?" asked Vinny.

"Over twelve years. I was one of the first studios on the island to shoot video. Shit, I used to get paid fifteen hundred a fuckin' job to do nothing."

"What ya mean?" asked Vinny.

"Shit," Sid continued, "I had this big fuckin' Quasar tube camera. We used to put in on a caterer's bar cart. I had a seven-person crew—a couple of guys would hold my lights, the others would follow me around the hall, pulling my cables.

"We set up a big fuckin' monitor on the table for the people to see. They would come over and ask us, 'Is this instant movie film, can you develop it here?' People loved that shit. We really made fuckin' money in those days."

Vinny laughed.

"The good old days," Sid said.

"Sidney, them days were something else. I mean what a bitch with the tube cameras and lights."

"Vinny, I'll tell you about a bitch with the lights. I was videotaping a Bar Mitzvah in '79 at one of the big hotels in the city. The boy's mother comes over to me and tells me turn off the lights."

"What?" Vinny could not believe this.

"Turn them off or go home," the bitch says. She says my lights are ruining the blue cast of the fluorescent bulbs she paid the caterer to set up. The lights were supposed to make everything blue. Ya know what I got, Vinny, when I turned off my lights?"

"Shit?"

"Worse than shit. When she came down to pick up the tape, I showed her where she ordered me to turn off the lights. Black, absolutely nothing on the remainder of that tape."

"Did she pay youse?" Vinny asked.

"Oh, yeah," Sid answered, "she paid…no problem. That story is one for the books."

Vinny, the videographer, was not a well-polished professional. He was short, heavyset, with a mop of curly black hair. His five o'clock shadow was showing, and it was still mid-morning.

"Where are youse located, Sidney?"

"South Shore in Elmont, Montclair Studios."

"I heard of youse, you're on Hempstead Turnpike between Plainfield Avenue and Elmont Road. Ain't there a baby studio there?"

"That's my partner upstairs. It used to be a nice area; we've been there thirty years."

"Do youse ever get any trouble from the niggers?" Vinny asked.

"Everybody over there gets some kind of trouble from them."

"They ever rob youse?"

"We were broken into once; they took some typewriters and cash. I don't keep any equipment there anymore, but they managed to get a radio slave unit and one lens."

"Them goddamn niggers," Vinny shook his head and said.

"Yeah," replied Sid, "goddamn them."

A skinny, shifty-eyed young man with short light brown hair approached, holding a nine-volt battery.

"This here is my assistant, Cosmo."

Cosmo smiled, and handed Sid the battery. "Pleased to make your aquain'ance," he said.

"Vinny," Sid produced his wallet, "let me pay you for the battery."

"Nothing doing, Sidney, I got so many of them things, as youse guys say it's a *Bruchat*."

"A *Mitzvah*," Sid corrected. He hated when *goyim* tried to speak Yiddish or Hebrew. "Well, okay," he grinned. "I thank you, sir; you are a gentleman and a scholar."

"Nah," Vinny replied, "This here is just a part-time job. During the week I drive an oil truck."

Sid shook his head and shuddered a bit, because he didn't understand what the hell this schmuck just said.

Sid changed the battery, fired the strobe, and the second light fired.

"Good, all set."

A bridesmaid entered the room.

"I'm Judy."

"Sid."

"Vinny."

"Everyone will be down in a minute. We're all ready to go."

That statement was a crock of shit. Nobody was ever ready to go.

"Very good," Sid responded, with a slight bow. He patted his assistant on the shoulder, "Let's get ready to go to work."

Chapter Four

S id Weitz looked sixty years old; people usually guessed that he was sixty. They were right, but so far nobody said he looked seventy. You could say that Sid was a nice-looking man; most people did say that. His wife, Norma, son Steven, daughter Linda, and parents said that he was nice looking. Sid hoped that Steve thought his dad was nice looking, because, everyone said Steve looked just like the old man.

Sid was five foot seven inches in bare feet; today the lifts he was wearing made him five foot nine inches. His waistline had a middle-age spread, but his face was trim. The wrinkles on the face were a result of age, wisdom, experience, and the aggravation that comes from being a parent, grandparent, and self-employed. Shooting years of outdoor affairs and squinting to keep the cigarette smoke out of the eyes, also contributed to the facial lines. The brown hair had long turned to silver. It was parted on the left and layered. The sideburns were short and the face was clean shaven. Sid did change with the times. From 1968 to 1971, there were long sideburns. From 1971 until 1980, the hair was worn longer, over the ears, on top, and in the back. There was a mustache from 1967 until 1973, then a beard for three years. The mustache came and went until last year, when it went, this time for good...too fucking gray.

The brown eyes used reading glasses for the past fifteen years; they now required distance glass for photographic assignments, as well as for driving. It is also nice to see where the hell you're going. The nose was average sized for a Jewish person and very straight. The lips were not very full and the teeth were still his own. Sid knew he didn't look like a movie star, but if he looked like a movie star, he wouldn't be shooting weddings. Sid sighed. *At least* he thought *I still have my health and my strength*. Health and strength, strength and health, that's what any old fart needs to survive anything.

Money is, of course, a big help. Money you have accumulated, saved, and invested through the years. If you were lucky, you had a good crooked stockbroker with a Ponzi scheme. Money saved, Sid had, but he would like to have more. Not just to leave the kids, but to have a nice, comfortable old age.

Today's job required formal wear. Most jobs Sid's studio covered required formal wear; occasionally, he wore a dark business suit. There were times he wore a light suit; perhaps his colleagues would criticize, but rank has its privilege. He was wearing a black tuxedo, white shirt, black suspenders, and a black clip-on bowtie. The breast pocket of the jacket sported a white handkerchief *a la* former President Reagan. Sid had removed his jacket and tie for the formal shooting session.

Sid's assistant Jeffery Glassman was identically dressed. Jeffery was twenty-three and a recent college grad. His bachelor's degree was in communications. He was thinking about working on his masters, and Sid encouraged that. Jeffery had been with Sid for five years now. He answered an ad for lighting assistant, took Sid's abuse, regarded the old candid man as a mentor, and was trained in all aspects of portraiture, candid work, and videography, as well as the business of running a photography studio. Jeffery was taught the folklore of the candid man and the history of how the Greater New York studios evolved. Why this smart kid wanted to follow in the footsteps of an old has-been candid man was something Sid couldn't understand.

"Better you should work for some of these arrogant schmucks on the North Shore or in the Five Towns who think that they're God's gift to the industry," Sid told his assistant on more than one occasion.

Those fucks, he told all the young people who listened, can afford to pay off the fancy Long Island Temple caterers to recommend jobs to them.

'Learn from the best,' was Sid Weitz's philosophy, so if the kid thought he was the best, what the fuck. But, he wanted Jeff to finish his master's degree in secondary art education and teach photography in the vocational high schools. If the kid wanted to be a schmuck and shoot weddings, better he should teach during the week and shoot as a part-time occupation. Better yet, teach during the week and spend the weekend making time with your girlfriend. At least as a school teacher, the kid would have a pension along with union benefits. Sid just had his Social Security, health insurance, and individual retirement account. That was supplemented from some stock dividends and a safety deposit box full of cash that he had stashed through the years. His wife, Norma, a bank executive, had her own individual retirement account, Social Security, and a pension from her bank. With taxes on Long Island so fucking high, they didn't think they would live in luxury during their retirement, but at least they would live. It was so fucking hard to survive with your own small business today. Sid wished Jeff could understand that.

Today, only the very expensive chic award-winning studios and the very cheap package deal studios survive. You're better off teaching kids. Why sink money into a business that is much too risky? Don't be a schmuck!

The young guys in this business today are college and art school graduates. The guys from Sid Weitz's time never really learned to pose or shoot. They invented the shit as they went along. They were mostly salesmen with terrific personalities, which accounted for their success as deal closers for booking jobs. Several of the old guys were very good, but they were really just slick oily two-bit salesmen. *Jeff had an education, he wasn't one of them, and should have nothing to with those lowlifes, me included* Sid thought.

But, at least I taught him, Sid rationalized; at least I'm guiding him so he doesn't make mistakes. Opening a studio now, in this economy, would be a mistake. Be a teacher, kid, at least it's secure. There were days, Sid believed, that the broad who delivered mail to his house had more financial security than him.

Jeffery Glassman was a good-looking kid, in Sid Weitz's opinion. He stood at five foot ten, had layered sandy colored hair and gray eyes. He had a small nose, but his face was a Jewish one. Jeff was a very good student and a fast learner. He picked up all the tricks of the trade that Sid taught him. He was now experienced enough to photograph and videotape weddings on his own. Sid needed a lighting assistant today, so Jeff was temporarily demoted. Normally on Christian jobs and small Jewish ones, Jeff did the stills and Sid did the videotaping. Occasionally they alternated. During the summer, Jeff spent his days shooting in-home baby portraits for Sid's second business. Happy Time Photographers was situated in an office above Sid's studio.

Sid's partner Lenny Schecter ran that part of the business. Lenny no longer shot affairs; all he was interested in was the babies. As a wedding portrait photographer, Lenny was average. As a baby photographer and a salesman, no one could touch him. As a person, he was a worm, a creep, a cheap bastard, and a real lowlife. Sid could not stand him, yet, he stayed with Lenny for thirty years because together with Carl Resnick, they built a successful studio with a great big following.

Carl Resnick was a great portrait photographer and a class act all the way. Carl won several awards; if anybody put Montclair Studios on the map, it was him. Carl was born in the Bronx, but was very well spoken; he sounded like a faggot, which he was not. He was a true artist. He didn't use profanity the way his two partners did. In 1980, he was fed up with Sid and could not tolerate lowlife Lenny anymore, so he packed up his wife and youngest son, moved to Arizona, and opened a studio. He operated under the name of Montclair Studios. The last they heard, Carl was doing well.

The bridal party entered the room. The bride was wearing a very expensive top-of-the-line white gown. The bridesmaids were wearing gowns of pink. Both mothers were wearing pink formal gowns. The men were wearing black tuxedos, and the groom wore tails. They were young educated professionals with money to spend…the kind of client any photographer wants.

The mother of the bride approached Sid. She was an attractive woman in her forties who was recently widowed. "Sid, I guess we're not going to take any pictures outside today."

"*Zoy gaytes,*" Sid replied, a Yiddish expression, which means 'that's how it goes.'

"What about pictures by the windows, Sid? We could at least see the grounds."

"Well, there's too much rain on the windows; you're not even gonna see the grounds and they're gonna be very blue. Jeff knew in business the customer is always right, but Sid was so frustrated with the surroundings he had to work with, Jeff figured Sid really didn't want to bother with creativity today.

"If it lets up," the bride's mother continued, "maybe we can go outside and take some pictures."

The rain looked like it was not going to let up during the course of this event.

"We'll try."

The groom's father, a tall athletic-looking man with a bald head, went over to where Sid and the mother of the bride were standing and introduced himself.

"Sid, I'm George, my wife's name is Frieda. What do you want to do first?"

"We're going to family pictures first, so we can let you go see your friends."

A little girl ran up to the groom's father. "I don't wanna get my picture taken, Grandpa."

"Shh," replied the groom's father, "I'm talking to the man."

"I don't wanna!" the little girl whined.

"Well you hafta!" was the reply from her grandfather.

Sid posed the bride and groom with both sets of parents, pressed his shutter button, but the flash unit did not fire. "Okay, once more, gang," Sid sang out jovially…nothing. The photographer looked at his strobe. "Hold on, guys, I have to change my cord."

Sid and Jeff walked over to the small table on the side of the room where the equipment case was.

"Shit, I hope it's just the fuckin' cord; lemme fire the test button." The unit emitted a burst of light. "Good, fine," the photographer mumbled. He rummaged through the case, pulled out a spare cord, and plugged it into the strobe. "'Kay, let's do it again." This time the main light on Sid's bracket and the second light, which was held by Jeff, fired. Success!

The family group photos went very smoothly. The photography of the bridal couple did not go very smoothly. Soon after the first few photographs were taken, the second light stopped firing. If there is one sure way for clients to lose confidence in their photographer, it is an equipment failure to occur right before their very eyes. A photographer can assure the people that this happenstance is trivial and he has a lot of backup equipment with him, but this really does not inspire confidence from clients. Any experienced wedding photographer knows that once a client loses confidence in you, the job might as well be over. The client will now watch carefully for any problems you as a photographer might encounter during the course of the day. As far as passing the proofs, forget about it! They are going to be looking for mistakes. Instead of being psyched to see beautiful images from their affair, the clients are going to be looking for everything the photographer did wrong, and they are going to find the mistakes, because they were so nervous because of what happened to you, they will notice small things, which normally they would not have noticed.

First the fucking cord wasn't working, now the fucking slave wasn't working. Once more a trip to the old equipment case.

Jeff was concerned for his boss. "What's the matter now?"

"Ahhh, pussy! The damn slave isn't firing. Let's plug in old standby for a while."

Old standby was a slave cell, which plugged into the second unit. This was used in the old days before the radio slaves. The cell needed to see a burst of light from the main unit. The radio slaves made double lighting of affairs easier because the slave cell didn't always fire when photographing outdoors because the sun interfered. At receptions, photographers had to ask guests to please refrain from firing their flash units because our lights would be triggered. It was more convenient to use a device that fires the second unit by sensing a sound wave from the first unit. In the old days when a photographer asked a guest not fire, the guest really got pissed off. Of course, the fucking guests fired anyway, which triggered the second unit, which caused the slave to never be ready when the photographer fired the main unit, causing an incorrect exposure.

Sid knew what the problem was, the cord which plugged into the radio slave unit needed to be changed. Later at the reception, he would do it. Now, there was no time. As the photographer disconnected the radio slave and rummaged through the case for old standby, he was somewhat frazzled by this. Sid farted. His assistant thought that his nerves caused him to cut one. The fart was not very loud and, fortunately, there was no smell. Sid must have known he farted. Jeff figured he was so involved in what he was doing, he probably didn't care about it. Jeff shook his head and hoped it didn't happen again.

"I'm glad this happened," said Sid, "you've never seen a problem on the job. You're gonna know how to handle it and not get upset. See, this is how a professional handles a problem."

Jeff felt some resentment toward Sid. He videotaped and photographed a lot of affairs and thought of himself as a professional.

"See, you know how to handle problems calmly and quickly now; you know what to do, so you don't get frazzled. I'm glad it happened."

Sid was wrong about Jeff not seeing any problems during his five years with Montclair Studios. He saw problems galore.

On one job they were shooting at a fancy Woodmere country club, Sid's strobe unit stopped working altogether. He didn't have a backup, so Jeff had to plug his strobe into Sid's camera and walk around with him, holding the light directly above him and be his main light. It was a very good thing that, at this point, the Bar Mitzvah was almost over. Jeff was surprised that the pictures came out as well as they did. He was also surprised that Sid wasn't sued. The clients thought their expensive, highly recommended photographer was being creative. They did not know that their photographer was trying to save both the job and his ass. Jeff recalled Sid farted during that incident, too, but the band was playing loudly so no one heard it, which was a good thing, because Sid was so frazzled, he really let that one rip.

The slave cell was working so the people were not really all that concerned. Sid Weitz was doing his best for an old guy who just went through hell.

"Sid, the bride's mother called out. Are you going to take any close-ups of them?"

When photographing a bridal couple, some photographers shoot full length, then move in for a close-up. Sid preferred to do the full lengths first and then do the close-ups.

"Eventually," was his reply to the mother of the bride. In his mind was, *Why don't you take a walk, lady, and let me do my fuckin' job*.

When it was time to shoot the bride alone, the bride's best friend entered the room, engaged the bride in conversation, completely distracting the little J.A.P. *Beautiful, just fuckin' beautiful* Sid thought. *Now this little creep is going to cost us time.* He knew he would have to step in and seize control.

"Amy, can you lower the bouquet please, darling. Amy, Amy! Hello, Amy! Look here.

Unbelievable fumed the photographer in silence, *unfucking believable*.

The bride came back to earth. "Oh sorry, Sid, you want me to hold the bouquet like this you mean?" She was making like the statue of liberty.

Sid leaned over and whispered to Jeff, "This bride is fuckin' stupid."

During the course of the portrait session, a bride doesn't really know what to do. It is the photographer's job to guide her. However, if you have a bride who happens to be fucking stupid, a person with a short attention span to boot, it will cause a portrait session to drag. Today Sid had a bride who was really fucking stupid.

The pre-ceremony session of the formals ended at eleven forty-five A.M. Now it was time to do the reenactment of the ceremony pictures, or, in this case, the pre-enactment. In order not to have the schmuck videographer interfere with the stills, Sid decided to do the ceremony photos beforehand at the pre-ceremony rehearsal. The Rabbi permitted photography during the ceremony, but Sid thought this would be better. He would just shoot the actual final blessing of the bride and groom, the breaking of the glass, and the kiss. The rest of the time he would just do the available light photographs, recharge his batteries, and wait. It was time to go up to the sanctuary to do the ceremony shoot. *Maybe*, Sid thought, *maybe I'll survive this wedding after all*. As he walked up the steps, the photographer wondered what else was going to go wrong today. He also knew he had to piss real bad. The problem with morning jobs is that during the shoot, the photographers always have to pee. Sometimes a great photographer can't piss when he wants to.

Chapter Five

S id briskly followed his assistant up the steps. He had to piss, but there was no time for pissing now. The bridal party and the photographer were ushered into the temple sanctuary by the banquet manager; he would be conducting the rehearsal for the ceremony. Vinny the videographer and his assistant Cosmo were already inside all setup.

Sid went over to Vinny to inform him that he would be shooting a reenactment and only some highlights of the actual ceremony. Vinny asked Sid if he wanted to meter the video lights for his available light photographs. Sid said he didn't need to, after all these years he knew what the exposure would be. The camera would be handheld; the settings would be one thirtieth of a second at f/2.8.

The banquet manager lined up the family outside the door of the sanctuary in the order in which they were to walk down the aisle.

The bride was concerned about her little niece Pia, who was fearful about walking down the aisle. Sid could only try to reassure the flustered bride. "Amy, I don't think the little one is gonna make it, but we'll try."

First Sid was to photograph the processional. He stood directly in front of the sanctuary entrance. Normally for a processional, the photographer stands center aisle; pre-focused at ten or twelve feet and photographs the subject when they reach the spot where the lens is focused. For a reenactment, the photographer would do well to stand in the doorway, because standing center aisle would show a lot of empty pews in the picture.

First, Sid photographed the grandparents of the bride and groom. In a Jewish ceremony the bride and groom's grandparents participate in both the processional and recessional. The great-grandparents walk down, too, if, of course, they are still living. Next, the ushers and bridesmaids were photographed. The little ring bearer and flower girl made it down the aisle with some parental and grandparental coaxing.

"Yippee, hippee," the photographer sang out, "the little ones made it!"

Sid wasn't concerned in what order the little ones walked down. That would be taken care of during the proofing. The little ones made it down the aisle, which was all that mattered. As long as the bride and groom were happy, everyone, god willing, was happy, and this made Sid happy.

The best man made his way to the *chuppah*. The *chuppah* was a canopy that was held up by four poles. The *chuppah*, also known as the 'tent of peace,' was what the bride and groom stood under during a Jewish wedding ceremony. The parents, best man, and maid of honor also stood under the *chuppah*, providing there was enough room for all. This was a very large *chuppah* on a large altar today...there would be room for all. The stands were high enough as to not obstruct a photographer's view. In olden days, the *chuppah* was held above the bridal couple by four men. This tradition still prevails today in the Chassidic and Orthodox sects of Judaism. Sid had photographed a great many of those weddings. A handheld *chuppah* could cause a photographer problems. If the men holding it up were not very tall, the *chuppah* could obscure the bridal couple. Sometimes a man holding one of the poles would have his arm tire during a lengthy ceremony. This would cause a section of the *chuppah* to cover the subjects, ruining the picture. It never failed to happen; the *chuppah* covered the subjects just as the photographer clicked the shutter.

The groom and his parents entered. In the Jewish faith, both the groom's parents walk down the aisle with him. Sid took four pictures—two close-ups of the groom looking at his mother, one of the groom looking at his father, and one full length of the three of them walking together. The next shot was the matron of honor.

The bride and her parents entered the sanctuary. The bride had the blusher part of her veil covering her face. The traditional picture of the bride walking down the aisle at a Jewish wedding calls for the blusher to be worn. Amy, the bride, had a difference of opinion.

"Sid," Amy whined, "can't we take the picture without the blusher?" Nobody's gonna see my face, do you know what I'm saying?"

Sid was shocked, for a Jewish girl to utter that dreaded phrase, "Do you know what I'm saying?" If this was a *shiksa*, well alright, but a Jewish girl? College educated? The little shnookie should know better! *Oy gevalt!* Where the hell do the kids learn to talk today? *I mean*, Sid thought, *I got a Brooklyn accent, but my kids always spoke well and used correct grammar*.

It is true that Sid Weitz spoke with a thick Brooklyn accent. His wife, Norma, was also from Brooklyn, but her accent wasn't as thick as his. Their son Steven and their daughter Linda were both born in Brooklyn, and reared on Long Island. They spoke with regional downstate accents. Sid was happy that the Weitz children articulated better than their parents. Many of Sid's Long Island clients found his gravelly voiced Brooklyn accent amusing. People often told him that his voice sounded like a cross between Humphrey Bogart and George Burns. People thought the way Sid pronounced certain words was hilarious. Coming from Brooklyn, it was given that Sid said foist, thoid, secont, terlet, fah Chris' sake, to mention a few. There were things that came out in normal conversation that caused people to smile. "Have a good toim." "I'll have the serlern steak," or his directions for traveling on the Island. "Take de Seaferd Erster Bay to de Longuilland Expressway." That one always got a laugh. The Brooklynese was part his sales technique. He sounded like a smooth personable salesman, which indeed he was. Saying "You got it, baby," to women in the bridal party to assure them they were posing correctly was part of his *shtick*. Often, Sid addressed young women as "Babe" or "Honey." He was not altogether sexist, but he had little tolerance for stupid broads.

College educated as Amy was, she was a stupid broad. She's a schoolteacher and couldn't even talk right.

"Can't we take the picture without the blusher?" inquired the bride once again.

"Well, you're going to be wearing it as you walk down with your parents, during the actual ceremony. You're going to look as you should in this picture."

"Nobody's gonna see me," the bride retorted, "I wanna see my face in the pictures; you know what I'm saying?"

Oy vay, there she goes again with the "You know what I'm saying?" Sid leaned his head close to Jeff and whispered in his ear, "Holy shit, this bride is fuckin' stupid. She's supposed to walk down the aisle with the blusher, they told her that. It's Jewish tradition, this girl is really fuckin' stupid, I wanna tell you."

"Tell you what we'll do, sweetheart, we'll take a picture of you walking down with the blusher and without the blusher; how's that, Amy?"

"That's a good idea," chirped the bride's mother.

"Well, I'm not gonna put any pictures in the album if I can't see anybody's face. If you wanna go ahead, I'm not, I wanna see faces," Amy replied.

"And a lot of light in the pictures," the groom's mother called out.

"*Oyyyy*," moaned the photographer

The series of pictures of the bride and her parents in the processional are a full length of them walking, the bride's blusher being lifted by one of her parents, and both parents taking turns kissing her on the cheek. Two quarter length photos, one of each parent kissing the bride were taken from the front. Then a repeat of this series with the lighting assistant standing in the second pew from the alter holding the second light directly behind the bride, at a slight angle away from the photographer's lens. Several full length kissing and veil shots were also taken. This backlighting method will cause the photographs to look very dramatic. The next photos were of the bride's Uncle Lou shaking hands with the groom. Uncle Lou was a stand in for his brother, the bride's father, who passed away two years ago. Photos of Uncle joining the couple's hands together, walking up to the altar, then the bride and groom walk up to the altar together to be married.

In a Jewish ceremony, the parents of the bride leave her at the steps of the altar. This is to symbolize the fact that she is no longer the responsibility of her parents; her husband was now to assume full responsibility for her. This is the way it is done in the Jewish faith; even today the Orthodox sects do not hold women in high regard. True conservative, reform, and reconstructionist sects now permitted women to join the rabbinate or to become cantors. However, this protocol of leaving the bride is the way it is done in all sects of Judaism.

Still, with all the *mishigoss*, Sid believed that being Jewish you could choose to live in the twentieth century if that is what you wanted. The Catholic Church, now that was another story. Being a photographer, Sid was very familiar with the Roman Catholic faith. He wished the Church would soon come into the twentieth century for the good of civilization.

The next series of photographs were of the reenactment of the ceremony—the ring exchange, the drinking of the wine, the blessings from the rabbi, and the kiss. In addition to shooting the actual kiss, Sid opted to shoot the reenactment of the kiss from the front of the bride and groom, close up. The actual shot of the kiss would be full length toward the altar. Sid also photographed the ring exchange and the drinking of the wine, both in front of the bride and groom, close up and full length before the altar. This was for variety and to make the clients order a lot of pictures for their albums, which would cause them to go beyond the contracted minimum amount, say thirty-six or fifty, thus running up a big bill, making a wedding photographer very happy and his bank account full of money. Sid charged twenty-two dollars for an 8x10, the processing lab charged him three dollars—this was a quality machine print, not a custom print. So, needless to say, if a photographer charged a correct price and held firm, and was able to book the job, the profits after overhead expenses were very, very damn high. A high profit for any business is good.

Film is the cheapest commodity for a photographer. If you want to sell, shoot! Don't shoot willy-nilly; take carefully exposed quality pictures with principal characters.

If, in your best judgment, you see something interesting without a principal, go for it! Don't shoot twenty pictures of the same person, but get at least one, because if you ain't got it, you ain't gonna sell it.

Bridal photography is a numbers business, sell, sell, sell! Get 'em to buy more! There are price shoppers who will stay at the minimum amount of pictures for their album. They will order a couple of additional pictures, if they order anything at all. If that's the way a job went, guess what, you didn't make any money on that job. If a photographer books a job of just stills for fifteen hundred dollars, and with all the additional prints can get the client up to five thousand dollars, which is what a smart photographer should do—keep getting the client's order up. If you cannot get the client to pay much, much, much more than what the job was contracted for, you're just not making money! Shit, you're not even getting by.

Now, Sid would keep the bride and groom alone for a little while to do some formal, romantic, and dramatic photographs at the altar. There would be a series where Sid turned off the main light on his camera and lit the bride and groom with his second light; this created very dramatic portraits.

Now it was time to go upstairs to a dressing room to shoot the signing of the marriage certificate. This was an important event in a Jewish wedding ceremony.

Once more up a flight of steps. Steps, steps, steps…Sid really had to piss now.

There were mirrors in the dressing room; Sid seized the opportunity to do some pictures with the bride, groom, and parents. Mirrors often made a lovely prop for wedding pictures.

As the couple was ready to sign the certificate of marriage, they encountered a problem. There weren't enough Jewish witnesses in the room to affix their signatures to the document.

Amy, seated at a small makeup table turned around and faced her photographer. "Sid?"

Sid was flattered and guilty. Flattered because this was the first time a bride had ever asked him to be a witness. Guilty, because, he told Jeff that Amy was "Fuckin' stupid." *I really shouldn't feel guilty*, he thought, *this girl is stupid, there's no doubt about that*.

"Can you do any better?"

"C'mon, Sid, you're my photographer, and you're a nice man, please."

Now Sid was really having a guilt trip. "Well, alright, here goes," Sid signed Sidney M. (for Milton) Weitz to the document.

There was one more photo opportunity in the dressing room. The rabbi held a brief pre-ceremony service, where he blessed the bride. Sid was almost certain that at twenty-eight our bride Amy was no longer quite innocent. In fact, he was sure that that Rabbi Hyman Lavinsky was the only hymen in room that was still intact. Oh, well, what are you going to do with children today? Sid was sure his daughter Linda had waited until the wedding. He wondered if his daughter-in-law Christine waited for his son Steven, He knew she supposedly had a past. Just a Jewish father's wishful thinking. His wife, Norma? Well, that was another story. Sid was in the army, it was during Korea, and who knew if he would live to get married…oh, well, that was a lifetime, two children, and two grandchildren ago.

Amy's mother lowered the blusher; the rabbi faced Amy, and placed his hands on her shoulders.

"Amy, I ask you to stop crying. Your father, may he rest in peace, is looking down from heaven and watching; I don't want him to think that he is the cause of your tears."

Sid had photographed with flash some parts of this service. When the rabbi looked into the bride's eyes, he pressed his shutter. Neither his strobe nor Jeff's fired.

Jeff leaned toward his boss, "Sid, there wasn't any flash."

"I know that," his boss replied. "I turned off my light; I was doing an available light."

Jeff was concerned. Sid usually indicated when he was going to turn off the strobe or do a special effect. Jeff was glad that this photograph was available light, instead of another equipment malfunction. *The old guy must be slipping* Jeff thought. Last week at the C. W. Post Interfaith Chapel, Sid walked outside to photograph the rice throwing, leaving his camera at the altar. Jeff brought it out to him; Sid was going to need it again before the day was over.

The brief service was over; it was time to go downstairs for the ceremony. Again, with the steps.

Sid photographed the bride and mother and uncle walking down the aisle from the back with available light. Then he entered the sanctuary and photographed some available light and a few flash photos from several angles, including some shots from an upstairs balcony.

The video setup was adequate. Vinny, the videographer, was handholding the video camera as he stood before the altar. There was a second video camera on a tripod in the balcony focused on the altar. The footage from the second camera would be edited in with footage of the ceremony from the first camera. Sid didn't know if Vinny's boss, Nick Tavella, charged extra to use a second camera at the reception. There would only be one camera taping the reception today. The people didn't want to shell out extra money and this reception, albeit a Five Towns Jewish job, didn't warrant a second camera.

Usually at a Christian ceremony, Sid photographed the parents in pews in available light or flash, if permitted. He didn't feel like doing it today.

Now that the available light shots were finished, and the ceremony had a while to go because Rabbi Lavinsky was a windbag, Sid had some time to leave the room. He had to go in to the banquet hall, change the battery in his strobe, and plug the used battery into the rapid charger. This device charges batteries in one hour. He was about to take a few photographs of the elegant table setups, but first he better take a piss.

Both he and Jeff walked into the men's room.

Chapter Six

Both Sid Weitz and Jeffery Glassman took a very satisfying piss. Wedding photographers often have to go long intervals without relieving themselves. A candid man learns to appreciate a good piss as one of the finer things in life. Jeff went to the sink to wash his hands. Sid walked to the door without washing his hands. Jeff looked at Sid, Sid shrugged, "What for? My dick is clean."

The room where the cocktail hour was to be held was as elaborate as the main banquet room for the dinner.

There were very long tables of fine gourmet kosher food. White gloved servers were waiting to place the food onto the guests' plates. In the center of the room was a white grand piano. The pianist was tuning up. Sid didn't know whether or not this pianist was part of the ten-piece band or not.

One thing about Jewish people who had money, they knew how to have an affair. The Jewish people who didn't have money, knew how to brag about having an affair. Either they bragged or they told their friends they wouldn't want to have something so big and tasteless.

The *goyim*? Well, the *goyim* with money, such as the privileged W.A.S.P.s and the Greeks knew how to throw a bash. The regular goyim? The Irish and the Italians, for instance, knew how to party, but always looked for a bargain. They were more concerned with keeping everyone's glass full of booze, than spending the money on photographs to preserve the memories.

When the glasses are empty and the food is floating in the toilet bowl, the pictures and the videotape are all that you are going to have left from the affair. The *goyim* want to go for the cheap wedding photography 'package deal.' They go to the studios that specialize in high volume, low-end affairs…and they have the nerve to say that Jews are cheap.

Sid walked into the main dining room, changed his batteries, and plugged his used ones into the charger. He set up an area next to the bandstand. The videographer's dolly cart was already there. Keeping the equipment near the band and away from the people was a prudent idea. This prevents theft, sabotage, or any other catastrophe a wedding photographer would shudder to think of.

The band was the Larry Epstein Orchestra. He knew practically everyone in the trade—bands, caterers, florists, limousines, disk jockeys, tuxedo rentals, and gown makers. Often times these vendors were a source of referral to Montclair Studios and Montclair Studios was sometimes a source of referral for them. This Epstein guy must be new or from an entertainment agency. A few members of the band exchanged greetings with the photographer. A gorgeous blonde went up to the bandstand; she was the lead singer. A lot of wedding bands employed lead singers.

"That girl is a piece of ass," Sid remarked.

"Norma would kill you."

"No she wouldn't, kid, besides my Norma is still a piece of ass herself…a fifty-five year-old grandmother and still a piece of ass. Ya know why?"

"Why?"

"Because she kept herself thin and stayed in shape."

"Oh."

"Yep, there's this kid, a college kid who lives across the street from us, he has all his life. A real nice kid, in fact, I did his Bar Mitzvah. Well, anyway, he always chats with Norma. He calls her Mrs.Weitz, but he wants to nail her."

"How do you know that?"

"I know; I see it in his eyes when they talk. I see he's always focusing on her knockers. He's always looking at her ass. Believe me, this kid thinks Norma's still hot. She still is…we're grandparents, but we still fuck like a couple of teenagers."

"How do you know they're not doing anything?"

"Nah, my Norma is not Mrs. Robinson. But, if she wants to give him some head, why not? He'll have some experience from an older woman. Then he'd know what to do with a girl his own age. When I was dating Norma, you know, when I was in the army, I banged an older woman; she taught me a few things."

"I hope you're joking."

"Jeff, do you bang that cute little girlfriend of yours? No pussy yet, my boy? Don't worry, you're young yet."

"Sid, come on."

"Okay, okay. In my day, you had to be married before you could have pussy. You couldn't have any pussy until you were married. That's what I told my son."

"Did he listen to you?"

"I doubt it."

"Still don't like your little *shiksa* daughter-in-law?"

"I like her; I like her, I just wish she was Jewish."

"How many months pregnant?"

"Six…going to be a girl…no Bar Mitzvah. The kid, I bet, will be baptized, you watch. Come on, let's get to work, we have a lot to do yet. There's the recessional, the receiving line, and *yachod*. I'll follow the rabbi's lead. We got some time, yet, the rabbi talks too much."

They photographed both the rooms from the entrance with a wide-angle lens—the table setups, the smorgasbord setups, and the chap playing the piano—more often than not, these pictures never made it into the album. The Yiddish clients expected it and the lower-class *goyim* didn't really care. Sid photographed the invitation and the wedding cake, then they both went back into the sanctuary.

Sid and Jeff knelt in front of the altar, waiting to shoot the breaking of the glass; it wouldn't be long now.

The glass was being wrapped in a cloth napkin, and the photographer and assistant stood up. The glass was placed near the groom's foot. SMASH! CLICK, FLASH! *MAZEL TOV!* An embrace, CLICK, FLASH, *MAZEL TOV!*, the big kiss, CLICK, FLASH, *MAZEL TOV!* APPLAUSE, APPLAUSE, *MAZEL TOV!*

It was over; the temple's public address system came to life with a lively rendition of *Od Yishama*.

For the recessional, Sid stood at twelve feet, pre-focused. The couple started walking up the aisle, CLICK, FLASH.

Perfect! Once more looking at the *mishpachah*, acknowledging their congratulations.

"Okay," the photographer called out, "look at the camera." CLICK, FLASH! "Now kiss!"

Sid jumped in front of them, kissing in front of the sanctuary door.

For Jewish weddings, photographers usually photograph everyone in the recessional. At Christian weddings, you just need the bride and groom; you can get the parents, too, if you want to get fancy.

Time for the receiving line. There would only need to be a few shots of this. Most of the time, receiving line pictures didn't even get into the album. Sid photographed using straight flash and bounce.

Sid and Jeff went through the line last. "*Mazel tov!* Good luck to you," was the wish from their photographer.

The rabbi appeared and led the happy couple to his study for *yachod*.

Yachod is a time for the bridal couple to be alone. This tradition is mostly observed in the Orthodox movement. In olden days, *yachod* was when the bride and groom consummated their marriage. This does not happen today. Although, there was this time Montclair Studios was shooting a fancy wedding at a big temple up in the Riverdale section of the Bronx. Sid was shooting the video and when the rabbi took the bride and groom to his study, Sid forgot to remove the wireless microphone for sound from the groom's lapel.

As Sid was setting up his video lights in the banquet hall, the public address was spewing sounds of ecstasy. Sid ran out of the room, and as he ran through the lobby to the rabbi's study, the temple rang out with cries and moans of, "UHNNH!" "OHHHH!" "OH YESSSS, BABY!" and, "EEEEH, EEEEEE!"

Sid's wireless mic was on the same frequency as the temple's.

Sid banged on the door of the rabbi's study.

"Go away, leave us alone," moaned the bride.

"Yeah, get oudda here!" the groom cried out.

"Hey!" he screamed at the top of his lungs as he banged on the door of the study, "Hey! You still have a microphone on! Everybody hears you, for Christ's sake!"

"For God's sake, Bruce! Wipe off your dick, pull up your pants, and give me the goddamn mic!"

There was somewhat of the same type of occurrence at a Catholic church in the Bensonhurst section of Brooklyn. Sid had already placed the wireless mike on the groom's lapel, when the groom went out to meet his friends.

"Hey, Tony, how the fuck you doin'?" the groom greeted his friend.

This was being broadcasted throughout the church as the guests were entering. Fortunately, the priest was a young Italian guy and found this very funny.

The bride's mother spoke, "If you boys would like to go have something to eat, the cocktail hour is just starting."

"Thank you."

"Sid," the groom's father spoke, "you're gonna do the tables during dinner, right?"

"Yes, sir!"

"And during the break in the reception, we are going to want some family photos—aunts, uncles, cousins, stuff like that."

"Absolutely!"

"Good, alright, we can go into the lobby or maybe outside; it looks like the rain is letting up."

Jesus, the 'prick head' isn't even paying me and he's calling the shots, still, Sid just smiled and nodded.

The damn rain was letting up. It wasn't going to be such a lousy day, after all. Sid and Jeff inched their way into the room where the hors d'oeuvres were.

Chapter Seven

The smorgasbord table at an elegant Jewish wedding is a beauty to behold. It probably cost more than the wedding albums. There was an abundance of both hot and cold meats, kosher pasta dishes, kosher Chinese and Italian dishes, salads, fruits, and Jell-O molds. A Japanese couple was preparing sushi; this was just for the cocktail hour. There was a large well-stocked bar at the end of the room, even though Jewish people are not known for drinking. Somebody was going to drink today, and the drinks at this place weren't watered down like at those shitty factory-type halls. This was strictly the good stuff.

Both Sid and Jeff had cokes. Sid seldom drank at all, and rarely had a drink on the job. To some extent, he was happy his son Steven had eloped with his *shiksa* girlfriend Christine. The Christians just have to get that Christ into that kid's name somehow. Christine's mother was Irish, her father Italian, and Sid knew how much those folks drank. That was why he was happy about the elopement. He didn't want to play host at an affair where the bride's little *shiksa* girlfriends would be running around the hall drinking their beer right out of the bottle. Was there any reason those people have to drink their beer from the bottles? Do it at home in your undershirt, that's alright, but for Christ's sake at a wedding…what a bunch! At least today everybody is going to drink from the glass.

"Oh, my God, Morty!" a female guest exclaimed, "They're having sushi."

"So what?" her husband retorted, "It's kosher."

"It is?"

"Sure—tuna, salmon, only the fish with fins and scales—see, there isn't any shrimp or squid, no shellfish."

"Oh."

"You wanna try some, Sarah?"

"What, are you joking?"

Sid tried some sushi, it was good. If you want to get stuffed, go to an Italian wedding. If you want to eat, go to a Jewish wedding. At an Irish wedding, everybody drinks, so they don't know how the food tastes. The next day the guests don't even remember who got married.

"It looks like Chateaubriand, this meat, but it ain't, 'cause Chateaubriand isn't kosher." Sid inspected the chafing dishes.

"How's the meat?"

"Good."

"What the fuck do you mean good, Jeff, it's terrific!"

The next thing they tried was the kosher chicken ratatouille. The thin crepe split and some red sauce bled down Sid's dress shirt. He tried to wipe it off, but the stain only spread.

"Can't take you anywhere."

"Well, I'm gonna go in later, tomorrow, so I'll put it through the wash in the morning."

"I thought we were closed on Monday."

"We? The fuck do you mean we? Anyway, you know why I'm going in…to close it out."

"Shit, Sid, you're really going to go through with it?"

"It's already been done, baby. Most everything has been moved out, thrown out, or sold. Some at the furniture is at the office in my house. Look, you knew I was serious. We'll talk about this later."

"You need help tomorrow?"

"Come over after one. I have some shit I'd like you to have. It ain't much, remember, I'm not retiring, yet; I'm gonna work out of my house."

"You'll still need me?"

"Nah, Jeff, I'm semi–retired, I just need to occupy my time and earn some dough before I can get Social Security, or until I can find a crooked stockbroker with a Ponzi scheme. I'll use you to shoot and tape and light for me, but it's over; it's finished and I'm finished"

"Sid, you're not finished."

"How many people did I tell you used to work for me in our heyday?"

"Thirty." Jeff doubted that was the truth.

"How many affairs did we average a weekend?"

"Forty-five." Jeff doubted that was the truth too.

"How many weddings alone did we shoot a year, not counting Bar Mitzvahs?"

"One hundred fifty, plus all the Bar Mitzvahs, made over three hundred; Sid, you told me."

"Damn straight. We booked three hundred…no…five hundred jobs. Lenny, Carl, and me each shot one hundred fifty ourselves. How many jobs have I shot lately?"

"Not many."

"Not many. In fact, now I shoot and tape so many jobs for other studios, when you assist me on those jobs, you really work for them. For the last year when I shot for Shiffman, Allonmar, and Liebmann-Rhett, that's what paid most of my fuckin' studio rent. How many people work for me now?"

"Just you, me, and Lenny."

"Lenny don't work for me, he's my partner. In fact, he's not my partner anymore and his staff has nothing to do with me. You're only over there part time, so it's just me."

"It's just you."

"That's right, and I'm getting old, I'm tired, business is dying, and Elmont is all *shvartzed up* now, so why should I stay? Remember the Jewish guy in Flatbush? The *shvartzes* walked into his studio and put a bullet in his head. You want me to end up like that putz Malkin? Malkin Photographers? He can't afford the overhead anymore, so now he shares a store with a guy who does tee shirts and monograms. You see how he displays the albums and frames in his windows? They're lying there amongst the fuckin' tee shirts."

"Do what you have to do."

"It's just time to go, that's all. Finish eating, we have work to do. We'll talk more about it tomorrow, I promise. If you ask me…teach. Shoot affairs or any commercial assignments part time from your home. Don't even bother opening a fuckin' studio; new studios don't make it these days, and us old-timers are going out of business. Have security and peace of mind."

"Yeah, yeah."

"Don't be a putz, kid. Do yourself a favor, do this shit part time, make a good living teaching photography, and hold on to your money. Don't piss it away on a studio. Get laid by your cute little girlfriend and enjoy your life. Listen to me, sweetheart, if there's one thing I know…it's this fuckin' business."

"But you made it, you survived."

"Why do you want to survive? Wouldn't you rather live? Living is a hell of a lot better than surviving, believe me."

"Sid," Jeff was almost pleading with his boss now, "You told me you made a good living."

"Then was then. It was a long time ago, it was the newness of this type of business. We used to tell them they needed us for that date. Now we're a dime a dozen—there are so many around, try to tell someone they need you. You know what they'll say? 'Fuck you! I don't need you, you need me! I'll get someone else, you fuckin' moron, you!'"

"So that's how it is, boss." It was a statement, not a question. Jeff's tone was somewhat contemptful.

"That's how it is. Today the clients know they wield power. Especially with this recession. Now they are trying to have legislation passed so they get the negatives. What? You won't give me the negatives? Fuck you! I'll get someone else. You can't give me a better price? I'll go with someone else with a package deal. What about my uncle has a good camera, or my friend takes good pictures, he'll do it. Sometimes today the way things are we can't always charge a good price to make a lot of money. Sometimes we're afraid to charge a good price because we're afraid of losing the job. Now, we let the goddamn public walk all over us."

Jeff seemed to be listening intently to his mentor.

"Remember, there are a lot of studios, part-time hacks, and bridal centers out there. So, your work better be worth the fuckin' price. If you aren't able to sell your work, well then, buddy, you better get used to spending Saturday nights at home jerking off. The era of the 'you need us' attitude is over, pal."

"I'll remember that, Sid. I'll try to take your advice."

"Don't try, take it!"

"We'll see."

"Oh yeah, you'll see. Come, let's go make a diagram of the guest tables, we got seventeen today."

Chapter Eight

In the elaborate banquet room of the Woodmere Reform Temple, Sid Weitz made a diagram of the guest tables. He did this by placing little circles, numbered one through seventeen, on a little piece of scrap paper. This enabled a photographer to mark off each table that was photographed. During the course of an affair, it was hard to remember if every table was photographed. In his forty years, he encountered a lot of, "My wife is in the ladies' room, can you come back?" A photographer had to remember.

The band was ready; the guests were entering the room.

The last check Sid made was the tiny video light he 'Velcroed' to his bracket. This helped a photographer to focus when shooting tables in a dark hall. The light was connected to the nine-volt battery that powered his strobe unit. Everyone was seated at their table. Sid put on his distance glasses and pre-focused on the area where the bridal party was to enter. After everyone entered, things would move fast.

First, the grandfathers of the bride and groom would stand at a small table and recite the *Motzi*, the blessing of the bread. Then there was to be a first dance followed by a *hora*, where the bride and groom are to be lifted on chairs, followed in turn by their parents. The toast by the best man was to take place later. At a Jewish wedding, the toast was made after dinner; at Christian weddings, the toast was made before dinner.

Sid had a 55 mm wide-angle lens on his camera now. It was easy to shoot receptions with a wide-angle lens, especially the candids. A wide angle allowed the photographer to move into the action rather than backing up to compose.

Vinny, the videographer, was already setup, the camera was on the dolly cart, and his lights were positioned. Sid prayed that this asshole wasn't going to get in his way. Even worse, this guy better not shoot any posed pictures over my shoulder.

The only people who knew how to videotape were those who photographed stills. That was not merely a belief of still photographers, that was a fact. All Sid knew was that this jerk better not follow him around all day and shoot his stuff.

"Alright, folks! Let's put our hands together," the bandleader addressed the crowd, "it's time to party!"

Sid photographed the entrance of the parents, the members of the bridal party, then the entrance of the bride and groom. The happy couple walked through an arch composed of members of the bridal party, set up by the maitre'd.

Sid positioned himself in front of the small table draped with a white linen tablecloth; a large challah bread on a silver platter, along with a salt shaker lay on the table. Both grandfathers smiled at the photographer.

"*Boruch atta Addonai elho-hainu melech haolam, hamotzi lechem menen h'aretz.*"

"*Omayn!*" called out all those who were present, including the photographer.

The first dance was *The Wind beneath My Wings* from the movie *Beaches*. The lead singer was very good, but she was no Bette Midler. He snapped several posed and candid photos of the bridal couple, parents, grandparents, and principals of the bridal party during the first song. The photographer then placed a fresh roll of 220 film in the Mamiya to be ready for the events to follow.

The band was blasting now, BOOM BA BOOM - BA BA BOOM BA - BOOM! "*Hava Nagila.*" The room was vibrating now; Sid had a pulsating feeling in his dick from the beat. The guests formed a single circle around the couple, and then there was a double circle. So many photographers hate double circle *horas*. This made it hard to capture the main principals.

Sid did not use a stepladder on jobs anymore. He just thought he was getting too fucking old to schlep a lot of shit. The stepladder was useful for the *hora* or shooting candids of disco-type dancing. It was nice to stand above the subjects, but you had to be careful not to get the back of people's heads. The ladder was good for doing things in tight areas, but when you get to a certain age, you don't want to kill yourself, regardless of how much the client is paying you. Without a ladder, the photographer had to get into the circle by tapping people on their shoulder, and gesturing with the camera. If this didn't work, the photographer just had to push his way in. A long time ago, when Sid was starting out, a Chassidic photographer in the Boro Park section of Brooklyn, a pious man, taught him how to handle people who push the photographer or will not get out of the way. The pious photographer told Sid, after the bride passes and the men start shoving, use your elbows and knees, but always with a smile.

"Elbow a man hard in his stomach, then smile and say, "Oh! I am very sorry." If someone stands in front of you, take your knee and slam it into his crotch. Then smile and say, "Oh, sorry! Are you alright?"

Sid had not elbowed or kneed anybody for a long time. He sometimes enjoyed giving a pain in the ass who jumped in front of him, a shot in the balls. In the early seventies when he was shooting with a heavy Koni-Omega Rangefinder camera, a bop in the back of an interfering guest's head did the trick.

The bride was being lifted up in the chair. Sid held his camera high above the guests the same way a newspaper photographer does. Jeff was not holding the monopod with his strobe high enough. The kid knew better, he was not paying attention.

"Jeff, damn it! Higher, hold the fuckin' light higher, you're lighting the bride's ass!"

Jeff, standing very close to Sid, raised his light. He was afraid that the people would hear the language that had no place at a wedding reception.

The *hora* medley continued. After *Hava Nagila*, the band played *Mazel Tov and Siman Tov*, *Rad Halaila*, *Shmelkie's Nigun*, and *David Melech Yisrael*.

This was a standard Americanized *hora* set, so there were a few important and popular *horas* that were played. Chassidic and Orthodox wedding have fifty-minute *hora* sets, not to mention the *mazel tov* dances the men do, which go on forever.

After the *hora*, Sid was still miffed at Jeff. He made the kind of mistake only an inexperienced light person would make.

"Unbelievable! The bride was up nine feet, you were holding the light at about five feet! Unfuckin'believable! What the fuck got into you? You disappointed me."

Jeff tried like hell to keep a straight face when Sid said "disappointed," because it came out "disapernted." The old guy was having a bad day today.

The people sat down and the serving staff was taking orders for the main course. Today's choices were prime rib of beef au jus, lemon sole, fresh young Vermont turkey, or breast of chicken.

At most Jewish weddings, the guests are more upscale, so caterers do not want the guests to be disturbed during the meal by the photographer. It was a good idea to do the photography and video interviews as soon as possible. He was pissed when the putz videographer decided to follow him around and videotape the table after he set it up. He was pressed for time and had to work fast.

As fate would have it, some broads at the tables had to go to the ladies' room, so there was going to be a good deal of backtracking. Slowly, but surely, the bride's dais and all seventeen of the tables were photographed.

Sometimes, photographing guest tables at Jewish affairs can be a grueling task. When you ask people to sit, they stand. Everybody there is a photographer, they all offer their two cents worth of advice on how to shoot, all because they won a ribbon from their camera club for taking a picture of a sunset with an autofocus camera.

Once, one stupid ass broad asked Sid if there was any reason why his flash was so strong. He told her this way the pictures will come out. He knew as long as you smile you can be sarcastic and get away with it.

The tables had large centerpieces right smack in the middle. The centerpieces blocked whoever was sitting behind them. An inexperienced shooter would shoot with the centerpieces right where they were. Even a lot of seasoned pros would attempt to shoot through them. This was a good way of doing it, if you liked shadows across people's faces. Other stupid photographers would take the centerpieces *off* the table. This was no damn good, because the clients paid a lot of money for their floral arrangements. Sometimes the flowers cost as much as the photography…he remembered the cost of flowers for his daughter's wedding.

There was a proper way to set up this type of shot and Sid Weitz knew how. The photographer places the centerpieces toward the end of the table, and moves the chairs so that the flowers are at the furthest end from the person in the last chairs. The expensive floral arrangement is not omitted from the picture, but there are no shadows across anyone's face.

Sid had an excellent time tested method of gaining a lady's cooperation for a table picture. He would ask the young lady to stand over there. The old hag's husband would always say, "This guy can't be the photographer, he's blind, he called my wife a young lady." The men at the table laughed and the old hag glared at her husband, but at least she would move to where the photographer wanted her to stand.

At the seventeenth table, the groom's father came over to check in with his photographer.

"Having a good time, George?" inquired the photographer.

"I sure am, Sidney, it's one hell of a bash."

"Glad to hear it, George, you should enjoy."

Sid raised his camera to his eye to shoot the table, when the groom's father asked the photographer an embarrassing question. "Sidney, are your lights working?"

"Come again?"

"I just wanted to know if you're having any problems like you had this morning."

"Everything is fine."

"You're not having problems with your lights or cords or batteries?"

"No problems."

"Is your flash going off?"

"Everything is bee-yoo-ti-ful!"

"Well, I just wanted to make sure."

"No problem, George, thank you for asking."

The groom's father turned and walked away. Sid muttered, "Fuuuck yoou!" under his breath. Jeff was standing close enough to hear; he hoped no one else did.

All the tables were photographed. The main course was being served. The band was taking a break during the dinner, except for a guy tinkling at the piano. Sid wanted to tinkle, too. They would wait in the empty banquet room across the hall.

He paused and lit a Viceroy. Family pictures, some romantic shots, some more candids, the toast, and the *M'zinka* dance set, and, with the toast, the job was winding down.

Photography was something Sid Weitz did by rote. In the last forty years, he had photographed God knew how many affairs. This did not include portraits, passports, and other shit. Everything was all routine for him now. He took a long drag on the cigarette. Everyone was eating; with camera in hand, he walked out of the room, it was time to take a break.

Chapter Nine

The cheap fucks who paid for this elaborate Five Towns wedding opted not to provide dinners for the band, the photography, or video crew. Sid sat at a large round table in the empty banquet room, with the members of the band. Vinny, the videographer, was not in the room, thank God. The band's piano player was not in the room, either; he was diddling on his keyboard. Sid and Jeff introduced themselves all around.

Larry Epstein, the bandleader, was a nice affable young guy. He and Larry exchanged business cards. They sat all around sipping sodas. Sid tried to keep from staring at the cute, little piece-of-ass singer. Vicky was quite a looker in that tight black dress. She was one gorgeous *shiksa*. His daughter-in-law Christine was a cute *shiksa*, but nothing to compare with Vicky. Vicky had beautiful, straight, pearl white teeth. Christine had crooked teeth, although they were not very bad. The blue collar *goyim* don't spend money for braces for their kid's teeth, they spend money on motorcycles.

"I never worked a job with you," the bandleader spoke, "but I've heard of you, you have a studio in Elmont."

"Yep," answered the photographer, "been there a long time."

"Sid, I grew up in Baldwin, I know your studio."

"Where do you live now, Larry?"

"Dix Hills."

"That's a nice area; I've shot a lot of jobs up there."

"Sid, there's a studio in town, Creative Imagery, do you know them?" Larry asked.

"Yes, that's Donna Frescatti. She's a nice kid; she used to shoot for me. She's not a member of my association, so I seldom see her, but we're still friends."

"I work with her sometimes," Larry continued, "she just got divorced."

"Good!" said Sid enthusiastically, "the guy was a real lowlife. She'd work all day so he could come home drunk and beat her up."

"That's terrible," Vicky offered her opinion.

"Terrible?" answered Sid, "Ya wanna know what her husband did for a living?"

"What? Tell me." Vicky was interested.

"He was a cop. A Nassau County cop…assigned to the domestic violence unit, yet."

Vicky shook her head in disgust.

"I'm trying to remember who shot my Bar Mitzvah," Larry spoke. "Some guy in Oceanside. He had a studio on Crest Road."

"I know who you mean," Sid replied. "A little guy with a hairpiece, a hunch back, what the hell is his name?" Sid paused for a moment, "Hmmm…schmuck…that's Alvin Bookbinder. Yeah, he's still around, works from his house now, he and his wife, Ida. He almost died a few years ago in a terrible car wreck. He was in a body cast, like a mummy, for months." He chuckled, "I went up to see him in the hospital; they didn't think he was going to live."

Vicky said that Sid must know a lot of photographers.

He told her that most of the guys he knew were either retired or dead.

"You said you know Alvin Bookbinder," Larry reminded him.

"Well," Sid answered in his gravelly voice, "he's the living dead; I rest my case."

The table laughed.

Vicky leaned toward Sid and he saw the tops of her creamy shoulders, and the outline of her sculpted breasts. Sid and Jeff exchanged glances, to let each other know that they both had boners.

"You're a member of the professional photographer group, right?"

"That's right," Sid replied pleasantly. "I was a member when we called ourselves L.I.P.P.A., The Long Island Professional Photographers Association. Now we're P.P.G.N.Y., Professional Photographers of Greater New York. We used to be a studio owners' association, but through the years we allowed candid people to join. I frankly thought that was a good idea. If everybody learns how to execute their ideas better, the industry benefits. Some shooters who don't belong think we're a group of arrogant, blue ribbon, over-priced, award winners who think our shit doesn't stink."

"Is it like that?" asked one of the musicians.

"Well, there are some people there like that. This association is the closest thing we have to a union. It used to be a strong powerful organization. Some view it as a backslapping professional clique, but it makes a shooter feel good to know that they belong. Also, they try to educate the consumer about our craft and what is quality. Nowadays, the association is bullshit; just a bunch of big egos."

"We belong," Larry spoke proudly, "to a couple of musical associations."

Sid voiced his approval. "Good for you, babe. You can't be an island unto yourself."

"So, tell me," asked Normy, the trumpet player, "do you do mafia weddings?"

"I've done a few," Sid admitted. "I haven't done any lately."

"They don't mind the pictures?"

"Nah, their main concern is being photographed by the feds waiting outside the hall. The feds try to catch them violating their parole. You just have to be careful."

"How?"

"Well, first of all, if you're shooting an Italian wedding and you see a table where only men are sitting, you don't shoot that table. You walk with your back to that table. When I was young, I was shooting this Italian football wedding in the East Bronx and…."

"What's a football wedding?" Vicky interrupted.

"That's where they chuck sandwiches to the guests," Larry explained, "it's very classy."

"Yeah, anyway," Sid continued, "a guy with a mustache and silk suit walks up to me. He asks me if I speak Italian. I says to him, 'Do I look Italian?' So he says, 'I'ma watcha you woik, you a berry a good photog-a-rapher. I'ma goona aska you one a favor. I wanna you remember dis a favor all a nigh' long. When I see a da proofs a dis a weddin', I don't wanna see no pictures a dis a table.'"

Jeff never heard this story before. True or not, he was impressed with the way Sid mimicked an Italian accent.

"Then he hands me a twenty dollar bill."

"You're kidding!" The trumpet player was splitting his sides with laughter, "The guy gave you money?"

"It ain't like the movies, they ask you nicely. Then they give, I dunno, twenty dollars for you being a good guy."

"Hey," the drummer spoke up, "why didn't you tell that guy, screw you buddy! Don't tell me how to take pictures!"

Again, a burst of laughter all around.

"It would say in the papers, 'Photographer found in Gowanus Canal,'" Larry called out.

"It would say, 'Photographer not found,' believe me," added Normy.

More laughter.

Sid held up his hand to continue.

All quieted down and listened intently to the old photographer. They were enjoying themselves.

"I used to shoot weddings for this mob boss, now deceased. He was a legitimate businessman, wholesale meats, also owned a casket manufacturing company. He used to come in to my studio all the time. I asked him the name of the groom, 'We can't tell you that.' I'd ask, 'Well, where is the affair gonna be and what time?' Then the boss would look at his consigliere, he would nod, so the boss said, 'Okay, we can tell you that.' They paid everything in cash. I figured in the sales tax, of course, seeing as they were law abiding citizens."

Everybody was cracking up now. Sid had fancied himself a raconteur.

"The weddings were a lot of fun. I saw politicians, actors, comedians, lawyers, singers, and cops...a lot of cops, after all this was the wedding of a legitimate businessman's daughter, why shouldn't cops be there?"

Everyone was hysterical.

"I used to tell my wife, Norma, if I'm not back by seven the next morning, call the FBI."

Larry turned to Sid, "But seriously, man, I hear things are pretty bad out there for guys in business right now. Financially, I mean."

"This isn't the heyday anymore, the 1980s are over. You get good times, you get bad times."

"Yeah, but Sid, I know so many of you guys went out of business in the last couple of years. What is it? Too much competition, the economy, what?"

"A combination of all those things. I'm closing my studio. I'm gonna work out of my house; I don't need a studio anymore, not for the amount of work I do anyway. My goddamn rent is up to sixteen hundred dollars a month, not including the utilities. The area I'm in, in Elmont, is very bad now. Once it was a Jewish area, but there aren't too many left, maybe a few down south by the cemetery. There are still a lot of Italians left, but I always catered to a mostly Jewish clientele. The blacks use very cheap package studios. Some even offer financing. Sure, I've done a few jobs for them, but I'm talking about the upscale ones, the Dr. Huxtables. The blacks in my area are mostly common law anyway. There is so much crime where my studio is, I just have to get out before I get popped or cut. I'd like to not have to kick the crack vials away from my front door. Part of the reason for my problems now is that my clients are afraid to come to the studio."

"How about the Puerto Ricans?" asked Larry.

"The PRs aren't as bad the *shvartzes*, believe it or not. They're smarter, they own businesses. They spend money on weddings, they're real party people, don't get me wrong."

"I know that," agreed Larry, "I've worked for them."

"Yeah, well, they're not so bad to do business with, they book...they tip big, and some of the girls are beautiful. The only problem is the PRs take three years to pick up their proofs."

"Didn't you have a baby studio, Sid?"

"We always had a baby studio. My partner Lenny Schecter ran it when he wasn't shooting candids. Thank God, the baby business kept him upstairs and away from me."

"You had another studio setup in the store?"

"Nah, upstairs was in-home baby portraits by appointment only. We'd sell the mommies packages. Lenny's moving next month. Happy Time is moving to Lynbrook."

"He doesn't shoot big jobs anymore?" Vicky asked, as she was leaving the room to make a call.

"Not for years," Sid called after her. He just runs the baby place. I bought him out of the candids; we have paperwork going on now. He's gonna buy me out of the babies. He tells people who call for a job interview with him, "Just show me a portfolio of babies and children. Don't show me any weddings or Bar Mitzvahs, none of that bullshit." When we were young, we needed each other; now we want nothing to do with each other."

Vicky was out of the room.

"Just babies, that's it?" Larry continued the conversation.

"Lenny just cares about shooting kids now, that's it? He's very successful, too. I can prove it; the putz has the Better Business Bureau and the Attorney General's Office after him. He caused my other partner Carl Resnick to move to Arizona. He couldn't take Lenny the lowlife. Carl was a class act all the way, born in the Bronx, but spoke like an Englishman. Twelve years ago, things really got strained because Lenny didn't want to get into video. He thought it was a passing fad. Ha, ha, passing fad my ass! Now, I swear there are more videographers out there than photographers. We were the first studio on Long Island to shoot video. Up until three months ago, I had a clause in my contract that said we would not book stills with outside video companies. We did that for the same reason a dog licks his balls, because we could! We had a great reputation. Now I'm winding it down, so I'm a bit more flexible. See that schmuck in there shooting the video?"

"Yeah."

"Well, he drives an oil truck. He works for this asshole, who used to shoot stills. Now he sends out video crews. These guys have no training, they get a lesson on how to operate the fuckin' camera, and how to compose, do tilting, panning, and close-ups, that's all. Some of the original videographers started as still photographers. They knew how to work with photographers. They never got in our way."

Larry nodded.

"I do video; I know I shouldn't block a fuckin' aisle with a fuckin' dolly cart, so the still man can't shoot. You know, I was doing this church wedding a couple of weeks ago, this fuckin' schmuck had this big fuckin' cart like I've never seen before. I asked him nice three times, three times, to please get out of my way. The cocksucker doesn't budge. He fuckin' sees I'm struggling, really busting my balls. So, what I do finally is tell him to get the fuck outta my way! Alright, the son of a bitch gives a little, but at the reception, the prick keeps blinding me with his light. He keeps shining it into my lens. The dirty bastard follows me around, and he shoots what I shoot!"

Larry looked surprised.

"That's right; he shoots the stuff I set up. Then a few days later, the bride calls me. She wants the proofs so the video company can use them for the opening of their video. You believe that?" Sid touched Larry on his forearm to emphasize his point. "She calls me so I can give them my pictures for her fuckin' video. Unfuckin' believable!"

"Whadja do?" asked the bandleader.

"I told her, if she puts my photography on someone else's video, I'm gonna sue her."

"You can do that?"

"Absolutely, I have the rights to those images. When it's created, it's copyrighted."

"So, if somebody tapes my band without my permission…?"

"I think so, yeah…maybe you can sue. My wife and I saw a Broadway play; the ticket said we couldn't have a tape recorder."

The band leader looked like he had learned something today.

"Larry, let me tell you, it ain't no picnic on the other end either."

"Meaning?"

"When you're shooting the video and you're working with a still man from somewhere else, some inexperienced guys walk right the fuck in front of you. It really pisses me off, when I'm taping a scene and somebody walks right in front of the camera. At least my studio handled my kid's Bar and Bat Mitzvahs and my daughter's wedding, so there weren't any problems." Sid paused and thought for a moment, "Well," he continued, "there was one problem at Linda's wedding."

"You must have driven your people crazy."

"I did, I did. I kept telling Harry, a retired Jewish New York City cop who's been with me twenty-five years, 'take a picture of this, take a picture of that. Pose this way; use my idea for the next shot.' He turns around to me right in front of everybody and says, 'Siiiiiid, leeeeeeave meeee alooone!'"

Larry laughed.

What Sid did not tell his new bandleader friend was the story that had become the talk of the industry.

Harry Lowenstein, had been a New York City police officer for thirty years, he had shot for Sid Weitz for twenty-five. Harry had shot for several other studios throughout the years, but he always had work from Sid, Carl, and Lenny at Montclair Studios. In their heyday, the owners of Montclair needed Harry more than he needed them.

Harry only shot with square formats; he was strictly a Hasselblad man. He was an honest cop, so his friends wondered how he could afford Hasselblad equipment if he was not on the take. Since he was one of Sid's best, Sid asked him to please shoot his daughter Linda's wedding. Harry agreed to help a man he thought was a close friend. At the end of the night, Harry handed Sid the rolls of exposed film and asked Sid for his paycheck.

"What!" Sid was exasperated. "Whaaaat! Harry, you don't shoot my daughter's wedding for me, as a friend!"

Harry did not get paid. He wasn't even shooting as a contracted studio. He thought he was shooting for a day's wage. The lighting assistant got paid; Sid told Harry that he wouldn't think of cheating a kid.

Harry told all his friends in the industry, "Sid didn't want to pay me for shooting his daughter's wedding, well alright, that's Sid. But the sonofabitch! I've known him twenty-five years; he could have at least given me a plate of food!"

"What was the other problem, Sid?"

"Oh, a 'vidiot,' a real shithead. When Linda got married, video was still very new. So, this guy who was supposedly very good wanted to shoot jobs for us, so I told him he could shoot my kid's wedding. Okay, so he gets to the hall, he doesn't even secure his light stands. My God, he could kill someone if a light fell over; he'd go to jail, so would I. So, I read the guy the riot act, he gives me an argument, but does what I tell him. But at the fuckin' reception, he shoots all wrong. Finally the straw that breaks the camel's ass is when he completely fucks up so many of my photographer's shots. I scream at him, 'I'm the father of the bride and I'm gonna beat the shit out of you!'"

"What happened?" Larry asked, he was enjoying Sid's tales.

"In front of my whole family, I take off my tux jacket and go after him. My mother-in-law looks at me and says, 'Oooh, common!'"

"Did ya hit him?"

"Nah, my wife grabbed me; Harry the photographer, he's a cop, he blocks me, says, 'Sid, I'm gonna book you!' So Norma calmed me down. I think the video could have been much better. I never used the prick again; I'm sorry I didn't punch him. As for Norma's mother, well, that wasn't the first time she said I was common."

"Who would ever think you could be common," Larry said straight faced.

"I tell you, my friend, it's getting hard to make a living doing this shit." Sid was still ranting about the 'vidiots.' That is the term Sid Weitz used to describe half-assed unprofessional videographers. "Three months ago, when I lifted the clause requiring only our video crew, some fuckin' vidiot bumped into me in a church with his cart. The fuckin' ass knocked me over, whap! Right in the aisle of the church. I went down; I thought it was the end of me. I should have killed the bastard."

Jeff excused himself to go call his girlfriend.

Larry excused himself to return to the reception to see what was going on. Sid lit a Viceroy.

Vicky came back into the room. "Those things will kill you."

"I know," the photographer admitted. "I'm quitting; it ain't easy. I used to smoke Pall Mall unfiltered a long time ago; I used to smoke a Pall Mall and a Kool at the same time."

Vicky was astonished, it showed. "My God, a menthol along with an unfiltered regular!"

"That's right," Sid smiled. "For years my little girl begged me, 'Daddy, quit!' I'm in good health, so far, so I'm weaning myself off."

"Weaning, I haven't heard that word in years." She sat down next to him.

"Years ago we adopted a cute little red striped kitten. The man at the shelter told us that the kitten was weaned. So my son Steven named him Weanus Catius. We all called him Weanus."

Hmmm, Vicky thought, *Weanus, that's a good name for a cat,* she said, "Weanus!"

"We called him 'Wean' for short," Sid was cracking up. Vicky found him charming. The people who didn't find him common, found him charming. "We sometimes called him Weanie or Weanaleh, because we're Jewish."

Vicky giggled, she was a bit flushed.

"A great name for a pussy cat, Weanus ain't. I was embarrassed to make an appointment for him with the vet. The receptionist called out, 'Mr. Weitz and Weanus!' My wife had to take him to the vet once, and she was embarrassed. On the phone, the receptionist asked her what the cat's name was, Norma gave our last name Weitz, and the cat's first initial, as W."

"What happened to Weanus?"

"He ran away from home, and never came back; held up his middle claw, and just took off."

"Why'd he run away?"

"Vicky, baby, you'd run the hell away too if some schmuck named you Weanus."

"Have any pets now?"

"Just a seven year-old female cat, grey striped, named Plucky. We named her that because plucky means spirited; she was a spirited kitten."

Vicky crossed her legs.

Sid put out the remainder of his cigarette. He offered Vicky a spearmint flavored Tic Tac mint.

She took two, so did he.

Sid did not use profanity in front of women. In all the years of marriage to Norma, the only words he ever said in front of her were, damn, goddamn, hell, crap, shit, bitch, sonofabitch, and bastard. There were also the Yiddish expletives *schmuck, putz,* and *momzer.* Never any words stronger than those, and although, said in front of Norma, never directed at her. Sid was fond of the word fuck, but only used it in front of his male cronies. He told his stories to Vicky without using explicit language. Women photographers who knew him knew he had a mouth, but they never heard him say anything vulgar. Some women photographers described Sid Weitz as earthy, but on the whole, he usually behaved himself in front of females.

Except for one situation, an incident that occurred a year ago. Sid was videotaping a Bat Mitzvah for another studio. He needed to pay off some bills. The studio gave him an attractive twenty-year-old girl to assist him. She was learning the ropes, and the studio was almost comfortable with sending her out on her own. She was told that she would learn a lot from assisting this old timer, as he was the first still photographer on Long Island to shoot video. She looked forward to working with him.

Sid screamed and yelled at that poor girl all night long from the beginning of the job to the end. She just couldn't aim the video light on the monopod where he wanted it. She moved in too close or back too far with her light. Sid opted to vent his frustration, rather than teach her. She truly felt that she wasn't doing anything wrong. *This guy is not going to let up on me* she thought.

She tried to be friendly toward this jerk, *maybe I'm messing up* she thought. She tried to make small talk with him during the break in the reception. His response to her was shrugs and sarcastic remarks. The photographer from her studio told this jerk, while standing at the smorgasbord table that he was going to pass on some of the delicacies.

"My doctor says I gotta cut down on the good stuff, Sid, too much cholesterol."

"What would you do if the doctor told you that about pussy?" That stupid jerk replied right at the smorgasbord.

The dance sets at the reception were a nightmare for the poor girl and he gave it to her. She started to cry. He actually had her in tears, which never happened before. He ignored her crying, muttering something about incompetence.

Sid had to drive the poor kid home at the end of the night. She had to endure his cigarettes; after all, it was his car.

"I'm a grandfather," he said, "two boys."

She did not reply

When he pulled into her driveway to drop her off, they made eye contact, something she tried to avoid.

"I'm sorry I yelled at you."

She made a face, a look of indifference, and got out of the smoky Chevy.

The next day, the studio owner told Sid that he thought he was very hard on the assistant, that he made her cry.

"She can tell you what she wants," Sid told the owner, "hey, it ain't my problem if the little broad is incompetent."

Vicky stared pensively at Sid. She sat next to him, her legs crossed. She was very close.

First Sid looked at her cleavage, then caught himself staring at her legs. He averted his eyes to the middle of the table.

"You married, Sid?"

"Yep, thirty-six years, same woman."

Vicky thought that she detected some regret in Sid's voice. "You don't sound too happy about it."

"I'm just tired, I am happy. My wife, Norma, is a super lady."

"Children?"

"Two, boy and girl. Linda and Steven, both grown, married, and out of the house, good kids."

Vicky nodded. "How old?"

"I just turned sixty and I'm a grandpa, two boys, my daughter's. My son has a girl on the way."

Vicky flashed her radiant smile, "No, no, Sid, I meant how old are your children?"

"Oh, jees, I thought you meant I look too old for this work. My daughter is thirty-one; her two boys are ten and seven. She wants more. Her husband is a foreign trade consultant; he's always traveling to China, Japan, Taiwan, all over the world. He better stay home a while, if they want to have any more children."

"How old is your son?"

"Twenty-eight."

"Almost four years apart."

"Yes, I was a struggling candid man, so we waited. In those days I had a monthly mortgage of fifty-six dollars; I was afraid I wasn't even going to make that."

"What does he do?"

"My son, the doctor! He's a resident in Brooklyn."

"So, they're not photographers?"

"Nope, my kids are very diversified in their professions. My daughter is an audiologist. Steven my son is working his *tokus* off all hours at the hospital. He's an osteopathic physician, specialty, pediatrics. He's young, yet. He might go into another specialty. They both used to assist me when they were young. Sometimes they helped me out in the studio. But, photography wasn't for them. I didn't want it for them."

"Your wife, Sid, is she a photographer?"

"No, she is a bank executive. She used to be a teller. Norma does take all the pictures when we go on vacation or at family circles, but not professionally. I tried taking some pictures last winter with her 35 mm when we went to Hawaii; they came out looking like shit."

"An osteopath, Sid, is that sort of a chiropractor?"

"No, hell no. It's the same as being an M.D. It's a different course of study with emphasis on the whole body, with a focus on manipulation of bones and joints. As a medical doctor, the only difference is that you have D.O. after your name instead of M.D."

"Oh, I love the way you talk," Vicky started jiggling her leg. "You said jernt, not joint."

"What are you going to do?" Sid chuckled, "I'm from Brooklyn. I also say foist."

"So, you're the only photographer in the family?"

"No, my brother Saul is a photographer in the city. He does commercial work only. You know, fashion, advertising, still life. If anyone asks him about portraits, weddings, or Bar Mitzvahs, he sends them to me."

Vicky noted that Sid said B' Mitzvah. All the photographers she knew said B'Mitzvah, not Bar Mitzvah.

Nobody comes to me for the kind of work Saul does. If someone wants something on a small scale done, we do it in the studio. On that level, Saul wouldn't want to bother with it. I have another brother, Seymour. He actually works for a living; he's a lawyer. Then there's my sister Helen; she married a stockbroker, their marriage has its ups and downs."

Vicky laughed at the pun.

"You got it! A lot of people never get that one!"

"I got it. You and your brothers all have the same first initial."

"Yeah, at family circles when we were kids, they used to call us the three *S*s. My father called us the three schmucks. My son is an *S* too, Steven, isn't that something?"

"But, I didn't think if you were Jewish you could have the same letters for you names."

"This is alright, because the Jewish names are different. My daughter ain't an *S*, we named her Linda. Norma's mother wanted us to name her Freda after her aunt. We hated that name, so we decided on Linda, because it means beautiful, like you, Vicky."

The old photographer could still charm a broad. That really made this cute kid blush.

"Sid, tell me how you became a photographer?"

This cute little doll was really very interested in this sixty-year-old candid man. The candid man did not mind at all, he liked her company.

This is one cute little doll, the photographer was thinking. Boy, if he weren't married....But, the photographer loved his wife dearly; she was his best friend. Not even one *shtup*, he was thinking, *be true to the only woman in the world who is stupid enough to stay with such a shit*, not one single solitary *shtup* with this cute Barbie doll.

"When I was young, my uncle gave me an old camera. He probably found it while breaking into somebody's apartment. I went around taking pictures as a hobby. Graduated Midwood High School, a guy who owned a camera store asked me if I wanted a summer job to pay for my hobby. So I worked for him, developing film, making enlargements, and selling cameras, projectors, and everything. It was working there I learned how to sell. Do you remember the old movie projectors, Vicky?"

"Yes, we had one, I recall."

"I met Norma; she was working in the bakery next door. She used to smile when I went in for coffee. Love at first sight, I guess. We became an item. All in all it was a good job, I became a good salesman."

The doll was a good listener.

"One day I saw an ad in the paper, 'Wanted photographer to photograph babies, buh, buh, buh, no experience, will train.' Had to have a square camera, which I did. A twin lens reflex, a Rollei. This outfit was called Lamar Photographers, down on DeKalb Avenue in Brooklyn. They started the baby portrait business. They started doing catered affairs, too. After a while, I shot affairs for them. Well anyhow, I shot twelve to eighteen babies a day for them, and then I had to sell the photo packages."

"I met this artistic fellow, Carl Resnick; later on, he was an award-winning portrait and candid photographer. Carl attracted the people to our studio, Lenny and I sold them the jobs. I also met Lenny Schecter there; he became a partner, too. It turns out I was one of the best photographers they had; the other top man was this guy, Hal Grossman. He left to become a movie photographer. He used to work for me years ago, too."

"Being a schmuck kid, I enlisted when the Korean action broke out. I didn't want to lose Norma, so I asked her to marry me. I wasn't expecting her to say yes. My parents liked her; her parents thought I was common. So, we got married, and I went off to war. I guess I wanted an adventure out of Brooklyn. A few of my cousins and some of my younger uncles saw action in World War II. I had some old uncles who were in the First World War. I figured enlisting was the thing to do. I made sergeant. Guess what, Vicky?"

"What?" she answered.

"I was in the infantry, so the gooks shot at us. I was winged, nothing serious, but Ike gave me a purple heart, but I ain't a hero. I was just a schmuck kid. I got my discharge and all of a sudden we had a little girl."

"Lenny and Carl stayed in touch with me, so we started our own baby studio. We even had a processing lab for a couple of years. I worked for a wedding studio in Brooklyn; candids were in their infancy then. Norma worked at the bank and we got by. I have to laugh now. There was no training to shoot affairs; nobody really knew what they were doing. We made it up, and the pictures back then looked crappy. It was all new; if something looked nice, we used it. If it didn't look nice, we wouldn't use it again. In those days, I shot five weddings a weekend. Three on Saturday, two on Sunday, and sometimes a Friday night wedding. Even now, I sometimes shoot two jobs in one day, but with all the time affairs take today, as you know, Vicky, it isn't common practice or a good idea to shoot a doubleheader."

"Well, gorgeous, I studied, I learned, and I refined. Then we followed the money and moved the baby studio to Long Island, from Brooklyn to Elmont. We bought a house in Hewlett, we're still there; we became suburbanites. When the store downstairs went out of business. Lenny, Carl, and I started the wedding and portrait studio. By then, Norma and I had our little boy. We were booming—we were high end, high price, high volume. Lenny shot affairs, but stayed upstairs and ran the baby business. Carl and I ran the studio downstairs. We had a big staff—those were happy times. I entered some print competitions and won some awards, but Carl was the big award winner. One year all three of us bought a Cadillac for our wives. Norma had a Sedan De Ville, and I drove a Mercury Marquis—those things used to look just like Lincolns. In fact, Norma and I had his and hers Lincolns one year. I couldn't believe it! What clients we had—the Long Island and Brooklyn affluent—doctors, lawyers, newscasters, actors, politicians, Mafioso. We constantly put away money for a rainy day, but we always had money in our pocket to spend. We sent the kids to private colleges, and our son to medical school with no loans, no tuition assistance. We took a lot of nice vacations in those days, too."

Vicky watched Sid lean back and close his eyes, reflecting on his career. She felt sorry for him. She also found this sixty-year-old grandfather very attractive.

"But then it all changed for you, Sid," she said very softly; it was a statement not a question.

"Gradually, things changed. A lot of studios went out in the last couple of years. I don't mean the new kids, I mean the guys who'd been around thirty, forty years. There were some retirements, a couple of the old guys died, but a lot of rough times."

"I knew a lot of photographers from working with the band," Vicky sighed, "how did this happen to your industry?"

"Well, first," Sid leaned closer to this cute doll to explain, "this isn't the heyday anymore. Things were always up and down through the years, the nineteen eighties were good. Although I'm a democrat, God bless old senile Reagan. I didn't vote for him, but God bless him."

Vicky laughed; this kid is a good audience.

"With old man Reagan, people were booking. I was spending money like it was going out of style. A lot of guys got greedy and overbooked, which caused problems. The quality suffered, and they were short of staff, so they often sent out people who had equipment, but no experience. Those schmucks overextended themselves, so they ended up with financial troubles and went bust. Then, we have those goddamn package deal studios and those one-stop, low-price wedding centers. People ain't gonna pay for a book of pictures that gets shoved away in a dresser drawer. The damn album gets looked at once a year, if even that much. That's today's philosophy. In the next few years, you watch, more studios are gonna go out. Only two kinds will be left—the established quality studios, which are very expensive and come highly recommended. These places will always book and get their price. We have a limited clientele, anyway our clientele only go with the type of service and style we offer, and the package people go to 'el cheapo.' That's the other type of photo studios that'll be around, the cheap, low-end package pirates."

"At least, Sid, you can take it easy now."

"We'll see, these damn Nassau County taxes are gonna bury us. Maybe Norma and I will move to Florida in a couple of years."

"Sid," Vicky placed her hand under her chin and started breathing deeply. Shit those women singers were good at that. "If you ever want to talk, I'll give you my number. Maybe you can come over for coffee. You're very interesting. I have an apartment in Oceanside. You can come over any time."

"No, honey," the sixty-year-old wedding photographer sighed, "I don't go with young girls. I'm strictly a one woman man. I love my Norma, I tell my troubles to her. We never had any problems with marriage; she understands me, I understand her. We are still very much in love, Vicky. You're a beautiful young lady. If I weren't married, I would go over to your apartment for coffee tonight. I don't think you'd enjoy a sixty year old, but I'm faithful, what can I tell you? I love my wife. I'm flattered you found an old fart like me attractive and worth your time. I thank you, Vicky, I really do, but I have my Norma."

"It's beautiful that you feel that way after all those years."

"To tell you the truth after all these years, when I'm not at home, I can't wait to see her."

"You're beautiful, Sid."

"No, but my Norma is. Very beautiful."

"I'm going to see what Larry is up to, you sure you don't want my number?"

Sid smiled and shook his head.

"See you inside," she said with a flash of a seductive smile.

"Besides," Sid quipped, "Norma has everything in her name—the house, the stocks, the bonds; Vicky, you'd have to support me. She also packs a good wallop."

Sid watched Vicky leave. *Nice ass* he said to himself. Norma has a nice ass, too. I married a girl with a nice ass. *She's my best friend*, the photographer thought. He always attributed a good deal of his success to her. He didn't think he would have made it in life if it were not for Norma.

Normy, the trumpet player, came back into the room. This guy looked as old as Sid.

"Not yet, they are still eating," he said. This guy was an old wedding trade veteran. "I guess you guys compete more now than in the old days. I know a lot of candid men from the old days, when I started playing in bands back in Brooklyn."

"What part, Normy?"

"East New York, you?"

"Midwood, off Avenue M."

"I know this guy in Merrick, Malkin Photographers, Franklin Malkin."

"I know him, too," Sid answered, "he's a real putz. He used to let his kids visit him while he was in prison."

"What did he go inside for?"

"Pornography, of course. He was always a lowlife. Years ago, he and his wife used to share a bungalow up in the country with my wife and me. His son used to take a pee on a tree outside, right in front of everybody. I half expected Franklin to do the same. His wife said it was no big deal, they were out in the country, and the little kid from Brooklyn was just experiencing the great outdoors. He could have experienced the great outdoors without peeing in front of my little girl. So what, we're all out in the country, he couldn't pee inside like a human being?"

"I also know Marion Studios in Brooklyn, on Flatbush Avenue in Mill Basin. They're still the biggest."

"Oh, yeah," Sid made a throw away hand gesture, "I shot for them a million years ago. Robert and Roberta Feinberg...Bob and Bobbie. They divorced a long time ago. Bob's father and uncle started a business. Their kids and nephews have a few studios of their own. Bobbie has her own studio. In fact, she works from the home they used to live in up in Brooklyn Heights; she won it from him in the divorce settlement. But, Normy, I lost a lot of respect for Bob Feinberg. He and his brother Howard broke into Bobbie's home.

They went through her drawers looking to see what they could find on her, you know, to screw her in the divorce settlement. It's funny they sit on opposite sides of the room at the dinner meetings and don't even acknowledge each other."

"Do you know Phil and Marcia Fruend?" Normy asked, "They're the same way, you know, the father and daughter team?"

"Oh," Sid shook his head," sad, that is so sad. They broke up. They ran a studio in Bayside. He opened a studio for her; she ends up suing him. I used to get a kick out of those two. I used to watch them argue right in front of the clients. Once in their studio, I heard, after the couple came back from the church for the studio formals, they were covered in rice. So, Marcia vacuumed it off. Phil was getting impatient, they were pressed for time, and he just wanted to shoot portraits and get the fuck out of there. But Marcia was going to have her way, so Phil hauled off and kicked their canister vacuum right across the floor of their studio. Bang! Right the fuck in front of the whole goddamn bridal party. She's on her own now, she's a *meshugina* anyway."

"Yeah," Normy agreed. "I know she used to treat her father like an employee, not as her father or the studio owner; it was disgusting."

Sid nodded, made a sad expression, and shrugged.

"But getting back to what I said before," Normy the trumpet player went on, "you guys are more competitive now than before, I see. You fellows really kick each other's ass. It's a real dog-eat-dog business these days. At least, that's what I hear from the other guys in the business. Everybody keeps lowering their prices to book."

"Normy," the photographer spoke, "there are package deal studios, which sell price, and then there are quality guys like myself. I sell value and quality, not price. By me, the value is we do good work and use only top of the line materials. If they can't afford that, they ain't my clients. True, my clients ain't spending like in the old days, but on the jobs I book, I make. If I lowered the standards of my product, I wouldn't have a product."

"Good, if you can make a buck."

"Well, it ain't ever gonna be the way it used to be in my business," he lamented. "There used to be a lot of good studios around and we all made money. There were clients. I dunno, it was like a large pot of clients, there were enough jobs for everybody, and people booked in those days because we told them that they needed us. Today they don't need us and they know it. So, naturally, we compete amongst ourselves now. But Normy, baby, ya wanna know who my real competition is?"

"Ya just told me the cheap package studios."

"Shit no, not them. My competition is the caterer, the disc jockey, the band, the limousines, the dress maker, the tux place, the invitation printers, the honeymoon people, and the fuckin' jewelers."

"Wait, Sid, I know a couple of bands who do video and pictures, but we're not into that, we just play music."

"It ain't that, it ain't that!" Sid shouted; he was quite pissed now. "It ain't fuckin' that at all."

"So what the hell are you saying?" Normy asked.

"I mean, it's all you guys, in general—my competition."

"How do you figure?"

"Look," the photographer motioned for the trumpet player to sit, "you guys cut into my fuckin' profits because you charge more than I do. I work fuckin' harder and longer at an affair than you. They usually book you before they book me."

"Sid, we have to charge to make a living, how the fuck do we compete with a photographer?"

"Wait a while," Sid growled, "clients spend on you people. The gown, the hall, the flowers, the band that they think is more important than pictures. Just a book of pictures that's gonna sit in a drawer. The stupid fucks don't understand that all you're gonna have left from the affair, are the videotapes and pictures. We try to educate them, tell them how important the pictures are. They ain't gonna have the food or cake again, because the next morning, it turns into shit. They ain't ever gonna dress up like that again. They ain't ever gonna listen to your band again. They ain't gonna remember one fuckin' song you played. The pictures are all that they're gonna have left. The memories, the pictures, ahhh…but now they want to spend on everything else. All the other bullshit! They tell me when they call up on the phone for a price quote, or walk into my studio; they tell me, 'We spent a lot of money on the gown, the hall, the band, buh, huh, buh, so we can't spend a lot of money on pictures.' Or, I love this one, 'We're on a tight budget. You have to give us a good price for the privilege of busting your ass, Mr. Photographer, or shoot the job at a loss. All just for the privilege we're gonna give you to bust your ass. We don't give a flying fuck about your overhead. Just give us a good price, and we'll let you shoot our affair, because we don't respect you. You're not a pro, you're a shit!' That's what the fuck it is!"

Normy stood up a bit dumbstruck; he really did not know what to say.

"I never spoke at length to a candid man, how was I to know what the causes of your problems are. But then again, I'm a part-time musician, so why should I give a fuck?"

"I'll tell you something else, Normy."

"I figured you would, Sid."

"You fuckin' book the people, come in and play your tunes, sing your songs, and then leave. We spend a few months to a year with the clients. It ain't a picnic if a particular client is a ball breaker. We book a year or more in advance, but the job doesn't end at the end of the day. Fuck no, there's the proofing, the editing, the video editing, the proof passing, masking the negatives, getting the pictures printed, getting the album to the bindery, handling God forbid any complaints—all that shit. All customer service, you know; what's breaking your poor hump really is customer service. This is a hard profession, I think just as hard as the poor little salesman who works at

Stern's Department Store selling mattresses just to earn his forty grand a year. This is considered an honorable profession. I break my ass because I'm the fuckin' best. Hey, it's what I get paid to do. The clients don't appreciate all the work that's involved. They think it's fun to take pictures and make videos. Of all the professionals they hire for their affair, we work the hardest, fuck the band. The photographer is the most important vendor; we work the hardest."

The prime rib of beef and the Vermont turkey was eaten. The dinner was over. The Meltzer/Scheiner wedding was winding down. Yet, there was still work for the photographer. It was time to go back into the room.

Chapter Ten

"Sid," the groom called out. It was the first time today that the groom addressed his photographer directly. His little J.A.P. bride is finally letting the boy speak. Well, those little Long Island princesses learn fast about taking control of their men. By a Long Island princess's tenth wedding anniversary, all the women in her family commend her on how well trained her husband is.

Norma Weitz was not a J.A.P. Sid would not have taken any shit off of her if she were. As their daughter Linda was approaching adolescence, she started to act like her snotty Five Towns girlfriends. Some weekends being grounded, a couple of wallops from her daddy, and an extra year of riding the school bus cured that bullshit. Linda didn't get a car to drive to school like her snot-nosed friends. She waited until college to get Norma's Pontiac Grand Prix. The little spoiled kids from Long Island have parents who think their behavior is acceptable. Sid thought parents ought to swat their kids across their designer labels. But, then again, where do the kids learn from? The parents, the nouveau rich elite of Long Island. Sid really couldn't hate these people. They were after all, his target market and best clients.

"Sid," the groom called out again; he was drawing closer to his photographer. "Sid, can I ask you a question?"

"You just did, babe."

The groom was taken aback; he did not know what to say next. He looked a bit intimidated.

"What can I do for you, Scott?"

"Amy wants to know if we can do the groom's pictures of the family and friends."

"Absolutely! We are running out of time, so ask her to have everybody out in the hall; now please, Scott."

"Now?"

"Yes, Scott, let's do it now."

"I'll tell everyone and get them together for you."

"Beautiful, Scott, I'll be waiting for you right here in the lobby."

Both Sid and Jeff waited for an eternity. They sat in leather club chairs. They both waited with equipment in hand.

"Talk, talk, talk," Sid grumbled, shifting his head side to side. "They're gonna go in a group to take pictures, and one guest is gonna go up to them and hold them up with bullshit small talk. C'mon, let's go, assholes," he called out, none too softly.

"Sid, this happens to us every time. It's part of the fuckin' job; you told me that yourself when I started."

"Part of the job shit!" replied the photographer, banging his fist on the arm rest. "I've waited like this for forty years. There ain't no cause to make a working professional wait like this; I don't give a fuck the reason. We had some of this shit at my Linda's wedding, but I moved everybody along. Aw, fuck it, this shit can't be helped. I didn't get my check, yet. Watch...watch...you watch! I'm gonna go up to the fuckin' mother of the bride and she's gonna stand with her guests saying goodbye for ten hours. Talk, talk, talk, you know what they say, Jeff?"

"What do they say, Sid?"

"The difference between British and Yiddish? The British leave without saying goodbye, the Yiddish say goodbye without leaving."

A large group of people jabbering away, led by the bride and groom, entered the lobby.

Sid stood up. "Is that people coming to take pictures? Hot diggity dog! It is people coming to take pictures."

"Can we take pictures outside now, Sid?" the bride's mother asked.

"Absolutely, Dorothy; it's really nice now."

The truth was, Sid did not really want to leave the nice air-conditioned hall to go outside. He selected an area on the pavement in front of shrubbery. The pavement was an ideal place to put the people, because the ground was still mucky from the rain.

Sid stood near the curb in a photographer's stance for a group picture, right leg slightly in front of left leg, crouching. Jeff stood at forty-five degrees to him, holding the monopod with the Matador strobe on top. They were double lighting outdoors. Sid knew photographers who used available light outdoors. This worked better with the Christian clientele. Sid used flash outdoors to fill in shadows. He preferred available light for effect during indoor ceremonies.

"Okay, let's go! Is everybody happy?"

Uncles, aunts, cousins, grandparents, nephews, nieces, friends, coworkers, and neighbors...each group had their chance to pose with the bride and groom. Sid just hoped these bastards would place a large order for additional photographs and extra pages in the album. It would be terrible, if these pictures just adorned a proof album.

The group pictures were finished. Back to the nice air conditioning.

"Alright, Amy and Scott, I'd like to go upstairs to take some pictures by the big window, and then finish up with some romantic pictures."

They rode the elevator to the second floor. Sid took a series of romantic pictures in full and three-quarter length. Had he brought along his 150 or 110 mm portrait lens, he would have done close-ups. He used mostly available light. Flash was used for the hands, rings, and bouquet pictures. Then there were some kissing pictures and silhouettes. Finally, there were the obligatory waving goodbye and carrying the bride over the threshold pictures. Sid fancied this particular waving goodbye picture unique. He had the bride and groom stand on top of the staircase. He stood at the bottom and shot up to the couple on top. Not every couple had a pose like this one, but not every couple was fortunate enough or smart enough to have hired Sid Weitz to shoot their wedding.

The job was winding down. Sid and Jeff stood at the side of the dance floor, watching couples dance to old big band standards and lively Latin numbers. One couple did a jitterbug to *String of Pearls*.

Since none of the main cast members were on the floor, Sid was not shooting. With the camera bracket in his left hand and a cigarette in the right hand, he grooved along with the music. His feet did a cha-cha. He and Norma used to dance a lot when they were younger. Now they would have time to go dancing.

The elaborate Viennese table was wheeled out. This was an important photograph, not to be placed in the album, of course, but to give the clients something to show off and brag about at the cabana club. Sid photographed the exquisite desserts, making mental notes of what he would have.

The cake was being wheeled to the center of the floor, and the bridal party was being called up. The cake cutting was another corny, yet traditional photo opportunity. Some Jewish couples did not have this ceremony. First, the setup poses were taken; then, the actual cutting and feeding of the cake to one another. This couple fed each other with forks from plates. This is the way upper-class Christian and Jewish couples usually do it. The *goyim*, for the most part, went wild with the cake cutting. They held a hunk of cake in their hands and smashed it into each other face. Sometimes things even got out of hand. There were times this stupid ritual got downright hostile and violent. Sid was thankful for that reason that his son eloped, because his *shiksa* daughter-in-law looked like a cake smasher.

"Reverse, reverse," Sid instructed as the bride switched to feeding the groom; reverse came out "revoise."

Sid and Norma cut the cake at their wedding, but they did not have an album. He could not afford one and he was in the business. Jack Bergman, owner of Bergman Studios on Newkirk Avenue in Brooklyn, was his boss at the time. He gave Sid and Norma a gift of six poses, plus group pictures of each side of their family as a wedding gift. They just had studio portraits done.

Sid's friend Hal Grossman, who was also working for Bergman, filmed the ceremony at the temple.

Jackie Bergman was a good man to work for. His two brothers, Leo and Stanley, were the real moneymakers in the family. Together, they owned Bergman Brothers Brighton Beach Funeral Home on Coney Island Avenue. It was one of Brooklyn's leading Jewish funeral parlors. They were still in business, with locations in Florida. Today it was run by Leo and Stanley's sons and nephews. Jackie Bergman's son was also a funeral director over there. He found it more lucrative than candids.

Sid had to admit they gave Jackie a nice service when he kicked off. He knew how Jackie went and did not want to go that way. Jackie Bergman, at the age of seventy-two, had a massive heart attack while shooting a Bar Mitzvah reception. The boy's father was a doctor, but did not want to touch Jackie, for fear of a lawsuit. So, Jackie lay on the floor in the middle of the candle lighting ceremony, turning blue. The Bar Mitzvah boy and his four-year-old brother got a kick out of that. The story was that the Bar Mitzvah boy called out, "Hey, Ma! Gimme your instamatic! I wanna get a picture of this guy. I could show it at school for science." The kid thought it would be cool to bring in a picture of some dead old guy with blue lips. There was never any confirmation that such a photograph existed, but Sid would not be surprised if it did.

It was time for coffee and cake. Sid needed some coffee and wanted a piece of cake. He also wanted an éclair, some chocolate mousse, and some cookies. He had a tall glass mug full of strong black coffee, with a dollop of whipped cream on top. Since this was a kosher affair, the whipped cream was not real cream, but what the hell, this stuff made from vegetable oil was not so bad, it just gives you heartburn at three A.M.

The bouquet toss, although standard at Christian weddings, was only sometimes done at Jewish weddings. They were not going to do the garter toss. The groom removes the garter from the bride's leg and tosses it to his friends. Sometimes, the groom had a pair of panties, which they pulled out. The garter toss was not done much at Jewish weddings; this was strictly for *goyim*.

Two chairs were set in the middle of the dance floor. The groom's parents sat on the chairs. The bandleader announced the *mezinka* set.

In the Jewish faith, whenever parents married off the last of their children, all in attendance formed a circle around them. The men patted the father on the back. The women placed flowers from the centerpiece in the mother's hair. There was a good deal of congratulating and kidding, a tremendous show of emotion. This just leant itself to photography; this was truly the stuff that good candids were made of. There were just some photographs that one could not set up. Some candids were even better than posed pictures, because they were real, and they captured the true essence of the subject, along with the true emotion of the event. Candid meant honest; the happiness displayed in these photographs was very honest.

The bride's mother was not seated for the *mezinka*. Her youngest son was not married, yet. Sid overheard her tell one of the guests that her son had not found himself, yet.

The bride's cute three-year-old niece, who was the flower girl, brought a cookie to the groom's mother. A fat woman danced her big fat ass right in front of Sid, blocking him. She shook her big fat ass, to and fro, not moving out of Sid's way.

"You fucked up my picture, lady; you're fucking me up."

Jeff heard Sid voice his frustration. Miraculously, the lady with the big fat ass moved out of the way. *Shit*, Jeff thought, *maybe she heard 'Mr. Classact.'*

The music of the *mezinka* medley was blasting; Sid's dick was vibrating once again from the beat and from the people dancing around the groom's parents. The band went into *Oz Azoy*. Sid had enough congratulatory candids so he waited. The band played *M'chutenista Meine* next. The guests were dancing faster now. When the band started playing *Chosen Kale Mazel Tov*, the bride's uncle took the bride by the hand and started to mimic a dancing Chasid, to the delight of the guests.

A couple approached the photographer to ask him why their auto-focus, 35 mm camera had stopped firing. They walked away disappointed, when after taking one look, the photographer made a 'who knows' face and shrugged.

Now the band was playing *Siman Tov*, and then started playing the *mezinka* very fast. Larry Epstein played a good klezmer-style clarinet.

BOOM BA BOOM! BA - BA BOOM BA - BOOM! The band was playing an encore of *Hava Nagila*. Both the groom's parents were lifted up on the chairs.

Sid held his Mamiya 645 up high. CLICK, FLASH, CLICK, FLASH! CLICK, FLASH, CLICK, THUMP, SHHHHRRRIIPP!

"Ahhh shit!" exclaimed the photographer. "This is my last roll of film. Aw, fuck it! Shit!"

"You took enough of them, Sid," Jeff yelled over the music.

"Yeah, fuck it," Sid agreed with his assistant.

Just then a couple came over to them. "Hey, Mr. Photographer," the man called out, "take a picture of us together." He was standing right on top of them.

Without missing a beat, Sid held the Mamiya up to his eye, placed his right hand on the back of the Armitar strobe, and fired the test button. The couple thanked him, then walked off.

"How'd you like that shot?" the photographer asked his assistant. "See that? See what I did?"

Jeff nodded. He saw Sid do that on a million jobs already. That was a good way to get rid of some photographically unimportant pain-in-the-ass guest, who probably wouldn't buy the fucking picture anyway. Most likely that picture would never be placed in the album. It would just sit the fuck in the box with all the other unselected proofs.

As the band played *Bashana Haba'ah*, they walked together back to the side of the bandstand to where their equipment was. The job was over, time to break down. Jeff stood watching the levity with the monopod in his hand.

"The job's over, Jeff, put the fuckin' light down and relax."

The *mezinka* dance set was over. The band went into *The Last Dance*. Vicky was singing the Donna Summer hit, that by now almost every American candid photographer was familiar with.

Sid handed Jeff the last roll of film to have been shot. Jeff placed the roll in his pants pocket. Any smart experienced photographer keeps the film on their person, not with the equipment. If the equipment is insured, and it bloody well should be, it can be replaced. Precious exposed film can never be replaced.

Sid placed his hardware and accessories into the battered Speed Graphic case. Jeff turned the strobe on Sid's camera off, then turned the unit on his monopod off. He also turned off both radio slave units. Their radio slave started to work after the ceremony was over, as they were on the same frequency as the temple's P.A. system. Sid took the 55 mm wide-angle lens off the camera and replaced the 70 mm standard.

Then Sid took the empty film boxes and wrappers and tossed them onto the serving tray with the dirty dishes. He emptied the small glass ashtray he carried in his case into the mug he drank his coffee from. The case was closed, everything was turned off, so all he needed to do was get his check.

The bride's mother was saying her long goodbyes to the guests. Sid stood beside her to make his presence known.

"Sid, you did a wonderful job. I'm going to thank Amy's friend Gail for recommending you."

"Thank you, Dorothy, I'm glad you approve. Amy's friend knows my brother Saul, the commercial photographer. He put Amy in touch with me."

"Oh," the bride's mother looked a bit confused, "I think I see what Amy meant now. She said this guy had wild hair; I guess she meant your brother."

"Yes, that's Saul, he has long hair. I'm a businessman; he's an 'artiste.'"

"Well, I will thank both Gail and your brother for the recommendation."

"Dorothy, do you know that I'm not going to be located in Elmont after tomorrow?"

"Yes, Sid, I remember you're going to be working out of your house in Hewlett. I have the directions, you're off Peninsula Boulevard. I live two towns away from you; I'll have no trouble finding you when I come to pick up the proofs. Same phone number?"

"Yes, for now I'll have call forwarding for the Elmont number."

"Here is your check. I'm sure the pictures will be beautiful."

The photographer thanked the bride's mother and shook hands with her.

The happy young couple, Amy and Scott, along with Scott's parents, Frieda and George, came over to bid their photographer goodbye.

The bride kissed her photographer, the groom and his parents shook hands with him.

On their way out of the temple, Sid and Jeff peeked into the sanctuary, to see which studio was shooting the evening affair. A photographer, a lighting assistant, and a poser were doing some romantic photographs in the sanctuary. Two videographers and their assistants sat in the pews watching. The photographer and videographers were all from the same studio.

"Ahhh, David and David from East Rockaway," Sid observed.

This studio was one of the leading Five Towns photography studios. For years, they were in competition with Sid. Although his studio was based in Elmont, in Nassau County's south shore, Montclair Studios was a Five Towns studio; Sid lived in Hewlett, Carl used to live in Lawrence, and they had offices in their homes, which made them Five Towns' photographers.

The David and David photographer had two light stands set up on the *bimah*, with two portable strobes and white umbrellas on top.

"Shit," Sid backed out of the sanctuary exit very fast. Let's get the fuck out of here before they ask why I didn't use an umbrella." He paused for a moment and said, "I didn't set up room lights, either. What? I'm gonna tell 'em I don't do that shit anymore."

Jeff walked with Sid to where he had parked Norma's new Nissan Stanza. Sid parked on the side street near the temple, so he would not have to give the kid a buck for parking his car. He placed his satchel, camera, and monopod in the trunk. In the trunk were a film bag and a blank check from Montclair Studios. He made it out to Jeff for seventy-five dollars. This was more than what Sid got to photograph his first wedding. Not only was the pay shit, he had to go back to the studio, go into their darkroom, and place the 4x5 size sheet film into holders for developing before he could call it a day. Jeff originally got fifty bucks. Some guys still paid their assistants that. The high end studios sometimes paid the assistants rather well—one hundred twenty-five, one hundred seventy-five. Sid was a high-end photographer and he loved Jeff, but he hated to part with money. Seventy-five it was.

Sid then picked up the empty order bag from True Color Professional Film Laboratories in Rockville Centre. He had used this professional photographic lab for the past twenty-five years. He had an open account and when things were busy, the lab gave him volume discounts on his orders. This lab had a night slot for customers to drop off the film on the way back from jobs. This would be Sid's next stop.

"Okay, *bubie*, see you tomorrow after one. Our last day of work…go find a real job. You can still shoot for Lenny if you want, but if I were you, I'd look for something better. Lenny's a creep, we both know that."

"Sid, you said we would discuss this."

"Nothing to discuss, babe, I'm closing the studio. The neighborhood ain't great anymore and I can't relocate because I don't have the business anymore. I'm gonna work from my house, and shoot for some other studios for extra dough. What I book, I book…what I make, I make…that's it." Sid closed the trunk.

"I'll see you tomorrow, Sid; drive carefully, huh?"

Sid could see the kid was upset with him.

"You too, baby, be well."

Jeff walked to his car. Most of the time Jeff rode in Sid's car when they worked together. Jeff got a phone call from his boss at seven-thirty this morning, telling him that his new Chevy was not kicking over and he should meet him on location with his own car.

Sid opened the left rear door of the Nissan, slipped off his tuxedo jacket, folded it, and laid it across the backseat. He unclipped his bow-tie and slipped it into the pocket of the folded jacket, and opened the collar and top two buttons of the dress shirt.

"Excuse me, sir," there was a tap on his shoulder.

Sid turned around. He was standing face to face with a heavyset man with curly, permed, grey hair and fat lips.

"I was at the wedding and I watched you work. You did a fine job. My daughter is getting married next May. Do you have a card?"

"Yes, sir," Sid closed the rear door, took out his wallet, and extracted a business card. Let me give you one with the new address, I work out of an office in my house now, in Hewlett.

"No problem," the man with the fat lips studied the card. That's not too far. I live in Merrick. I have my practice in my home, I'm a dentist. The name's Dr. Cain."

They shook hands.

"It's good you work out of your house. Years ago," the dentist spoke, flapping his fat lips, "when I had to make my son's Bar Mitzvah, I walked into this studio near where I live. The studio was very big, so I told my wife this guy is going to charge us a fortune. So we listened politely, then we walked out. We found a guy working out of his house, who was willing to give us a good price."

You prick, you obnoxious South Merrick fat fuck, Sid thought.

I remember you; it was a couple of years ago, but I remember your fat lips now, Doc! With all your money from stealing your patients gold fillings and crowns, you wanted a bargain, you fuckin' cheapskate.

"Well, anyway," the dentist flapped his fat lips, "we thought this other guy took nice pictures, but he moved away. Last year, my oldest daughter got married at The Lake's End up in Roslyn?"

"Oh, yes."

"Well, we used the Lawrence Studio."

"That's Hal Grossman, but Hal isn't there anymore. He broke up with his partners. He and his son Gary both left; the partners all sued each other."

"Yeah, right, so Hal charged us a fortune. Okay, so maybe I'll have to tell more people they need a root canal this year. Maybe I'll have to find more cavities in patient's mouths, you follow? I'm gonna make my money back, drillin' and fillin'."

Sid nodded

"Now this daughter who's getting married next year, she's a college graduate, but she can't find work, so she sorts contest mail for a big company. The reception is going to be at The Lake's End again. This Grossman spent forever taking the goddamned pictures so we missed our cocktail hour. You worked fast, which is why I approached you."

"Well, I'm fast, I'm invisible, I'm a nice guy, and I do a good job."

"Yeah," Dr. Fatlips continued, "I'm going to give you a call. We'll get together and if you want the job, you'll give me a good price, okay? I have a lot of affluent patients and friends from where I live in Merrick. I'm active in my temple; I'll give you referrals, but you have to work with me, understand?"

"Yes, Doc."

"If you give me a price that I want, you may have this big fancy wedding. If you don't quote me a nice price, you can stay home that day. You can work with me, just think of all the people I know from where I live in Merrick, South Merrick, I have a waterfront house."

"I'm looking forward from hearing from you." *Drop dead* is what Sid was thinking.

"Take care and we'll be talking soon." The flabby lipped dentist got into the red Jaguar parked behind Sid. Obviously, this guy did not want to give the kid a buck to park his car either.

Sid returned the wave he got from Dr. Fatlips and his wife as they drove off. He opened the driver's side door and got in.

"Fuck you," Sid said softly, "the fuckin' date is gonna be booked when you call, you fat piece of shit. I don't need a job from you, douche bag."

Everyone wants a bargain, he thought as he drove away, *that's just human nature. People are shits; there is no doubt about that.*

There was this young fellow who came into the studio a couple of weeks ago with his fiancée. The kid was a civil engineer. He told Sid at the moment he was living at home with his family, which consisted of ten children, a mother, and an illiterate father. Sometimes people start telling a photographer their life story. Being a good salesman, he listened to both Tony and his fiancée Donna. All these Italian kids who came into the studio were Tony and Donna.

He's making a lot of money as an engineer, buh, buh, buh. He wants to spare no expense for this wedding. He booked the reception at the Colonnade House in Massapequa, and hired the Gaspar Greco Orchestra. Gaspar Greco was in demand for Italian weddings, people spent money for him; he was good. When Gaspar belted out *Al di La* or *Love Me with All of Your Heart* the crowd went wild.

So, this Tony tells Sid he wants to save money on pictures. He wanted good photographs and video, but the party itself was more important than the photography.

Sid felt that Tony owed it to him to book his studio. After all, his tax dollars went to provide schooling and public assistance for all those kids that his old man was responsible for. An illiterate father, huh? Well there is one thing that Tony's old man knew how to do. If you ain't gonna book me, then let the Pope pay for my property taxes, to put your siblings through school.

Tony did not like the price, because he called to tell Sid he and Donna booked a bridal center. Sid thought their work sucked, so did every other legitimate photographer who was familiar with that place. That stupid kid, money was no object for everything else. When it came to the pictures, the memories of the most important day of your life, since you got your first Camaro Z28 IROC, you gotta have a cheap package deal. Oh, well, no big loss. His fiancée Donna had a mustache, which would have required extensive retouching. Showing an album of a bride who has a mustache is not all that visually appealing.

"Bargains, bargains, everybody's looking for bargains," he sang out as he drove toward Rockville Centre. He popped a cassette into the tape deck. He sang along with George Burns. The song was *Eighteen Again*. Sid Weitz played it often, now that he understood the lyrics.

"Sorry, George, I'm too fuckin' depressed to hear that one today." He ejected the cassette. "I love you, George, may you live to be a hundred, but I just can't bear this one right now."

He passed the signs of the times as he drove—a vacant luncheonette, and an empty Pontiac dealership. He passed more signs of the times—bridal shops and tuxedo rental stores that were offering large discounts at the height of the season. Holy shit, if these vendors had to give discounts this time of year, business must be very bad. Everyone was hurting, not just the photographers, but the entire wedding trade. Businesses all over Long Island were hurting.

Sid knew for sure the only ones making a living were politicians, actors, authors, civil servants, drug dealers, and Nassau County cops.

He just passed two blue and orange striped Nassau County patrol cars parked in a 7-Eleven parking lot. The cars were positioned so the drivers could talk to each other. *They're probably laughing about how we pay them eighty thousand a year to do nothing.* Sid wished the little foreign man behind the counter would *shvitz* on their jelly donuts.

Man, it was tough to run a business today, any business. Open your own store if you don't mind struggling for the American dream you'll never live to see. Butt your head up against the store, work hard night and day, and then what's you reward? Getting shot by a desperate crack head. The economy was bad, people ain't buying, and that's not good.

Sid pulled up to the processing lab. The protective metal grate was down, but there was a slot for photographers to put the film envelopes. He left the motor running, got out of the car, and placed the precious parcel of memories in the chute. Going to the lab during business hours was, at times, a social function. Photographers got to bump into colleagues and old friends. This was a place to catch up on goings on in the industry, swap war stories, and bullshit. Photographers, firemen, and cops just loved to sit around and bullshit. Why not? Bullshitting was something to do when business was slow.

Back in the car, Sid turned on a soft FM station, which played the type of music heard in a dentist's office. He wondered if that dentist with the big fat lips played this station in his office.

He was relaxed now; the day was turning into a warm sunny day. Right on time, oh, great one, right in time for evening. With all the problems, he knew he shot a good job. Now he was on his way home to Norma. He made her nervous this morning when his brand new Chevrolet Caprice did not start. It was five o'clock; maybe they would go out to dinner tonight.

Sometimes he called Norma from location; today he did not. 'Chinks' or sushi or Italian tonight. Maybe a diner.

Sid pulled the black Nissan Stanza into the driveway alongside the light blue Chevy Caprice. It was a practical car, albeit a luxury car; it was, however, merely a Chevy. It resembled an unmarked police vehicle, which deters carjacking. Sid decided on another Caprice because he needed a large car, but did not care about making an impression anymore.

"Uh huh, aha," Sid mumbled, "I wonder what the fuck was wrong with it. I'll probably have to pay for towing. Fuck General Motors!" he shouted

Chapter Eleven

Norma Weitz was tired, unusually tired for a quiet Sunday. She did not have to go to work today, but spent most of her day at the Chevrolet dealership three towns away. She had to wait while the customer service department repaired her husband's brand new Chevrolet Caprice. She really felt sorry for Sidney. He just spent five hundred dollars to fix his well-worn nineteen 1984 Chevrolet Caprice. The damn car broke down on the Belt Parkway near Kennedy Airport. They were on the way to see Sid's parents, who lived in the Midwood section of Brooklyn. Shortly after they pulled off the parkway, an identical light blue Chevrolet Caprice pulled up onto the grass behind them. A young uniformed N.Y.P.D. Highway Patrol officer got out. He saw a Jewish couple from Long Island leaning up against the car. He looked disappointed.

"Oh, I thought you were on the job," he said.

"No, I'm on the grass," Sid replied.

"Does this mean you won't help us?" Norma asked.

"Oh, yeah, ha, ha, right," the cop said embarrassed. "I'll call a tow. Jeez, whaddaya think about these Chevys, huh?"

When that car was deemed unrepairable, Sid sold it to a college kid. The boy's father examined the car and asked how much.

"Five hundred dollars," Sid informed the man.

"Five hundred for a car that's seven years old."

"I just put money in it; I had it fixed up."

The man looked at the rusting rear door. "It looks like shit."

"You're right, mister, it does look like shit. So, give me five hundred dollars and you got yourself a great second car, a real good station car. You got yourself a great car for your son when he comes home from college."

The man bought the car.

Sid ran out and bought another Chevy Caprice—it was adequate for his photographic and video assignments. He thought about a Cadillac or Lincoln, but he did not need to impress anybody anymore. He really wanted another convertible; it had been a long time since they had one. He wanted a two-seater with a small trunk, but he was still working and a heavy car had its advantages, so another Chevy it was. Although Sid was not crazy about the new 'jelly bean' of the new Caprice. Earlier in the year, Norma's 1988 Lincoln Mark V was having engine trouble. They gave their daughter the Lincoln, so she and her husband would not have to have the expense of replacing one of their cars. They heard many good things about foreign cars, Japanese especially. Sid remembered when foreign cars were not very attractive and not as popular. They decided to give the foreign markets a try. Being Jewish, Sid and Norma ruled out German cars. The French, Italian, and Korean cars did not appeal to them. The English cars were either very costly or not big enough. They liked the Swedish cars, but decided on Japanese. After all, Sid never had trouble with his Japanese cameras. Norma loved her Nissan Stanza. Sid liked it, but thought it was too small, although it was a mid-size. It was also very pricey, over ten thousand dollars…the same as they had paid in 1982 for their Buick LeSabre coupe. Sid knew, in retirement, he would not be trading cars in every two or three years. He had to choose reliable ones and keep them running.

The new Chevy needed a minor adjustment and the battery cables had to be reconnected. Now it was running as perky as a new car should.

Norma Weitz hated to see her husband aggravated, because of one important reason—she was in love with him. As abrasive as he was rumored to be throughout the industry, she loved him and tolerated his faults.

She never told Sid he had faults because he truly believed he did not have any. How can a man who is so talented and successful have faults? Whatever works for him, had been her position for over thirty years.

He certainly had his share of aggravation today. Now he can come home and relax. She hoped that she and Sid would make love tonight. He had been so tense lately. She believed by making love to her, Sid kept his mind off his troubles before going to sleep. He had troubles for sure, as he was about to close a studio, which had been once very successful. She felt guilty about admitting to herself, a fifty-five-year-old grandmother, that she was feeling horny. She made an exaggerated salute, *here's to you, Dr. Ruth*.

Norma was a very supportive wife, as was Sid a supportive husband. She was always very proud of the work displayed in her husband's window; very proud of his awards and accomplishments, she was married to the best portrait and candid photographer and event videographer on Long Island.

Norma Weitz was dressed in a knee-length, form-fitting beige skirt and white blouse. She sat without shoes in stockinged feet on the white leather couch in their den. The door connecting the den to Sid's home studio was open. Sid would walk from the driveway through the side entrance, through his office, put his equipment down, wash up, sit with her on the couch, and watch television. Sometimes they would talk, sometimes they would neck.

The Weitz entertainment center was located in the den, although they had several radios, televisions, and stereos in other rooms throughout the house. The Weitz family music and literary materials were kept in the den. The taste in music varied. Sid loved jazz; he had recordings by Dizzy Gillespie, Charlie Parker, Billie Holliday, and Bessie Smith among other jazz greats. There were also recordings by The Boston Pops, Mitch Miller, Tito Puente, Glen Miller, Doc Severensen, Herb Alpert, The Manhattan Transfer, The Baja Marimbas, Andy Williams, Vic Damone, Al Martino, Eddie Fisher, Roy Clark, Lawrence Welk, Frank Sinatra, Dean Martin, Tony Bennett, Sammy Davis Jr., Perry Como, Jerry Vale, Bette Middler, Barbra Streisand, The Beatles, Steve Lawrence and Eydie Gorme, Jack Jones, Dinah Shore, and Tom Jones. There were several recordings of Bach, Motzart, Brahms, Schubert, Bizet, Stravinsky, Debussy, Revel, Tchaikovsky, Chopin, Mendelssohn, Vivaldi, Verdi, and Liszt among the pop records.

The books in the library were of such authors as Ernest Hemmingway, Robert Louis Stevenson, Mark Twain, Philip Roth, Ian Fleming, John Gardner, Steve Allen, George Burns, Dr. Benjamin Spock, Dr. Ruth Westheimer, Gwen Davis, Charles Dickens, Ed McBain, Richard Cameron, William Shakespeare, Neil Simon, Lawrence Sanders, Joseph Wambaugh, Dennis Smith, Desi Arnaz, Sam Levinson, and Elie Wiesel.

Their children's diplomas adorned the walls of the den. Pictures of the family hung on the wall, and were displayed on tables and dressers throughout the house, such as Steven's Bar Mitzvah portrait, which was taken by his own dad. Norma remembered the day the portrait was taken at the studio. Steven kept making faces, and sticking his fingers in his nose. Sid kept yelling, "You're frustrating me, man, you're really frustrating me. Keep up the shit, kid, and I won't let you go to your own fuckin' reception." Norma heard this while waiting in the reception area; it was the first time she heard him use that expletive on their son, but he had it coming.

When Steven was younger, he was hell on wheels. When Steven was twelve and Linda was sixteen, he pulled a stunt that would never be forgotten. They had first driven to the studio to pick up the proofs of Linda's sweet sixteen. Norma had some shopping to do. When she had finished, they drove home. At the time, Norma had a 1973 Cadillac Fleetwood; it was a large car. Linda was sitting up front; Steven was sitting in the back eating a Light N' Lively black cherry yogurt. He lowered the window and threw the container at a man working on an old Mercury Cougar in front of his house. The container flew through the air, spilling some of its contents on to the back of the man's flannel shirt. The airborne container continued over the man's head, hit the headlight, and the remainder of the yogurt splattered onto both the front of the car and the man's shirt. Norma saw the event unfold through the rearview mirror she reached into the back swatting Steven as she drove.

"You fuck!" It was the first time Steven and Linda had ever heard their mother use such a word. "You fuck, you lousy fuck, you fuckin' fuck; fuck you, you little fuck."

Steven laughed hysterically; Linda covered her face in shame.

"FUCK!" Norma yelled as she turned to him.

"FUCK!" Steven yelled back, making a touchdown victory gesture.

"FUCK!" they both yelled together.

Norma stopped the Caddy down the road, got out, walked to the middle of the road, faced the victim, and spread her arms out wide. She explained later, this was to show the victim that the person, who did that, was going to get it.

The man stepped into the middle of the road and made the same gesture.

Norma got back into the car and drove off. When Sid came in the front door wearing his leisure suit and his 'I made money today' smile, Norma attempted to tell him what his son did.

Sid held up both his hands, shook his head, "I don't want to know from." Sid felt the less he knew about his son's antics the better.

Norma was concerned. Steven was doing very well in school and appeared to get along with others. There was a repeat performance a week later. Norma was driving Sid's 1973 Cadillac Eldorado convertible coupe. It was a cool fall day, so the top was up. Two teenage boys on bicycles were peddling on the street toward oncoming traffic. Steven saw a golf pencil on the floor of the car. He lowered the window and threw the pencil out at the two cyclists, without Norma seeing. At a red light, the two irate young men knocked on the passenger side window. Norma asked what the problem was. One of the young men told her that her son just threw something at them and could she please open the door so they could kick her son's ass. Norma shook her head, told them that she would take care of it, and drove off. Their pediatrician referred them to a reputable clinical psychologist, who was an adjunct professor at one of the local colleges.

At the introductory session, Norma explained to the doctor how well Steven was doing in school, how nice and generous he was.

"Of course, Steven is generous," the psychologist replied, "he gives people yogurt, he gives people pencils."

Norma reminded the doctor that it was not her son's generosity that brought them here.

"Steven," the psychologist said sternly as he looked at him, "you simply cannot throw things at people from moving vehicles; not only is that antisocial behavior, but you can get locked up."

Norma looked at her son and nodded.

"Over the summer," the psychologist continued, "somebody threw a can of soda at me. I was going to a Bar Mitzvah with my wife one Sunday, and we were getting into my car in the driveway, when a young boy on a bike rode by and threw a can of soda that had been shaken up at us. The soda splashed all over a light pinstriped suit I was wearing; my wife tried to run after the boy, I wanted him locked up."

"Was that you?" Steven asked, sounding both awe struck and satisfied with himself.

The psychologist promptly asked Norma and Steven to please leave his office and to please pay the receptionist on the way out for both the therapy session and for the dry cleaning of his suit

On the way home, Norma realized what a small world it really was. She remembered Sid coming home from a Bar Mitzvah, telling her that the uncle of the Bar Mitzvah boy apologized for being late, because he had to change his suit when some street urchin threw a soda at him.

Norma told Steven that she would tell Dad that the psychologist told her that her son was a normal red-blooded American boy who liked to release tension by getting off a good prank once in awhile. She told him that Dad did not need to know that they were kicked out of a psychologist's office. In return, Steven would agree to suppress his rowdy behavior. Steven agreed to his mother's conditions and never terrorized a pedestrian or cyclist again. Today, Steven was a resident in pediatrics, go figure.

Years later at breakfast, Norma read an article about that prominent psychologist's death. He was trying to talk a patient standing on an eight-story ledge out of jumping. The doctor leaned too far out of the window while sitting on the window sill, and fell eight stories to his death, probably ruining yet another suit. The patient, realizing that jumping from a building was a horrible way to die and that life was worth living, went back inside.

Portraits of their daughter Linda that were on display, were of her as a Bat Mitzvah girl, on her sweet sixteen, various graduation photos, and as a beautiful bride. Except for the graduation portraits, the photos of Linda were taken by Sid at the studio. Norma would not permit Sid to work at their children's affairs; Sid did, however, shoot all the portraits at the studio. Norma did not have a problem with that, they were intimate photographs, and Sid was the best photographic portrait artist on Long Island.

Now the walls and dressers were adorned with pictures of the grandchildren Peter, nine and Alec, six. Peter called Norma 'Grandma' and called Sid 'Sid.' Alec called Norma 'Gam' and Sid 'Poppy.' When he first started to talk he called Sid 'Poopy.' Sid was very close with Peter and did not mind him calling him by his first name. Peter loved to go to the studio to watch his grandfather work. He was proud of his grandfather's work.

"Sid," Peter asked last week, "are you going to shoot my Bar Mitzvah?"

"Hell no, kiddo," was his grandfather's reply. "Harry has that unenviable task. I'm gonna spend the whole day dancing with your grandmother. I might even dance with you."

"Harry, the cop? He's real old."

"Pete, don't you want to give this poor *altacocker* something to do? Gotta keep him working or he'll go senile. He doesn't chase *shvartzes* anymore. That's what happens to us old photographers, we get senile. Besides, Harry's younger than me."

Mark Sossin, Linda's foreign trade consultant husband, was a fine son-in-law. He got along well with his in-laws. He and Sid sometimes played golf together. They were thankful for Linda's happiness.

Peter told people his father and grandfather played "sonofabitch" when they went out golfing, because they said that word a lot.

Their daughter-in-law Christine Copobianco was a sweet girl, but not what they wanted for their son. Steven met Christine when he was an intern; she sprained her ankle and he taped it up.

Christine was from the eastern end of Long Island. Her mother was a waitress, her father an auto mechanic. Christine had a college education, still she was working part time at a fast food restaurant.

At one point in their relationship, Steven told his parents that Christine and her parents were having trouble with the wife of one of her former high school teachers. The wife accused Christine of having an affair with her husband. She was telling Christine's parents that their daughter was a slut. The Weitz's did not need a slut for a daughter-in-law. Sid believed if a married woman was accusing this girl of being a slut, it was probably true. Christine was a flirt and she came on to men, especially Jewish men, which is how she hooked Steven Weitz. She dumped a business major working at the hamburger joint for Steven. Steven assured his parents that this woman was crazy. Her husband dated Christine years after high school during a temporary separation, but that was it. It must be nice when a teacher remembers a former female student working in a burger joint and asks her out.

Christine was Catholic and did not look at all like a Jewish girl. When Sid was first shown a picture of her, he remarked that she looked like a real *shiksa*. Sid and Norma were not happy about the fact that their grandchildren might be raised as Catholics. Christine's parents were not all choked up about their daughter marrying a Jewish boy.

One day when things between Christine and Steven were getting serious, Christine's parents invited the Weitzes to dinner through their daughter. Sid never liked driving on the Long Island Expressway. Going out to exit 63 did not help matters any.

The Copobiancos, Christine's parents, had a beautiful colonial house with an in-ground swimming pool. Sid and Norma saw a bunch of cars, a motorcycle, and a tow truck in the driveway. This somehow did not surprise them. Nor were they surprised to find the Copobianco family had two dogs, two cats, and a rabbit. They were greeted at the door by Mary, Christine's mother. Christine's mother was a pretty woman of forty. She looked like her daughter—wavy auburn hair, green eyes, and teeth, which could have used braces twenty years ago.

"Hi, did youse find the house alright?"

Even though there is no such word for the plural you, Christine's parents used the word 'youse.' They soon found out Mary used the word youse even when addressing a single person.

"Sid, can I offer youse a drink?"

Christine's father, a tall brawny man in his forties with a Sonny Bono mustache tried to be friendly. The problem was he did not try very hard. Her father wore a mechanic's work shirt with "Sal" embroidered over the pocket.

During dinner, Christine's younger brother, Sal Jr. entered the dining room and grunted what sounded like a greeting. He was wearing a 'Twisted Sister' tee shirt with the sleeves cut off. He did not seem to want to have anything to do with his parents' dinner guests. The conversation was cordial, but strained. Sid and Norma enjoyed their hostess's London broil. Sid was surprised they did not serve a baked ham.

"Sid," Sal spoke, "Christine tells me you're in weddings."

"Well, Sal, I'm a photographer; I have a studio, but we photograph affairs for the most part."

"You're a photographer," Mary replied, "oh, youse take pictures?"

Sid smiled as he answered Mary, "Yes, well that is a major part of the job."

"I guess you do a lot of Jewish jobs," Sal spoke as he swallowed a gulp of beer from the bottle. "A lot of Bar Mitzvahs, huh?"

"I do a lot of Jewish jobs, Sal; I work for anybody."

"We went to a Bar Mitzvah once," Sal said, "in Dix Hills at the big conservative temple?"

"Yes, I know that one, I've shot there."

"We have Jewish next-door neighbors," Mary offered, "they're lovely people."

"Who? The Friedmans?" Sal leaned across to his wife. "They're always looking to make trouble. Remember the crap they gave me about all the cars in the driveway and all the cars I fix up on the front lawn."

Mary scowled at her husband.

Sal tried to redeem himself. "It ain't against them people being Jews; they just like to make trouble. They ain't bad people, they're really okay, but sometimes they give me a pain."

Norma spoke softly, "There are people like that in every faith."

Sid held his tongue for his son's sake, but he wanted to ask Sal if he was baptized by Father Coughlin.

Mary looked like she was happy for Norma's statement.

"Youse are right, Norma, there are troublemakers in all faiths. A family of niggers moved into the house across the street. They're very nice people; alright, the husband comes across smug, like because he's successful. The Friedmans weren't very friendly, so I went over to see them. They were alright," she shrugged.

"I work with a couple of niggers," Sal said. They're nice guys, but that doesn't mean I want them to live near me. They're nice if you know a couple one on one, but as a group? Forget about it."

Christine and Steven were growing very uncomfortable.

"I mean no offense," Sal continued, "but birds of a feather flock together. If I'm a sparrow, I want to live with a sparrow and not a crow. No offense to the crow; I'm sure he's a very nice bird, but let him flock with his own," Sal looked at Christine and Steven as he spoke.

Steven and Christine ran off to Lake Tahoe, Nevada, together, and got married. Now they were happy and living in Forest Hills, Queens. Norma got

Sid to take a formal wedding picture of them at the studio. The Weitzes and the Copobiancos seldom saw each either, which was probably a good thing, because they had nothing in common.

Norma walked into the den bathroom to freshen up. They had installed the bathroom in the den when Sid built an extension onto the house for his office. There were two additional bathrooms in the home studio—one in the reception area and one in Sid's private office. There were seven bathrooms total in their house. Not bad for two kids from Brooklyn.

Norma gazed into the mirror. Unlike many women at the age of fifty-five, she was pleased at what she saw—smooth, tight skin. Norma Levine Weitz was five-foot-four, two inches shorter than her husband. She had reddish brown hair and green eyes, greener than her daughter-in-law's. A lot of people took Norma for Irish. She had smooth red lips, not very full yet not very thin, and a small nose, which was natural, not a result of cosmetic surgery. Her clothing size was petite; she was curvaceous, yet small. She was weight conscious—although she was careful, she was not always on a diet. Her daughter Linda inherited her petite figure. Norma discovered that Sid was attracted to women who were petite, with compact breasts and small shapely buttocks. Sometimes Sid looked, but he never touched; he was a faithful devoted husband. Norma knew that she was beautiful before she met Sid. After she met Sid, not a day went by when he did not make her feel beautiful. She was still able to wear form-fitting clothing without any help from a Playtex eighteen-hour girdle that so many grandmas her age needed. When a woman is a fifty-five-year-old grandmother and she was still able to turn heads, it was very satisfying.

It was five-thirty, Sid should be home soon. She wanted him to be relaxed and hoped that everything went well for him today. She missed her husband when they were apart; now they will have more time together. Sid's decision to close the studio and not relocate to another storefront was a painful one for both of them. They had their years of success, and Sid still had a following, but not like the old days. The industry was changing, soon film would be obsolete. Jobs would be recorded electronically. Electronic imaging will forever change photography. Videographers can record affairs, and then sell clients still prints of their electronically produced images.

There was a lot of competition from package deal studios; it was time to go. She was proud of her husband's accomplishments and she still got a thrill from looking at Sid's portraits, albums, and videotapes. She always looked at the window with pride. She wasn't sure his partner Lenny's wife felt that way, but Lenny could not shoot like Sid.

The telephone rang as Norma clicked on the television to watch HBO. Their home phone number was unlisted, so whoever was calling would most likely be a friend or family.

"Hello," Norma picked up before the machine, which Sid called their electronic secretary.

"Hi, Mommy, how are you?" It was their daughter Linda. She and her family lived out in Suffolk, in Bright Waters, a section of Bay Shore. Their house was for sale. Mark had to relocate to Boston.

"I'm fine, darling, how are you?"

"Okay, I'm pregnant, Mommy. You can tell Daddy it's official; they think a girl this time, I held off telling you until I knew. I know he wants a granddaughter this time."

"Steven and Chris are having a girl, but you're right, this will make Daddy very happy."

"Alec, I'm talking to Gam, go play with Daddy."

"How is Mark and my beautiful grandchildren?"

"They're fine; they're going to watch a Disney tape. Daddy didn't want to take us to see Disney movies, because he thought Walt Disney was an anti-Semite."

"Daddy thinks every Christian is an anti-Semite. He had no problems buying those Mercurys and Lincolns from Henry Ford. Sid's a complex man. So what's new?"

"Nothing much, just doing some packing. How's Daddy?"

"He's fine, but he was crazy this morning."

"When is he not crazy, what happened now?"

"He had trouble with his new car, which was good for an episode. Otherwise, he's fine. He shot a Bar Mitzvah in Brooklyn last night, a little *momzer*, I hear. He shot a wedding today in Woodmere; he should be home soon."

"Is Daddy smoking?"

"Daddy cut down a lot, he's trying to quit. He switched to light and ultra light cigarettes for a while; he said they made him smoke more. He really doesn't smoke in the house anymore, I won't let him. I know he smokes when he's on location shooting and in the studio, but not a lot."

"Mommy, not a lot is still too much."

"I know, I know, but he's gonna quit, I promise. I'll kill him if he doesn't. Look at me, I was a social puffer—I puffed from time to time, never inhaled—I quit altogether back in 1963 when the first health report came out, never puffed again. God knows I had the temptation in the house. If I can quit, Daddy can quit."

"If Daddy wants me to come in with Mark tomorrow to help him pack up, the offer is still good. The boys can lend a hand."

"No thanks, honey. Daddy wants to go in and say goodbye to the place himself. He sold the studio furniture and threw out the old stuff. All his equipment and the albums are here. He wants to give his assistant some items and see what Lenny wants. He's gonna give you the frames you wanted in the window. The photographs are faded, so he's gonna throw them out. Oh, they're gonna disconnect the phone tomorrow. There'll be a recording telling people to call the office here. Steve asked him for the old studio answering machine because he has a new one at the number here. He told them to come over Saturday and take whatever they need."

"Daddy still doesn't like Chris?"

"He likes her; he just wishes she was Jewish."

"Do you talk to Chris' parents at all?"

"Eh, we talk, we don't talk. They don't call us, we don't call them. Her brother is getting married soon. Chris told us they're gonna call. Daddy will shoot it for them; he really doesn't want to, he won't make a dime, but he'll do it. He say's if he does a good job, maybe Chris' father will refer him to Patrick Buchannan.

"Oh, my God," Linda laughed heartily. "That's funny, but Pat Buchannan doesn't have kids."

"Yeah, I know."

"Is Daddy still upset about us moving to Boston? We're coming back to have the baby here; I want my doctor."

"We'll both miss you. He's a little sad, but not upset. He says next year, if Mark has to stay in Tokyo for a while, we'll fly there to see all of you. Next summer he won't be very busy, so the trip will be good for him."

"I'm going to get back to Mark and the kids. But, if he needs help tomorrow, tell him to call."

"I will, Linda."

"He has two years until Social Security; I hope business will be good for him."

"It's never gonna be what it used to be. But listen, what is? I'm still working at the bank. I can quit with my pension, but no Social Security, yet. Also, I have to occupy my time, but we'll see; maybe I'll get out with pension and work here with Daddy. For now I'll support us, we have money saved, we get stock dividends, and interest on a treasury bond, so we'll get along; you shouldn't worry. Besides, Daddy said some studios have dates to send him out on. He's a top man so they'll pay him a top wage."

"I'm going to miss that studio, Mommy."

"Well listen, it was probably one of the best looking photography studios on Long Island, everybody in the business said so. He was a few stores away from a busy movie theater; people saw that big double store when they drove by. People saw the stunning photographs in that big glass façade as they walked by. When he started with the video, he put a couple of monitors in his windows showing scenes from affairs. But the area went; he probably should have gotten out years ago. All Daddy's neighbors sold out or retired; there aren't any white people there anymore. The clients don't like to drive over there to see him. He thought about relocating to a nice office in Plainview, but for what? Everyday another studio closes. Daddy doesn't need such an overhead now. He's not happy about the way things are, but he's had his heyday, and he's grateful for the good times. So listen, it's time to take it easy."

"I guess you're right, Mommy. Well, I'll let you go; give Daddy our love, maybe we'll come over Saturday also."

"We'd love that, darling."

"I was just thinking that's what Daddy should have done; he should have named the studio for the front windows and called it Photography at the Glass Façade.

"Well, Lenny's wife, Sherry, picked the name Montclair. God knows why. I could never stand her, that woman gives me a pain in my ass. Carl's wife wanted to name the studio after the place in England where Shakespeare's plays were performed."

"I'm going to go, be well, Mommy."

"You too, darling, goodbye."

Norma hung up the phone. HBO had a comedy special coming up. She heard the chirp of the Nissan's burglar alarm in the drive way.

Sid entered the door on the side of the house into his home studio. He placed his equipment on the floor of his private office near his desk, went into his private bathroom, peed, and washed up.

Norma was sitting on the couch in the den again when he walked through the adjoining door. Their eyes met. They smiled at each other, a lot of old married couples seldom smile at each other.

Norma saw that Sid looked very tired; yes, it was time for him to take it easy. She was happy he was home.

Chapter Twelve

Norma and Sid embraced and kissed, theirs was one marriage the flame had not gone out of. Sid tasted of nicotine.

Norma smacked him on the arm. "Damn you, Sidney!" She always called him Sidney when she was miffed at him. "You've been smoking, probably all day, I bet!"

"I only had a couple of low tar Merits," lied Sid, he had been smoking more than a couple of high tar Viceroys. "I ain't gonna have any more tonight."

"You're damn right, you ain't."

"I was uptight, so I smoked a little, what can I tell you?"

"A little is too much, my love," Norma retorted. "Quit! That's what I want you to tell me."

"I'm gonna quit altogether."

"Sidney, you've been telling me that for years."

"I'm gonna quit, I tell ya! I know you can beat the shit out of me; I'm an old man who's no match for you. Meanwhile, I cut down a lot. You know, these days my clients get bent out of shape if I smoke in my own studio. Years ago, smoke used to fill banquet halls; they put cigarettes in glasses on the tables during both the cocktail hour and the reception. They passed out cigars, boxes of Nat Sherman's. Now brides request that there are to be no ashtrays on any tables. How goddamned inconsiderate that guests who drove all the way for the privilege of writing a check to the lucky couple have to go outside to smoke."

"You better quit, I want you to see sixty-one; shit, Sidney, I want you to see eighty-one. Please, love, if not for me, do it for our grandchildren. You know Linda confirmed what we were thinking. She is pregnant and the doctor thinks it will be a girl, we'll see. She and Mark want to name a daughter Rebecca."

"Becky is a nice name for a Jewish girl. I promise I'll quit. *Oy* I gotta sit down; I feel like a grandpa, I'm tired. In a little while I'm gonna change; we'll go out to eat."

Norma sat down on the couch next to Sid. She was aroused by the way her husband smelled after a hard day's work. The scent of his shirt was a mixture of cumin and chili powder. The first time they made love was after Sid shot a wedding. He had a weekend pass from the Army. She knew he was going overseas and she might never see the man she loved again. So, without the benefit of rabbi, *chuppah*, or the breaking of the glass, they spent a night together, and then got married. She never forgot that spicy male scent; it always turned her on.

"You feel like Mexican food tonight, love?" she asked.

"*Oy*," Sid groaned, "I couldn't take that tonight. Last time I had that stuff, I lit a cigarette afterwards, and with all that gas in me, I was afraid I'd blow up like a Bayonne refinery. You wanna go out for 'chinks'?"

"So, how was the wedding?"

"The usual big ostentatious Five Towns affair, you know, like what we made for our daughter. Only it wasn't too big, because there was only a best man and a matron of honor. Their video crew didn't get in my way, they were fairly decent, and so I have no complaint with Nicky's people."

"Nicky?"

"Nick Tavella, remember him from Brooklyn? From when I used to work for Benny Garfine, may he rest in peace."

"Oh, the photographer who was once a mailman?"

"Yeah, that's the one, Nick Tavella and his budget-priced videos."

"The bride was beautiful, Sid?"

"Jewish brides are always beautiful, I told Steven that when he was little."

"Don't start again, Sid," Norma warned, "it's over, they're married, they're gonna have a baby. We accept it, they love each other and that's the end of it."

"Well, anyway, today I got at least three hundred shots. Look, babe, I like Christine—she really is a sweet kid, it's just not an easy thing to swallow. She and I are friends, you know that. I hope they don't give that kid some *goyish* name like John or James."

"The baby's a girl, Sid," she reminded him, "and our rabbi's son-in-law is named James and he's Jewish."

"Even worse," Sid grumbled, "they'll name her something like Kathleen, Ann Marie, Philomena, Tricia, or God forbid, Mary after Christine's mother as in Mary Mother of Jesus. Watch, watch, you watch, Steve is gonna make sure they give that baby a real Catholic name just to aggravate me."

"*Gavolt*, Sidney," Norma placed her arm around her husband, "sometimes you're a real *nudnick*. Don't upset yourself, you have to live and let live."

"Sure," Sid agreed, "but when are they going to let me live."

"You're tired, honey, go change...we'll eat."

'I am tired, that Bar Mitzvah last night was a pain in the ass. I'll drop the film off at the lab on Wednesday when I pick up the wedding proofs. What about my car?"

"I had the car towed to the dealership. The saleslady, that nice Eve Massengil, took care of the whole thing. It was just a small adjustment with the starter. The car runs beautiful now, I drove it around. If you want, I'll take your car to work and you can have my car."

"No, you drive it, you're used to it." Sid was getting testy now, "I know we're insured for towing, but I'm gonna make them pay! Goddamn it! I should have bought another Japanese car. This won't be the end of it; it's gonna keep breaking down, and I'll end up having to buy yet another new car."

"Sid," Norma was getting tired of her husband's complaints, "Eve Massengil was so nice, she said how sorry she was and took care of the whole thing. It happens, what more do you want, you wanna get a stroke over it?"

"I feel sorry for that woman," Sid replied, "to go through life with a name like Eve Massengil. Was she named for a douche bag?"

"Oh, Sidney."

"Well, at least her name isn't Schmuck; I heard of a judge named Peter Schmuck...Peter, yet. What about the actor Peter O'Toole? Groucho Marx used to say that was a double phallic name."

"Tell me about last night," Norma sighed.

"Last night the Bar Mitzvah was at Brooklyn's Congregation Beth Affluent; they had an orchestra and a DJ, same company, the Dick Marcus Orchestra and Entertainment. Richie Marcus sends you his love, by the way."

"How old is he?"

Sid paused to think, "I think he told me he was sixty-six. He has grandchildren older than ours. But man! Can he still play the trumpet? He blows and sounds as great as he ever did, and he still croons, too...Richie's expensive, but he's worth it. He's always booked, always in demand. Remember, we couldn't get him for Linda's wedding."

"I remember, but Toby Tobias was just as good," answered Norma.

"Last night the smorgasbord alone was over ten grand, easy. They had a caricature artist, a mime, a couple of clowns, a magician, a balloon artist, and to top it all off, they hired Alan King to do a 45-minute standup routine."

"Some bash," Norma observed, "but, Sid, you can't complain, these are the jobs you want to book."

"True, these are the moneymakers. Also in attendance last night was a congressman, an actress, a singer, a playwright, three anchormen, and two anchorwomen...you know that beautiful Jewish woman on Channel Nine I like? The Boro President of Brooklyn...some people asked for my card, we'll see."

"If they need, they'll call; if they can afford, they'll book," she said.

"Listen," he said, "listen to this...the kid who parked my car said the photographer from last night drove a Jaguar. How's that for *chutzpah*? So, I says, 'I'll bet the photographer from last night tipped you too!' and I drove off."

Norma laughed at her husband. He really did have a wonderful sense of humor and could certainly deal with a little snot nose.

"When we were leaving last night, those little bastards called out, 'You guys suck,' right in the damn lobby. It wouldn't have bothered me, but I'm sixty years old, and I don't think I shoot the greatest jobs anymore."

"How was that Italian wedding you shot Friday night?"

"I told you."

"You didn't say. You went right to bed, then you went to the studio yesterday and, from there, to the Bar Mitzvah."

"Well, the hall was crap, the people were nice—they knew of my reputation, they wanted a quality photographer, so they hired one." He smiled and kissed Norma lightly on her lips.

"No problems?"

"Yes, problems—shitty background."

"Didn't you carry your portable background and stand?"

"Nah, I'm too old. Christ, remember when I used to set up room lights in the banquet room? Remember when I used to bring umbrellas and stands and tripods on location? I used to triple light the ceremony and sometimes the reception."

Norma nodded.

"I'm too old to *schlep* that crap, forget it."

"Why did they pick a shitty hall, Sid?"

"Her dad is the post commander and the guy who handles the catering is his brother-in-law."

"How was working with the lucky couple?"

"Nice, both good kids. Both schoolteachers. Her name was Jeanette, I forget his name. She kissed me goodbye, and gave me a long hug. I guess she felt I was close to her on her special day, a real sweet kid."

Norma leaned against Sid and placed her head on his shoulder. Her hair smelled of honey shampoo. Sid wondered if it was the shampoo—Norma was such a nice person, maybe it was her sweetness he smelled. A man who thinks of his wife as a nice person first, a friend second, a sex partner third, a good mother fourth and, finally, a good grandmother—has a happy marriage.

Sid considered Norma a good lover. Linda and Steven were products of their lovemaking. She was always there for him.

Norma also considered Sid a friend and a lover; she needed him to make her laugh.

"Oh, Sid," Norma exclaimed, "look who's on HBO!"

Sid put on his metal-framed distance glasses he always kept on the den coffee table. He turned up the volume of their large Mitsubishi television.

"Oh, it's him! What's he got to say tonight?"

The him was Sid's favorite 'borscht belt' comedian. This guy spoke with a heavy New York mockie Jewish accent, although he was not from New York. He was very clever and controversial; he claimed he wrote all his material. Sid and Norma had been fans for several years. They saw him on their honeymoon up at Grossinger's in the Catskills. They thought he was funnier than the guy who insults people. He was ripping into the nation's elected officials. Sid and Norma laughed heartily at his comments on various campaign rhetoric. They laughed when he mimicked speech patterns of candidates for public office. They winced when he referred to a southern governor, who was planning to run for president, as a lying bastard; and laughed when he mimicked some pop singers.

Then, this comic spoke about his recent marriage. After forty years of bachelorhood, he got married. He made fun of lavish catered affairs on Long Island. Sid laughed hard.

He made fun of the way guests eat at Jewish affairs. He made fun about how today's Bar Mitzvahs resemble a three-ring circus complete with clowns.

Then he started talking about paying a price to hire a photographer. Both Sid and Norma leaned forward.

"Albums he showed us—this is flush, this is reversible, this is expensive—but I'm the best; meanwhile, this schmuck was confusing us."

"Oh, my God, I can't believe this," Norma was laughing hysterically now.

"Shhhh, wait, wait; this I gotta hear," said Sid, "the sonofabitch."

The comic started dancing his trademark dance around the stage.

"Anyone who says a wedding is supposed to be a beautiful experience never had wedding pictures taken. Anybody here use a wedding photographer?"

There was a chuckle from the audience in response to the comic's query. A few hands went up.

"Good, I'm not alone," the comic continued. "All we wanted was a beautiful picture of the two of us and he hochked us, and posed us, and blinded us, and twisted my head this way, and moved our shoulders that way, and put our hands that way."

He was now gesturing and contorting himself. The audience was enjoying this routine. Sid and Norma were laughing, too.

"Listen, the truth is the truth," commented Sid.

The comic continued, "He told us for the price we were getting an award-winning photographer. I don't know about his pictures, but as a pain in the ass, the guy wins an award."

The audience was hysterical now.

"All day long, it was look at the camera, now look at each other, and look at me; and kiss her, now kiss him and look away, not like you're looking away, but like you're looking at the camera, but not like you're really looking at the camera. Turn to the side, no, not your side, my side; put your hand under her arm and turn to me and look away. Put your arm around her waist and your hand in your pocket; look into each other's eyes and take your hand out of your pocket; and don't stand like that, try to stand like this; but don't look here, look there."

The audience applauded in agreement.

Sid and Norma were laughing very hard. He wondered how many of his colleagues were watching this guy tonight.

"When they show this during the week, I gotta tape it," he told her in between laughs.

The comic was not finished, yet; he was still dancing around.

"Look at the bouquet, but not like this, I mean like this and look away from the camera. Okay…now let's go outside to do pictures because it has stopped raining. Now let's go inside because it's too hot! Now let me take off my jacket and change film. Now let's change locations, but not there…there's too much sun and not there…there's too much shade and a lousy background."

The audience was really eating up this routine.

"I want the video man to stand on the right and shoot to the left and I want everyone to look at him, but not like you're looking at him, and pull up your pants and tuck in your shirt, and tell the rabbi he's in my way and shouldn't be in the picture, and tell your aunt to stop taking pictures, she's bothering me."

They were laughing; this guy was hot tonight.

"At the reception," the comic continued his monologue, "he did the tables and made everybody crazy. Everybody sitting down, stand up; everybody standing up, sit down. Everyone on this side of the table, move to that side of the table. Everyone on that side of the table, move to this side of the table and everybody look at me, smile, and hold it because I have to change film, I have to change batteries for my flash, and I have to change my lens."

The crowd at this casino was roaring, why not? There were a lot of snotty Jewish people from the Five Towns area of Long Island on junkets to Atlantic City tonight. *I bet some of my clients are home watching this now*, Sid thought, *or even there in person*. Sid wondered if the *goyim* who had used package deal photographers got these jokes.

"I hope somebody took a picture of my reception, because I didn't see it…I was too busy taking pictures. My friends told me the food was terrific and it was a beautiful wedding. Now I know why people buy wedding albums, so they can see what their weddings looked like because they're never there, they're too busy taking pictures."

That line brought the house down. Sid and Norma could not catch their breath. Their sides ached.

"The pictures in the albums are supposed to be for memories. For memories? Listen, I don't remember anything, because that sonofabitch kept making us run out of the room!"

The audience in that Atlantic City showroom applauded wildly. Hell, they were giving the guy an ovation.

Sid caught his breath, he was laughing very hard, and then he started to cough.

"Alright, alright, enough already. I'm gonna go upstairs and change then we can go out for 'chinks'."

"He was funny tonight," Norma assessed, "he got your shtick down pat."

"The hell do you mean my shtick, it's an exaggeration based on something he saw or perceived. Evidently, he did not like his photographer because my father always said, 'In jest there is truth.' Enough of this crap for one night. I'm hungry; those cheap bastards didn't feed us. I'll be right down," Sid trotted upstairs.

The phone rang, Norma answered. "Hello."

"Hello, Mommy, were you watching HBO?"

"Yes, Linda, Daddy and I saw him; we laughed."

"How is Daddy?"

"He's pooped, but he's feeling alright; we're going out for 'chinks.'"

"Well, I hope he wasn't too offended."

"No, Daddy's a big boy, he can take a critique. But, he probably thinks that his impression of what's his name, that country western singer with the beard, was funnier."

"I'm sure."

"I told Daddy it's official, you're expecting. He was happy, he loves his grandchildren. Now we're going to have two girls."

"They say *maybe* a girl, Mommy; I hope, we'll see. At least you'll have one granddaughter for sure. I'll call you tomorrow. I think we will come over Saturday, then Mark is off to Antwerp."

"We'd love that. Don't forget the boys."

"Give Daddy my love."

"I will, honey, good night."

"Good night, Mommy."

"Who was that who just called?" Sid called from upstairs.

"Linda, she wanted to know if we were watching HBO."

"Christ!"

Within ten minutes Sid came downstairs. He was wearing a pair of brush denim jeans, which he bought back in the mid-seventies when they were in style. He also wore a yellow Izod Lacoste golf shirt with a little alligator on the front and a pair of worn white leather Hush Puppy loafers without socks.

"I'm gonna shower when we get back; I'm starving, let's go."

The Caprice rode very well and they were happy about that. They ate at the new mandarin Chinese restaurant on Broadway in Woodmere. The food was very good. They did not cook with MSG. The place also offered low-salt or no-salt cooking. The waiters were pleasant, and the prices were reasonable, for a change.

After they ate, they drove back to the house, got undressed, showered separately, but got into bed together, naked.

Both Sid and Norma were very tired. They were not too tired for each other. They made love like a couple of teenagers, but with the adeptability of experienced adults.

Chapter Thirteen

M ontclair Studios was closed on Mondays, but Monday was not always a day off. Film had to be taken to the lab, proofs and finished photographs had to be picked up. Photos had to be sent to the album bindery, videotapes needed to be edited, and there were supplies to be purchased...so many things that could not always be done during business hours.

The staff of Montclair was happy to set up appointments with prospective clients on Mondays. One of the partners met with the people. Hey, if it meant booking a job and making a buck, to hell with a day off.

Mondays were also good for booking family portraits, as was Sunday. The studio was closed on Sunday, too, but that was also a good day for making appointments and shooting groups and portraits, when the photographers were not out on location.

Monday was always a slow day.

Sid Weitz hated Monday.

As he shaved in the bathroom, he played the small radio, which was on a shelf. The last of Sid's favorite dentist office FM music stations was starting to switch to a more contemporary format. This upset Sid very much. They were taking everything away from him. The station was playing a tribute to Monday—*Rainy Days and Mondays*; *Monday, Monday*; and *Written on a Manic Monday*.

Sid Weitz always hated Monday.

Most people hate Monday.

Fuck Monday.

Sid Weitz began the first day of a new week sipping a mug of coffee in his kitchen. His wife, Norma, sat across from him, sipping her coffee. They were eating toaster made blueberry waffles, without syrup. They did not think these waffles needed any. Sid had finished reading the *New York Times*; he was reading *Long Island Newsday*.

"Christ, look at this, babe," he complained to Norma, "our beloved county executive, who wants to run for governor in two years, is raising our taxes for a change. What the hell do we get in return for our taxes in Nassau County anyway? Another little playground in an affluent neighborhood that is never used? What else—new signs to be put up on all county property, with the names of the supervisors, council, clerk, and receiver of taxes—like they're doing us a favor?"

"What are you going to do?" Norma asked.

"Move to Florida before these taxes choke us. Really, last week in front of the store, some county workers came to fix the street. Fix the street, my ass. You know what those guys did? They spent a half hour bending over showing us their ass cracks while they tore up the street, then they spent three days sitting on the curb eating lunch. That's right; they tore up the street even though there was nothing wrong with it. After they patched up the goddamned street, it looked worse than before. When we go to the town pool, ever notice they have men walking around with Styrofoam cups?"

Norma nodded.

"Well, these men get paid a hell of a lot of money just to walk around all day long to see how many kids peed in the pool. They get the job because they know someone in the Republican Party and they kick back part of their salary to finance some big shot's campaign."

"But, you know what's worst of all? The cops. These goddamn Nassau County cops—the most overpaid, underworked police force in the country. They spend their day giving people road directions. Remember when the studio was broken into? What did those guys do? Nothing."

"It was some cash and office supplies," Norma replied. "They really didn't get much."

"That's what I told you, I didn't want to get you upset. Truth is, the sonsofbitches also got a studio Mamiya RB-67, one Mamiya 645, a couple of lenses, and some radio slaves."

"A 645, oh Sidney, you didn't tell me."

"It was an older one; I used it primarily for studio work. I didn't remember what my insurance covered, so I didn't want to worry you."

"Oh, alright, but you got a settlement."

"Getting back to all this Nassau County bullshit, the cops did nothing. I called the precinct and the cops came, the Nassau detectives came and did nothing. The cops who took the complaint were very nice, but they were just cops. Then this Nassau County detective came over. This guy was a real red-faced German anti-Semite. He treated me like a criminal and not the victim. Harry Lowenstein was over at the studio when the detective came. When Harry flashed the shield, he bristled, told Harry he wants to ask him some questions because he is a photographer for this studio, and there is a world of difference between a patrolman and a detective so he can put his shield away, because this investigation does not concern the N.Y.P.D. He thinks maybe I took the stuff for the insurance. He suggests maybe Harry is a bad cop who broke into the studio. He kept referring to Harry as Lowenstein really accentuating his name. Then he says people in my line of work should be charged with highway robbery. He's standing there; his German face is getting all red, complaining about how his daughter couldn't afford a photographer for her wedding because we charge so much money. He's supposed to be investigating my complaint, and the bastard is calling me a crook. When I went up to the squad to get the report, I asked Harry to come with me. He introduced himself to the bulls, they were cordial, but when he asked the investigating detective how the case was coming along he turned away from Harry. Harry said he'd like this guy to run a red light in his sector or for his son to drive drunk on his shift."

"Calm down, Sidney, you complained."

"Complained nothing. I told his captain who was a Jewish guy bucking to be Nassau County's first Jewish police commissioner, I didn't like this detective's treatment. He tells me that he probably had a bad day He said the detective wanted to help me, he really didn't mean to offend, but he has bills from his daughter's wedding, and he never displayed any anti-Jewish feelings in front of him. Then he tells me his son got Bar Mitzvahed recently and he felt that the studio that shot the job had ripped him off, too."

Sid sipped more coffee.

"Listen, hon, these Nassau County detectives, who I think Hitchcock portrayed as the morons they are in *North by Northwest*, make over eighty grand a year and they can't afford wedding pictures? I get these freakin' police charities calling my studio every other day…every other day, harassing me to contribute to their bullshit organization. Even Harry tells them to screw off. I read in the paper last week a lot of cops out here retire on pensions worth over a hundred grand a year. This doesn't include all those clowns who finagled a disability retirement. The last thing these Nassau County cops need is charity."

"I liked that restaurant last night."

"Yeah, Norma, that was very good 'chinks.' The prices were reasonable and the waiters weren't arrogant. Remember the place we took my sister to? It was a Saturday night, very busy. That little chink waiter kept rushing us, he wanted us to get out so he could get another tip from the next party. The damned food was so salty. The Chinaman got tired of pouring water for me, so he put the pitcher on the table. He said, 'You drink a lot of water.' I wanted to kick that little chink in the balls. I gave him a lousy tip. Maybe Saturday when the kids come over, I'll take everyone out. You don't mind having 'chinks' again?"

Norma shook her head 'no.'

"You sure you're not going to need any help today, love? I could take off."

"No, you go to the bank. I got up early and put some boxes in the car. There isn't a lot to take, most of it is here… a lot of the crap was thrown out or sold, which is good, because we never fixed that old burglar alarm after the theft. Those thieves didn't even have the decency to reconnect the wires when they were finished."

Norma laughed.

"I just have some odds and ends to take care of and then I'm outta there. Lenny's moving the baby office to Lynbrook next week. I didn't tell you? Lenny found a suite in a nice office building. Now, I have to make money to survive. I read in the papers our stocks are all down, so I hope I get customers from working here in the house."

"Your brother-in-law is a good stockbroker, Sid, why not give him a call," she suggested.

"Oh, no! I don't want a good stockbroker," Sid waved his hands and shook his head. "I want a crook! I want a Ponzi scheme."

"Well," said Norma, "if you don't need my help, I'll get ready for work." She leaned forward and kissed Sid, "I'll see you later, relax."

"I'm relaxed."

"Be calm."

"I'm calm."

"Try not to worry about anything, it's going to work out alright," Sid wished he could believe that.

"I'm not worried."

He was worried plenty.

"Sid, aren't you going to get dressed?"

"I am dressed—this is my last day, nobody is coming over, what the hell difference does it make what I wear today?" Sid said with a shrug.

Sid Weitz was not dressed the way he usually was to go to the studio. His usual code of dress was a business suit or sports jacket, sometimes slacks and shirts, cardigans and turtle necks in the cold weather. Since Montclair was once a high-end studio catering to an upscale clientele, Sid dressed for success. Today, he did not give a shit about dress or success.

Today, Sid was clad in white polyester shorts with a trouser type waistband, a blue and white 'American Film Classics' tee shirt, white cotton sweat socks, and new white deck sneakers. On his head, he wore a medium blue baseball cap with white lettering that read, VIRGINIA SLIMS across the front. Sid was not sure where he got the cap. He did not smoke Virginia Slims cigarettes, nor did he ever attend a Virginia Slims tennis open. But, it was a good hat to shield his face from the sun. He already had a pre-cancerous growth removed from his face last year; he did not need any more. It wasn't a cancer on his face his wife worried about. In his profession you, unfortunately, had to spend time in the sun.

Sid eased his Chevy Caprice out of the driveway. So far, the car was running well. Today he was going to his studio for the last time. This trip, which had been part of his daily routine, would not be taken any longer. Sid knew he was going to miss going to work every day, for awhile anyway.

Sid turned on to Peninsula Boulevard and headed toward Sunrise Highway. As fate would have it, there was a crew from the public works department displaying their ass cracks as they tore up the street.

A nice-looking Irish broad was waving a red flag, directing traffic. Sid checked her out as he drove by. She was cute in her tank top, but she had an angry face; he assumed she was a *farbissen shiksa. Still*, he said to himself, *the crew ought to put this broad on the jackhammer so she could display her ass crack while he had to wait for the oncoming traffic.*

On the way to his studio, Sid passed three studios, which appeared to be thriving. These fellows always had work, especially here in the Five Towns. He knew that in these times, their situation could change, but they seemed to be holding their own.

Two weeks ago, a part-time photographer who was working from his house in Suffolk County came to the studio to buy some vinyl and leather bound album covers that Lenny bought a while back. Lenny bought those cheaper grade albums in keeping with the changes in their area. Sid did not really want to book the cheaper jobs at prices that range from nine hundred and ninety-nine dollars to sixteen hundred dollars. But, what are you going to do? It helped to pay the rent for that big studio for the last couple of years. Times are hard and a buck is a buck, and right now everyone has to take a little less. Clients today know that if they walk out of a photo studio, most likely, the photographer will not be shooting a job that day, period. Who taught clients how to get the cheapest packages they could? The photographers—they lowered their prices, gave their work away, compromised on everything— resulting in everyone lowering their prices, knocking the whole industry on its ass. The clients are the ones who manipulate the industry today.

These inexpensive albums they had at the studio were not needed now. Sid placed an advertisement on the bulletin board at the lab. A photographer called and asked to come over to look at them. This photographer explained that, initially, he started out offering only custom bound library albums. The bound albums were made at a bindery. The prints are textured, then sprayed with a protective lacquer, trimmed at the sides, and then the edges are gilded before they are placed into the album. The print actually becomes the page. For an extra charge, the client could have a border around the print.

There are borders for various print sizes. The reversible album does not have to be turned to view horizontal or vertical photographs; also, reversible albums are larger than flush, as extra leather is needed for the larger pages. Flush bound albums with vertical and horizontal prints have to be turned for viewing. As the years go by, flush albums often chip at the edges.

Some binderies years ago, offered a smaller border, known as a panel album. This was not Sid's favorite. Although there was a border, the album had to be turned for verticals, as it was primarily for square photographs. Montclair Studios had not offered a panel album for years.

This young *goy* from Suffolk saw his plan to go high end and offer expensive leather-bound albums backfire. He was in the wrong area. People who live out in the boondocks don't spend money. They only show interests in beer and motorcycles. This putz had to switch to package deals if he was to survive.

"I don't understand what happened to the business," the photographer said as he wrote Sid out a check. "What the hell happened to this business?"

"I wish I knew," was Sid's reply.

Sid felt sorry for this poor putz. He only knew from selling package jobs to *goyim*, and things were bad for him. Sid catered to the affluent, both Yiddish and Goyish, and now it was pretty much over for him.

Sid pulled over on Sunrise Highway and started to cry. He took out his handkerchief and wiped his eyes, and then regained his composure. For Sid Weitz, photography was more than a business; it was a way of life. That was true for most of his fellow candid men. His top candid man, Harry Lowenstein, could understand that; for him, being a cop was more than just a job, it was a way of life, even though he was Jewish and not a third generation *Mick*, he knew what it was to have a job that was also a way of life.

It was an interesting forty years, anyhow. If he wasn't getting the blood sucked from him from a Jewish mother who wanted her way, he was being strangled by Italian clients who wanted a package deal. Photographers were told today the clients wanted the negatives and to hell with his copyright.

He thought about a Bat Mitzvah he photographed ten years earlier. The girl's mother wanted an Art Leather reversible album, not a Library Bound reversible album. When it was time to pick up the completed job, the mother said that was not the album she wanted. She claimed she contracted for a Library Bound reversible album. Sid asked his receptionist to produce the contract. It stated that this woman did indeed contract for an Art Leather album. The woman said she would be right back with her copy of the contract. That was very nice, calling a man a liar in his own place of business, when he knew damn well he was being honest and could back it up in writing. The woman came back with her copy of the contact, which she should have had with her in the first goddamn place. It confirmed that she had contracted for an Art Leather album. Sid half expected her to rewrite her copy to get what she wanted. She did not even say she was sorry for being so snippy.

Clients are like women; you can't live with them and, sure as hell, can't live without them.

Another Bar Mitzvah mother squeezed blood from him, too. She told him he could photograph the ceremony in the reform temple on Saturday. He photographed the posed formals in the sanctuary on Friday morning. The boy's parents were put out because the rabbi was not available. Sid ran through the final arrangements with the rabbi right before the service. He knew he would not be allowed to use flash on *Shabbat*. The rabbi told Sid he would only be allowed to take three pictures. He did not know that. He thanked the rabbi for that information; he explained he otherwise would have shot a lot more. The rabbi told Sid that he would have been thrown out. The rabbi wanted to know why the photographer did not check with him the day before when he was here taking the formals. The photographer reminded the rabbi he did not wish to make himself available. This did not endear the photographer to the rabbi, nor to the boy's mother, for that matter. She did not want the photographer to know about the three-picture-only rule; she wanted photographs and to hell with the temple.

Then there was the time in a temple in Brooklyn, in Brighton Beach, the groom's father had a disagreement with the rabbi, so he laid him out during rehearsal right on the *bimah*. The rabbi had a heart attack. The groom's father was arrested later on. If Harry Lowenstein had been shooting that job, he would have made an off-duty arrest of his client.

So many war stories. Maybe retirement was the time for him to write a book about the last forty years. Fiction or non-fiction, that was the question. He did not know the answer. Not yet, anyway.

He pulled the Chevy back out into traffic. It was time to retire and take it easy; shit, after forty years, he earned it. He did not need the aggravation anymore. He could not take the aggravation anymore.

So, what happens now?

Well, now he goes in to clean out the store and take life one day at a time as he works out of his house.

People were just not booking photographers like they used to. Or, was it just him. He did not understand what happened to this business.

What the hell did happen to this business?

Chapter Fourteen

Lenny Schecter sat at his large oak desk in his private office, sipping a cup of coffee. He was deciding on how he should identify himself today, to people who call on the phone. Should he say he's Mr. Cohn, or should he be Vince Venezia? He always used names; in this kind of numbers business, it helped to be someone else on the phone. Salespeople often used phone names. Especially, if the state attorney general's office, the department of consumer affairs, Channel Two's Roseanne Colletti and Arnold Diaz (the Channel Two troubleshooter and the 'shame on you' man), were also receiving letters from somewhat less than satisfied clients.

Lenny was looking over a large quantity of orders of baby portraits for Happy Time photographers. He swiveled from his desk to look out of the window at the street below. Hempstead Turnpike was once one of the finest shopping streets on Nassau County's south shore. Now, it was a real mess. His brand new white Lexus stuck out like a sore thumb. Lenny did not have a 'no radio' sign in the new car; he figured those little car thieves did not know how to read. Next week, Happy Time Photographers would be located in a modern office building in Lynbrook. Whatever was left of Montclair Studios would be in his former partner's home in Hewlett, and good luck to him. The wedding portrait line was a bitch today. Everybody buys baby pictures.

Lenny had not worked downstairs in Montclair Studios for the past five years. He would still shoot an affair if Sid needed him to. At the age of sixty-one, Lenny had no desire to shoot candids. He only wanted to rake in the bucks from the baby pictures.

Sid and Lenny had two very successful photographic organizations, in spite of the departure of their talented partner Carl. It was time for Lenny to drop the candids completely. Sid wanted to take his money out of the baby studio. He no longer had the patience to oversee in-home baby portraits. Lenny thought that running a baby studio would be ideal for Sid at his age.

"Why do you want to shoot those goddamn weddings and B'Mitzvahs?" Lenny chided Sid in exasperation, when they were dissolving the partnership of Happy Time Photographers and Montclair Studios. "Shit, you're gonna be sixty years old, you still wanna run around and chase limousines and run up and down steps? You wanna run to the park and take pictures and bend and *schlep* shit and struggle with rotten B'Mitzvah boys? You wanna be Harvey Shiffman in Woodmere; he had a heart attack, and he still shoots? You're outta your fuckin' head, man."

Sid told Lenny that he was going to be working a lot less and he was still in good shape.

"What are you Sidney, a *nar*? Ya wanna be a *nar*?"

Nar was a Yiddish word for 'fool'; it was short for *narishkeit*, which meant 'foolishness.'

Well, if Sid wants to be a fool, Lenny thought *let him. It's his fucking life; I'll stay in babies and stay healthy and make money.*

Lenny Schecter was wearing light gray gabardine slacks, a dark blue pullover golf shirt, and white moccasins without socks. In the next room, there were six women calling mothers of babies from sheets of leads, to set appointments for their pictures to be taken. Out on the road, he had several photographers shooting babies and small children. Also, out on the road today, were several salespeople hustling portraits from the sittings.

By three o'clock today, Lenny will have cleared a couple of thousand dollars. Even though Happy Time no longer photographed schools, camps, athletic teams, or proms, the children's pictures alone carried the business. Pictures for *pishers*, that is where the money is. Lenny knew he must be making a shitload of money, because he was forever fielding calls from the Better Business Bureau and Channel Two's Roseanne Colletti. Her, he did not mind—she was cute, he liked her. It was that fuckin' Arnold Diaz he could not stand. Today was going to be a good day. Every day at Happy Time was a good day. Downstairs at Montclair, you got depressed.

Lenny Schecter looked like the creep he was thought of by his colleagues in the industry. He had a large nose and beady eyes. His voice was the same gravelly Brooklyn accent as Sid's. Years ago when Lenny used to answer the Montclair phone, clients could not tell if it was Sid or Lenny who answered. Only their wives could tell. Carl's voice sounded different. His added class to the studio. Lenny used to tell Carl he sounded like a faggot.

The main difference between Sid and Lenny was, Sid had his own hair, and Lenny wore a very obvious hairpiece. Lenny wore it to the studio and out on shoots, but he never wore it in his house. Lenny thought he might stop wearing the damn thing soon. Sid knew what Lenny looked like without it. He was very bald and even uglier. Sid told Lenny he should never go out without the rug.

Lenny wanted Sid to have all the equipment from Montclair—the only thing Lenny wanted was a wall frame that hung in the reception area that his mother liked.

Lenny sold a spare button making machine. The photo buttons, mirrors, magnets, and pendants that the machine produced were very big sellers for Bar and Bat Mitzvahs, sweet sixteens, sports teams, and birthday parties. They had booked 'photo favors' as a separate coverage. Those favors were sometimes sellers with wedding and baby clients. There were two old Crown Graphic press cameras, which were modified to make passport cameras—one for color, one for black and white. Those two went quickly. Everything from the studio, which was not needed, went very quickly. Why not? Lenny marked everything only twenty-five dollars. Neither Sid nor Lenny were looking to make a lot of money on the old studio equipment. They first thought it would be better to sell that stuff to another photographer, who might be able to use it, rather than toss it out for the garbage man. Whatever they made was found money.

Other twenty-five dollar items that went were video camera brackets, camera brackets, album stands, posing stools, posing desks, posing benches, prop chairs, tripods, monopods, old portable strobe units, old 'potato masher' strobe units, old studio lights, old backgrounds, and light stands.

The fifty dollar items went very quickly, too. A sixty-inch metal office desk with a swivel chair, a modeling light, a video light, a heavy video tripod, a dolly for video, and a simulated marble posing column.

There were other studio accessories priced much higher, such as a motorized background for studio portraits, and the studio lighting equipment. These items were purchased by other studios earlier in the year. The photographers who bought the lesser priced items were younger, less established shooters who were looking to buy studio equipment at low prices. The equipment did not have to be pretty and it was not, but it had to work, and it did.

The old studio furniture was sold through an advertisement in the *Buy Lines*—that shit was reasonable enough to sell quickly, and it did. Lenny and Sid divided up the money. In addition to getting his fifty percent of the sold items, Sid got back the fifty percent he put into Happy Time Photographers. Lenny got his fifty percent back from Montclair Studios. Sid and Lenny were now finished as partners, but what a run they had!

Both the wedding and baby studios did very well. Then the times changed, the area changed, the economy changed. Lenny grew tired of being a candid man in the seventies. In addition to supervising the baby studio, Lenny wanted just to work in the studio as a portrait photographer. He did not want to learn how to shoot and edit video along with Sid. Lenny already knew how to shoot movies, what the hell did he need video for? Besides, Lenny thought video would never catch on. The fact that nobody had called the studio to book weddings for years did not bother him one bit. When the studio first started to offer video in 1976, Lenny shot the affair with a movie camera. After the film was processed it was transferred to videotape, either a VHS or Beta. The following year, video cameras were phased in.

"Alright, I was wrong about the video," Lenny later admitted. "It did catch on. Only now everybody and their uncle are doing video. There is just too much competition out there." Lenny agreed to go along with Sid years ago on all his ideas. Offering photo favors, switching to color film, double lighting on location, getting rid of the tungsten studio lights, the 8x10 and 4x5 view cameras for studio portrait work. He even went along with Sid when he wanted to dump the Speed Graphics and the Koni-Omega camera with their 6x7 negative size, in favor of 6x6 and 645 medium-format cameras, which were easier to handle. Lenny even kept quiet when Sid wanted to change the manual potato masher-style strobes in favor of the portable made for the trade automatic Armitars.

Lenny did think that photo favors were actually a good idea. A Montclair photographer would set up an area at a reception and shoot folks with an instant camera, and process the novelty items on location. The clients loved the cute frames or the little key chains. But, then again, if that concept did so well, why the fuck did we sell the button making machine?

However, the video, that was the last fucking straw. Who the hell needed it? So much money and equipment always needed to be upgraded…fuck that shit. Why the fuck should he piss away money on expensive equipment that had to be upgraded every week. No thanks! *If Sid wanted to offer video at Montclair Studios, let him do it without me*, Lenny thought. *Let him spend his own fucking money on that shit. All I want to know from is the high volume baby sales.*

Lenny did, at first, get some satisfaction when Sid had to upgrade his video wares with the frequent changes of technology. It pissed him off somewhat when Sid took it all in stride. He grumbled a bit, then reasoned that it had to be done for business. Still, Lenny was relieved that the money for this fucking studio was not coming out of his pockets.

One of the telemarketing gal-Fridays walked through the open door into Lenny Schecter's office. She was a cute little black girl with a slight Jamaican lilt, who Lenny wanted desperately to bang, but was afraid of his wife, Sherry.

"Lenny, Tony called. He said he just broke his record for last month. He said the baby's mother bought everything from him."

"Beautiful, baby, beautiful. Tony's beautiful and so are you. Is Sid here yet?"

"No, I don't think so; there doesn't seem to be anyone downstairs, yet."

"Ain't you glad, Geneva; ain't you glad that I took you away from those crappy department store baby studios and gave you a real job?"

Geneva smiled and waved to Lenny as she left the room.

Cute little girl, very cute, lovely accent, Lenny said to himself. *She knows I want to get into her; I haven't had a cute little shvartze girl since the army. If it wasn't for old fat ass Sherry…eh, what the hell, fuck Sherry. Shit, I'd rather fuck Geneva…all in good time*; he let out a soft wicked witch of the west laugh, *all in good time.*"

Lenny lit a Montecristo cigar. He used to smoke cigarettes a long time ago. He had tried to convince Sid to switch to cigars, but Sid did not care for them. He joked that if he smoked cigars, girls would not want to kiss him. Lenny favored the high grade cigars, but was not above buying the cheaper drugstore cigars, if that was all that was available. He liked cigars. *I'm losing my partner; he could have been in clover with just the baby pictures, but the putz wants no part of it, he wants to shoot affairs. It's his goddamned life,* Lenny reasoned, *he knows what he's doing; he used to be very successful…used to be!*

The baby studio was a success because Lenny and Sid knew all the wonderful tricks of the trade. They trained their salespeople to use all the nice tricks. There was a way to get a hesitant mommy to buy a package. The salesperson would keep on dropping to the lowest-priced package, and then at the lowest-priced unit, he or she would take out some money, maybe a twenty dollar bill and place it into the order bag. The salesperson would tell the mother that they are laying out the money, and the client will be able to reimburse the salesperson when the pictures are delivered. The "I'm laying out my own money" bullshit worked. Sometimes a mother would decide after setting up an appointment, she did not want pictures, after all. The photographer informed mom that, if she did not allow him in to take the pictures, the studio would not pay him. Most of the time it worked.

Lenny's phone rang; he placed the Montecristo into the ashtray and answered.

"Happy Time."

He listened, picked up the Montecristo, and puffed.

"No, ma'am, we don't shoot weddings. Which number did you dial?"

"I see, you want the number for Montclair Studios downstairs. We have the same address and same exchange number."

Lenny listened again.

"I see, you remembered Montclair from your cousin's Bat Mitzvah; you're looking for Mr. Sid Weitz."

Again, Lenny paused and listened.

"What? No, I'm the guy with the hairpiece; I did the stills, I guess Sid did the video. Huh? Salt and pepper hair and a beard? Yes, that was Sid; that was a while ago, he doesn't have a beard anymore."

Once again, Lenny paused.

"Right studio, you just got the partners mixed up. Sid has his own hair; I'm the guy with the rug. I'll give Sid the message when he comes in, honey. He'll probably get back to you tonight, *muzel tov*." Lenny hung up.

Today would be the last day Lenny would work with Sid in the studio. He just wished Sid would not hock him all day with the wedding and Bar Mitzvah bullshit. Happy Time had a lot of appointments to make for baby pictures. He thought he might take Sid out to dinner with both their wives and pick up the check, but why bother? Sid was not really retiring, yet, and Lenny hated picking up dinner checks.

The phone rang again

"Hello, Roseanne," Lenny said when the caller identified herself. "We are giving that couple who complained about us back all the money. You know, Roseanne, the lighting they use at Channel Two does not do you justice. You're such a beautiful woman. I miss you on the weekend anchor; *oy vay,* when they replaced you with the little cute Puerto Rican girl on weekends, you started going after honest businessmen like me. What, I told you, honey, I'm working it out; the couple will be satisfied, I promise you. Yes, you have my word. By the way, do you send out autographed pictures?"

Chapter Fifteen

Sid Weitz needed a pack of Viceroys. He knew he really needed a pack of Viceroys, like he needed a hole in the head, or, God forbid, a hole in the throat. He turned right off Hempstead Turnpike on to Elmont Road. A little Hindu had a discount store where he could buy his cigarettes. The discount store was formerly owned by a Jewish man, who opened the store the same year Sid opened the studio. Today, in an effort to cut down his intake of nicotine, Sid was going to buy Viceroy Ultra Lights. To compensate for inhaling a lower content of nicotine, Sid would buy one hundreds instead of his usual king size. Quitting was hard, he knew that. He tried to quit so many times.

Elmont Road was a wide intersection that began up in the Village of Elmont and ran all the way up to Floral Park. If you made a left-hand turn on to Plainfield Avenue, you would pass Montclair Studios. Sid would drive through the parking lot, behind the stores, and come out on Hempstead Turnpike so he could park his car in front of the studio. The one good thing about the building the studio was in was there was plenty of parking. Long Island clients did not want to walk. They wanted to park as close to the store that they were doing business in, as possible. If a Long Island consumer cannot find a parking space, they just drive off and shop somewhere more convenient. Hempstead Turnpike was sometimes too busy for a sane human to attempt to cross. The studio was on the left-hand side of the street.

Sid double parked in front of the discount store and dashed in. He knew he would not get a ticket for double parking, because in this neighborhood, the fat assed cops were scared shitless to be out of their cars. More often than not, the bastions of this county would be chomping down donuts, and trying to make time with a cute counter girl. Sid believed that between the village cops and the county cops, he would be better protected by an old box of leaky condoms.

On the left side of Elmont Road was an off-track betting parlor. All the local horse players, con men, daydreamers, and lowlifes congregated in front of the place. One might think that these characters would much rather gamble than pursue gainful employment. Come to think of it, that was a reasonable assumption. Next door to the O.T.B., was a barber shop formerly owned by an Italian, and presently owned by a Haitian. This barber shop no longer styled razor cuts, layer cuts, or shags. The sign in the window announced the shop specialized in afros, dreadlocks, and high tops.

On the right side of the street, was a jewelry store that now carried mostly costume jewelry, and a luncheonette, which was famous for serving thick sandwiches. Next to the luncheonette was a ladies' hair salon. Once the salon served a white clientele, now it catered to women of Hispanic origin. Then there was a dress store, which had once sold top-of-the-line women's wear, now they sold *shlock*.

Sid entered the discount store. Strangely, the store smelled of tea and curry. The little Indian man looked up and smiled.

"My friend, my friend, please come on in, come on in."

Sid and Norma noticed that tobacco shops, stationery, discount stores, and gas stations were being taken over by Indian immigrants. The Indians were associated with convenience stores the way Greeks were associated with the ownership of diners.

"Hello, Sanjay, a pack of Viceroy Ultra Lights, please, the one hundreds."

"Sid, I hear this is to be your last day here, you retire?"

"Semi-retire, how much do I owe you, Sanjay?"

"You a very good photographer. I see the window of your photography studio. You are very good."

"How much?"

Sid was double parked, he did not want to tempt fate on his last day here, some restless, fat-assed cop might drive by and give him a ticket.

"For you, my friend, on the house...no charge to you. Is your partner to retire, as well?"

"From weddings, yes; he's moving the baby studio to Lynbrook next week."

"He does very nice baby pictures, I see in the window."

"Sanjay, baby, I'd love to chat, but I gotta go." Sid extended his right hand. "It's been nice knowing you, *bubeleh*, take care and keep smiling."

"I keep smiling; you take care too, er, boobaloo."

Sid dashed from the discount store to his double-parked car. There was no ticket. He drove down Hempstead Turnpike, turned left into the parking lot, exited on to the side street, made a right, and parked at the end of Plainfield Road. There were no parking spaces left in front of the studio. As he backed the Chevy into the space, a beautiful black woman about six feet tall wearing her hair up in some sort of African style, wheeled a shopping cart in back of the car. Barely wearing a tank top and tight white stirrup pants, she crossed, oblivious to the back-up lights.

"Come on, Cleopatra Jones, look where the fuck you're goin', mama," Sid called out. The windows were up, she did not hear.

He walked back to the studio. How the block had changed in the last thirty years. He did not go into the studio, but walked back down the block, recalling the merchants who used to be on the block.

He passed the home repair contractor and the small tire shop. The studio was next; Lenny's big new white Lexus was parked in front.

"I see Schecter, the schmuck, has his Lexus today," he said out loud, "he probably got tired of driving his wife's Cadillac Seville with the Rolls Royce grille."

Continuing down the block, next to the studio, was an income tax consultant, a printer, an electronic equipment store, an insurance agency, and a bank, which until last month, handled the Montclair Studio account. Sid had already transferred his share of the business assets to a branch near his house. After the bank were a travel agency and a printer. The printer handled Sid's business printing, as well as the invitations for his children's affairs.

The pizzeria once was owned by an Italian man who served Italian specialties. Now, the place was owned by a man from the Dominican Republic. In addition to pizza, the house specialties were Spanish. Sid and Lenny had eaten there after the Dominicans took over, the pizza was the same, and the Latino specialties were really very good.

In between the pizzeria and the travel agent, there was a public coin telephone. A black woman with a child in her arms was using it. There was a black man wearing a cap with X on the front standing next to her yelling.

"You wanna go to fuckin' court?"

"Alright," replied the woman without emotion.

"I'll get my lawyer and we'll go to fuckin' court!" he screamed at the top of his lungs.

Sid expected gunfire to erupt at any second and was ready to hit the ground like he did in Korea. Instead, the man who was probably the common-law husband turned and ran across the street into the tavern.

Next to the pizzeria was a large discount store that was part of a chain. The building used to be the old Argo Cinema. The old movie theater closed five years ago. It was once a very nice neighborhood movie. In recent years, a low element frequented the theater. People got tired of enduring all the pot smoke. Neighborhood movie houses were folding all over Long Island. Just as the discount package studios were hurting established photography studios, cable television and video rentals were destroying movie theaters. Today, the phrase "at a theater near you" meant a drive to the next town for a suburban experience. The marquee of the old movie house was now the sign for the discount store. The two large front windows, which once displayed movie posters, now advertised sales on bargain *shlock* merchandise.

Next to the movie house, was a videotape rental outlet. This store opened up before the movie theater closed. People who stood on line to see a movie would sometimes change their mind, stop in, and rent a tape.

Next to the video store was a shoe store that sold ladies shoes and handbags. This store also once carried quality merchandise; now like the rest of the stores on the block, it carried *shlock*.

Above the stores were offices. The two offices above the store that housed Montclair Studios were occupied by Happy Time Photographers and the local Little League and youth outreach.

In between the printer and the electronics store was an alley that led to the rear parking lot. This alley was once used by patrons of the movie theater and shoppers, as well as the staff and clients of Montclair Studios.

The alley was a shortcut to get to one's car. Teenagers and amorous adults used to step inside for some kissing, and folks ducked out of the rain while walking or waiting for the bus. Now the alley stank of urine, cheap wine, and God knows what else. The concrete walk of the alley was littered with crack vials. Forget the shortcut; a long walk might save your life.

Sid walked to his studio. The large white electronic sign over the store read MONTCLAIR STUDIOS, in big, black block letters. Under the word STUDIOS, there was a second line, which simply read PHOTOGRAPHERS.

The remaining pictures in the large front windows were faded from the sun. Many of the outdoor photographs had a green cast. Many of the pictures looked like they were taken in 1969, which in fact they were.

Sid unlocked the door and entered the studio. It had the musty smell of age and inactivity. The rust color carpeting, which ran through the reception area, had long faded. At least the expensive wall paneling held up. There was a small corridor at the entrance; upon entering the studio, one would have to turn right to go into the reception area. On the wall facing the entrance was a cutout in the paneling. This accommodated large picture frames, containing portraits, which were changed periodically. The reception area had recessed lights in the ceiling. This big glass façade was something to behold in her heyday.

There was just a small dented bridge table, along with two broken folding chairs, which was all to be thrown out at the end of the day. All the studio furniture was gone. Most of the shit was so old, it was thrown out. On the old bridge table was a telephone answering system. This item had been promised to his son Steven. The sign that posted the studio's business hours had also been thrown out. This was the end of Sid Weitz's source of happiness, aggravation, creativity, and craftsmanship.

This studio housed three decades worth of creative expression. This was the end of Sid's home away from home, maybe even the end of his real home.

Lenny Schecter entered the studio from the little alcove in the hallway, which contained the stairs that led up to the baby studio.

"Good morning, Sid, fuck you," he called out. Lenny and Sid often greeted each other this way. They often greeted colleagues this way. "I got a couple of messages for you here. First, the man from the realtor is coming to put the sign in the window."

"What sign?"

"Ya know, the vacancy sign. Then the guy from the phone company is gonna stop by to disconnect the phone wires. Fuck, they'll never rent this place. You also had a call from a broad by the name of Stacy Levin, says we did her cousin's Bat Mitzvah. She thought you were the guy with the hairpiece."

"I'm not, you are," Sid replied.

"Damn right, and I'm gonna stop wearing this fuckin' rug soon. I only wore it to shoot jobs or here at the studio. But, I tell ya, I'm not wasting my time with it anymore. I mean I never wore it in the house, at this point of my life I don't need it anymore."

"Yes, you do, Lenny," answered Sid, "you do need it, believe me, I've seen you without it. I really don't think you should go out without it; you look just a little bit better with it and you happen to be very bald."

"Fuck you," Lenny grinned at Sid, and blew a puff of cigar smoke into his face.

"Let's see, Levin, Levin," Sid recollected, "I remember, it was in Little Neck, a cute kid. I did the video; I talked you into doing the stills. I think I frightened her with your *punim*. It was a year and a half ago, remember?"

"You want me to remember everything?" Lenny was exasperated. "You fuckin' expect me to remember a job I shot last year? I can't even fuckin' remember a job I shot last week."

"I remember this one, Lenny. I remember a lot of my jobs."

"Yeah, you remember a job you shot in 1974, you're terrific, Sid."

"How did she sound?"

"She sounded like a broad."

"Shit, Lenny! I mean was she interested or was she pricing?"

"Oh, she sounded interested, man. Yeah, she praised our work. I think it's a hot lead. Let me give you the number."

"Give me the number."

"I'm gonna give you the number."

"Give me the number!"

"I'm giving you the number!"

It was like old times.

Sid told Lenny that he would call this young bride-to-be tonight.

Lenny told Sid he did not care.

Their nice Jewish mailman Bernie Gottlieb came into the studio. Bernie was a tall man with big bulging eyes, a pickle nose, and a neatly trimmed mustache. He was one of the few letter carriers on Long Island who still wore the traditional service cap with the patent leather visor and postal service shield.

"Hi, fellas, how are you? It's going to be goddamn hot today, and me, I gotta walk around on these streets where the *shvartzes* shoot at each other."

"Bernie, it ain't only in the streets, *bubie*," Sid replied, "the *shvartzes* shoot at each other in the housing projects, too."

"They also shoot at people sitting out on the stoop from speeding cars," Lenny added.

"Yeah," Bernie laughed, "maybe a crack dealer will wing someone from United Parcel."

"Just look up when you walk past a tenement, Bernie," Lenny advised. "A welfare mama might toss her little brown baby out the window onto you."

"They don't toss their babies out windows anymore," Sid commented, "now they drown them in the bathtub or just beat them to death."

"Or scald them, or leave them alone in the apartment with a book of matches when they go to the bar," Lenny said contemptfully.

"My nephew, the city housing cop, told me last year they found a newborn in a trash compactor that wasn't operating. Last month, he and his partner found a baby in a garbage can, complete with umbilical cord," said the mailman.

"So what?" asked Lenny. "So what? Those kids would have ended up on the garbage heap anyway."

"That's right, Lenny," Bernie responded, "the *shvartzes* are animals, so let them live like animals. They should all shoot each other, not us."

"Today is our last day here, Bernie," Sid said.

"I'm gonna miss you guys, no kidding. I've know you guys a long time. I remember you had another partner. When I started on this route, Sid had a beard."

"We all three had beards, for a while."

"You and Carl had beards longer than I did," Sid corrected.

Sid handed Bernie a plain white envelope containing a twenty dollar bill.

"Thanks, fellas, I really appreciate this. I retire next year myself. That is, if some animal doesn't kill me, or God forbid, a *meshuga* postal worker with an Uzi."

"Bernie, *zie gezundt*, be well, keep smiling."

"You too, Sid, you should have health. Good luck to you, huh? You too, Lenny."

Bernie shook hands with both Sid and Lenny, handed them their mail, and left.

"So, how much did you give that putz?" Lenny asked.

"Twenty."

"Oh, holy shit! Give 'im ten fah chrisses sake!"

"He's a good man, Lenny, he was reliable; I like him, the best fuckin' mailman we ever had."

"A good man, my ass!" Lenny shouted. "He inquired for his son's Bar Mitzvah and later on had the *chutzpah* to ask again about his daughter's wedding. He sat down on both occasions; Estelle and I showed him albums, videos, and gave him a bottom line price. The bastard never booked, fuck him!"

"So he found something in his range, why not? He told me the receptions were not very large or lavish. He couldn't afford us...I understand, we got all the affluent *yids*. So, with all those big shots we had, with all the *gonser moochers*, you bitch and moan over a mailman? He knew us...he was too embarrassed to tell us we were out of his range."

"Yeah, sure, you understand," Lenny was shouting now. "You understand so good we're outta business."

"Look, Lenny!"

Both Sid and Lenny were standing nose to nose now.

"Lenny, I'm gonna tell you something. Being partners with you for thirty years was no picnic. We had a damn good operation, me, you, and Carl. But, it was not all fun and games, I want you to know!"

"When I wasn't correcting your mistakes or apologizing for you."

"What the fuck do you mean, Lenny?"

"Sidney, Sidney baby, our clients always told me that you were rude to them. You were even rude to them at their receptions. You had this chip on your shoulder, but Carl and I put up with it. You weren't always rude, but more often than not, you shot off your mouth, Sid."

"Well, Lenny, we both know that a lot of our clients and their guests were so fuckin' stupid. I couldn't take their shit. I didn't intend to offend if that's how it came out, but those people shouldn't be so fuckin' stupid."

"Sidney," Lenny spoke again, "you were a good candid man, a good video man, you were good at running the studio, you were always a good closer, but down here with the candids, you caused a lot of hard feelings. Not only by being rude to clients and guests, but also taking an attitude to our colleagues in the trade. You ain't the most liked member of our association."

"What did I do to those fuckin' prima donnas?" Sid asked.

"At our associations monthly dinner meetings, you would always tell everyone they were wrong."

"They were."

"You criticized everybody's print in the competition," Lenny started to laugh. "You criticized with such venom the technique of others. You discouraged the young fellows trying to break in, instead of helping them, you *fagin* them your knowledge. Someone once commented that you were an arrogant bastard. The wife of one guest speaker you openly criticized, said, 'That man should only bleed from his ass.'"

Sid shrugged and scratched his balls. He was not making a gesture at his partner, his balls itched.

"Sid, you were always correcting everyone, disagreeing with everyone. You know, I'm surprised there's anyone left who still talks to us. The president of your video association calls you 'Mr. Personality' behind your back."

"Sometimes in front of me, too."

"Sid, I had a lot of trouble getting assistants to light for us because of you."

"Because of me?" Sid snapped, "Shit, what did I do to our lighting assistants?"

"Sid, you'd scream at those people at receptions, right in front of the clients and all the guests. Once it got back to Carl that you told an assistant to hold his fuckin' light straight when you were shooting a table. Shit man, right in front of guests. I had to place an ad in the paper for assistants every other week. People would answer the ad, go out with you, and then quit. Nobody quit when they went out with me, Carl, or Harry, or Marty, or Freddie, or Susan, or John, or Donna."

"It's my fault the people I took out on jobs were fuckin' incompetent?"

"It's your fault, Sid, you didn't train them properly. Those people don't know what to do the first time out. They don't know where to light. They don't know to stand on the side of the shorter person. They don't know not to aim the flash at your lens...come on, what's the matter with you? It's up to us to tell them how. How Jeff likes you and stayed with you is a great mystery of life, I'll never know. Remember the girl you took as an assistant?"

"What girl? Sid asked Lenny. "I don't remember."

"I know you don't remember," Lenny shouted back, "you never remember anyone you gave the business to."

"I don't remember!"

"Okay, you were covering for another studio, I don't remember who. They needed a man to do video, they called you. They gave you this girl as an assistant...a sweet young kid, I heard. She was also interested in getting into stills. They told her she'd learn from you. I heard you screamed at the poor girl, you yelled at her, cursed her, screamed and screamed, and that she was in tears by the end of the job...the studio you went out for told me this."

"Lenny, you would have tried to get into that little girl's panties."

"I wouldn't have humiliated the kid in public, though."

Sid turned around, then turned back to face Lenny.

"She didn't know what to do. She didn't know how to hold the fuckin' light the right way, when to move in, when to move back, fuck, I could have gotten shadows on people's faces and you want I should worry about making a stupid, goofing girl cry? Better the clients should cry?"

"You should have taught her and gone over it with her, Sid."

"She should know it if she does video, she should have known how to light a video job, Lenny."

"You could have been nice to her."

"I'm nice to my wife, my children, and grandchildren, so what do you want? Leave me the hell alone."

"Schmuck," stated Lenny as he puffed his cigar.

"*Oy vay!* I can't take anymore," Sid groaned. "Oh, fuck it. I don't wanna discuss it anymore, I'm retired."

The front door opened and in walked a tall skinny man in glasses; he was carrying a FOR SALE OR LEASE sign. He walked to the front window.

"I take it you're the weasel from the realty office." Sid called out.

"I beg your pardon?" the man responded meekly.

"Yeah, well," Sid continued, "just hang up your sign and get the fuck outta here, okay? Because we're very busy."

The man taped the sign in the front window and left without acknowledging Sid or Lenny.

Lenny shook his head in disbelief and disgust. He smirked as he puffed his big cigar.

Sid lit a Viceroy Ultra Light.

The front door opened and Jeffery Glassman came in.

"Ah, so good of you to join us, sir, an honor," Sid greeted him.

"Good morning, gentlemen," Jeff said

"Gentlemen, where? Where?" Lenny said looking around.

"Okay, kid," Sid sighed, "c'mon, we have some work to do, yet."

Chapter Sixteen

J effery Glassman tugged at the visor of Sid's cap.

"Virginia Slims?" Jeff inquired.

Sid replied, "I don't know where the hell I got this hat. It keeps the sun off my face."

Sid removed the cap and tossed it onto the bridge table.

Lenny took the picture frame that his mother wanted out of the window, removed the photograph, and placed it on the floor.

Sid removed the photographs his daughter wanted. Those were very expensive gold-plated 8x10 size frames and one 5x7.

"Yep, these are the ones she wants for her new family room. They're moving to Boston, Lenny, I told you."

Lenny grunted.

"She has a big house with big rooms."

The remaining frames that were taken out of the studio's two large front windows were placed into a cardboard box.

"What about the pictures, Sid?" asked Jeff.

"Eh, they're all so old and faded, throw 'em out. Here, throw out these old sample albums while you're at it. Put them in the box marked 'G' over there."

"G?"

"Yeah, 'G' for garbage."

The front windows were empty, which was alright, because nobody looked in the windows anymore. After today, anyone who looked in the window wouldn't see anything, except a vacant store.

Lenny took an automobile windshield scraper, and scraped off the sticker on the door that displayed business hours. After doing that, Lenny handed the YES, WE'RE OPEN/SORRY WE'RE CLOSED sign to Jeff.

Sid handed Jeff the sign that read, INSTANT PASSPORTS WHILE U WAIT, COLOR OR BLACK AND WHITE.

"Keep it, keep it, you're hell bent on opening a place. What am I gonna do, put it on my front door?"

"Well, that's that," Lenny called out, "I'm gonna go upstairs to where the real business is, if you gentlemen don't need me anymore."

"Lenny, you don't want the rest of the frames from the window?"

"No, what the hell do I need with them? We use different frames for baby pictures. You take them, Sid."

"Jesus, I got boxes of frames sitting in my garage right now. You take them. Jeff."

"You sure?" asked Jeff.

Both Sid and Lenny nodded that they were sure.

"Is there anything you want?" Sid asked his former partner.

Lenny extended his lower lip over his upper lip, closed his eyes, and shook his head. For Lenny this meant no.

Sid knew all of Lenny's gestures very well. His wide sneery grin to express satisfaction with himself, his shrug to say, "What do I know? His closed-eyed slightly opened mouth shudder to express disgust or disbelief. Sid had seen all of those gestures for the past thirty years, and was sick of them. Yet, he knew he was going to miss all the expressions coming from Lenny's ugly face.

"Just come on up and tell me when you're leaving. Take what you want or give it to Jeff."

Lenny turned and walked upstairs.

"Sid, hey!" Lenny called down from upstairs.

"Yeah?" Sid called back.

"The shit that's lying around, you'll throw it out."

"Absolutely, I'll take care of it."

"You're gonna spend the summer shooting baby pictures for that asshole?" Sid asked Jeff.

"I need the money, Sid." Jeff replied.

Sid sighed, then expelled a deep breath. "Yeah, I guess right now you do need the money. Look, don't let him take advantage of you and work you too hard, or send you into bad areas to shoot. Remember, you have proms and sports leagues to do for my friend up in Albertson."

"He wants me to shoot some reunions and school pictures in the fall."

"He told me he likes you're work, kid. Lenny is a real cheat, you gotta watch him. Lenny and guys like him always get the best of a deal; I want you to know that. If he gives you any trouble, call me and let me know. I can handle Lenny. I never let him get away with any of his shit. Better yet, if he gives you any shit, quit."

"Shooting babies for Lenny is only temporary, Sid," answered Jeff, "don't worry, I can handle Lenny, I'm not about to take any shit from him; I never took any shit from you."

"When did I ever give you any shit?" Sid demanded.

"You've given me shit, not a lot recently, but there were times you've given me shit, Sid, believe me."

"You mean there were times when I criticized you, rebuked you, showed you a better way to do something?" Sid was laughing, "Maybe in the beginning, I yelled at you a little bit, which is normal in teaching. I remember once, when you weren't paying attention to me, when I was teaching you how to do Rembrandt lighting for portraits, I gave you a 'hello, is anybody home' knock on your forehead. Also, once when you complained about something I critiqued you on, I said 'Don't be a schmuck.'"

"It was great experience learning from you, Sid, but all I'm saying is that Lenny wasn't the only one around here who gave me shit, sometimes it was you."

"Alright, alright," Sid shrugged, "sometimes it was me. Holy shit! You sound like my son now. I gave him shit, I tried to teach him. When he was an intern, I told Norma let's charge him for rent. She agreed, she said we'll save the money for him. I said no, we'll spend it on ourselves. He and some young doctors rented an apartment; he couldn't believe the cost of living. Steve asked, 'Dad, do you know how much toilet paper costs?' I told him, 'I know how much toilet paper costs, do you know how much it costs? Because, I ain't gonna buy it for you.' He says, 'It's expensive,' I told him, 'so, don't wipe your ass.' I gave him shit; I try to teach my son about the reality of fuckin' life and I gave him shit. I'm happy he did well, he's a doctor; I taught him about life, still I don't think he likes me very much. I can't say I'm sorry, Jeff, because I really don't think I gave you shit. So, if I did, I did."

"You did, I just wanted you to be aware of that," Jeff said.

"Okay, so now I'm aware," Sid answered back. "But I have to tell you, I think I was right."

Sid sat down on one of the old decrepit folding chairs at the bridge table. He motioned for Jeff to do the same.

"Jeff, listen to me. If I was critical of you, it worked. Man oh Manischewitz, I wish I had the photographic education that you did, when I was coming up. But, shit, I'm one of the old guards of this fuckin' industry. I molded you into a fine photographer and videographer. I taught you very well for shooting portraits and candids, so whatever teaching method I used, it worked. See, my boy, even without a college degree, I have a professorship. So, if I taught you well, how could I have been wrong? Nu?" Sid shrugged.

Jeff rolled his eyes, sighed, and imitated Sid's shrug.

"You're right."

"Damn right, I'm right. By the way, you happen to be fuckin' right about what you said. It was a great experience learning from me. I happen to be the best in the business. I'm fuckin' great! What I taught you is worth thousands of dollars. Go on; go to a Monte Zucker or Denis Reggie seminar. They'll show you some of their work, but by me you learned the truth about everything. What can you learn from attending a Don Blair or Stephen Rudd lecture? I ain't gonna say *bupkis*; you'll learn some technique. Who knows? Maybe you'll learn how to shoot a wedding picture on rocks in California, with a sunset on the Pacific Ocean as a background. What I taught you about shooting and about the industry you couldn't have learned anywhere else—not from a photography school, not from books, not even from any other studio in the business. My father always says I teach too much. But, I always felt, if everyone would take the time to learn the right way of doing things, this industry would be better off. Not every experienced photographer would teach you the way I've taught you, or what I've taught you. I don't care if this guy has a big fuckin' studio and wants to train you to light for him or shoot for him. He wouldn't have taught you the way I taught you. Established candid men *fagin*, you know it means 'deny' in Yiddish. Why the fuck would they want you to have their know-how? I remember, after Korea, I tried to get a job at one fellow's studio. The cocksucker did not even want me to see his camera room. God forbid, I should come away with the knowledge of how to set up one. See, you're a hell of a shooter. You had a great teacher, you learned from the best, remember!"

"I'll remember," Jeff answered.

"Yeah, remember. When I started out, I was taught some basic lighting and posing techniques. In the old days, nobody really knew what the fuck we were doing. We—the old-timers, the founders of this industry--practiced, refined, and turned candid photography into an exact science, which is what you have today. Today, you're taught all the techniques of shooting affairs. But, guys like me," Sid paused to light another Viceroy. "Guys like me, the so-called old-timers, we invented this. Okay, today, you got some award-winning shooters who travel the country lecturing, selling their books, posing guides, videos, and equipment, which is manufactured for them. They endorse equipment for which they are paid a lot of money. They will charge you hundreds of dollars to teach you, what you learned here for free. Then you'll go out and say, 'I'm gonna shoot like these guys.' Forget it; you ain't gonna book like them, because you ain't them, just some small-time putz who thinks he can shoot like them. Ya know how these people make their money? From their lectures, not their shooting. They have studios and a staff to run it for them, that is, when the staff is not filling phone or mail orders for videos and books. If you're a big shot and want to book one of those guys personally to shoot your affair, you pay ten thousand bucks for one album, for openers. Don't laugh, Jeff, I know a photographer who did that for his son's wedding."

Jeffery sneezed.

"Salute! See you sneezed, this is the truth," Sid went on. "Alright, this guy and his son are both award-winning prima donnas. A real putz, the way the father struts around. He made a Bat Mitzvah girl cry during the candle lighting ceremony, putz kept hollering at her. So he paid this bigger prima donna over ten grand to shoot his son's wedding."

Sid paused while that revelation set in with Jeffery. The kid looked astonished.

"I heard that the over-priced fag's pictures came out lousy. I asked Larry, you know, he's the father, to show me the album, but he keeps pushing me off, he's embarrassed. He keeps changing the subject, telling me about his goddamn parakeet. Anyway, *boychick*, these schmucks book, they shoot, they make. I could probably do what they do—write books, make videos, travel, and lecture, but I didn't. It was not for me."

Sid paused; the kid was listening, not staring off into space.

"But, my friend, let me tell you, I was one of the best on Long Island and Brooklyn for many years. So please, don't say I gave you shit. I helped to mold you and your career. You learned from Sid Weitz, Montclair. You learned from the best."

"You're the best, Sid; I never said you weren't. You're one hell of a teacher and as a photographer, you're fuckin' great. You always say that about yourself, so it must be true." There was some guilt in Jeffery's voice.

"Thank you for the compliment," said the photographer to his assistant, "this was almost as kind as the first time Norma's mother said I was common."

"I really mean it, Sid," continued Jeff, "I know we're going to work together again. I booked a couple of jobs on my own. Stills and video, separately; I haven't booked both together, yet. I told you about the jobs I booked."

Sid nodded.

"Happy for me, boss?"

"So, you want me to light for you now? Maybe I will, if I get really fuckin' bored. You ever realize the word ass is in assistant?"

"I could not have done it without you. So, if I never thanked you for teaching me, cultivating and motivating me, giving me advice, telling me the secrets of the trade, being there for me, holding my hand, sometimes kicking my ass, and for being a friend, maybe my best friend, I thank you. Thank you for everything, Sid."

Sid placed both his hands on the bridge table, leaned forward, and smiled at Jeff.

"You're welcome, baby; just remember to thank your parents, too."

Jeff leaned across the table, looked Sid in the eye, smiled, and said, "But, you still gave me shit!"

Sid took the cigarette out of his mouth and shrugged. "Well, what are you gonna do?" he said.

Sid then started to laugh.

"What's so funny?" asked Jeff.

"Shit."

"Huh?"

"Shit is funny, it happens to be a funny word."

"Shit is funny?"

"Yes," Sid was laughing hard now. "Shit is funny, only if you say it, not if you step in it."

They were both laughing now.

"*Oy, oy,*" Sid laughed outloud, "*oy, oy, OY!* Jeff, I gotta tell you about shit."

"What is there to tell?"

"No, no, no, about my son Steven, when he was a kid. My parents used to own a private home on East Twenty-Third Street in Brooklyn. This was the house I grew up in. Well, anyway, Steven must have been about three or four, and we were visiting for the day. Well, Steve was standing by the screen door in the front of the house. A kid carrying a surfboard walks by. I dunno, the kid must have been about seventeen. I still remember what he looked like—tall kid with short blonde hair and metal-framed glasses. So, he walks by the house, and my cute little Stevie yells out, "HI-YA, SHIT!""

Jeff was lying forward onto the table; his face was beet red from laughing.

"The kid turns toward Steve, made eye contact, and walked on his way in disgust. He just kept staring at my little boy, walking and nodding his head with a disgusted expression on his face."

"He's your kid, Sid," laughed Jeff.

"I know that," Sid laughed back. "I saw it from the living room window."

"What did you do?"

"Nothing, I was too busy laughing. Just like I'm laughing now, although it was not really very funny now, was it? Norma ran over, and *potched* him in the *tokus*. When Norma's mother heard about this, she told Steven not to talk like that or people will say, 'Ooh common, like they do when your daddy talks.'"

"What did your parents say? He did it in front of them."

"My mother was somewhat shocked and amused. As for my dad, well, he thinks good manners is keeping the dining room window open when he eats, so as not to offend a guest, when he farts," he laughed.

"Your father is like that?"

"Yeah, always was. Sometimes when we had company, my mother would serve him, put something on his plate, and he would shove aside the food on the plate with his hand to make room for the other stuff. In restaurants, if he did not like something, he'd call out, 'Waiter, what is this shit?' My father is a character, alright."

"You know the old saying, Sid, 'Like father, like son.'"

"Nah, I'm not as crass as that crazy old bastard."

Jeff was listening intently. Most people listened to Sid Weitz's stories, he fancied himself a raconteur. Most people he knew did think he was good storyteller and a good talker. Jeff was a good audience, maybe this is why Sid loved the kid—a raconteur needs an audience to be a raconteur.

"Let me tell you another," Sid went on. "Near my in-laws there is an Orthodox synagogue on East Thirteenth Street, off Kings Highway. They have a lovely catering hall...did we ever shoot there together?"

Jeff shook his head 'no.'

Well, you should see it, it's very nice. Anyway, it was a Sunday afternoon in July. Lenny was doing the stills, I was filming the job. I used a Bolex movie camera with a lens turret. My assistant waited for me in the hall with all the lights set up. This was back in 1969, there was no video. I parked my car on Avenue P, around the corner from the *shul*. I had a '65 Pontiac Tempest convertible back then, I remember. So I, as I walk to temple that morning, I pass this man, paving a sidewalk in front of his three-family home. The house was on the corner of East Thirteenth Street and Avenue P. The wedding ended about four-thirty, five o'clock. I'm walking back to my car, in back of these two men, who were guests at the wedding. I recall, one guy was holding onto this other guy who seemed drunk. The man who was drunk, was tall, bald, and had a beard, and yes," Sid recalled, "he was wearing a tan suit. Well, this man stops where the sidewalk was roped off. He pauses, looks down, and jumps over the rope making a swan dive right into the block of wet cement."

Jeff was enjoying this.

"So, the big fat Italian man who owned the house runs out, as the man he was with and some of the other guests help him up. The schmuck says he's alright and walks off with his friend. I only wish that the fuckin' movie camera was not packed away."

"What did the man who owned the house do?"

"Nothing, he got down on his hands and knees and repaved the blocks that putz ruined."

"You tell good stories, Sid," said Jeff.

"Yeah, I'm a regular fuckin' Steve Allen, I really kill this, kid," Sid said to no one.

"Enough already. Like you said, we have work to do, yet," Jeff reminded his boss.

Sid got up and walked into the camera room section of the studio. This was the area where portraits, family groups, and pre-reception formals were taken. On the floor was a box that contained a button and mirror machine. Sid gestured to Jeff.

"Take it."

"Thanks."

"You can make photo buttons, photo mirrors, for keepsakes and party favors. Lenny and I made a shitload of money doing this at B'Mitzvahs. I have a friend who only does party favor photos on the weekend. He gets a lot of work from referrals, he runs ads. We worked a job with him, remember?"

"Uh, huh," Jeff replied and nodded.

"Actually, we worked with him twice on one job. Andy did the favors for us with this machine when we couldn't get my friend. Andy is a candid man who knows how to compose and shoot. My friend is a weekend favor hack. He stood there with his Polaroid…okay, kid, look at the camera…and takes the pictures with a little flash unit. Later on when we looked at the pictures he put into those frames, did you notice how off center most of them were?"

"Yes, they sucked," answered Jeff.

"They did. It was the success of a mediocre photographer that caused me to buy a couple of these machines, and offer novelty photos and favors. In fact, one slow winter, I had a couple of photo favor jobs, where the people had already booked a studio, but hired us to do the favors. Take the machine, as a businessman you should always look to make more. Take my advice, Jeff;

I used to serve on a businessman's committee back in the '60s at the photo association. I like my friend, but why should he, a part-time nothing, make money with his photo keepsakes? Better I should learn how to do it, offer it as a service from my studio, and put the money in my pocket. The same with video, why should some unqualified prick who advertises in a shopper's guide, some shit who low balls clients for inferior work, make money? Fuck him, I do video, too—quality work. I want to put bread on my table, why should I be restricted to stills so he can also be at the reception making the money that I should be making? You know, it used to be the same with movies in the old days. You have to explore every possible way of making money, Jeff, in any business. Why should you allow your competition to make money off of you? If the competition does make money off of you, then it's your goddamned fault."

Jeff picked up the button machine and moved it to the side.

"Lenny sold the newer electronic machine we had. Who knows when I'm gonna do favors again."

"What else are you getting rid of?"

"See that modeling light over there? Sid pointed to a light on a stand, "I need it to give to the garbage man. Also, take the posing stool and posing desk. Take it, Lenny sold one set, one set I kept for myself."

"Thank you, Sid. I appreciate this, I really do."

"Well, you're gonna need this stuff to run your own business." Sid said somewhat mockingly. "Only, don't let the idea of having your own place go to your head. Don't be such a big shot in the beginning and don't get big eyes too fast. I still expect you to shoot and tape, even light for me from time to time."

"Definitely."

"Damn right! And when I need you, I expect you and I don't give a shit how fuckin' big you might be. You happen to have been the best assistant I ever had in the whole fuckin' forty years of business."

"Feel guilty about shooting for myself now," Jeff lowered his head.

"Fuck, you should, you're gonna compete with your wise old mentor."

"My wise old mentor named his cat Weanus."

"My son did that! I wanna give you these things."

Sid handed Jeff two ancient Crown Graphic cameras that were modified to shoot passport and identification photos. They were old, yet very workable.

"Here, take them both—one for black and white, one for color. This guy used to modify these old things for us. I think the cost was seventy-five bucks each. Today, a new passport camera goes for about four hundred. Lenny sold two modified Polaroid Land camera passport jobs we had. I'm gonna keep the fancy one in my house. You know, just in case somebody calls me out of the phonebook and asks if I do passports."

"Do they work?" Jeff asked.

"What the hell do you mean?" Sid replied, somewhat offended, "Of course, they work. What the hell do you think I've been using here?"

"Sid, I don't know what to say."

Sid dismissed Jeff's gratitude with a wave of his hand.

"Hey, *bubie*, ya wanna know who came in here for a passport picture?"

"Who?"

"The Jewish guy who used to be on Star Trek," Sid smiled as he recalled, "I duuno what he was doing here on the Island. Jesus! It must have been twenty years ago."

"Mr. Spock?"

"No, no, no, the other guy. The one who had another show where the cop he played was always jumping onto speeding cars, which is bullshit because Harry Lowenstein told me he'd never think to jumping on a speeding car; real cops don't have stunt doubles."

"Him?" Jeff was surprised.

"Yep."

"What did he say?"

"How much is a passport photo?"

"That was it?"

"That was it. They're just people like us who sometimes need the services of a photographer. They can afford our services, too," he smiled.

"Oh."

"You know, I took pictures of celebrities at weddings. You saw those albums. I showed you the one of the garden wedding I did years ago. The one who used to play Ninety-Nine on television posed with the bride and groom. She was in the park that day; I don't think she was a guest. The actress who played a mermaid gave me a hard time at a wedding I was shooting. She kept asking me why I didn't have a Hasselblad. I did not want to get thrown out, so I kept my mouth shut. Celebrities sell, Jeffery. Norma and I, back in '77, went to Roosevelt Field Mall when Desi Arnaz came to autograph his autobiography. Norma took a picture of us together. I used to have it hanging up in the studio. This was before I met you."

"What did he say to you?"

"Desi Arnaz? He said, 'Who you wan' dis wan to,' and 'Thanks, amigo.'"

"I guess people were impressed with celebrity albums."

"Yes and no. Sometimes people will think if you were good enough for some actor, you're good enough for them. Fair enough, but don't forget my clients in Cedarhurst, Great Neck Estates, or in Kings Point are worth more than some actor. So, they don't really give a shit, unless they socialize with that crowd. I was trying to book an affair, not book those actors a part in a movie."

Sid opened a paper shopping bag with a department store logo on it.

"Here," he reached into the bag, "you need video lights? I got some video lights."

He and Jeff both reached into the bag and took out the lights.

"Here, take," he handed Jeff the bag. "These I don't need anymore."

He took out a very small light. "This one you use on the bracket of your still camera, for when you photograph the tables. A great focusing light. I was shooting this *goyish* wedding at one of those shitty Mafia halls out in Suffolk. The maitre'd tells me, 'I hope you can see what you're shooting, because the bride's contract calls for low lighting.' Then the bastard leans over and says twenty dollars might bring up the level of light for me. So, I take this thing out of my pocket, put it on my bracket, and say, 'How about twenty watts?'"

"I'll remember that," replied Jeff.

"Yeah, remember that," said Sid, "you shoulddda seen the look on that prick's face."

"I think I'm gonna have trouble booking video with stills," Jeff lamented.

"Sometimes you will have trouble," Sid replied, "I wanna talk to you about video. Until recently, we had a policy here, as you know, Jeff. If you booked someone else for the video, we would not book the stills."

Sid sat down on the camera room floor. He motioned for Jeff to do the same. They both crossed their legs Indian style.

"In the last decade, the wedding centers that offer one-stop shopping were born. Then there's the four hundred ninety-five dollar video package in the shopper's guides. These vidiots cater to a Christian crowd, not necessarily the blue collars. This way of business changed things for us. When we first started shooting video, 95 percent of our jobs booked stills and video. Now, it's a fight. The Jewish clients will take your whole enchilada if you're recommended and have a track record. The Gentile mentality is to go one place for the lowest-priced package deal they can find. Jeff," Sid looked right into the young man's eyes, "this will cause you problems. I think we talked about this before. Today, you can't always successfully tell people, if they book another video company, you won't book the stills, or you could end up losing the whole fuckin' job. What will you do if you can't book another job that day? You need that date booked. You're home that Saturday night jerking off and your landlord is hollering, 'Where's my fuckin' money? Who gives a shit about you? Pay me my rent, or get the fuck out.' The people will go to someone who is flexible, or to someone who just shoots stills. See, Jeff, we're between a rock and a hard place. We can't tell people they need us, we discussed that, remember?"

"Yes, I remember."

"Okay, 'cause this isn't the '50s or '60s, or even the '80s. For so many of us the heyday is over. I said people today don't like policy dictated to them. They say, 'Fuck you, I'll go to someone else. Don't tell me I need you, who are you to tell me that. You need me.' I tell clients…for flowers, I would go to a florist. For music, I would go to an orchestra. I tell them if I needed video, I would go to a photographer. Notice how I say video first?"

"Yes."

"I tell people how important it is for the person doing the video and the person who does the stills to be from the same place. You need to explain that when you and your mother are cooking in the kitchen, you try to help her, but you get in her way, because you're doing different things. When a videographer and a photographer are from the same studio they are doing the same thing. They do not get in each other's way, you follow?"

"I follow," answered Jeff.

"But today, *bubie*, everybody screams, 'I can get it cheaper.' And, in our business, the Gentile mentality is getting it cheaper. Why do you suppose Kmart opened in Levittown and *not* by me in Woodmere? Know your market. But, lately, the Jewish clients are getting like the *goyim*."

Jeff listened.

"You know that for the most part, the Jews don't *chondle* you—that means 'bargain with you'—as much as the *goyim*. The Jewish mothers you deal with a very demanding. They want quality for their money and they'll cut your throat to get it. The *goyim* want to bargain with you for everything. The Italian clients gotta have a package a deal, ya know what I'ma sayin'?"

"I know, Sid."

"I'd rather do Jewish affairs, you know that, Jeff. It's not that the jobs are easier, they are demanding, although there isn't any drunkenness. I've had to deal with price-shopping *goyim* who wanted a good price. They didn't hear one fuckin' thing I was saying. They only wanted to know, how much? They did not even look at the pictures. Jewish clients want quality and are willing to pay for it. True, there are quality conscious *goyim*, but lately they have not been coming in. Granted, these people are a hell of a lot better to work for. They care about quality and will spend on the right studio, like they are Jewish. Those folks will book your video and even order additional pictures from you, too."

"I know, Sid, we have to target the right clients, you asked me once why do they sell Rolls Royce cars or Mount Blanc pens, 'because there is a market for them,' you said."

"Absolutely right. You have to look for the people who are looking for you, get me?"

A nod.

"Don't try to book if you know you're not gonna book. Crackerjack salesmen say you cannot prejudge people, I know, but you can. You must qualify people to set up an appointment. Don't run after the package deal crowd who wants the cheap vinyl slip in albums, if you're selling quality work in bound albums. Don't chase after the people who want a two hundred dollar camcorder produced tape, which they are given at the end of the reception. You never lower your price for anyone or for any reason. Never compromise your work. If you use multiple lighting, which is more expensive than single lighting, so be it, tough shit. Once you lower prices, or compromise your policies, clients will no longer respect you. If you're a professional, why would you want to deal with those who have no respect for you? Those jobs will end up sending you to the emergency room, I guarantee. This does not mean you do not give the client value. You always give the client value, for the price. You can negotiate for additional items that cost you very little, but will make the client happy. You just never negotiate to lower your price—you're like a doctor, not a beggar. You offer the quality stuff; you have to know your market. Go in one direction, if you go in too many directions, you'll end up with nothing, *bupkis*." Sid placed emphasis on *bupkis*, which is a Yiddish word for 'nothing.'

"You're a good teacher, Sid."

"Be a good student, Jeff, *shaddap* and listen. You gotta have a marketing plan, remember that. If you don't have a marketing plan, you got nothing."

"I understand."

"I hope to God you do, because I don't want to see you land flat on your ass. You're a good kid, but you're young, yet. If it will make you feel better, I don't know everything either. I just don't tell the schmucks in the trade that; let them think I know it all."

Jeff smiled at his boss.

"But, I do know more than you, so be careful."

Again, a nod.

"And, never trust anybody. That's what my father used to say to me, 'Never trust anybody, you hear me, anybody? You think someone is your friend, not so; that person just wants for himself, not for you. Trust no one!'"

"I hear you."

"Good boy. By now, you know a lot of photographers like shooting Jewish affairs, because we work right through the reception. They don't drag on or get boring. The only Jewish jobs that drag are the Chassidic weddings where they have fifty-minute dance sets. At *goyishe* weddings, the band puts on recorded music and goes to eat; at Jewish weddings, we work straight through and photograph the tables, with maybe a little break during dinner for soda or to *gay pishen*, but that's all."

"Yeah," Jeff agreed, "I know, sometimes, I just wish Christian weddings would move faster. We go to the park, and sometimes we have a lull because everyone goes back to the bride's parents' house after church."

"Exactly, but one good thing about working a Christian job, is that you'll always eat. At Jewish affairs you won't eat, because those places charge over a hundred a plate, sometimes two hundred, maybe more. I think where we had my daughter's wedding—temple Beth Affluent of Woodmere—it was two fifty a couple, and that was already over a decade ago. The *goyishe* halls try to sell clients on giving the band and photographer dinner. At the prices the Jewish halls charge, they ain't gonna want to feed us, who the hell are we? There were a few who fed me through the years, but, I said, a few. Remember what I told you when you started working here?"

Jeff took a long breath and sighed, "Eat a lot of food at the cocktail hour because they probably won't feed you at a Jewish job, and with goyishe jobs, you never know."

"Good boy, you pay attention. And, I want you to know this; you shouldn't worry about the package deal. An Italian part-time photographer, who works from his home, he'll tell the clients, 'I have a low overhead, I'm not expensive.' Oh, and I love this one, 'I'm a part-time shooter, so I'm not looking to make a lot of money.' Bullshit, if you shoot for a studio or for yourself, you should try to make as much as you can, especially if you're good. These morons are ruining the business for us; I'll say that until the day I'm planted in Beth David. When these part-time, package deal schmucks say, 'Why do you want to pay for your studio's location, or plush furniture or fancy chandelier or carpeting,' these people like getting ripped off, that's why they use those studios. My ass, Jeff! Always present yourself professionally. Your studio should be a fancy showplace, like this one used to be. Clients don't come to big studios because they like to be ripped off, that's pure, unadulterated horseshit. That's an anti-Semite's view of how it is. People who want quality, who are willing to spend for it, come to big studios like me, because they want someone who is a success, not a part-time hack. Legitimate high-priced studio owners, like myself, do not, I repeat do not, rip clients off; we just will not stoop to the 'what's your package, what's your price, package deal mentality.' Upscale people want to walk into an elegant studio, with a good track record. Go find an upscale person going to a low-end package deal hack, they don't. Only the low-class shits use those assholes. This is not a question of saving money; this is about paying for quality. There is nothing wrong with being an expensive studio, as long as your work is worth it. Never accept the 'let's keep this package to the bare essential.' Fuck that, baby; you won't make any money with that low conniving crowd. I hope the package deal morons never learn this, because I don't want their clients, trust me, neither will you. Don't worry about not being the lowest bidder. Sometimes you're better off not being the lowest.

Jeff looked as though Sid's sermon of wisdom had sunk in.

"Well, it is now two-thirty," Sid looked at his gold-tone Dufonté watch, by Lucien Piccard, "so take your stuff and go. You've kept me too long and now I'm all fucked up. I got a lot of things to do."

"Okay, Sid, thanks for all your words of wisdom. I'll call you next week. Thank you for all the stuff."

"Was I right? Don't answer, Jeff, I'm always right. Remember, I told you most studios won't hire you if you shoot in six forty-five. I said get 6x6 square, and make it a Hasselblad. Clients know what a Hasselblad is, trust me. Shoot with a 'Hassy,' they think you're good. I know you wanted a Mamiya 645 like me, but I said 'do as I say, not as I do.' I was right. I've been right about everything."

"Thanks again."

"Don't mention it, kid. Be well and keep smiling."

Sid smiled at Jeff.

Jeff smiled back at Sid.

A younger version of Sid Weitz walked through the front door.

"Hey, Steve, what are you doing here?" Sid called out, happy to see his son, the doctor.

"Just coming to help you, Dad. I called the house, you had already left, and Mom told me you were here. I haven't been in this place for quite a while, so I wanted to see the studio one last time."

The junior Weitz was much more verbally articulate than the senior Weitz. "Where's Lenny?"

"Upstairs."

"Good." Steve hated Lenny's guts. He always thought Lenny was a creep. Sometimes he thought Sid was a creep, but not as big a creep as Lenny.

"Steve, you know my protégé, Jeff Glassman, don't you? Jeff, you know my prodigy, Steven?"

Jeff and Steve shook hands, which was hard for them to do, because Jeff was holding all the stuff Sid had given him.

"Jeff was just leaving," Sid said. He looked at Jeff and said, "Go." He pointed to the door as he said it.

Jeff looked at both Sid and Steven, nodded, and then left.

Sid took off his distance glasses, laid them on the bridge table, looking at his son, while rubbing his eyes. Sid grinned, looked at his son, and shrugged.

"Nu?"

Chapter Seventeen

"You're happy to see me, Dad. I'm surprised; lately you haven't been happy to see me."

"I'm happy to see you, son," Sid said very cordially.

Steven Weitz looked at the cigarette butts in the ashtray and shook his head disapprovingly. "I thought you quit smoking those goddamn things."

"I cut down a lot and I am quitting. I had a nerve-wracking morning; the weekend was rough, too. I guess Mom told you that I had some shit yesterday with the new car. Right now, I've been worrying about what I'm going to do with the rest of my life. How I'm going to pay these high Nassau County taxes, how your mother and I are going to eat until I become eligible for Social Security, trivial bullshit like that."

"Dad, your so-called trivial bullshit is no excuse for your smoking."

"Look, Dr. Weitz, I'm sorry you don't approve of my lifestyle, I am going to quit. I can't afford it anymore. Next week, when all this crap is over, I won't be so keyed up."

"How do you sleep at night?" Steven asked his father, very concerned.

Sid put his hands together sideways, and cocked his head to mimic a person sleeping, "Like this," his dad replied.

I'm trying to find out how you're feeling, Dad," said Steven

"How do I sleep at night? Jesus, you sound like your mother's fat ass cousin Esther, when I told her I voted for Nixon."

Steven sat down at the bridge table across from his father.

"So, Doctor, how is everything? What's new?"

"You tell me, Dad, you're the man with the news."

"Who am I, Jim Jensen? What news? You tell me." Sid gestured up to the heavens.

"Well, Dad, nothing is really new with me."

Dr. Steven Andrew Weitz, twenty-eight, a physician completing his residency in pediatric medicine, was a younger, less abrasive version of his father. He was Sid's height, but somewhat trimmer. He had his father's features, yet he was somewhat better looking. *This was due to Norma,* Sid thought. Steven's hair was the same cut and texture as Sid's. The shade was the dark brown Sid used to have, more than a decade ago. Steven had a full mustache, which was to make him look older because he did not want his patients to call him a kid. When Steven first began his internship, elderly patients asked him how old he was, where he went to school, where he studied *Torah*.

Sid moved his chair next to Steven.

Steven hugged Sid. "It's good to see you, Dad, really. Christy sends her love."

Steve called Christine, Christy. *She was an adorable young woman.* Steve thought, *somehow her crooked teeth made her adorable. They weren't very crooked, she looked like a Christy.*

"How is Christine feeling?" Sid never called his daughter-in-law Christy— only Christine—which was fine with Steven. Christy was his special name for her. Sometimes he called her "bunny nose," because of her naturally small nose. There was genuine concern in his father's voice, maybe even, a hint of affection.

"She's fine, Dad, but she's getting very big."

"Yeah, when your mother was pregnant she was very big. Both times, with Linda and you. Linda was very big with Peter and Alec. Did Mom tell you about Linda?"

"No, actually Linda spoke to Christy; I know, they think this one is going to be a girl. Linda said Rebecca was going to be the name."

Both father and son stared across the table at each other.

"Nu? You throw anything out your car window lately."

"Holy shit, Dad, I was kid; let's forget about that."

"Yeah, you're right; I used to call the tobacco shop about Prince Albert in a can in my day."

"So, Dad," asked Steven, "how were your jobs this weekend?"

"Ho, ho, ho," Sid laughed mockingly, "when were you ever interested in my photographic assignments?"

"I've always been interested in what you do. I just don't understand photography that much. You know, Christy and I bought another camera last week, our old one fell apart."

"Another pocket camera?" asked Sid.

"No," said Steven enthusiastically. "It's a single lens reflex auto focus, auto exposure with a built-in flash, not quite a point and shoot."

Sid nodded approval.

"You know, the kind people hold over your shoulder when you're trying to shoot."

Sid made a "What are you going to do?" face.

"How were the shoots, Dad?"

Sid lit another Viceroy.

Steven shook his head.

"Rotten kid, rotten to the core; will probably be a successful, lawyer or slumlord some day," his father answered.

"Oh, I see, he was one of those Bar Mitzvah boys from hell."

Sid nodded ruefully.

"I wasn't all that bad."

Sid shrugged, neutrally.

"I mean, how bad could I have been? You had this old man with a Jewish accent who kept telling me to 'shmile.' The old guy kept pinching my cheeks. Harry was a guest. I was afraid of him, he was a cop. How bad was I, Dad?"

"Eh," replied Sid.

"Tell me about the little bastard, Dad."

"He was a little rich kid from Manhattan Beach. A brat, a little Lord Fauntleroy. He picked up my camera, I asked him, very politely, to please not touch my equipment. The little snot nose said, 'Trust me, Sid.'"

Steven giggled.

"Yeah, every time I told the little *momzer* not to touch my gear, he says, 'Trust me.'"

Steven sighed.

"He reminded me of a friend of yours, that little snot nose who moved to the city. I forget his name, but once I took you and him out for 'chinks,' he had the *chutzpah* to order eggrolls during the meal. Then that little shit, looks at me as if I was some kind of stupid putz and says, 'It's not complete without eggroll.' Remember what I said to him?"

"I remember, Dad, you asked him how he'd like to pay for the complete meal."

"Goddamn right. So then this kid starts to fiddle around with Jeff's video equipment. Jeff did the videotaping saturday night."

Steven nodded, waiting for his father to continue.

"Well, I asked that little snot not to play with the monitor," Sid continued, "that little wise ass told me to shut up."

"Oh, my God," Steven laughed, "he didn't."

"He freakin' did!" Sid said, laughing along with him. "The little shit rolls his eyes, as if I was the one who was annoying him, sighed, and said, 'Shut up.' Where do kids come off behaving that way?"

Steven shook his head in disbelief.

"What are you going to do?" Sid philosophized.

"How was the reception, Dad?"

"The standard nouveau riché ostentatious affair, the kind to which rabbis are starting to raise objections. They had a sixteen-piece orchestra. Remember Dick Marcus from Douglaston? He played at your B'Mitzvah. This job was wild, but not as wild as that little brat's job, the one I had in New Jersey. They had some big hotel, with a separate room for the kids to play arcade games on video machines," Sid shook his head vigorously.

"Well, Dr. Steven," Sid's tone of voice was business-like now, as he looked his son in the eye. "Why did you feel you had to *schlep* out from Queens today to see me?"

"I told you, Dad," Steve was also using a stern tone of voice, "I wanted to see the studio one more time, and Mom said you might need some help. I wanted to see the old studio one last time."

Sid slouched in his chair.

Steven realized how old his father had become; his father looked his sixty years. Steven wondered if he would look that old when he was sixty.

His father extended his arms in a gesture for his son to look around.

"I can only remember two times in the recent past when you came in. Once for your Bar Mitzvah portrait, again for your wedding portrait. Christine looked very cute in that cocktail dress she bought for the pictures. You showed me the pictures of the ceremony in the Las Vegas chapel. She was a beautiful little bride; I'll give you that, Steve. You brought her in with her parents, Mr. and Mrs. High Society of Suffolk County. Your mother, Linda, Mark, and the boys came over. Lenny took a picture of us standing together, like we were one big happy family."

"I thought we were," Steven answered. "Linda played a *hora* and tarantella, from a tape you used for your video editing. We danced in a circle here in the reception room."

"Someday you may understand what I mean."

"I think I do understand," Steven looked uncomfortable.

"When you came in for your pictures, do you remember what you said to me?"

Steven shook his head 'no.'

"You said, 'Gee Dad, you and Lenny are letting the place go.'"

"I knew you were ready to call it quits, looking at all the faded pictures in the window. This used to be a beautiful studio; you kept it so neat."

"How would you know, you never wanted to come here."

"My friends in school told me, Dad, you did most of their Bar Mitzvahs, confirmation portraits, and sweet sixteens. You even shot the affairs to which I wasn't invited. They brought pictures to class to show everybody. I used to tell everybody—everybody, students, teachers, custodians, and the guy who drove the bus—that my father took those pictures. I was proud of your work."

"Yeah, now I'm ready to take it easy. I earned the right to take it easy, didn't I?"

Steven nodded his head 'yes.'

"Certainly," Sid agreed with his son's head shake.

Steven smiled; he loved the way his father said certainly. It came out, "Coitenly."

None of Steven Weitz's friend's made fun of the way his father spoke. Most of his friend's fathers spoke with heavy pronounced New York accents, as well.

"In a couple of years, I'm gonna get my Social Security, and I have a bit of money stashed away. Your mother is going to keep working for a while, so I'm gonna let her support the two of us. Technically, I'm still in business, I have some jobs lined up, and some new jobs will be coming in."

"Right," Steven stood up from the table, "and other people want you to work for them."

"A few photographers I know want me to shoot stills and videotape for them, strictly on a per diem basis. I ain't gonna shoot for *shlock* places, only for quality places that can afford to pay me what I require.

"At this point in my life, I could never work full time for a studio again. There are some places that would like to have me, but at this point in my life, I couldn't take it."

"Mom told me you could afford to shoot a lot less or even get out altogether if you wanted to."

"Now, Steve, it's very expensive to live here on Long Island, especially in the Five Towns. I'm always gonna have to work for expense money. I put both you and Linda through school and I helped you both out with cars when you started out. Last year we gave Linda another car, our Lincoln. When you went to medical school, we took some loans, but I helped as best as I could. It was easier for me to make a living then."

Steven did appreciate all the help from his father. He did not believe the old man believed him when he said he did.

"I'm gonna try to take it easy, relax, and enjoy my semi-retirement. When I work, I work. Mom and I plan to do some traveling. Last spring, we went out to California. It was great, no business hassles. In Los Angeles, we visited all the cemeteries where all the actors are buried. First, we went to Forest Lawn Memorial, the non-sectarian one. Then Mom and I went to Hillside Memorial, which is the big Jewish cemetery. We went into the mausoleum where Jack Benny and his wife are. It was very interesting. We saw who was Jewish."

"Who was Jewish?"

"You'd never believe it, Steve. Remember the actor David Janssen? He's in there. So is Vic Morrow, from the TV show *Combat*; he was killed making that Spielberg movie. We saw so many others; your mother knows who else, she'll tell you. We haven't gone dancing in years, now I'll have time to enjoy my grandchildren.

"That's what I wanted to talk to you about, Dad. Christy and I decided to have a Christening and a Bat Mitzvah. We'd like you to oversee the Christening pictures," Steve paused, "and the Bat Mitzvah…"

"Shoot Bat Mitzvah, if I'm still alive," Sid cut his son off.

"Dad, for Christ's sake," Steven scolded his father, "what the hell do you mean if you're still alive? Of course, you'll be alive. I don't like the way you've been talking lately."

"A Christening and a Bat Mitzvah—the best of two worlds—how quaint can you get?"

"Dad, that's the way Christy and I worked it out. We think this is what will be best for us and our daughter. I'm sorry if I hurt you and Mom, but Christy and I love each other and that's it. I thought we straightened all this out months ago."

"We did, we did," answered Sid, "it's all straightened out. I happen to think it sucks, but it's all straightened out."

"Look, we thought you might like to shoot or videotape your granddaughter's christening…"

"My granddaughter's christening!" Sid exclaimed, waving his arms in mock joy, "my granddaughter's christening. I'm gonna have to get used to saying that, 'my granddaughter's christening.'"

"Look, Dad," Steven was raising his voice to his father now, "I know you're upset. If this upsets you, don't come, we'll…"

"You'll what?" Sid shouted back, "you'll hire another photographer? Look at this, my son is threatening to use another photographer. Go hire Hal Grossman, I think you can afford him since his partner, the other Hal, Hal Strickland, sued him out of the partnership. Go have your in-laws call a package deal studio. I'll be there, *boychick*, your *shiksa* wife is carrying my granddaughter. Watch, watch, you watch, with my luck, she'll grow up to be a nun."

"Sometimes your warped sense of humor gives me a pain in the ass, Dad." Steven rubbed the bridge of his nose.

"Yeah, that's right; she'll either grow up to be a nun or a biker chick. It will be up to you, Steve, to tell your daughter not to call her grandfather a 'joo.'" He accentuated the word Jew for a tough sounding effect.

"I guess this isn't the time to tell you the name Christy and I decided on for the baby."

Sid stubbed out his cigarette. "It isn't, but why don't you tell me anyway, Steve-a-reno. Let's see," Sid looked at his watch, "you haven't given me any aggravation, for about ten seconds."

"Angela, Dad. The baby's name is Angela, after Christy's paternal grandmother. Angela Victoria Weitz."

"Angela!" Sid cried out, "Christine's grandmother? I met her, she's still alive."

"We can do it that way in her faith, Dad. We thought about naming her Sydney, but we knew in the Jewish faith, the namesake has to be dead to do it."

"Why, is Christine wishing?"

"No, Dad, she loves you, only you don't believe it. Christy wants to love you, but you won't let her."

"I like her, I guess. As for love, I don't know, yet. Your mother loves her, isn't that enough for now?"

"No, Dad, it isn't."

"Tough shit, don't fuckin' tell me who I have to love, okay?"

"Okay."

"Shit, naming the baby after Christine's grandmother, the woman walks around in tight jeans, wearing a Met's tee shirt and cap."

"She's not that old, Dad, she has the figure for jeans and she loves the Mets. Are Grandma and Grandpa coming to the Christening?"

"Your mother's parents will; they're crazy George McGovern ass-kissing liberal masochists. My mother? Maybe. My father? Never."

"Why not?"

"Can you see my father, Burton Weitz, in a church? He's never been in one, and at this stage in his life, he's probably not going to want to set foot into a church, especially for his great-granddaughter's christening; oh, my God, Steven!" Sid stood up.

"Sorry, Dad, but I had to tell you."

"I'm sorry too, Steve. Sorry for you. I hope the rabbi at Angela's Bat Mitzvah will be able to figure out her Jewish name."

Steve smiled and chuckled. "I don't think there is a Jewish name for Angela, Dad."

Sid was feeling faint now; he wanted to kill his son.

"Damn right there isn't a Jewish name for Angela," he snapped. "At her Bat Mitzvah, the rabbi will call out come forth Angela, daughter of Christine. Oh, my God, Steven! Steven, oh, my God!"

"Maybe our daughter won't want a Bat Mitzvah."

"She won't want one if she wants to be a nun."

Sid took a deep breath and lowered his head. He felt like an old man.

"Dad, I know this is hard for you, but everything will work out."

"Oh, Steve, I hope you're right," Sid's voice was breaking, "I hope so."

"Don't worry, Dad, everything will be fine, you'll see."

"I ain't worried, Steve. Here, help me take this old bridge table and these shitty chairs out back for the garbage."

Sid and Steven spent the next hour and a half taking out garbage. At the end of those ninety minutes, the studio was once again an empty store. There were no pictures, no fixtures, and no furniture. Just empty walls and memories of an era just ended.

A large black man with a utility belt walked into the studio.

"Yes, sir," Sid called out, "may I help you?"

"Good day, I'm here to disconnect some wires. I have to go out to the main box to check on some things. I'll probably have to climb up and check on the lines also. I believe the office cut you off last week."

"Sure, right out back, help yourself."

The telephone man was from the Islands, he seemed like a friendly sort. "Thank you, sir; I'll try not to take up your time."

"Take as much of my time as you want," Sid called after the man, "I'm retired."

"When is Lenny leaving?" Steven asked.

"Next week he's moving to a big office suite in Lynbrook."

"Dad, Carl was classy, but I never understood how you put up with a creep like Lenny all these years."

"Neither did I. Carl was a classy gent, that's true. But, Lenny was my business partner, not my lover. Whatever he and I did, it worked."

"I know what you did worked," Steven acknowledged his father's success. This studio was an industry legend, Dad. I remember the good times. You and Mom gave Linda and me a great childhood. I had more than a lot of kids I knew. I had the opportunity of growing up in 'The Five Towns.'

"My son, the doctor," exclaimed Sid.

"With a *shiksa* wife," Steven shot back.

Both father and son laughed, although for Sid, this was not something to laugh about.

"Steven, when the economy improves, my business will get better. It will never be the way it used to be, but things will be better."

"I know, Dad," Steven sounded sympathetic, "I've seen a lot of studios close to where we live in Queens; you probably knew some of them."

"I knew all of them."

"Why are there so many closings? Every time I drive on Union Turnpike in Queens, or Merrick Road here in Nassau, I see so many studios that went out."

Sid shrugged and shook his head. "Who the fuck knows. Today, only the top level, high-priced studios with big name recognition and a society following survive. The low-priced, package deal places and bridal centers are doing well, too. I mean, the bridal centers that have not gone bust and screwed the clients out of everything; you've seen that on the news, right?"

"Yes."

I explained all this shit to my assistant, who wants to go out on his own now. You are lucky to be a doctor. It isn't as easy for doctors today to make money, but you probably won't have to put up with this shit, so you're better off. Guys like me, competitive high-end photographers, have trouble surviving because of this. I used to tell clients, as far as the quality studios go, I'm the most reasonable. Today people call up, they only want to know the price. The attitude is 'I can get it cheaper.' Unfortunately, they can get it cheaper, that's why a lot of old candid men are closing. Cheaper doesn't mean better. I have had couples or even B'Mitzvah parents come in here, flip through the albums, and not really watch the videos, only interested in the bottom line. For some, they were not very concerned about quality. Their position was, a picture, is a picture, all pictures are the same. I told them, in that case, they were not my clients. 'I'm not for you and you're not for me,' I said. Once I had this young couple here, I dunno, they tried to use a ploy to get me to lower the price. They kept bitching they didn't like my work. They bitched about the price, but mostly they were overly critical of the work. I showed them albums of several different shooters who worked here at the time. I told them, if you don't like my work, the best thing for you to do is walk. They were offended, I said, 'I'm not trying to be nasty, I thank you for coming in, but the best thing for you to do, is walk.'"

"What happened? Steven asked.

"They walked, it wasn't a good match. In this business it works both ways; you have to pick your clients, too. I guess it's true in every business."

"In theory, Dad, you're right, if you don't starve to death first."

"Shooters don't have it much easier today. If you want to shoot, or video tape for that matter, shoot for a high-end studio—if you're good enough—or for a package deal studio. Because today, these places have all the bookings. Even some top high-end shooters are going out to shoot for these package places. I know some top men who are struggling, so they lend their talents to *shlock*; they go out for the whores who ruined the industry they love so much and shoot for a mere two hundred dollars, if even that. This big studio on the North Shore, which was taken over, then went into bankruptcy, laid off this fellow I know, a top man. Poor bastard shoots for whomever, and for whatever. Shit, this guy loved to shoot as much as life itself; he lived to shoot. He needs the work, so he does what he has to. It's sad, it sucks, but if you're a shooter, these studios are the ones who give you bookings to go out and shoot jobs."

"I never thought it worked that way," Steven said with a surprised look on his face.

"Because you're not in the industry, but that's the way it works, my boy," his father answered.

"Explain more to me, Dad; I never knew much about your business."

"If you want to make a living shooting, you get a job with a busy studio— someone who is more successful than you are. After all, you want to work for somebody with a lot of jobs to send you out on. Okay, this place has more dates booked than you do, as an independent. I don't care if this is a cheap or expensive studio; he has more work than you have. He needs your services, you follow?"

"I think so."

"He pays you to shoot. All these places have dates booked, the rest of us struggle. We lower our prices, behave like whores, and some go out of business. All the brides go to these places to book, all the B'Mitzvahs. So, if we need a job or if we like to shoot, we go to these places and ask the fortunate owner for permission to photograph affairs. We need his jobs because we cannot get our own."

"I see," said Steven, somewhat confused at the old man's logic. The old man was very bitter these days. He knew his marriage to Christy did not soften the old man's outlook on life. *Maybe when Christy and I go over Saturday, I'll talk to him about getting some help*, he thought. *I will have to take him aside. If I suggest counseling in front of anyone, he'll flip out; for spite, he won't even consider it. I'll have to talk to Mom about it*, he figured. Linda would be there too; they both might have to confront the old man themselves. He was so depressed lately, such a *ferbissen*. Steven could not recall when the old man was ever bitter, he was always upbeat in the heyday, but this is not the heyday. If the old man does not tone down and cool it, Steve feared, he could become a basket case. He used to seem so upbeat when it came to shooting jobs. He loved going to work at the studio every day. Whenever the old man had to go on location, he put the whole world on hold while he was working. Now his attitude was, let's get the damn job over with.

Steve tried to understand why his father was bitter. Maybe, he has the right to be. The old man had a business for three decades, now it's gone, he understood that. The fact that an only son married outside his family's faith caused some bitterness, that too was understandable.

He was not paying attention to his father, who was still speaking. The old man was rattling on; he did not speak anymore, he just rattled now.

The old man was argumentative with Mom a lot these days, too, Steven noticed. They usually got along well, now he challenged and disagreed with everything she said. This behavior was a major concern for both Steven and his sister. Steve was upset with himself, because he never used to think of his father as "the old man," let alone refer to him that way. But the truth was, Sid was acting like an old man. Steven was somehow angry at his father, although he did not quite know why. He was very worried for Sid; he understood why he worried about him.

The old man was rattling away. *I guess this is the mid-life crisis* Steve figured. He wished this was something that he would not, someday, have to go through. *I hope, I won't be this way when I'm sixty*, he thought. Then Steven remembered both his grandfathers, who were now both in their eighties. Both men had a better outlook on life than his sixty-year-old father.

"Hey, you listening to me?" Sid asked Steven.

"Yeah, Dad, I'm listening," Steven focused back on his father.

"You're fuckin' lucky you're a doctor. Okay, at times, you have to be a salesman; if you're a surgeon, you gotta sell. You always have to be a businessman. But, believe me when you work in a sales job, you're gonna grow to hate people. You're gonna see what kinds of bastards people really are. Last week some old sounding broad left a message on the machine. She says it's nine A.M., she says, and she wants a call back as soon as possible before ten this morning. My fuckin' machine says hours are eleven A.M. to five P.M.; we're not here this early. I return the bitch's call anyway. She answers, tells me she changed her mind, she doesn't even tell me why she called. Maybe I should open up earlier? I used to when I was younger. Most studios on the Island don't open until either ten or eleven in the morning. Nothing much happens until then. At eight A.M., Lenny opens the baby studio, because that business starts early, His photographers are out on the road early. I wondered if that old hag even listened to my message and heard the hours of operation."

"Dad, I see all kinds of people, too, real lowlifes. When I was an intern in the emergency room, I dealt with every low down drunk you would ever want to see. They brought this foul-smelling Puerto Rican man in; he fell in the subway because he was so pickled. One detective asked me for his report, 'Do you think this man is inebriated, Doc? His partner says he ain't inebriated, he's Puerto Rican.' I deal with all lowlifes, Dad, on both sides of the law."

"When you're in sales, you'll hate people. Then after a while, you'll go crazy. Remember the character Willy Loman? Now I hate selling, back then, I did the hard sale, and my partner, class act Carl did the soft sell. Now I gotta sell, sell, sell, and close. I get aggravation because I did not want to lower my prices and get the redneck wedding."

"Rednecks...here on Long Island?" Steven asked, he looked bewildered.

"Oh, absolutely," continued Sid. "In the blue collar parts of towns here on Long Island, not just down south or out west. You know you're in a redneck town when you're in a restaurant and all the men wear tee shirts to eat out...towns where they keep campers in the driveways. Those, Steve, are redneck areas. Especially Suffolk County, all the way out east where your in-laws live. The boondocks, exit sixty three on the Long Island Expressway."

"You sayin' Christy's parents are rednecks?"

"They are, Steve, believe me. Two dogs, two cats, and a rabbit in their house, feh! Five old cars, one tow truck, three motorcycles in their driveway...they're rednecks. You don't make any money from that crowd, so I don't go after them. I knew this photographer, a part-time shooter, from out east who caters to the rednecks; he doesn't get rich, but at least he works."

Steven started laughing.

"What's so funny?" his father asked him.

"Nothing."

"C'mon, tell me!" Sid demanded.

"I remember what you said to Christy, when we first started going out."

"What did I say?"

"It was cute. She was talking to you about the upcoming holidays. She said she wasn't sure of what to get her father for Christmas. She told you, she might get him a chrome rear end cover. Remember what you said? We were having brunch at the dining room table."

"I don't recall what I said."

"You said, 'Why, does your father have a metal ass?"

"I didn't know it was for the rear of a motorcycle. What do I know about motorcycles?"

"But," Steven continued, "you say my in-laws are rednecks."

"Well," Sid, wiped his forehead, he was perspiring now, because the studio was very hot. He and Lenny sold the air conditioners weeks ago, since they were not planning to be around for the hot weather. "I don't mean it as a knock, I mean it as a fact...your in-laws are rednecks. If I wanted to knock them, I would call them *goyim*."

"You do call them *goyim*," Steven winced.

"Yeah, because your mother and I have nothing in common with them; neither do you, Steve. Why the hell did you stop dating that beautiful Gayle Eysenberg from down the block? I liked her, and Mom and I had things in common with her parents."

"You had plenty in common, you both drove a Cadillac. We broke up, that's all; it didn't work out. That is all in the past, I don't want to get into it."

"I'm sure you don't, Steve; she married a nice Jewish boy, but her parents were pissed about the breakup, they didn't call me to shoot the job. Just as well, because, frankly, I would have eaten my heart out. Jobs from your in-laws I need like a swollen prostate. You can shoot all the jobs you want with that crowd, but you won't make money. If you're in business, making money is the name of the game, Doctor."

"Dad, I understand."

"Good, I'm glad you understand. My business is a numbers business. So is yours, Doctor, if you get the sickies, you got the numbers. Today, everything is price. Today, people come in with price lists from other studios, not so much to compare, but to squeeze you. Doctors have this problem, too, now. Open a nice practice down the street; you'll have the no appointment needed, walk-in doctor's office. Then you got those HMOs. Getting back to my sales, you know what this guy is charging, is this person just as good, does he produce the product as well as I do? Today, people come in and play photographers off against each other. For example, if I tell them this coverage, with a fifty-page, eight-by-ten bound album, is two grand, they tell me the guy down the block says he'll do it for five hundred. I know damn well that the other guy would not do it for five hundred, but, they think I don't know, so they play us off against each other. They don't realize we talk to each other; they think that competitors don't call each other up when someone bullshits us. I had a situation where these rich Jewish people came in for a B'Mitzvah, so they go to this fancy studio in Roslyn before coming to see me. They show me his contract, I think they already booked Barney; I don't know, maybe it was a price quote on his letterhead. Anyhow, they show me some unbelievably low prices. So I get suspicious and I ask Adrienne, she was our manager at that time, to schmooze them while I call this studio. I knew Barney, he was not cheap, so in my office I noticed that these rich, Roslyn Estates assholes put whiteout on the studios prices and wrote in their own prices, bastards! I get Barney on the phone, we talk about this. So I put him on hold, go back out front, tell those *schnorrers*, that someone wants to talk to them on the phone. You should have seen the looks on their, flabby Roslyn Estates faces. Liars hate being called liars, especially successful ones."

"What happened, Dad, they book you?"

"No, in fact I asked them to leave."

"It's in every business, Dad."

"You're right, Steve, although some businesses more than others. That's why I say, you're going to see what bastards people really are. He looked at his son and smirked. Especially doctors, doctors are the cheapest and lousy tippers."

"Thanks a lot."

"You're welcome. Steve, you know all this. You know how snooty a lot of your colleagues are, especially the young snot nosed doctors, who think they know everything, but don't know shit. You've seen it, you grew up in the Five Towns, and those are the folks I worked for. Understand this, you're gonna want to have your own practice one day. Today, when you go into business for yourself, you butt you head against the wall. Today, it is not only hard to get started, but to survive. Believe you me, you're clients only want what's best for them in the long run, they don't care if you eat or not."

"In any business," said Steven. It was not a question; it was a confirmation of what his father just said.

"Today the best jobs are computers in the private sector or civil service. The federal government jobs, the state jobs, county, and city jobs. Good pay and benefits, along with great pensions, even for those who had the sit-on-your-ass-do-nothing jobs. At my association, a lot of photographers are former civil service, and this economy doesn't affect them all that much. Look at Harry the cop; he earned his patrolman's salary, while earning a lieutenant's salary by shooting for me and others. Look at the fuckin' pension he retired on, he even ended up with more, because Harry retired on disability when that dumb ass rookie broad he was partnered with, accidently blew away the young woman who called out to them in the hallway when she heard the perpetrators that they were chasing out on her fire escape. Civil service gives great disability; it's probably the only job where an employee prays for some type of injury. In civil service you'll never get rich or be an entrepreneur, but at least you don't have to invest any money and you don't starve."

"I know," Steven agreed.

"Here in Nassau County," Sid went on, "if you have a town job or county job, you make out alright. You have to be a registered republican, because the party owns all the county's services. You have to be willing to volunteer time and make contributions to someone's campaign."

"A kickback," Steven interjected.

"They prefer to say contribution; it sounds nicer, especially at party official's indictments. You have to go out and campaign for the politicians, and you get rewarded with nice jobs where you do nothing. You know, a park recreation supervisor, or you could sit at an intersection all day long to determine if a STOP sign is needed. See you make a lot of money for just doing nothing. These employees have nothing to worry about; their boss will never go out of business."

"I know all that, Dad, I know about the system. I am not a business owner, but I am not an ignoramus."

"That's debatable, son. Out here, you take a civil service test, but I wonder if it really means anything. If you're a registered republican, willing to make contributions and get out and work for the party, then you're in, you get hired, and you get promoted. It works the same way in Brooklyn; you just have to be a democrat. It's a nice way to make a living, if you have the job."

"Dad," Steven put his arm around his father's shoulder, "you did what you wanted, you were very successful, and you had your run."

"I did, you're right," Sid leaned up against the bare reception room wall. "Did you know this county has a photography staff? The city of New York must have one, too, I guess."

"What is that?"

"Some guy, who shoots affairs as a sideline, told me he has this job. You ever see the pictures of our elected officials in the papers giving people awards and bullshit citations?"

Steve said he had.

"I thought the newspaper sent someone, but the town or county has a photographer who rides around with the county executive, the town supervisor, or even council members, taking pictures of them all day long as they go around handing out awards. So we have photographic proof that our elected officials are spending their whole day jerking off, when they should be working."

Steven shook his head in disgust. "What a racket."

"Damn right!" Sid cried out, "Damn right. But, as I said, those people have nothing to worry about, not even the schmucks who can't put two words together, they have security. It's a disgusting practice, but what the hell; they don't stay up at night worrying."

Steven looked at his wristwatch. It was a simple Timex. Some watch for a doctor, his father commented. He told him that he would give him a nice Pulsar quartz that he never wore.

"You gotta go?" Sid asked.

"Yeah, I have some forms to fill out, and then I'm going to pick up Christy. She wants to work at the burger place for one more month."

"You're both still coming over Saturday?"

"Oh, sure, we told Mom it was definite."

"Good, we'll go out to dinner, all of us, my treat, as usual. Linda and Mark are coming with the kids. Your mother and I found this new place. It has very good 'chinks' and the prices are reasonable."

"Dad, don't say 'chinks.' Remember what Nana Sadie told me when I was little?"

Sid winced. "What the hell did she say?" he whined. "Oh, yes, she said I was common. Thanks a lot, pal."

"She told me don't say 'chink,' it isn't nice; she told me to say Chinaman."

"*Oy*, that mother in law of mine is something else, I tell you."

"I know she is," Steven agreed. "We'll be over Saturday…you don't have any jobs?"

"I have to videotape a Greek Orthodox Christening in Merrick in the morning. They booked a photographer from Astoria; the people called me out of the *Yellow Pages*. They told me the Greek DJ will videotape the reception, so I hit them for six fifty for an edited ceremony only with a super VHS camcorder; I'll set up the lights myself, no assistant. The Greeks don't mind the video lights in the church. I'll edit the job myself and pocket the cash. This should be an hour and a half, tops. So, come over at noon, I should be back by then"

"Okay, at noon. Do you still need the answering machine?"

"No," Sid turned around, "where the hell is the phone guy? There was a black fellow in here a while ago. He was going to disconnect, I dunno, the jack, or some wires and shit. I guess he's working outside, still. Oh, well, take the machine. This thing has a day time stamp for the messages."

"We can use it for our apartment." Steven turned it on, "You have a tape in here, Dad. You also have a message, I think."

Steven pressed the playback button. There was only one message. A young boy's voice saying, "I want your pussy, I want your pussy and your tits." *Must be a Bar Mitzvah boy screwing around*, Steven thought.

"Schmuck kid, I dunno who it is." Sid was tired; he wanted the day to end.

Steven unplugged and picked up the answering machine.

"Thanks, Dad."

"You're welcome, son."

Both father and son embraced and kissed.

Sid held the front door open for his son, watching as he walked across the street to where he parked his four-door hatchback Volkswagen Golf. Sid helped his son to pay for the car. He told him that he would have given him the '84 Caprice, had there been anything left of that car internally.

Sid shook his head, a son who drives a German car, with a *shiksa* wife and a baby girl named Angela.

"Why me?" Sid asked out loud.

"Excuse me, m'frien'," a deep voice called out.

Sid turned around startled. It was the man from the telephone company. It had been a couple of hours.

"Where were you?" he asked the lineman.

"Oh, when I was out de' back way, de people in de pizza parlor were having trouble wit' der lines. De office told me to check it out. Me an' another mon fix de lines. I think dey were chewed up by rats."

"Shit! I ate there a couple of times! Holy shit!" Sid screamed.

The telephone man laughed.

Sid felt like retching.

"I did what I had to do at the box. De office turned off da phone. Nex' week, de mon in de office upstairs jus' has to call de office to disconnect."

"Okay, good enough," Sid opened the front door for the phone man. "Thank you for coming."

"You're welcome, good luck to ya."

The studio was as hot as hell now. It was not even a photography studio anymore. It was just another vacant store in the neighborhood. Sid looked at his watch, everything that had to be thrown out, was thrown out. There was nothing left to do. It was time to go.

He stood at the front door and locked it, even though there was not anything left to steal. He took one last look at the store, which had been his second home, perhaps even his first and only home for the last thirty years.

He had started here shooting weddings and Bar Mitzvahs, portraits on black and white film, and color movies. Later on, this studio introduced color film "For the Look of Life," for candid coverage. This studio started incorporating video in 1978. This very store had been the first studio on Long Island to offer video coverage.

"*Oy*," he sighed. That summed it all up. There was nothing left to be said.

No memories, just vacant wall that required spackling, nothing left here— just a big sign outside above the façade, which would be left up. The big electronic studio sign was the landlord's problem now. Let that prick worry about it. Let him pay someone to take it down.

"Nothing left to do," he said out loud to nobody.

There was one more thing to do.

Sid sighed again.

"Time to go upstairs and talk to Schecter, the schmuck," he said out loud, again to nobody.

Sid picked up his blue Virginia Slims baseball cap. He had everything; he would leave by the Happy Time Photographers office exit. He walked to the stairway in the reception area and went upstairs to say good-bye to the baby studio staff, and to talk to Lenny.

Chapter Eighteen

S id paused at the second floor entrance of Happy Time Photographers. He listened to the secretaries on the phones, setting up and confirming sitting appointments with mothers. Secretaries were filling out job assignments for photographers and processing order forms from the outside sales staff. There was the sound of typing, pens scratching, phones ringing, and happy chatter—quite an operation—reminiscent of the portrait studio downstairs, when things used to be busy. The smell of brewed coffee and bakery cookies wafted through the entrance. The outer office was not as neat as it usually was. There were packed boxes of frames, film, folios, which were cardboard frames for photographs, vinyl slip in albums, and order forms.

"Hi, Sid."

"Good morning, Sidney," a few of the girls called out as he entered.

The lighting for the Happy Time staff was bright. Lenny was a fucking cheapskate; Sid knew that, the whole world knew that. Bright light yielded a much more pleasant working environment, so the cheap bastard spent a little more on electricity; he could overcharge clients to make up the revenue loss.

The mood at Happy Time was upbeat, unlike the somber mood at Montclair Studios downstairs had experienced for the past five years. When Carl, Sid and Lenny's former partner, sold out eleven years ago and moved to Arizona, he thought Montclair would be finished in two years. He and his wife were surprised the studio lasted as long as it did.

Here the money was flowing as if Reagan was still the president. Here the phones were ringing; the buttons were all lit up with customers calling to order pictures from the sittings. Sid could not recall when was the last time he had put a client on hold to answer a call from another client. The phone at Montclair did not ring as often as it used to in the old days. This was very depressing, for any kind of a business...operating a business and getting no calls, or worse, getting all the pain in the ass calls.

Sid was afraid to answer the phone in recent years. Every time the goddamned phone rang, the party on the other end wanted to sell, not buy—bullshit charities, police support groups, all kinds of bridal advertising, which always proved to be fruitless, chemical salespeople, insurance agents, and distributors for crap they never used.

The insurance agents were a royal pain in the ass. One guy was a part-time photographer, whom Sid knew. He was always calling to sell him a policy. Sid saw this schmuck's work, he was better off selling insurance. The stockbrokers were worse. Sid did not need some shithead stockbroker wasting his time about mutual funds, stocks, and treasury bonds. So far, no stockbroker called with a good Ponzi scheme on which Sid could make money. His brother-in-law Arnold Lieber was a stockbroker and a very successful one. Nevertheless, Arnie was a pain in the ass. When his baby sister Helen, a gorgeous girl, married Arnie, Sid bought some stocks from him to help them out. He had nothing but the utmost contempt for Arnie back then; he considered him a loser. When Helen and Arnie announced their engagement, Arnie's father, Izzy Lieber, who owned a string of filthy, neglected nursing homes, asked if they would get a good deal on wedding pictures. He assured Izzy that his sister would get a great deal. He told the old *goniff* that he was honest, unlike the way he ran his nursing homes. Imagine, bilking defenseless old people, so he could drive big Chryslers while they lay in their own piss and shit. When Izzy died, Sid and Norma went to the funeral, not out of respect, but just so Sid could walk back to the grave after the cemetery service, and go "chop ptu," and spit right onto Izzy's box.

It never failed these days. Every time the studio phone rang, it was either a cheap bastard price shopping, or some fucking peddler selling. Today those fucking solicitors were getting very aggressive. What were these telemarketing firms doing, recruiting bums from the subway? Last week, a sale rep from a maintenance supply company called back after he was told that the studio did not need any cleaning chemicals. Evidently, Sid had been too abrupt for the sales rep's liking. Sid picked up the phone a second time; the man who had identified himself as Ron from Alton Chemicals, was shouting and cursing at Sid.

"Listen, you homo," the sales rep admonished, "you hang up on me one more time and I'm gonna come over and put a used scum bag over your head, you asshole."

"Why don't you come over, you pussy-licking lowlife, take a look at good salesmanship, you shit head," Sid replied, then hung up. He really wanted that shit to take him up on his offer to come over.

Sid seldom said, "Sorry, we're not interested," to those pains in the asses. Now, he merely said, "Fuck off," and slammed the phone down.

For years, the staff of Montclair Studios avoided quoting prices on the phone. Especially, since this was not a package deal studio. Montclair relied on reputation and recommendation, rather than price. Sometimes, they would have to ballpark a prospect to get them in. Sometimes an 'about' worked. "It's 'about' twenty-five hundred." An 'about,' but never an 'exact.' Today was another story. Today, price governed if a prospective client came in. They did not waste their time on someone they simply could not afford. What photographer, by the same token, would want to waste time with someone they were going to lose anyway? Today, only price shoppers and solicitors called the studio. Christ, it became depressing after a while. Sid became adept at singling out those who were calling to sell him something. The salesperson always asked to speak to the owner or the manager. Any person in business knows that these are the only people who have authority to make a purchase. The rep always asked, "How are you doing today?" as if he or she really gave a fuck about Sid's well being. Sometimes if the seller asked for Sid Weitz, he would ask the caller to call back at six this evening. The studio closed at five. Another fun tactic was to ask the caller to please hold. Sometimes that poor seller held forever. At times, the seller redialed and asked for Sid, he asked them if the boss picked up. When the caller said that he did not, Sid asked the caller to hold again. This sometimes went on for hours. There were, however, the undaunted few who kept it up, to no avail.

In the heyday, the studio had salespeople call engaged women and mothers of B'Mitzvah celebrants. Sid even made a few of those calls himself, and he was quite good at it. But when nobody is buying what you are selling, another party calling to sell you something you do not need is extremely frustrating and time consuming. Sid was, yet, somewhat happy that somewhere out there in our recession stricken economy, at least some salesperson was working and making a living. Perhaps just by working, that person, however, had a reason to get out of bed in the morning, for a while, anyway. Things could get better, but first we have to vote out Bush.

Geneva Collins, a beautiful young black woman who was a Happy Time secretary, came over to Sid. On occasion, she worked at Montclair; she was one terrific secretary. She was a college graduate, who had booked sittings for a department store baby studio. She was waiting for a better job in office management. Sid assured her she would advance, baby studios were a good place to start. Even the actor Dom DeLuise was a baby photographer. He told her, "You'll be an office manager for some big firm one day." Geneva told Sid maybe she would write a book about a baby photographer. Sid advised her it already had been done. He told her about the movie *Easy Money*, where Rodney Dangerfield played a slovenly baby studio owner. The movie was not far from the truth, except for the end. What candid man would ever come into such great wealth? Perhaps, a candid man who wanted to write a novel based on his experiences in the industry. Geneva was a very pretty, innocent kid; he did not like the way Lenny looked at her.

"Hi, Sid, how are you?" she asked. She had a beautiful, slight Jamaican lilt. She sounded more continental than Caribbean. She had a soft voice, the kind that a young college girl would have.

"I'm fine." He smiled at her.

Geneva stifled a giggle, because his response came out, "Oym foine."

She was a sweet little girl, everyone in the office said so. Sid wondered what his reaction might have been, if his son Steven had married her instead of Christine. Would he refer to her as his "*shvartze* daughter-in-law?" He felt better about her as a daughter-in-law than Christine. Maybe because Geneva spoke much better than Christine. "I'm going to miss you, Sid. You were a pleasure to work for."

"Thank you, honey; I'm going to miss you, too."

"If I ever get married, Sid, I promise I'll call you; you're an excellent photographer."

"I know that," answered Sid. They both laughed.

Geneva Collins was wearing a form-fitting white dress blouse and tailored black slacks, designed to feature her assets. She did not have the figure that most of the black women in the neighborhood had. She was very trim, yet shapely. Her skin was the color of coffee ice cream. Her lips were not very full, nor too thin; her nose was small and very cute—it was natural, there was no cosmetic surgery—it looked like Norma's. Her hair was straight, black brown, and she was wearing it up today. Although Geneva was black, she caused many white men to turn their heads. She knew this and never let on, for this was a result she desired.

"Geneva, come with me out into the hallway."

In the hallway, in private, Sid gave her some fatherly advice.

"Watch out for Lenny, hon." They faced each other. "He's a schmuck, and he really wants to have you."

"I know, I know all about him. I think, Sid, you want me, too. I like you, so that's fine with me." She moved a little closer to him, almost pressing against him.

"I told you when you worked downstairs, as my secretary, I only have eyes for my wife, and I love you like a daughter."

"I hope not like your daughter-in-law." She blushed.

"Listen, Lenny's cheated on that fat *grubba tokus*, tub-of-lard wife of his before. Be careful, he likes his women young and beautiful, so start looking for a better job as soon as you can. Watch him, because Lenny's a *tzadic*. You know what *tzadic* in Hebrew is?"

Geneva said that she did not.

"*Tzadic* is a righteous man. Lenny is righteous, he would never defile a Jewish girl; you, however, he wants to make you howl like a dog for him. It's true; he'll nail you first, and then fire you."

"Uh, okay, thanks for telling me, Sid. I'll start looking elsewhere, thank you." Geneva sounded shaken, better now than after Lenny tries something with her.

"Don't trust that bastard; I've been partners with him for thirty years, and I still don't trust him."

"Sid, I'll be careful," Geneva vowed. "I promise. He makes me sick."

"Lenny makes everybody sick; they should put his picture on a bottle of syrup of ipecac. He drove our other partner Carl to Arizona. He claims I did, but he was the one."

"Take care of yourself, quit smoking, and be nice to your daughter-in-law."

Both Sid and Geneva embraced and kissed each other on the cheek. They hugged again, very hard.

"I will be nice to Christine and my schmuck son, I'll try." Sid placed both his hands on her face and kissed her on the mouth, she responded. This was not a heavy soul kiss; it was more of a show of affection. Maybe an 'it might have been' kiss, no tongues, a slight, exchange of saliva.

"I have to be nice to my son now. I can't cast the first stone. If I weren't married, kid, I'd want to be with you. I know I'm too old, but still."

She hugged him once again. "I know, Sid, thank you for taking care of me, and for being a friend. I love you," she started to sob. "I'm going to go down for lunch, take care."

"Stay out of that Dominican pizza joint," he called after her, "I hear they have rats."

As he stood in the hallway with an erection, he watched Geneva walk down the steps. Sid felt mixed emotions; he was going to miss that sweet little girl, and he had just cheated on his wife. He did not know what bothered him the most. He was a bit disappointed in himself. He always thought he was better than Lenny.

When Sid walked into Lenny's private office, he found him standing at his desk in agony.

"My ass itches something awful," Lenny complained.

"Maybe you have worms," Sid suggested.

"Nah, this morning I took a real heavy crap; I guess I didn't wipe too good. We're all out of those moistened towelettes. It really itches up there."

Lenny picked up a stainless steel letter opener that looked like a dagger. He stuck it down the waistband of his pants and proceeded to ream the crevice of his ass.

Sid was ready to puke up the coffee that he drank this morning and every meal he had eaten since 1947.

"Ah, that's better. I'd use my finger if you weren't in the room; see, I'm a gentleman."

Sid really felt nauseous now. In thirty years he saw Lenny do some low class things, but this was a world record.

Lenny tossed the letter opener onto the pile of order forms in the middle of his desk. The secretaries and sales staff had to handle those. *Poor Geneva*, he thought.

"Nu, aren't you gonna scratch your balls?" Sid asked him.

"My balls don't itch."

"Lenny," Sid stared right into his partner's beady eyes, "I'm gonna get something offa my chest and tell you something I never told you. You're a fuckin' schmuck."

Lenny sat down and laughed. "Sid, you called me a fuckin' schmuck in 1961."

"Good," he pointed a finger at Lenny, "I revise it for 1991."

"Why you mad at me? What the fuck did I do? You blame me because your outta fuckin' business? You fuckin' shouldn't. You were always so pessimistic with a chip on your shoulder. You always had to put a fuckin' twist on everything."

"A twist?"

"Yeah," Lenny was shouting now. "If I said the sky was blue today, you'd say, weeellll, maybe not blue, sort of cyan; you always did that. Carl and I wanted to do everything we could for our clients, Sid. But you, baby, you always took the position it was them and us. You always had a chip on your shoulder to our clients, Sid. A lot of our brides hated you, by the way. You told them they were wrong. I spent thirty years apologizing for you. Carl was lucky; he got out and moved to Arizona. I hear his Montclair Studios in Arizona is doing quite well, even in this economy."

"You told me this bullshit, this morning," Sid shook his head sadly. "You're getting senile, Lenny. I think when you lost your hair thirty-five years ago, you lost your mind, too."

"You cannot alienate clients. It was a shame that you spent your whole career and wasted your talent doing the wrong thing. I don't know how you stayed in business so long."

Sid laughed at Lenny, then made his usual shrug.

"Carl had to balance us out, that was his job," continued, Lenny. "I ran the baby and school part, you handled the business and the hustling part, and Carl handled the portraits and the artistic part. He was the classy guy who worked with our clients, you were the candid man. For the most part, you offended the people. You offended all our colleagues. What can I tell you? You can't take morons. You have to tell other photographers when they're wrong. Because of your shit, there was a lot of good talent that did not want to shoot for us, upstairs and downstairs."

Sid sat down in the clients chair across from Lenny. He lit up a Viceroy.

"You should hear the stupid ass things some of those idiots at our photographic and video associations said. They were wrong, I tell them they are wrong. If they have a stupid idea that is wrong, I tell them, they are wrong, okay? Somebody ought to. I never say it isn't their right to be wrong. The Constitution of the United States guarantees your right to be a putz. I point out the fact they are wrong not because I *think* they are wrong, but because they *are* wrong! If they don't want me to tell them that they are wrong, they should learn the right way and think before they talk."

Lenny shook his head, "*Oy*, Sidney, Sidney, you make me crazy. All I'm saying is that we work for the clients. They are not our opponents, they are not against us. They want what is best, some want it cheaper, some trust the more expensive studios."

"Bullshit!" Sid was screaming at the top of his lungs now. "Bullshit! Bullshit! They *are* our opponents. They're against us when they call up and ask the price, and when they come in and sit down. They keep on fuckin' asking if we can do better, after we explain how much it costs for us to produce a job, how much time is involved, and that our prices for our service is bottom line. They are coming up with a reason for not using us. Jesus fuckin' Christ, Lenny, they don't say we want to use you. They fuckin' say, why the fuck should I use you? Why should we let you shoot for us? It's up to us to tell them why we should shoot their fuckin' affairs, you know that man!"

"I know it's changed, Sid. A man uses one of the prima donnas from the Five Towns or the Gold Coast up on the north shore, to do his boy's B'Mitzvah. They charge three grand for one book."

"More," Sid interjected.

"More," Lenny went on, "okay it was a beautiful job, shot by Hal Strickland from Lawrence or Ramon Roméro from Great Neck. But for the second or third kid, the man ain't gonna pay that kind of money. The big important job for the firstborn was done already. Okay, he doesn't want *el cheapo*, so he goes to a mid-level place, or an accessible high-end place like us. When he comes to us, we have to let him know we're on his side. We try to give him a nice mid-level price he can afford."

"Lenny, cut it out, you're wrong, The bastard is coming in with the attitude, that if we don't beat the price of the guy in Great Neck, who shoots just as good and does the same custom bound albums we do, he's gonna go to 'el cheapo,' or maybe his Uncle Charlie, fuck us."

"That's the way it always was," Lenny groaned, "only now it's more competitive."

"I tell you, Lenny, there is them, and there is us. They need us for the date of their affair, we can't say that to them anymore. We know how to shoot, they don't. They can have a relative shoot, bullshit. We know all the mechanics, the technique, they don't. They better be fuckin' able to afford quality photographers like us, if they don't want to go to a *shlock* package deal place or to an independent hack. We ain't gonna take one penny less. We didn't have to worry about someone walking out the door. We always ended up with the right client. We never fuckin' took one penny less, if they didn't have a photographer…" Sid shrugged; his shrug meant 'what can I tell you?'

"Today, our business is harder than ever before," Sid spoke again. "Look at the way everybody is cutting everybody's throat to book. For old candid men like us, Lenny, for us *altacockers*, it was more than a career, it was a way of life. Now look, the mid-level wedding studios are folding some high-end, too. Moonlighters are offering affordable video, we're in trouble, and we know it. What's more is the public knows it, the part-time hacks know it. Some old-timers told me they want to get out soon for other reasons. Some told me they're getting too fuckin' old to shoot. You know, guys our age, who started when we did."

Lenny said nothing; he just relit his cigar and nodded.

"Some old-timers we know didn't have any children to pass the studio on to. You know my buddy in Oceanside, he married late and he has no kids, just him and his wife. He's doin' alright, not like he used to, but he works. He told me they would like to sell the studio or at least the corporation, because they have no children. This is the beginning of the end of photography, Lenny. See all the electronic imaging and computer shit that is coming out? I'm in the business forty years. In forty years, there won't be any photography, there won't be any film, everything will be imaged on a piece of electric foil, or a computer disk. Fuck, it's here already! I saw a camera in an article. It was an electronic imaging camera. It's here, not for us old farts, who started with Speed Graphics, but it's here. Soon, Lenny, there'll be no photographers, only imagers. No more candid men, no more sitting at the P.P.G.N.Y. dinners swapping stories. Our way of life is over. Electronic imaging, watch, it's gonna be used in baby photography, too."

"Yeah, progress; some lady last week explained what paperless proofs are, where the proofs don't leave the studio. In theory, it sounds like a good idea, who knows? Not for us, we're too old for high tech shit. A lot of the younger fellows are using this at their studios, I hear. I even heard about video proofing to see how portraits will look. Big shit, Carl always used to shoot a fuckin' Polaroid."

"It was a way of life," Sid continued, "the only way of life I knew. I'm going to miss it. I don't give a fuck what anyone says, photography is an honorable profession. That's what Max Cohn always says at the association dinners, after he gets through reading the photographers prayer. He was, I think, the most honorable man in the fuckin' profession, I give him that. I loved it; I should probably sell my equipment and move to a retirement condo in Florida with Norma, but no. I love to shoot. Young people who open studios today have to learn computers and imaging. What we did was like being in Vaudeville. We were all actors, we performed our shtick, but like Vaudeville, our industry is in trouble, too. We had the good old days. I wonder if these kids, who bought out the old-timers will be able to look back on the good old days."

"Sidney, if you don't know it, I gotta tell you what helped to wreck you." Lenny stood up again. "It was the fuckin' video. You wanted to learn it and shoot it, I said fine, not with me. You pissed thousands away in video and believe me, you didn't fuckin' need it. You pissed money away on video cameras, decks, dolly carts, monitors, lights, all kinds of fuckin' bullshit equipment. You cost Carl money before he asked you to buy him out. At his place, he recommends video people; he isn't a putz who has to control everything. This fuckin' problem, I have to laugh at those poor stupid dicks. This is the fuckin' reason why clients hire a studio to shoot the stills, but they'll hire a video production company to shoot the video. People don't want to give all the money to one person. What if they think your stills suck? There were times when Carl did."

Sid held up his middle finger in mock disgust.

Lenny returned Sid's gesture.

"They should worry about the videotape you made for them, too?" Lenny wanted to continue. "I sure as hell wouldn't tie all my money up with one person for stills and video. That, I think, is too big an investment for a client. Carl said that too, years ago."

"Ah, bullshit! You're wrong," Sid imitated Lenny.

"You're wrong!" Lenny imitated Sid.

Lenny shouted again, "Ya wanna know why photographers can't always book stills and video? It's too much money to ask. That's right, even for some of the rich fucks. If you try to push the video you can lose everything. There were times when you, no we, lost everything. If you lost a sale, partner, you flushed my money down the crapper, too."

Sid just stared at Lenny without saying anything. Lenny found this refreshing.

"Man alive, daddy-o, you should have just stayed with stills, you wouldn't have to worry about the video. If you got a *photography studio*," Lenny accentuated photography studio, "you lose stills, you're up shit creek. But you're never wrong, so you don't listen."

"Good thing, Lenny, because this studio made money with video. Hey, putz!" yelled Sid, "I made a lot of money in video. We were the first studio to do video on the Island, don't hand me any crap."

"Made shmade," the putz hollered back, "you didn't need it! The video hurt us more than it helped us. Video people said they'd give us a commission for every job we referred to them. You said, 'Sorry, we do our own video, we don't work with outside video companies.' We wouldn't even book the stills if customers wanted to use another place's video. That was my money you were turning down; hey, I was your partner. You have some fuckin' nerve. You always did!"

"We made a big shitload of money doing video," Sid protested. "We always had jobs. My original tube camera looked like a car with its fenders falling off, I worked so much. I wore out an editing system in our first year of video. I made us money, as a videographer, I'm fuckin' great."

"Fuckin' asshole!" Lenny shot back. "You didn't need to get greedy on the video. Today, if you charge two grand for stills at a wedding, then ask the clients to give you another grand for the video… No way, Sidney, no fuckin' way. You can't ask people to spend another grand on top of two grand, they won't."

"Whoa, baby, we did movies, you used to shoot fuckin' movies more than you shot fuckin' stills."

"Movies were different, it was really photography, and movies were art, not bullshit electronic manipulation."

"You're entitled to your opinion, Lenny baby. What can I say, except, *cock a mun*." In Yiddish *cock a mun*, means, 'shit on you.'

"*Cock a mun* back at you, Sidney the right. Other studios have. Remember what Grandma used to say, you *nar*, 'You can't have both.' That's the way it is today, old friend. I told a new kid, if you want to be a shooter, you have to decide if you want to do stills or video. You could maybe do both if you just want to work for a studio. Shooting both makes you marketable in that respect. If you want to open your own studio, then I say it's one or the other. Try to book both, you'll get nothing."

"You don't think we were successful in video..we were successful in video. I know I was successful in video. Video jobs paid for your new fuckin' Lexus."

"Yeah, whatever you say. I don't care anymore, Sid, whatever you say."

"I'm glad you agree, Lenny."

"And, don't fuckin' give me any more crap about how you got into video because the stills were becoming too physically demanding for you. You said you'd do the video and hire people to shoot the stills. If you didn't want to work too hard, why didn't you retire, or just work in the studio and not go out, like me."

"Lenny, for the last time, I never wanted to stop shooting stills. I liked shooting stills and video. I wanted to take it easy, not stop going out. We made money offering both; that, my toupéed friend, is the end of it."

Lenny snorted, as he threw his cigar stub in the ashtray. "Yeah, you're fuckin' right, that is the end of it."

"Shit," Sid whined, "I don't wanna discuss it anymore, I'm retired."

"Yeah, you are. Let me tell you, the baby studio has been carrying the wedding studio for the last four years. Your partnership here kept you going downstairs."

"I don't agree with you, Lenny, but who the fuck cares anymore?"

"Yeah."

"I'm going home," Sid said wearily, "to my second home; for thirty years this place was my real home. Thank God Norma understood that. I'll come by next week to see your new office and to go over some things. You can tell me all your new telephone names. By then, I should know when the landlord will return our security deposits."

"Jesus," Lenny drew a breath, "after all these years."

"I'll go over all that shit next week when I see you."

"Do we have to pay Carl any security refund money?" Lenny asked.

"Fuck him!" Sid replied.

"Alright," Lenny sighed. "Sidney, good luck with your new studio location, or retirement, or whatever you want to call it."

"It's a little of both," answered Sid.

"It's a little bit of both," repeated Lenny.

"Good luck on your new office and the baby business, that's where you say the money is."

"Yeah, that's where the money is, Sidney."

Lenny extended his right hand across the desk, offering it to Sid.

Sid looked down at the letter opener on the pile of papers that Lenny had scratched his itchy ass with. He looked at Lenny's hand.

"Are you kidding? Feh!" Sid said disapprovingly and left Lenny's office.

Lorraine, a twenty year veteran secretary at Happy Time Photographers, came over to Sid. She was a fat blonde *shiksa*, but very likeable.

You boys were yelling. It sounded like the old days. You get along with your wife, your kids are out of the house, who are you going to fight with now that you don't have a partner?"

"Hee, hee," he laughed, "it's gonna be nice. I still have the bitch who takes her dog over to shit on my lawn."

"Good luck, Sid, stay in touch with us."

Sid and Lorraine hugged.

He hugged and said his goodbyes to the other four Happy Time secretaries. He took one last look at the baby studio, then went downstairs to the empty store. The vacant store had been one of the most highly recommended and regarded studios on Long Island and the Greater New York area.

As Sid Weitz walked down the steps to the studio, he heard an echo. It was the sound of emptiness.

Sid stood in the vacant store. He had butterflies in his stomach, he felt very lonely. He looked out the large front windows into the street. Some people walked by, nobody stopped to look. There wasn't anything to look at.

There was a time when passersby did stop to look. People looked at and admired the beautiful large framed photographs along with an occasional leather bound album in the window. People who lived and worked in the area waved to studio staff, they waved back. Other merchants stopped in to chat. Sid often chatted with the other merchants, sometimes had a cup of coffee with them. Other portrait or candid photographers stopped by to look in the windows when they needed inspiration, or just wanted to see what they were doing and showing.

People used to walk into the studio for passports, portraits, baby pictures, or to inquire about coverage of weddings and Bar or Bat Mitzvahs.

People brought old photographs in to be restored. Sometimes folks came in to have pictures framed or their videotapes copied. Some came to have their old home movies transferred on to video tape. This was before Sid relocated his editing equipment into his home. He knew few people, if any, would bring movies for him to transfer now. This service he offered may not be a way to make a living, it did, however, provide him with some extra pocket money. Extra money always helped, especially in recent years.

Now nobody came in or would ever come into this studio again. Not here, anyway, but somehow the new location just was not the same.

This was the end of a long career and a way of life.

Sid knew two men who were former candid men. One man works as a salesman in a camera store, the other man bought one. He did business with both of the men from time to time. They always asked how things were in the candid line.

Sid asked if they missed being shooters.

They both told him that they did not miss it. The salesman told him he was glad he was out of it, that he hated every minute of it; he said he would never go back to it. They were both good shooters, yet they were glad to be finished with it.

To some extent, that was the way Sid felt today. He used to love the business, now, he loved and hated it. He knew photographers who loved to shoot, but hated the business end. So many youngsters, who became full-time photographers, quickly learned that this business was not all fun and games and blue ribbons from print competitions.

For a lot of the ageing candid men, this was a hard business to get out of, shooting was in their blood. However, more and more people were leaving the industry, professing to not miss it.

Sid Weitz bad been self-employed for most of his career. There were times when he thought owning his own business was like driving a car on a muddy road. You drive down the road; your car gets stuck in the mud. So you try to get out, but every time you grind your wheel, you go deeper and deeper into the mud. You don't get out, you get frustrated. He knew there were times he kept getting deeper and deeper. What business owner never spent time merely spinning wheels?

He thought Lenny was wrong. It really is them and us. We have to make a living, so we need to have a certain number of bookings, with a huge batch of additional orders. The client needs a photographer, but they want to get everything they can from the photographer they hire. He knew most consumers were this way, as he too was a member of the buying public. The client wants quality…well, maybe not every client, either Jewish or Christian, wants the best studio. Sid knew, after all, everybody who had lasted for a long time, high end or low end, could be considered good. If not good, then professionally competent. Even the prima donna award-winning shooters did not shoot that way on every job. Sid knew for a fact some of his stuck-up, award-winning colleagues shot bread and butter jobs. As far as those shits were concerned, it was more myth than man. More reputation, salesmanship (or salesmanshit) than artistry. Sid knew his studio was legendary, and that reputation was well deserved, so fuck everybody else. As for the other schmucks, it was more showmanship, than competence.

Sid Weitz, his former partners Carl Resnick and Lenny Schecter, came from the old school—the school of hard knocks and Speed Graphics. When you came right down to it, the regular professionally competent candid men were the backbone of this industry. As far as that faction went, when you've seen one sample album, you've seen them all. If you happen to be a good photographer, that should not be a problem. Shit, if you were as good as Sidney Weitz, one sample album was all you needed. Most studios have the same poses in their albums as everyone else, even the studios that claim to be unique. The basic poses clients expect are both time tested and universal. Everybody shoots the same, whether a photographer claims there is an exact science or not. There is really one way to shoot a wedding or a Bar Mitzvah. As for portraiture, there are only so many, industry standard lighting techniques, yet everybody says that they are the best. How the hell can that be true? Sid Weitz was the best. He told people he was, so it must be true.

Hiring a photographer comes down to three criteria—who has the best value for the price, who you like, and who you trust. A fourth criterion might be who is in your range. If pictures look good, they look good. What the hell does the public know about judging the quality of photography? Any professional's work is going to be far more superior to a layperson's snapshots.

Clients are hard on us today, more than ever, that is a fact. Maybe they are against us because they know that they need us. Maybe photographers are necessary evils. The limo driver isn't, the band leader isn't, the tux renter isn't, but we are.

Them and us.

Us and them.

Could this be the reason why Sid's friend Harry the cop, became a photographer? Or, was it the other way around? Harry once told Sid and Carl he equated arriving at a bride's house for the family pictures, with answering a family dispute call. He never knew what to expect. It could be routine and go well, or the shit could hit the fan.

Clients today see us as adversaries; it was not quite like that in the old days. We compete with the caterer, the band, the florist, the gown manufacturer, and the jeweler for the customers' money. They spend their money on those folks, not us. Us they fight with.

The phone rings, the bride-to-be on the other end, informs us she has set her limit for the photography.

"We're lookin' for a photographer, but we don't want to spend a lot of money for pictures, ya know what I'm sayin'?"

The photographer knows what she's saying.

She wants us to give her a price she can live with, never mind how much it costs us. We know quality photography does not come cheap. They don't care, why should they? They have uncles who take nice pictures.

When a bride says this, we start out with a negative. Today, one has to be a crackerjack salesman to turn this negative into a positive—a good salesman, never mind being a good photographer. Today, when a client starts out with a 'no,' try, just try, to turn a no into a 'yes.' It is very hard.

"We don't want to spend a lot of money on pictures."

"My uncle has a good camera; he knows how to take nice pictures."

"I can get the video cheaper."

"We want a package deal, with everything thrown in—all the proofs and all the negatives."

Maybe they would like us to throw in all the equipment while we're at it? Them and us.

Us and them.

That is the way it was in this business today.

Why?

Sid supposed what an old appliance salesman told him years ago was true. When someone is on the paying end, they always get their way. The customer may not always be right, but they always get their way.

Montclair Studios had its heyday, made its mark, and left its legacy. There are only so many studios that thrive today.

In the last few years, a lot of studios closed.

In the coming years, many more studios will close. Still, life will go on. People will get married…boys and girls, Bar and Bat Mitzvahed. Families will need portraits, vacationers need passport photos. Maybe not from Montclair Studios, but from someone. As in every business, there will be survivors.

Today was the end of an era…

For Sid Weitz, the smooth veteran candid man, today was the end of a way of life. He never imagined how the last day would be. No hail and a small farewell.

When your work is complete, it is time to go.

Sid picked up the boxes and walked to the entrance of the Happy Time office.

It was time to go.

Sid stepped out onto the sidewalk and locked the door, which lead upstairs to the baby studio. He did not give a rat's ass now, if somebody broke in and burned the place down. It was just an empty store.

Sid checked the adjoining door, which was the entrance for the studio. He noticed Lenny had already removed the Happy Time Photographers sign on the wall near the office entrance. Lenny wanted to relocate, he was getting paranoid. In this neighborhood, who could blame him?

He stood back and looked at that big empty glass façade. He felt like crying, but did not. There was no point in crying now.

He thought, as he stood looking at the empty windows, *I always put up a façade. I kept my cool, most of the time. I smiled at clients when I really wanted to tell them to get the fuck out of my studio. We have to hide our feelings to be successful. We hide our feelings, not to cause those we love concern. Thank God humans don't have glass façades, just photography studios.*

Sid knew his family worried about him; rightfully so, he busted his ass for them. He had some problems, but who didn't?

He never thought that his façade was glass. He was a salesman, sometimes a psychologist, as people looked to him for support. Nervous, worrisome clients looked upon him as the voice of reason. Sid Weitz had a façade of stone. It was starting to crack and crumble in some sections, but this was due to normal wear and tear caused by age. It was a fact, when structures got older, they grew less stable.

He opened the trunk of the Chevy and put the boxes in. There was a small cardboard box, containing two Armitar strobe units with Lumedyne reflectors.

Why didn't I take them in the house he wondered? Maybe I am getting senile, he thought.

No, wait. They were left there because I did not know I was going to use Norma's car on Sunday.

So why didn't I put them in Norma's car Sunday morning?

Screw it.

He figured he was lucky that the guy who repaired the car didn't rip them off.

Inside the car he turned the air conditioner on, turned on his favorite soft FM station, which was the last of the 'dentist office' stations left.

The air conditioner was working fine.

On the radio, Tony Bennett was crooning one of his recent hits.

He shifted into drive, and drove once around the block when he noticed a parking space behind Lenny's car. He drove his Chevy Caprice towards Lenny's white Lexus, at a slow even crawl.

THUMP!

The connection was not hard enough to create a dent, just enough to produce the desired result.

The alarm on the Lexus went off—the siren wailed, the horn honked, and the headlights flashed.

"Heh, heh, heh," Sid laughed out loud, "take the letter opener out of your ass, Lenny! Come on down and turn off that goddamn alarm, it's giving me a headache."

Sid made an illegal U-turn on Elmont Road and headed to Hempstead Turnpike. He made a left, headed west toward Hempstead to Peninsula Boulevard. That street would take him home to Hewlett.

On the radio, Dionne Warwick was singing *Forever*. Sid liked that Burt Bacharach song; he remembered when it came out back in the'60s, when his studio was busy, when he bought his wife a mink coat.

Traffic was surprisingly light for a late Monday afternoon. Too early for vacations and school was still in session.

Sid Weitz was driving home, just like any suburban husband, at the end of a work day.

Chapter Nineteen

S id Weitz did not go directly home, he had some light errands to run. He pulled into a shopping center on Peninsula Boulevard, in Hewlett. As he walked to the store, he saw an altercation unfold.

A young affluent woman pulled her Porsche into a parking space reserved for the handicapped. A middle-aged man in a mid-size car took exception to her actions.

"Hey! That's parking for the handicapped, don't you know that?" he yelled out his car window.

"Fuck you!" replied, the affluent-looking young woman. Sid noticed she looked very healthy, too.

The man who felt it was his place, as a respectful citizen to chew out this horrible offender, zoomed into the parking space next to Sid's car. He swung open his door and smacked the new Chevy.

Sid ran over to inspect the damage to his car. The man stepped out of his car, glaring toward where the inconsiderate young woman was parked.

"Look at what you did!" Sid shouted as he ran over.

"Yeah, right," the man answered, "I told off little miss designer jeans. Some people are totally inconsiderate to others!"

"Yeah, tell me about it!" Sid replied angrily. There wasn't any damage to the door of the new Chevy.

Oblivious to his own actions, the considerate gentleman walked off.

Sid went into the CVS Pharmacy to pick up some toilette articles. A young mother was with her small daughter in the men's needs section. The little girl, a toddler, was opening the items on the shelf. Her mother was either unaware, or did not care.

A middle-aged female salesclerk in a red company jacket approached them.

"Please, don't let your little girl open the products; we cannot repackage them!"

"What do I care?" her mother snapped. She then picked up the little girl and walked away, offended by the clerk's rudeness.

As he attempted to pay for his purchases, an attractive woman in a denim outfit with an armload of baby items cut through the line, elbowing her way in front of Sid.

"I'm in a hurry," she justified her actions, "I have to pick someone up." She threw all the baby supplies onto the counter. "I'm late," she said, "I'll just take this." She held up a bottle of shampoo.

"Kinder, gentler nation, my ass," Sid muttered.

He drove leisurely, down Peninsula Boulevard, making a right turn onto Chesterfield Road, his street. As he drove, he was blocked by two large Mercedes Benzes—one silver, one black—he recognized the cars from the neighborhood. The cars were facing opposite directions, in the middle of the street. The two women were talking to each other.

"Fuckin' broads," he said out loud, "they stop right in the middle of the street to talk." He gently honked the horn. The Mercedes did not seem to notice the Chevy.

"Broads!" Sid said out loud. "Arrogant sluts, they park in the middle of the street and talk. They always cut in front of me on the highway, without bothering to look or signal."

He leaned on the horn this time.

The woman in the car that was facing down the street refused to yield. She stuck her hand out the window, signaling him to drive around.

He stuck his head out the window, "I can't go around, you're blocking the road, this isn't a kiddie car!"

That car moved up a bit and to the right, allowing the Chevy to pass. As he passed, the woman in the Mercedes that faced forward gave him a dirty look. He returned it.

Sid drove a short way up the curvy road, then pulled into the driveway of number 51 on the left-hand side of the street. He saw that his neighbor from across the street was walking her dog on his grass. He was forever chasing this woman, since her son brought the dog home from college. *Der Cubana Yid* was how he referred to this woman, a Cuban born Jew, who had lived on the block for twenty years. He had nothing against the Labrador retriever, he just did not want to clean up his shit.

He jumped out of the car and ran up to her. His neighbor, Isabel Kofsky, stood on the side lawn without a pooper scooper. Even with a pooper scooper, people should take their dogs to shit in the street, not on someone else's lawn.

"Hey, please!" called out the photographer to his neighbor. Although she was about fifty, she looked as if she was in her early thirties. "Please don't let him make on my lawn." The dog looked up, wagged his tail, and kissed Sid's hand.

"Leesing," Isabel replied in her thick accent, "he haba to go. So, I take heen pora walk. But we no make nuthin' on jour grass."

"You always bring him over here, for Christ's sake! Walk the dog in the street and carry a pooper scooper! Look!" He pointed to the ground, "Look, that's his crap!"

"Those are esteeks from a thee trees. We no make on jour grass, jou jused to haba beeg dog, he jused to barak all a thee tine. All a thee tine, all a thee tine, I here a heen barak."

"We *had* a dog, sweetheart, from 1970 when you were still on your first husband, until 1983. He only used to bark when your kids ran on my front lawn. We never took her to crap on your property."

The dog licked Sid's hand once more.

"I walk a thee dog, but he no make here!" She walked away.

Sid watched her walk away in her tight white jogging suit. *Nice*, he thought, *a nasty bitch, but nice.*

"Keep your damn dog off my grass, or I'll call the cops!" he yelled, after her. "They have a special 'shit squad' out here; they crack down on people like you! Any more crap over here, I'll sue! And keep your kids off my lawn, too!"

Her kids were out of the house.

"Hey, Sid," a familiar female voice called out.

It belonged to Shannon, his letter carrier. She was an attractive, voluptuous, thirty-something-year-old woman. She walked across the street to him. She had reddish brown hair worn in a shoulder length perm and brown eyes, which she always hid with mirrored sunglasses. She was wearing her summer uniform, grey shorts with a United States Postal Service tank top. Sid loved it when she wore the tank top; she had the chest for it. Everyone on her route liked her, especially the men. She was friendly and a bit of a flirt, although she had been married for over a decade. She was known for feeding the stray cats along her route.

"Hey, Shannon," he turned around, "why so late today?"

"I was in court today, at Tina's husband's sentencing. The judge sentenced him to life, the bastard."

Tina was a clerk who worked at the local post office. She was a beautiful, perky, petite brunette, who was well liked by all of her customers. Last year, her husband beat her to death in a jealous rage. Although, she lived several towns away, her death affected the town in which she worked.

Sid knew Tina professionally; she was his favorite clerk. Often, he shipped photographs to the bindery from his local post office. Once, she dropped a box of photographs, and he kidded her about ruining somebody's entire wedding. She thought he was serious. She apologized profusely. He told her was joking. She was very sweet to deal with, and she was very efficient in handling Sid's business mail. She knew he was a photographer, but did not approach him when she became engaged. This was just as well; he could not deal with the heartache of having a bride who was brutally murdered, especially by her own husband. He would have never been able to look at those negatives again. It is a lousy feeling for a photographer, who records a groom's promise to love, honor, and cherish his bride, in the sight of god, family, and friends, then beats her to death. Murdering your spouse is a hell of a way to honor, until death do us part. Sid had friends in the business that lost clients to tragic deaths. So far, his studio had not been touched by tragedy.

"Life, good!" Sid replied, "I hope he meets a lot of interesting new friends in the shower."

"I wanted to thank you, Sid, for all those frames and picture folders you left out for me last week."

"My pleasure, Shannon. I had a lot of good stuff at the studio. I closed it, and I didn't want to throw it out. It was top quality stuff, so I thought you might like it."

"I do, thank you so much. I didn't know you ten years ago; I should have used you for my wedding."

"Ignorance is not an excuse, honey. You should have used me, but I don't think you could have afforded me."

"You're probably right. So, you're retired now."

"No," he lied, "I closed up the studio because I don't need such a big expense anymore. I'm sixty; I want to take it easy. I don't work during the day that much. I just shoot candids now, when I work. I'll be working out of the house here. You may see an increased volume of mail here, as I had everything from the studio forwarded to the house."

"Oh, no problem, Sid," Shannon replied. She was a nice kid.

"How is your album holding up?"

Sid sent Shannon's wedding album into the bindery last summer for an emergency repair. Her dog teethed on a page, but since the studio was out of business, the negative was not available. The dog's damage was not great, so a repair was made, and the album was as good as new.

"It's holding up great. I'll see you tomorrow, I guess, take care, Sid."

"You too, beautiful, see you."

Shannon continued on her route.

Sid went into the house, carrying boxes of stuff from the studio. He walked into the kitchen. Norma was home, she poured him a glass of home-brewed iced tea.

"Thanks, hon."

"You're welcome. So, how did it go today? How's Lenny?"

"It went like the last day, and Lenny's disgusting."

"What happened, love?"

"Lenny stuck a letter opener up his *tokus*."

Norma spluttered the iced tea she was drinking, and she turned around to spit into the sink.

"What did he do that for?" she asked.

Sid sat down on a kitchen chair at their rectangular table.

"I dunno," he shrugged, "I dunno, I dared him."

"You did not." Norma said, matter-of-factly, standing at the sink.

"Maybe that was the only part of his body he could stick it in. Can we change the subject?"

"I didn't bring it up, honey bunny, you did."

"So, now I wanna drop it. I left the mail in the foyer. Shannon came late today, she was in court. They sentenced Tina's husband today to life, *L'chaim!*" He raised his glass to toast the sentence.

"Good," Norma replied, "I hope he meets some interesting new friends in the metal shop."

"In the shower," he corrected her.

"You going to the association dinner tomorrow night?" she asked.

"I wasn't planning to, but why not? It's been a while, I'll put in an appearance and say hello to all the schmucks. You wanna come with me?"

Norma paused, thought it over, and then shook her head 'no.'

"Maybe next time," she said.

"I'm tired."

"Take it easy, love," she said, "go rest."

"I'll need all the rest I can get. I'm gonna have to fly or drive to Boston now, whenever I want to see my grandchildren."

"Steven is thinking of taking a pediatric position in Atlanta next year, in Georgia."

"I, I, I know where Atlanta is!" Sid sounded exasperated, "I, I made it through high school."

"He thinks it could be good for them."

"Great," Sid gestured upwards, "now I can fly between Boston and Atlanta to see our children. We won't even have to unpack our suitcases."

"Sid, it's not like we can't do that now."

"I suppose." He finished his iced tea, handed her the empty glass, and with a courtly bow, said, "And now, madam, if there shan't be anything else, I shall take my leave. I have to move my geriatric bowels."

"If you're going to use the one in our bedroom, I kept the seat warm for you."

"Oh, then I'll use the one in the hallway."

Norma made a face; Sid smiled and left the room.

Sid locked the door, pulled down his shorts and undershorts, and sat down on the toilet.

"Ahhh, sanctuary at last."

Chapter Twenty

While Sid Weitz sat on his toilet in Hewlett, New York, plopping away his troubles, a successful portrait wedding studio functioned in Phoenix, Arizona.

Montclair Studios of Phoenix, Arizona, was thriving. Business was just a bit slow, due to the economy. Granted, the studio was not as busy as it had been during the go, go eighties, but just the same, there was a steady flow of business.

The Montclair Studios of Phoenix was run by Sid Weitz's former partner Carl Resnick, his wife, Cynthia, and their son Jordan. Jordan Resnick was the Resnick family's third generation photographer. Carl was the second, and Carl's father, Heinz, was the first.

Heinz Resnick, who people said looked more like a math professor than a photographer, was born in Berlin, Germany. He moved to the United States as a young boy with most of the Resnick family. His mother's family came over early, as well. Most of his family did *not* perish in the holocaust. They considered themselves among the lucky.

Heinz Resnick, Carl's father, now ninety-five, lived in a retirement condominium in Phoenix. A widower for five years, he had been retired from the photography business since 1975. He just decided he was too old at that stage in his life to shoot. He was proud that his son Carl and grandson Jordan carried on his craft. He was also proud that Carl's daughter Marra was good at being a trial lawyer. Heinz had a daughter, who had three children, and he was proud of what they had accomplished in their careers. He visited his son's studio twice a week, but only as an observer, never as a photographer; he enjoyed his retirement too much to work.

After apprenticing as a photographer, Heinz opened a photography studio in the early 1930s in the Bronx. His cousin Josef Wexler was his partner. Until they closed the studio in 1970 because their area became high crime,

Resnick/Wexler Photographers located on the Grand Concourse, was one of the most renowned photography studios in the Bronx and beyond.

Carl learned well from Heinz and Josef, but ended up going into a partnership with two young men he knew from shooting part time for a baby studio in Brooklyn.

Carl's Long Island studio was beautiful Heinz thought. He could have done better in his selection of partners; those two chaps, Sidney Weitz and Leonard Schecter, came across as vulgar and somewhat corrupt. Sidney photographed nice candids, his movies were adequate, and his portraiture passable, but not of Carl's quality. Heinz assessed Leonard as a good movie photographer, his baby portraits were very good, and his candids adequate; his studio portraits were, however, *dreck*. He told Carl not to let Leonard take any studio portraits. Sid and Carl made sure Lenny seldom did.

In 1971, Heinz Resnick photographed a few portraits, weddings, and Bar Mitzvahs for his son's studio. He did not care very much for Lenny or Sid, especially Sid, who could say the 'F' word one hundred times a day. Who could take such a lowlife, what kind of parents did such a boy have? Heinz met Norma, Sid's wife. He did not feel sorry for her, a Jewish girl married to such *shlub*. He figured, if Norma married Sid, she probably was not any bargain either.

After eleven years of partnership, Carl and Cynthia decided to move to Arizona, they liked the dry warm climate. Carl asked Sid to buy him out. Sid bought him out without any problem, although he was very surprised at his partner's decision. Heinz was happy that his son did not have to work with such a lowlife any longer.

Heinz gave Carl all of his equipment, except for the Hasselblads purchased back in the seventies, the stuff was old. Carl did not use the older equipment these days, but he kept it with pride, showing it off to friends and family. Heinz and his wife followed their son to Phoenix and they enjoyed living there, the climate of Arizona was more agreeable to them than the climate of Florida. When Sara Resnick died three years ago, Heinz walked into the condo and found her lying on the kitchen floor; the entire family flew back to New York for the funeral. The Resnick family maintained a plot in a Jewish cemetery in the Midwood section of Brooklyn.

Heinz received his son's former partners with their wives. When Carl entered the lobby of the Garfine Brothers Funeral Home in Brighton Beach, Brooklyn, Heinz thought he was going to join his wife. Sidney Weitz, dressed in a navy blue three-piece suit, went up to Carl. With a lit cigarette in his left hand, he offered Carl his right hand.

"Carl," Sid called out, "Carl, baby, sorry about your mom, *bubie*."

"Good to see you, Sid, thank you so much for coming," Carl tried to sound sincere. He moved away from him quickly, kissed Norma Weitz and Sherry Schecter, and shook hands with Lenny. He then darted off to see other friends and relatives and get away from 'Mr. Couth.'

Heinz knew those two morons' success was owed to his talented son. He was happy for his son's prosperity in Arizona, and was glad he was far from those lowlifes.

When Carl Resnick opened his Phoenix studio, he was still legally a partner in the Montclair Corporation. He used the name of Montclair Studios. Since he did not have a conflict in the state of Arizona, he planned on using that name anyway. The price he got for weddings and, yes, Bar and Bat Mitzvahs, were comparable to the high-end prices on Long Island.

Carl ran the studio and, at the age of fifty-five, he still photographed a fair amount of jobs himself. His son Jordan, daughter-in-law Karen, and four other people—three men and one woman—photographed portraits and candids for him. Carl did not offer video at the studio; he referred clients to a videographer. In return, the videographer paid Carl a commission and worked rather well with his studio staff on jobs. He knew Sid did well with video in New York, and the video added to Sid's legend. Video was, however, too much of an expense for him; he believed video detracted from his photography. Both he and Lenny told Sid they could have done without the video, but as usual, 'Sidney the Right,' had his way. And Sid said, "Let there be video...."

His wife of thirty-five years, Cynthia, managed the studio and acted as the receptionist. When Carl first met her as a teenager growing up in the Bronx, her name was Henrietta Bronstein; however, Henrietta liked the name Cynthia better, it sounded classy. Since the name change, she was always Cynthia—not Cindy, not Cyn—it was Cynthia. She cringed when Sid used to address her as "Cindy baby."

How a beautiful girl like Norma could put up with such a turd, was something Cynthia could not understand.

When they were in partnership with Sid, Cynthia was fond of telling friends in the trade, "Carl has class, all of it high, and Sid has class, all of it low." Lenny, she did not even care to think about. His wife, Sherry, was equally crass and uncouth.

Cynthia often described Carl and Sid as "The Odd Couple," they played off one another to the advantage of the business. It has been said that opposites attract, the marriage of Ted Turner and Jane Fonda, pretty much proved that theory. They're being opposites, in a way, was responsible for the studio's success. Cynthia found Sid repelling; she hoped that did not mean that they were not opposites.

Carl was the elegant photographic artist. Sid was the smooth talking hustler. Lenny was the movie supervisor and manager of the baby studio; he liked working upstairs, which was alright with both Sid and Carl. Carl was a portrait artist. Photographers would come to see Carl's work in the window display. As a portrait photographer, Sid could not touch him. To this day, the portraits on display at the studio were Carl's. Perhaps, Carl was the legend, Sid was the myth. Sid handled the business aspects of the studio's operation. Cynthia acknowledged that Sid had a good head for business, not that Carl was lacking. This was the way everything worked out. Sid was a good candid photographer, but Carl was better. His wedding, Bar Mitzvah, and portrait work won awards. The truth was, while Carl was over there, he was the main attraction at the studio. Most of the success for which Sid took credit, was attributed to Carl's artistry. Carl had a big high-end following, and Sid was too wrapped up in himself to see that.

Carl was a better customer service representative than Sid. At night, after hours, Carl drove around servicing the clients all over the Island, Brooklyn, Manhattan, everywhere. Sid sat on his arse in his private office at the studio, playing big shot, counting the money.

The Resnicks and the Weitzes socialized minimally. Cynthia wanted it that way, because she did not think it was a good idea for partners' spouses to be involved with each other. Cynthia thought it was a good idea to keep socializing to a minimum, because her poor Carl had to see Sid every day. Sid was a bit different when they socialized. He could be charming when he wanted to be. Sid could talk about almost any subject, and usually did. He was also a good storyteller and could be very funny, at times.

Carl had rough times, on occasion, carrying his two low-class partners. Sid had to put Carl down if he did not agree with him. He put everybody down to hide his own failings and insecurities.

One morning upstairs in the baby studio, Sid started up with Lenny over who knew what. Carl was upstairs doing some paperwork. He approached Sid with a technical idea he had. Sid disagreed; in fact, he really gave it to Carl, calling him a schmuck in front of the entire office staff. After Sid left the office, Carl stood there burning with anger and a wounded pride.

"One day," Carl said burning with rage, "one day, I am just going to tell that man, to, to, just fuck!"

The office staff sat silently in shock. It was a shock reminiscent of when Clark Gable used the word damn in *Gone with the Wind*.

With more pride than embarrassment for venting his anger, Carl turned to the office staff. "I bet you didn't think I knew that word!" he said, then stormed out of the office.

After Sid decided to incorporate video, Carl decided enough was enough, or as they say in Yiddish, *genug shoin*! He did not tell Sid to fuck. He asked him to buy him out, and Sid agreed. He told Sid he was moving to Phoenix, Arizona. Sid could not understand why; why would a classy Jewish man like Carl want to move to a place full of gun toting *goyim*, rattlesnakes, and Barry Goldwater?

Sid paid Carl off with a weekly check. Cynthia and Carl agreed that their business dealings with Sid were honorable.

When the Resnicks first moved out to Phoenix, they called the studio Montclair West. They told clients that they used to be partners with a studio on Long Island, which they called Montclair East. They told clients that they were no longer associated with the Montclair East Studio. They did, however, refer New York relatives of their Arizona clients to Montclair East. Some former Long Islanders who were transplanted to Phoenix remembered Carl's

Long Island studio. Sid referred relatives of his Long Island clients to Montclair West. There did not seem to be any hard feelings toward one another. Still, Carl was happy to be far away from Sid.

Carl's thirty-year-old, third generation photographer son Jordan, held Sid in higher contempt than did his father. Lenny was a jerk, a real low womanizing amoral smoothie. As far as Sid was concerned, Jordan thought he was an animal altogether—his insults, put downs, arrogance, temper, and foul mouth—all those qualities added up to Sid Weitz. Jordan found nothing at all charming about Sid.

When Jordan was a lighting assistant for his father and trainee photographer, he had a lot of exposure to Sid. Jordan was a very good impressionist since childhood. He started doing imitations of Sid. Everyone connected with the trade loved it. At association dinners, other photographers came over to him.

"Do Sid, do Sid!" they begged.

Jordan was always happy to oblige. He made his face take on Sid's expressions, and turned his youthful voice into Sid's. He sounded like Sid, speaking in a gravelly, George Burns/Humphrey Bogart accent.

"Harvey, Harvey, fuck you, Harvey!" Jordan said to the photographer who asked for the impression. "How are your balls? *Oy*, had dis wedding last noight, da band troid to give me shit. So oy told the fuckin' band, 'Oy don't give a shhhiiittt, where ya hafta set up, oym takin' moy fuckin' pictures right here.'"

"You sound just like Sid!" they exclaimed. "My God, Carl's son sounds just like Sid."

He was told his impression of Sid was uncanny, but warned not to do it in front of the *ferbissen*, he might kill him.

Jordan did the impression of Sid while pretending to smoke the ever present cigarette Sid always carried. He made all of Sid's facial expressions, shrugs, and body movements. Jordan was happy to be far away from Sid, too.

The Phoenix Montclair Studio was located on a busy main street in the heart of the city. It had a large glass façade, for people to see the artistic displays as they passed by.

Carl Resnick, an elegant man of fifty–five, finished a portrait session of a young woman and her three-year-old daughter.

Carl was five foot nine, had neatly coiffed, thick gray hair. A thin mustache highlighted his face. He wore a black Alan Stewart pullover shirt he had picked up in Florida. gray Docker pants, and gray pigskin loafers rounded out the day's wardrobe selection.

"Alright then, Jill, your previews should be ready next week. We really must get your husband in here one of these days; I have not seen him since the wedding."

Carl Resnick was born in the Bronx, but he did not speak with a Bronx accent. He practiced elocution as a young man. He spoke with an artistic sounding elegant voice. Both Sid and Lenny kidded him about the way he spoke. They said he sounded like a "fag."

Carl was not gay, far from it. He just sounded that way…that was the way all artists were supposed to sound. Carl seldom looked at women, because he found the right one thirty-seven years ago. He dearly loved his Cynthia. Carl truly believed that behind every great man, stood a great woman.

"I will try to get Tom in for a portrait; I want one of him."

Cynthia, seated at the desk in the reception area, took care of the young lady's deposit.

The young lady and Carl thanked each other. He opened the front door for her as she left. The man was class all the way.

Cynthia Resnick, the former Henrietta Bronstein, smiled at her portrait artist husband. She looked as radiant as ever. He met her at New York University—he was an art major, she an education student. Carl was the only partner who had a college degree. Two, for that matter, he held a bachelor of arts and a master's of arts degree. Cynthia also held an undergraduate and graduate degree. Lenny dropped out of high school to take baby pictures and shoot candids. He used to joke, they kicked him out of Erasmus High when he turned thirty-five. Sid claimed to be a high school graduate, and although Carl never saw Sid's diploma, he gave him the benefit of a doubt.

Cynthia had black hair with gray highlights, worn up. She was wearing a gray mid-length skirt with a matching jacket and pink blouse. She always dressed conservatively at the studio. She was very pretty in a demure sort of way. She was also fifty-five, but managed to look a decade younger.

"I was talking to Heshy Adomovich yesterday," Carl informed Cynthia. "He's still in Oceanside, but wants to retire. Heshy told me Sid finally closed the studio. He and Lenny dissolved their partnership. Old Sid is going to be like a fish out of water, even working from his house, if he gets work."

"Poor Norma," Cynthia said, "she needs him home all day like Bush needs Quayle. Why don't you call Sid up, Carl? See what he is doing."

"Frankly, I don't care what that primitive 'vulgarian' is doing, I simply don't care."

"Are you not interested in what he is doing now?"

"In what he's doing? He could be sitting on the commode right now, for all I care. Heshy told me what that wolverine has been telling all our friends!"

"What is Sid saying now?"

"He told everybody that I'm senile. He says I sit around my house and I don't know where I'm at?"

"Oh, Carl, you cannot pay attention to anything he says."

"I should thank him for doing the industry a favor by retiring. Anyhoo, Heshy told me things are not going all that well on Long Island. So many of the established people are retiring. Heshy told me there was a palace coupé at the Lawrence Studio. The two Hal's sued each other over God knows what and dissolved the partnership."

"Oh, God, I thought they were so successful."

"They were quite successful, creative, and innovative. They were also very greedy; mix that with big egos, and it is a bad chemical reaction, a combustion, if you will. Sid was that way. I have no desire at all to speak to him. If he and Norma, whom I like, were to come out to Arizona on a trip, perhaps, but I would require an adequate supply of Alka Seltzer."

"What else is new on the Island?" Cynthia asked.

"Franklin Malkin closed last year. I asked Heshy if his son still urinates in public."

"Does he?"

"No, which surprises me, because he was so much like his degenerate, pornographer father."

"Darling, you were one of the few elegant men in the business. Sid was, as our grandson says, a *scuzz*. But you played them off against each other and it worked. We were the envy of so many studio owners, because our phone always rang, and we all drove Cadillacs or Lincolns. Sid was a brilliant businessman and a good closer. He did have a good head for business, not that you did not, Carl. However, you were the true artist over there, and he knew that. I think Sid resented your talent, which is why he called you putz and schmuck."

"And 'F.'"

"And 'F,' he could not deal with the fact that you were so much better as a photographer, even back in the old days when you shot with a single light. You were the main attraction at the studio, everybody said, "Montclair Studios, oh, yes, Carl Resnick and Sid Wietz." She accentuated *'and'* after her husband's name. Sid was a character, people got a kick out of him, but were really not in love with him."

"You're right, darling, you're right. I tell people, to this day, I was not Sid Weitz's partner, he was *my* partner." Carl accentuated the word, *'my.'* "He was just a baby photographer and a candid man with a Speed Graphic and a dark suit."

"I do not think that Sid did all that well after you left, in spite of what he claimed, even with his precious video. You are a success; he is a has been. You are a class act; he is a *shlub*, probabaly born that way. Perhaps, Carl, it is time to bury the hatchet. After all, his names could not hurt you; you are so much better than he is."

"Yes, Cynthia, perhaps you are right. Perhaps, next week I shall call the wolverine, if only to tell him how well I am doing."

"You have every right to tell him of your prosperity."

"Damn right, Cynthia, damn right and balls! Also, I'll tell him, Heshy Adomovich told me Steven married outside the faith, our children did not. Let me aggravate him and make him uncomfortable."

"He has some zings coming to him, the moron."

"I think I shall enjoy talking to him, somehow. Perhaps one day, the wolverine will come to Phoenix. I should like him to see the way a photography studio should be."

Chapter Twenty-One

Tuesday morning started out dull for Sid Weitz. He did not have to drive to work anymore, he just had to fight the traffic to get into his office off the den; he already set up his basement as an editing suite and stockroom. He did not have any work to do in the office in his house. No paperwork, no editing videotapes, no editing proofs, and no cropping negatives for printing. He had no appointments that day. Norma left for work, and he was bored because neither the business phone nor the unlisted home phone rang. Tonight, he was going to his photography association dinner.

Two hundred thirty bucks a year for membership was getting too steep for him. He planned to apply for retired, or lifetime membership status, why not? He was old enough for retirement; he had been in the business a lifetime.

At ten-thirty A.M., Sid went out to get the mail. He was wearing a pair of denim shorts, a green tee shirt, white sweat socks, and his blue Kmart sneakers.

Shannon, his letter carrier, had just arrived. Sid was a bit disappointed, as she bounced up the front steps. She was not wearing the tank top today. She was wearing a plain light blue tee shirt that outlined her youthful breasts.

"Hi, Sid, how you doin'?"

"Hi, beautiful, I'm still alive."

"Oh, stop, do you want me to put the mail in the box, or from now on, do you want me to put the mall at the side door, by your office?"

"Nothing has changed, put it in the box. I installed this package box underneath, last month."

"I noticed it."

Shannon was wearing her mirrored sunglasses. Sid hated talking to people in those things. He liked to make eye contact with people.

"That's really for UPS, they ship my albums. If you ever have a heavy package, get me, I'll carry it up."

"Oh, Sid, that's alright, I need the exercise."

No you don't, Shannon, you're *zaftig*, leave yourself alone. I just don't want you to lift something that might be too heavy for you."

"So, how do you like your first day of retirement?" she asked.

"I'm not retired; I work out my house now, but I'm not retired. I wish everyone would stop saying I'm retired. By the way, has anyone ever told you that you do a great Rosie O'Donnell impression?" Shannon sounded just like the comedic actress, but it was not an impression, she really sounded that way.

"A few people told me that," she laughed. "Here's your mail." She stood very close as she handed Sid the mail, and he did not mind.

The mail was mostly bills and advertisements that would be tossed in the garbage.

"Thank you."

"You're welcome," she replied, "have a good day, Sid."

"You too, kid."

Sid watched Shannon jiggle down the steps on her way.

He went back into the house. Their seven-year-old gray striped cat Plucky, was sitting on the small table by the entranceway, waiting for him. Plucky always waited by the door when the knob was turned, she also ran to the phone whenever it rang.

"You're cute," he said looking into her green eyes.

She meowed at him, then extended her nose upward, and he extended his nose downward, until both noses touched.

"Now leave me alone, Plucky, I have things to do."

Sid spent the remainder of the day throwing out old negatives and old albums he should have thrown out a long time ago. Some studios keep negatives forever. Some throw the negatives out after five years, if they have not received an order from the clients. He also threw out some old proofs that he found. The proofs were from the days when Sid did not include the proofs with the coverage. Initially, he was not happy when studios started to include proofs with the albums. This decreased sales of additional photographs. Large proofs were also a problem. Sid's preview photographs were $3^{1/2}$x5 size; the larger 5x5 size, cost the studio orders for extra prints.

When Norma came home, he had already showered and changed for his dinner meeting. He wore beige gabardine slacks and a white short-sleeve dress shirt made from a satin-like material. He wore a dark brown sports jacket over it, without a tie. He was also wearing, oxblood colored loafers and beige socks.

Norma had dinner by herself after Sid left. She wanted him to get out and enjoy himself. She just hoped that he would not be depressed by the other photographers who were doing well. Most of the tales of well doing were bullshit anyway, he told her. She also hoped that he would not pick on anyone tonight. She told him to be nice to his friends, but he told her that nice is for eulogies.

Sid drove the Chevy, which was still running well as a new car should, from Hewlett to West Hempstead. The Association of Professional

Photographers of Greater New York had their meetings at Gustav's for the past six years.

Gustav's Old World Restaurant was a German restaurant with catering facilities. He had photographed several affairs there through the years. Gustav's advertised as "The Home of the World Famous German Prime Rib." The food was good, although sometimes on the heavy side. Sid liked German food, it was Germans he hated. The owner of the restaurant, a flabby fifty-ish man, Gunther, asked Sid once if he wanted to try his German apple cake. He told Sid that this delicacy was baked in an old-fashioned German oven. Sid replied that some of his relatives were also baked in one.

Gustav's was on a side street off Jericho Turnpike. He found a parking space in front. Upon entering the restaurant, he noticed they had a good crowd for a Tuesday night. He walked upstairs to the banquet room, where the dinner meetings were held. An association board member was handing out tickets for the door prizes, checking the membership list, and another was filling out nametags. Sid said hello to the men, though he did not know either one very well. He paid his twenty-five dollars for dinner, on top of the two hundred twenty-five dollars a year. He was a little pissed about the dues. Some of these people made every single meeting of the year. He assumed they were all working. He wished the 'krauts' would have a decent dessert tonight, for a change. A nice Bavarian cream pie, a Black Forrest or a German chocolate cake, or one of their ice cream parfaits, and not too stingy on the salad serving tonight. He hoped, tonight, there wouldn't be any apple pie for desert—twenty-five dollars for dinner, a meager salad serving, and apple pie for dessert, what a gyp. He really hated that shitty apple pie, but his mouth watered with anticipation of a plate of succulent German prime rib.

Ramon Roméro, the Argentinean boy wonder, walked past with his latest conquest on his arm. Ramon, in Sid's opinion, was something else. He was a partner with Gordon Liebmann of Liebmann Royce Photographers in Manhasset. He was born a master photographer and Casanova. Sid knew the story of how Ramon maneuvered his first wife out of alimony, so he could marry his current love interest. When he got tired of the second wife, he dumped her, too. He met this very attractive young Jewish woman. She looked like she was too smart for Ramon; she looked like she was divorce literate. Sid laughed at himself about that. He guessed she had a good lawyer to call when her restless tom cat once again begins to prowl.

Ramon and Sid walked toward each other, and they shook hands. Ramon was a six foot tall, handsome, Latin leading man type. He was believed to be in his fifties, and his jet black hair was now medium brown, an indication of a dye job.

"Haloo, Eseed," Ramon still sounding like he just got off of the boat, greeted his old friend, "I a no esee jou por a berry lon' tine, whoa hoppen?"

"Same old shit, Ramon, *mucho mierda*. I see you brought your new wife; man, you're not that much younger than me."

"Jou met a Allison las' tine?"

"Yes, she's very attractive and very young."

"Oh, jess," Ramon grinned with pride, "jung, I a like a my whemmen jung, eet keeps me jung. Her moother an' her fathre, no like a me so much. I know you don' haba thee estudio any a morea. Jou worka froom jour house now?"

"I got tired of all the fuckin' rent, Ramon. I wanna take it easy now. Besides, I wanted to take a few adult education courses. I was thinking about a pastry baking class, or a course in computers. The only problem is the class I'm interested in takes place on Tuesday nights, which would preclude my coming to meetings."

"Well, Eseed," Ramon replied, "liseng, eefa jou wanna take eet isy why nod? Jou woraka hard, jou can a relax now. I'll a talk a to jou later, I'm a gonna go watch a my wife," he said with a wink.

"I think your wife better watch *a jou, amigo,*" Sid retorted.

Ramon Roméro winked again and walked off.

Sid felt a heavy arm around his shoulder.

"Shidney," he heard a familiar voice, "where have ya been?"

The voice sounded familiar, yet, very different, so when Sid turned his head to the left, he was shocked. The man who had his arm around his shoulder appeared to be an old friend, Abe Susskind, owner of The Roslyn Studio. Abe and Sid had known each other since the mid-1950s. They shot a few jobs for each other years ago. Sid's Montclair Studios and Abe's Roslyn Studio were comparable in price and quality.

"Abe, what happened?"

Abe Susskind was a burly man slightly taller than Sid. His bushy hair was dark, even though he was sixty-four. He had a big beak of a nose, so he was often told he looked like the star of the television show *Taxi*. He was one of the best photographers in the business. In the '50s and '60s, Abe Susskind was an innovator. His methods modernized candid photography. He perfected the double lighting method, and he was the first photographer on Long Island to use a second light on location. His methods are still in use today by photographers all over the country.

Abe Susskind removed his arm from around Sid's shoulder and turned to face him with some effort. "Oh, Shidney, I hadda shtroke; it washn't a bad shtroke, but still," Abe shrugged.

"*Oy vay*, Abe, I didn't know, when?"

"Two months ago. I wash shopping in the shupermarket; I went to the courteshy deshk to ashk a queshtion. I tried to talk, but I shaid, ahhh, wah, wah, wah, waaahhh?"

Abe sounded like a trombone when he said that. The stroke did affect Abe's speech, that was obvious.

"So I realized I had a shtroke, I checked out, got in the car, drove home, put away the grosheries, got my wife, and drove to the hoshpital."

"Jesus, I'm sorry to hear this, Abe."

"Thank you. Before I got shick, did you get my meshage? I ran into, your neighbor, Bill Kelly, the lawyer."

"*Oy*, yeah, Bill told me he saw Abe Susskind at the marina having work on his boat, Abe says 'fuck you.'"

"No, no, no," Abe shook his bushy head, "I told Bill, 'When you *shee* Shid Weitz, your neighbor, tell him that Abe Shushkind shaysh fuck you, with love.'"

"That's something you would say; right back at you. How's Anita?"

"Feeling better, thank God, the operation worked out for her. Now I'm the one who's shick. I shold the building. I heard you closhed the shtudio. Lishen, I didn't need shuch a big overhead, anymore either, at my age."

"Abe, are you going to retire now?"

"Yesh and no, Shid; I can't shoot anymore, I'm not well enough. I can't lift things; I can't move my arms up very high. Alsho my shpeech was affected. I'm afraid that shome drunk will come over to me at an affair and ashk, why do you talk sho funny, what are you, retarded?"

"You worked enough, Abe."

"Enough and too long, but I'm downshizing, as they shay, on the newsh today, I'm not out, yet. I'm gonna shell the corporation to this young man, who shoots for me. I am going to keep a hand in it. I can take portraits, sho that's what I plan to do in my house. I moved a cushtom lab into the housh, machines and everything. I can shtill print, sho I'll do cushtom printing for shtudios and for competition prints. I'll work."

Phil Fruend, the owner of Celebrity Photographers in Bayside, Queens, lumbered over. Phil, also a member of the trade's old guard, was downsized, he gave up his studio, but not just due to the economy, he broke up with his partner, his daughter Marcia; he suspected her and her husband of stealing money from the business. Phil told Marcia, after numerous discrepancies, that he was going to control the money. By the end of the day, Marcia had moved equipment out of the studio and Phil found the ledger book in a wastepaper basket. He and his daughter dissolved their partnership and sued each other for a large sum of money.

"Hi, Abe, you look good."

"I feel good, thank God," Abe answered Phil.

"Sid, I hear you're gonna be a grandpa again, *mazel tov*.

"Thanks, Phil, yeah this time girls, they say—both my daughter and daughter-in-law."

"I don't think Marcia is ever going to give me grandchildren; lawsuits, yes, grandchildren, never."

Phil Fruend was also a burly man about Sid's height. He had short gray hair, parted on the left, and combed to the side. He also had a large nose, on which thick eyeglasses rested. He too was an excellent, award-winning photographer. He knew Sid from business, but they were acquaintances, not friends. Sid did not care about Phil one way or the other. Sid once told another photographer, "Phil Fruend is a schmuck with a big nose, and when he works, his nose gets in his way." Sid often complimented people this way.

As they were standing there, Phil's thirty-three year-old daughter entered the hall with her husband. Marcia Fruend Faulkner was a blonde woman, who looked a bit like Phil. She wore her trademark red beret and long skirt. She acknowledged old family friend, Abe Susskind, with a nod, and nodded at Sid, walking past her own father without an acknowledgement.

"Hey," Phil called out to her, "you don't know your own father!" Embarrassed, Marcia turned around. She mumbled something about not knowing that her father was going to be here. She asked who brought him.

Marcia's husband, Baxter Faulkner III, stopped in his tracks. He was a tall blonde, very wealthy-looking young W.A.S.P. He glared at Phil, and Phil looked as if he was going to hit him.

"Shit, Phil, take it eashy, don't yell," Abe admonished his friend.

"Excuse me, Abe," Phil turned to face his friend. In a firm voice, he said, "You always used to yell about everything. You always yelled at your studio, and you're telling me I shouldn't yell?"

"That's it!" Abe Susskind threw his hands up in the air as far as he was able. "I gotta take a shit, talk to you later, Shid." Abe Susskind left the room quickly.

"You robbed me, you both stole from me!"

Max Cohn, a past association president and industry legend ran over.

He was a six foot two, well-built, seventy-two year-old man. Max looked scholarly, with his brushed back white hair, neat mustache, and metal-framed glasses. He had heart problems, so he did not need excitement like this.

"Phil, we don't discuss these things here!" he reprimanded his old friend.

"Why did you steal from me, your own father?" Phil ignored Max. He turned to his son-in-law Baxter, "Why don't you steal from your grandfather? He's a millionaire!"

Jerry Silber, the current president of the association and member of the new guard of photographers, was a tall, balding, thirty-something year old, who wore his chestnut-colored hair in an Art Garfunkel hairstyle, came over when it looked like Phil was going to take a swing at his son-in-law. He tried to find out what happened from Marcia.

"My father is having one of his episodes," Marcia told him.

"Listen!" Jerry Silber warned Phil Fruend, "I'm going to throw you out!"

"I'm a founder of this association!" Phil protested.

"I don't care if you're the founder of my ass, I'm throwing you out!"

"Who's gonna do it?" Phil challenged.

"I will!" Jerry responded.

"Tell me something," Phil asked, "why do you wear your hair in that stupid Simon and Garfunkel style?"

"I like it!" Jerry Silber snapped, mortally offended.

"I don't!" Phil snapped back.

Sid was enjoying it. Phil almost beat up another association president thirteen years earlier, because the man bitched when Phil helped himself to a piece of apple pie before it was served. He loved it when photographers lost their cool and squared off with each other. He wanted to lay odds; Phil decks the kid in one round.

"If you want to stay, you better behave yourself," Jerry Silber said authoritatively. "I want you to stay away from your daughter."

The crowd dispersed, and Phil remained standing next to Sid. Sid looked around for food.

"Some fuckin' cocktail hour! Where are the fuckin' snacks, weenies, anything?"

"She hurt me, Sid; everything I did, I did for her. I opened the studio for her, Sid. I liked working out of my house, and I had a good business over there. I gave her training, I sent her to work for top studios so she could become a master, I bought the top-of-the-line equipment for her, and look, she turned on me! I ask you, Sid, is this the way a daughter treats a father?"

"No, Phil, it is not." Sid took a cocktail wiener from the tray of a passing waiter and dipped it in mustard.

"Let me tell you something, Sid." Phil popped a cocktail wiener in his mouth, "Abe Susskind wasn't too nice to me, either. He was my best friend. Abe was like a brother to me—he broke me into the business. We were close, he taught me, he respected me enough to take my advice—I got him to switch to Mamiya 645s when he was shooting with a square system—he did not like that much. But Abe made a schmuck out of me too many times."

"I had friends use me, Phil; there just has to come a time when you say no more."

"We were like brothers. In fact, he gave Marcia her first camera. He was a professional photographer before I was. He was a fascinating person to know, we used to spend time together. He was such a good friend, but he wasn't there for me when I needed him. I always shot jobs for Abe when he called. I always helped him out. A few years ago, when I wasn't feeling well and was depressed, I asked Abe to shoot a job for me. He told me he couldn't do it. I asked another time, to maybe come along on the job to help me out. Abe asks, "Why? You want me to hold your hand?""

"I told him, 'Yeah, that's exactly what I want you to do, hold my hand! I did so much for you,' I told him, 'I thought you were my friend, Abe, I guess you're not.' He said he had to go."

Sid listened and shrugged, not knowing what to say.

"I called him another time when I needed a candid man to cover a job, and he told me three weeks in advance he was taking Anita out for dinner. I asked him, 'You know in advance when you go to eat out?' He said he was taking Anita out to dinner that night, and that was it."

"*Zoy gaytes*, baby, Abe is that way. I never trusted him that much."

"Well, Sid, you know what they all say, 'Abe Susskind, always gets the best of a deal.'"

"Listen, Phil, you're a good man. You got a rotten daughter and a friend who is a prick, what can I tell you, baby?"

"When Marcia got married, back when I had a daughter," Phil continued, "we sent Abe an invitation, and he sent it back marked, 'will not attend.' No gift, no explanation, just 'will not attend.' I shot his daughter's wedding, and I made no money on the job. If Abe didn't send a gift, he could have sent an explanation."

Sid made one of his trademark shrugs.

"You're an honorable man, Phil, not everybody in the business is as honorable as you. Personally, I think you should give your daughter a kick in the ass."

"I can't, Sid, she ruined me, but I can't hurt her. She and her husband stole from the studio. Even before that, she wanted to be a big shot. We did heavy volume Jewish jobs, but the neighborhood was not all Jewish. She charged too much money for our area, and I got hurt. I wasn't trying to be a big shot, I was happy with our moderate prices, but she wasn't. She ruined everything, it wasn't just her stealing."

"When you have kids, Philly, you never know what you're going to get."

"You were lucky, Sid."

"Bullshit, Philly, my son isn't any fuckin' bargain, he married a *shiksa*. Alright, she's a nice kid, but you should see her parents, feh! What's the matter, he couldn't find a Jewish girl? Not in our neighborhood? Not in Hewlett, for Christ's sakes. He found one once, I thought, I guess she was too affluent for him."

"Yeah," Phil Fruend lamented, "children and friends, friends and children, fuck 'em both!"

"Here, here!" answered Sid.

Phil went to get a coke, and on the way he said hello to Harvey Shiffman, of Shiffman Studios. Phil claimed Harvey was cold to him, since the break up with his daughter. Marcia Fruend hung around Harvey's studio during the day, telling Harvey of all the horrible things her father had done to her. Sid would have told Marcia to respect her father and get the fuck out of his studio, and he really did not like her father all that much. Phil told Sid a few months ago, he had to call Shiffman Studios for information about something, and Harvey's wife hung up the phone on him. He wanted to know what Marcia was telling them he did to her.

Sid went over to say hello to Harvey Shiffman. He grabbed a cocktail *kinish* from one waitresses' platter and a baked clam from another.

Harvey Shiffman smiled when Sid came over. They had known each other for forty years, since they both shot for the same studio. Harvey was a part-time photographer in those days; he used to be a kosher butcher. Sid knew him from Brooklyn; when they were kids, Harvey used to run his father's butcher shop. Phil Fruend had known Harvey Shiffman a long time, too. They were in economics class together at Brooklyn College.

Harvey Shiffman was Sid's age and still going strong, even after his health problems flared up. Harvey Shiffman had silver hair that was thin on top, worn swept back. He let the hair in the back grow down to his shoulders. This was contrasted by a neat mustache. He wore a shirt and pants that were held up by paisley suspenders.

"Sidney, how are you, kid?"

"I'm fine, Harvey, *mazel tov* on your second heart attack."

"Thanks, Sid, I'm sure."

"You know what they say, baby, the third time is the charm."

"Kiss my *tokus*, Sid, I feel great. I bet I can run your nicotine-stained ass off. That operation made a new man out of me."

"Back to work already? No shit!"

"Well, I go a few times a week for therapy group. They're my age, but they all look and act so old. So on the first day, the therapist introduces me around. 'Group,' she says, 'say hi to Harvey.' They all said hi. Then she says, 'Harvey, this is the group, say hi to the group.' So I say, 'Hi, fuckin' old guys!'" He waved his hand in greeting.

Sid laughed.

"My son helps me run the studio and shoot, and he handles the video production over there; I'm not ready for retirement, yet. No one comes up to me on location to ask if I talk funny because I'm retarded, like Susskind. I think a heart attack is better than a stroke."

"One is probably as good as the other," answered Sid.

"Shit, we got old, pal," Harvey said, "listen to us; we're comparing heart attacks to strokes, debating which is better."

"Listen, baby, if shooting is too fuckin' strenuous for you, you can always go back to being a butcher...how much stress is in puttting the liver through the grinder or chopping the flanken?"

"Sid, you're a philosopher, you and Brother Theodore. Now, I spend my time running seminars for the young people. Old-timers attend, too; by this industry, you are never too old to learn."

"How did the studio lights work out—the ones you bought from me, the Bogens?"

"They work fine. I never thought you would quit, I thought you would relocate to a nicer area."

"I relocated to my house. I'm too goddamn old to open another place; I don't need such an expense. I'm glad you like the lights. Did I ever steer you wrong?"

"No, sweetheart, you never did. Do you ever talk to Carl out in Arizona?"

"What the fuck for?" Sid raised his voice slightly in distaste. "What has he got to tell me? He's gonna tell me, he saw Barry Goldwater in a restaurant? Fuck him! I gotta spend money to hear how well he's doing?" Sid took a mini potato pancake from a waiter's platter.

"Look who's here," Harvey grinned at Sid, "Regis Court and his child bride."

"Holy shit!" Sid faced Harvey Shiffman and began to laugh. "I love that name, Regis Court. He came to a costume party one year wearing a jogging suit with his jock strap on the outside. Shit, we fuckin' elected him president for that."

"He's older than us, and he married that beautiful kid," Harvey laughed, too. "He and Ramon Roméro, with twenty-two year-old wives, they're in better shape than us, baby."

"Bullshit, Harvey. I can still ball my wife like I did when we were first married. It doesn't take me two hours to cum; I'm like a top-of-the-line power pack, I can recycle in a few seconds and get it up again. She's in good shape, too; Norma keeps up with me without having to fake it. She never faked it in all the years we were together."

"So, do you enjoy working in the house? At least you can get out for a break. Last night, I saw my first movie in four months; I can't always get out, you know, we practically live at the studio."

"What did you see?" Sid asked.

"We saw that new Schwarzenegger flick, *Total Recall*, you see it?"

"No," Sid replied, "I saw a scene last week on Letterman. I gotta pay seven dollars and change, to see two women kick each other in the cunt for ten minutes? If I want to see that, I can take my wife to Loehmann's on sale day and see that for free."

"Shit! Hal Strickland, Mr. Five Towns himself, is coming over."

"That's good, because his partner, Hal Grossman, just walked in the door. I'm gonna say hi to Hal. Harvey, baby, I'll catch you after dinner."

Sid approached Hal Grossman, a man in his fifties, about five foot eight, medium build, bald on top, with wavy chestnut-colored hair around the sides of his head.

"Hal Grossman," Sid called out, "the old movie photographer, how are you?"

"Fine, Sid, but I haven't done movies in a century. I only shoot stills."

Hal Grossman started out as a movie photographer, but later moved on to stills. His movie skills enabled him to train videographers and editors to work for his studio. He had won many awards as a photographer. He was considered one of the best, and he was the most famous candid photographer in New York. He had won even more awards than his former partner, Hal Strickland. Hal Grossman and Hal Strickland worked for a studio in Brooklyn, owned by a degenerate gambler. He could not afford to pay his photographers their wages, so he paid them in studio equipment. Finally, to take care of the debt, he transferred the ownership of the studio over to the two Hals. They took a fairly well established studio and transformed it into one of the biggest, innovative, trendsetting studios in the region. They even named the business Trend Photographers. As Hal Strickland said at the inception, "A trend is not a fad. A trend sets standards." This studio's goal was to set the highest standards and creativity in the business.

They did set the trend with a studio in an affluent section of Brooklyn and one in the Five Towns on Long Island. They became the most prestigious studio in the whole area. In addition to outdoing each other in caterer selections, parents hire Trend Photographers as a symbol of status. This, of course, drove other well-known artistic, high-end photographers absolutely insane.

When Trend Photographers became the most prestigious studio in the entire area, the two Hals made sure other photographers knew that.

Since the dissolve of the partnership, Hal Grossman worked the lecture circuit. He was also shooting independently, and he did well due to name recognition. He was also a spokesman for a professional film processing lab. His duties included picking up film and dropping off finished proofs and photographs from the lab. From award winning photographer, to delivery boy, this is what the poor bastard was reduced to. Hal Strickland loved it, he wished nothing but ill on his former partner. He prayed his ex-partner should only drop dead on one of his jobs.

"I'm semi-retired now, Hal, you working?"

"Oh, sure, Sid, still shooting, my son is still shooting, too; we're both on our own, not because we don't get along like the Fruends, we just have our own followings and a lot of work. I'm moving out of Brooklyn, my wife and I found a nice house in Lido Beach, and I'm going to work from the house. I'm a new grandpa, so we plan to do a lot of babysitting."

"*Mazel tov*, baby, *mazel* and *brucha*. You should plan to do a lot of babysitting. At first, Norma and I did not plan to do a lot of babysitting, but," Sid shrugged, "we ended up doing it. I guess that was the same way with our parents. Now my daughter is moving to Boston, my son and my *shiksa*-in-law might move down to Atlanta, so any babysitting will be if Poppy can get a good deal on an airline ticket."

"We plan to sit, Sid, I love my little guy, but you know all about that, you're a veteran grandpa now."

"Hear your ex-partner is thinking about selling the studio. He wants seven hundred fifty thousand dollars, I hear. He says the reason is, he has no children, like the rest of us old candid men, and he's getting on in years."

"He has no children because he was always a numb nuts!" Hal angrily retorted. "I taught him how to be an artist, never mind a photographer. When I first met that schmuck, he didn't know a camera from a hole in his ass."

"I feel that way about my partner Carl. He was an okay candid man, but I taught him how to photograph well."

Yeah, right, Hal Grossman, thought. *Bullshit, Carl was an artist, Sid was a candid man*.

"Good evening."

The voice belonged to Regis Court, a tall dapper sixty-three year old. Both Sid Weitz and Hal Grossman shook hands with him. Regis Court wore a brown herringbone sports jacket and cognac colored pants, and he carried a pipe—the look fit his image, he resembled a college professor more than a photographer. He claimed he could shoot a job with a pipe in his mouth. Sid believed him; he shot jobs with cigarettes going all the time.

"I have to tell you what happened, Sid."

"What happened, Regis?"

"One of the younger members told me I have a very charming daughter. I told him, 'You just made her feel good, but now I feel like shit…she's not my daughter, she's my wife.'"

"So what?" replied Sid. "Let him go on a date with her, provided he promises to have her home in time to put you to bed."

"You have to hear what happened to me at a wedding last week in Manhattan."

"I don't have to do anything," Sid replied, "except croak and pay taxes, neither of which I plan to do anytime soon."

"I had my camera case with my back-up Hasselblad and all of my accessories stolen from a church. We were working at the altar, I had the case in the back, and someone grabbed it and ran out."

"Did you finish the job?" asked Hal Grossman.

"Yes, first I told the bride what happened to my back-up equipment and film, and explained my light person had the exposed film on her. The bride hollered at me, the theft was not really my fault. I told her, 'Don't yell at me, I'll leave right now, and you'll not have any pictures.' The little shrew apologized to me."

"How did you get through the job?" Sid asked.

"I sent my assistant with my camera on to the hotel. I stopped at a big camera supplier; this was Sunday, so all the Chassid stores were open. I bought film, and my assistant had a spare strobe unit and power pack in another case. Later on, I called my wife and she came over with an extra Hasselblad I had in the house, an extra wide-angle lens, and an extra portrait lens just in case it was needed. The following Tuesday, the cops recovered my camera; this junkie left it in the back of a car he stole. It seems that chap stole from guests during temple and church ceremonies before, but usually coats and such."

"You're a lucky man," Sid said, shaking his head while eating another baked clam and cocktail wiener. "You're fuckin' lucky you got the job done and your camera back."

"I told the bride that this job will be shot. I executed my duties."

"I never had anything stolen from me on a job. I know sometimes you have to concentrate on what is going on, or in your situation, you might not be able to be near your equipment, shit happens. I try to be fuckin' careful." Sid went on, "My studio was broken into, but on jobs I have been lucky."

Hal Grossman spoke. "Once, on a job, some man picked up my video man's lavaliere microphone. The guy put it in his pocket. My video man took the receiver, put on the earphones, and walked all around the hall until he zeroed in on the person who had it. The man claimed he saw it on the floor and he was holding it for him. He claimed he was going to give it back."

"So you gave the man the benefit of a doubt," said Regis Court.

Hal nodded.

The president of the association asked that everyone please take their seat for dinner. Sid sat at a table with candid men he knew, such as Phil Fruend, who was trying to avoid his estranged daughter and Abe Susskind. There were also some young, new faces Sid did not recognize.

The president started to call some raffle ticket numbers for the door prizes. Sid won a golf umbrella from Kodak. Abe Susskind won a bounce reflector card for a strobe unit. He laughed, because according to industry folklore, Abe Susskind invented that device.

Industry legend Max Cohn recited the Photographer's Prayer. He always recited the Photographer's Prayer, it was tradition.

"Oh, God, as I bring my subjects into focus and prepare to make each portrait, never let me forget that I am creating treasures for some family, a keepsake for loved ones. Make me sensitive to the qualities and virtues of others that I may draw out into light the beautiful, radiant belongings of their hearts. Help me, O Lord to be an artist collecting beauty of every soul, the glow of youth, the wisdom of age, the gentleness, the strength, the laughter, or the tears of each life that is precious in thy sight. Deeper than the means of livelihood, give me the perspective to see my photographer's art as a service to others, making life richer and more memorable. And, dear Lord, between the lights and shadows, the ups and downs, and the rolling years, keep me from getting out of focus or off center so that my life and work may be framed with dignity and colored contentment. Amen."

There were responses of amen, and the Hebraic *oymain*.

Several in the membership found the Photographer's Prayer to be moving and inspiring; others thought it was a crock of shit.

The president took the mic again and continued with some announcements. All the members talked during the announcements, which often pissed off the speaker and anybody else who wanted to hear the information. Sid half listened, this bullshit was not of any importance to him, he didn't give a fuck about fishing trips.

An angry-looking, old gray-haired waiter approached Sid's table.

"*Ve heff no pgrrime grrip*, tonight!" he barked.

"I was in the mood for German prime rib," Sid called out. Some people at the table, who had not grown up in Brooklyn, chuckled when Sid said German, as it came out *Joiman*.

"*Ve heff no pgrrime grrip!*"

"What do you have tonight?" Sid challenged the old kraut.

"*Ve heff, lemb shopps, fillet of shcrodt, biff shtoganoff, unt, ve heff, jaeger schnitzel*, it is pan cooked veal cutlet."

"I waaanted prrriiime riiib," Sid answered the waiter.

"*Zere is no pgrrime grripp, I shaid!*" barked the waiter.

"Okay, take it easy, I'll have the lamb chops," Sid said very soothingly.

"*Lemb shopps, veggrry goot.*" The waiter wrote down Sid's order.

"But I really wanted the prime rib."

"*Gut deem it!*"

"Shid, cut it out already," mumbled Abe Susskind, who was sitting next to him. "The old prick might spit in our food."

"Yeah," added Phil Fruend, "look, the old bastard is mouthing, 'sonofabitch,' when he writes."

Whether or not the old bastard spit into the food, Sid did not know, but the lamb was excellent. During dinner the talk was shop, trade gossip, and goings on in the photographers' personal lives—who retired, who still worked, who opened up and where, who was charging what, and who died.

Dessert concluded the meal, and the angry-at-the-world waiter returned.

"*Epple pie is dessert!*" he announced.

"I hate apple pie," Sid provoked the man, "don't you have any Bavarian cream pie or ice cream parfait?"

"*Epple pie is dessert!*" the waiter smacked his hand with his order pad.

"Do you have any blueberry pie?"

"*Epple pie! Epple pie is dessert!*"

"Does it come with whipped cream?" Phil Fruend asked.

"*Vis out!*"

"I hate apple pie," Sid complained. "First you had no German prime rib," he challenged the waiter once more, "now you make me eat apple pie, without even a dollop of whipped cream, yet."

"*Och!*" The waiter stormed off to get the apple pie. After the pie was served, the old waiter began pouring the coffee and tea.

"*Dekeffenated*," he announced.

"May I please have regular coffee?" Sid asked.

"*Ja, ja, ja, I get you gregular!*"

"*Danke schoen!*"

Sid looked at the pitcher of milk on the table, and as the coffee was poured into his cup, he inquired, "Excuse me, *meine herr*, do you have half and half, or maybe a non-dairy creamer?"

"*Milich,*" the waiter abruptly shook his head 'no.'

"No half and half?"

"*Chust milich!*"

"May I ask you a question?"

The waiter paused.

"Do you know how many men are on a baseball diamond?"

"*Nein!*" the waiter shook his head.

"That's correct!" Sid replied.

The old waiter angrily walked off. Since dinner was paid for, with the twenty-five dollars, gratuities were included. This was a good thing, because Sid would not have given that nasty old cocksucker anything.

"Now, I have the time to relax," Sid told his friends as he leaned back. "I promised my wife we would go into the city during the week. She wants to go on Fifth Avenue, to Museum Row. We think we'll visit the Jewish Museum."

"What do they have at the Jewish Museum?" a young woman photographer whom Sid didn't know, and was not a member of the tribe asked.

"A display of Jewish cavemen, what do you mean what do they have? They have artifacts and shit."

"I love walking on Museum Row," Phil Fruend volunteered. "It's a great place to spend a day. They have the photography museum that is something to see."

"There's the Irish museum," Sid spoke again, "they have a sign out front, TOUR BEGINS AT TWO-THIRTY P.M., BRAWL BEGINS AT THREE."

The table cracked up at that one. He remembered his friend Harry the cop telling him, one Italian cop he worked with told him on his day off he took his girlfriend to the black history museum. He told Harry, they saw a special showing, the white motherfucker exhibit. He told Harry they saw prehistoric switchblades and food stamps. He said they even had a welfare check on display, dating back before Jesus.

Harry asked his coworker if he saw any prehistoric black men with holes in their skulls, from being shot by prehistoric, racist cops.

Dinner was over, the members milled about bullshitting, before the start of the seminar.

Ray Cimino, a renowned children's portrait photographer stood by himself. A young enterprising up-and-coming portrait and candid photographer, Dean Gershon, went up to him.

"Hi, Ray. I sat at a table with the guy over there," he subtly pointed, "I met him at catering halls a couple of times, who is he?"

"Oh, the guy with the big mouth, that's Sid Weitz, stay away from him! He isn't anybody for a young artist, like you, to know or to emulate."

"He seems to be quite verbose and entertaining," Dean said.

"Verbose, he is. I've known him for years, he even shot a video for my family, he says, 'Do I know Ray Cimino, oh, yeah, the big fat bald guy!'"

Dean laughed and shook his head.

"Sid's a character, he and his partner Carl were legends for a while, and deservedly so. They did well out here on Long Island, they had a big Jewish following in Brooklyn. They had an office there, too. Carl was the legend, Sid was the hustler."

"Sounds like a character," Dean said, "I sat at his table tonight."

"Oh, a character alright. Sid is a brilliant businessman, but the credit for the great photography work at his place goes to Carl; I'm surprised he lasted all these years without Carl."

"I guess he has a magnetic personality, Ray."

"When he wants to be magnetic, Dean. Carl brought the customers into Montclair Studios. Granted, he was the first photographer on Long Island to shoot video; Sid's a pioneer. All the studios followed him with video, even Hal Grossman and the other Hal at Trend Photographers. Trend claims to be the industry leader, but they followed Sid. Sid is a terrific video man. Hal

Grossman asked Sid to teach him all about in camera edits. Hal Grossman asked Sid for knowledge, and Hal used to be the best movie photographer around, in the old days."

"He actually calls you the bald fat guy?"

"Oh, sure, Dean. He's a great video man, a brilliant businessman, I'd even say a very good photographer, but he is a character with a big mouth."

"I guess you know him, Ray."

"Yes, he was a top studio owner, but Sid Weitz is the coldest, meanest, most ruthless sonofabitch to ever hold a camera. If you agree with him, you're smart; disagree with anything he says, you're a schmuck. He drove his partner to Arizona; Carl was an elegant man, I don't think he could take Sid's mouth anymore. Carl told me to get away from Sid. Once Carl said, 'Sid's mouth is like a 7-Eleven store, open for business, twenty-four hours a day.'"

"He sounds that way."

"He *is* that way. He used to be known as the crazy man of Hempstead Turnpike, I guess now he'll be known as the crazy man of Hewlett. He and his wife drove matching Lincoln Continentals one year, big ego. I would have nothing to do with him, if I were you. Years ago, he wanted to sell a Bronica system he used, but didn't care for. He told this young guy it was for sale. Every time he called Sid up, Sid told him a couple of weeks, I have to catalog everything, I have to take it out of the closet and pull it apart, I'll get in touch with you next week, I promise, you're on my list, baby, my wife and I have to go to Europe, I swear I'll call you when I get back, I was going to get the stuff ready, but first, I had to work in the garden."

"What happened?" Dean Gershon asked.

"The young fellow bought nice new Hasselblads. Sid probably has those old Bronicas in his closet, unless some putz called and gave him a bid, sight unseen, who knows? Once another young guy said he wanted to buy Sid's corporation. Sid told him he would rather pay to keep the charter, and put all of his equipment out at the curb for the garbage man, rather than sell to a nobody like him."

"Sounds like a class act."

Sid Weitz walked past Dean Gershon on the way to the seminar area.

"Well, baby, are you learning?" Sid asked as he playfully slapped Dean Gershon's face back and forth. Dean did not appreciate that. Sid enjoyed giving the young know it alls a hard time. The old-timer walked off telling him to learn from the best.

Max Cohn warned young photographers to be careful. "Sid Weitz will tell you to follow me! Then you'll fuck up!"

As Sid walked, he grabbed Max Cohn by the arm.

"Max Cohn! You're still alive; you must be about a hundred fuckin' years old!"

"Still alive, Sid, not a hundred, still active."

"Still work, Max?"

"I don't shoot any more candids or portraits, Sid; I leave that to the young blood. I just custom print photographs now."

"Max, baby, you ought to retire; you're too fuckin' old for any of this shit."

"I like to do my printing, I stay active in the associations, nationwide, the state chapter here in Nassau, and out in Suffolk where I live now. I wouldn't want to leave the business."

Sid sat down in a chair in the seminar area.

Max Cohn walked up to Dean Gershon.

"I saw you talking to Sid Weitz before, young man, if he asks you for any favors, do yourself a favor, tell him, 'Fuck you.' I know him and I really don't *dislike* him, but he's a creep."

"He comes across like one, Max."

"I don't dislike Sid, I just don't respect him. He and I used to have studios down the road from each other, one town apart; I never had a person come to me after going to him. I think most of his work, at that time, was in Brooklyn. He had an old Jewish clientele. Last year he didn't come to too many meetings, he wasn't working too much. I called him and tried to cheer him up, but he didn't want to be friends, he just pushed me off. I don't think Sid wants anything from anybody. That's his way, he pushes away friends. By the way, did he ever tell you what he calls video men he doesn't like?"

"No, Max, we didn't talk about video."

"He calls them vidiots—that's his word—vidiots. Stay away from him, and you'll do alright."

The seminar, aptly enough, was about marketing to get the type of clients you want and getting them to spend in a recession. Sid thought this might be a little too late for him, along with some of the other poor bastards in attendance tonight. However, semi-retired is not dead, so he listened intently.

He left during the print competition, because it was the same shit. People were handling photographs for the display with white linen gloves. Judges who probably knew less than the photographers, who took the pictures, scored the prints.

Brides and grooms, posed in archways or in the middle of an arboretum. Children and young women photographed with either high key lighting or dramatic lighting. The same old shit—Hal Grossman, Ramon Roméro, Abe Susskind, or Marcia Fruend would win the blue ribbons anyway, as if they needed any more.

Sid was interested in the green ribbons in his bank account, instead of blue ribbons on his wall. You can attract clients with the blue ribbons; if you want to eat, you need the green ribbons. When you are old, you need the green ribbons you have accumulated through the years to be sent to you in a monthly check. Without a check, a nursing facility will not allow you the privilege of laying on bed sheets soiled with your own bowel movements, hooked up to a pee bag, wondering if your kids who grabbed as much as they could before the home got its cut, will come to visit. Green ribbons are important; why else does a man lying in the intensive care unit watch the stock market report? Blue ribbons were nice for any artist to have, but in real life it all came down to the green ribbons.

He drove home to Hewlett at eleven o'clock. Two hundred twenty-five dollars to pay for the privilege of a twenty-five dollar dinner and seminar that you have to watch from sitting in the back or off to the side. *Fuck it*, Sid thought, he would not rejoin, he was too old for the association, too old to be a candid man, and too old for the aggravation of owning his own business, and the problems of going to work every day.

He pulled into the driveway, slipped into the house, and turned on the small black and white television in the kitchen. Nothing on Johnny Carson interested him tonight.

Norma was asleep, so he quietly changed, washed, then got into bed and drifted off to sleep.

Chapter Twenty-Two

Retirement was not as bad as Sid imagined. Saturday the children and grandchildren came over. Sid kissed Christine and addressed her as beautiful.

Alec, the three year old, showed his karate moves to his poppy. He thrust his right hand hard into Sid's crotch, causing him to double over in pain, grabbing the dining room chair for support.

"Alec, don't hit Poppy in the ballsies!" Norma reproved her grandson.

Their children, Linda and Steven, talked to Sid about getting some counseling to make the adjustment to a slower lifestyle. Sid politely told them to mind their own business.

He and Norma took the kids and grandkids for Chinese food. Sid told his eldest grandson, Peter, to order the twice-cooked pork. He told him that twice cooked made it kosher.

Monday morning, Sid lay on a chaise lounge out in the backyard, watching the planes fly over Hewlett on the way to Kennedy Airport. He wore a pair of blue bathing trunks and a red polo shirt, with sandals and a light blue pork pie golf hat.

Norma went to say goodbye before she left for work. "Take a dip, honey," she suggested.

The Weitzes had an in ground swimming pool. It was not a large one, but it sufficed.

"Later, I might."

"No smoking, Sid."

"Just one, I promise."

"No!"

"Maybe I ought to switch to a pipe; you don't inhale with a pipe, you smoke mostly for the taste. You remember Regis Court, he smokes a pipe, and he's older than me. He told me it relaxes him, he said he just had a physical and he's in good health. His doctor told him, a pipe in moderation won't hurt him."

"Now that you're home during the day, you can visit with your girlfriend," Norma said coyly.

"Holy shit!" he called out in shock, "who's my girlfriend?"

"Our buxom mail lady."

"She's married, besides she's too young for me. She's a big girl," Sid gestured to his chest, "I like petite broads, like you."

"You watch her walk away, when she hands you the mail."

"I like to watch Shannon jiggle, she does that very nicely. She's cute, but she's a young lady and I'm an old man, so I look. Old men like to look, but I don't touch."

"You better not touch," Norma warned. "Seriously, you touch her and I'll touch her," Norma swung her right fist, "then I'll touch you!" She made a snipping gesture with two fingers.

"I only think about you, darling. I think retirement ain't gonna be so wonderful."

Norma kissed him on the lips, as she walked away, Sid watched. She was wearing form-fitting tailored slacks.

"Hey, baby," he called out, "you still got it! I like to watch you jiggle away, Grandma!"

Norma flashed him a radiant smile before leaving.

Sid spent most of the morning snoozing in the backyard. He was retired, so he did not go inside to pee, he watered the flower bed instead.

The following Saturday, Sid shot a wedding. He accepted an assignment from a jerk he knew, who owned a package deal studio in Suffolk County.

The studio, a low-end studio, did not use double lighting. He went out on the job alone. He carried a back-up camera in his case, with a spare strobe unit in the car. He used just his 80 mm lens and his 55 mm wide-angle lens.

The reception was being held in a hall in Copiague; it was an afternoon job. He decided to wear a business suit. He had on a charcoal gray, three-piece suit, but since it was a humid day, he left the vest in the car.

The bride lived on the south shore of Suffolk County in Babylon. Sid had a shock when he walked into the bride's home. There was a mural of Italy or Sicily on the living room wall. Underneath the mural, was a functioning waterfall, full of sudsy water. On the other side of the room, there was a hanging lamp that circulated red-colored mineral oil. What great backgrounds to work with!

The bride's father and her brothers stood in their kitchen in their tuxedo pants and tee shirts, drinking beer from the bottle.

"Wanna beer?" asked the bride's father.

"No, thanks," the photographer responded.

The bride's father was a stocky, dark-haired man in his early fifties. He spoke with an Italian accent.

"Dese a doctora spenda five minoots wit a you, den a dey charge a lot of a muna and a dey drive a da beeg a Merchedez."

Sid, being the father of a young doctor, was pissed off by the tail end of the conversation he had heard. Meanwhile, these folks who lived in a big house wanted a cheap package deal.

The father of the bride asked Sid where he lived. Sid did not volunteer the town; he merely told him that he lived in the Five Towns.

"Oh, a da Five a Towns, I was the cesspool contractor over a dere. I did all of a da sewer hookups."

Sid remembered this man from over twenty years ago, but did not tell him that.

The bride's father asked Sid where he came from originally. He told the man he was originally from Brooklyn, Midwood, the Kings Highway vicinity.

"Oh, I used to live in a Brook-a-leen. My neighborhood is still a good, 'cause we don't a let a da jigs in. My brudder lives a dere, his next a door neighbor bought a his nephew's house, crossa da street, and a sold it to paisan. We keep a the neighborhood. His a neighbor was a showin' a da house to a blacka guy. My brudda went crossa da street, he tells a da man, ay atsa matta, you sell a to black a guy. He tells a my brudda he ain't a black, he's a Dominican. My brudda says, I saw him, he's as black as a shit. If a you hard up for a the cash, we'll buy a you house."

Although Sid lived in a Jewish area, he knew of this practice.

"Atsa whadda we did," the bride's father continued, *"we buy a the house. Brook-a-leen, she's a beautiful, you could walk a around everywhere in Brook-a-leen when we was a keeds, remember?"*

"Yes, I remember," he answered.

"Ay shoo, you a remember, you a maybe my age. We kepta my neighborhood, it's a still nice."

It was a fairly big traditional Italian wedding, package deal aside. The bride was very pretty and a rather intelligent, well-spoken accountant.

Driving home, he passed another low-end studio. He knew the owner from running into him in the processing lab. If a customer complained about one of his photography or video packages, the studio owner bluntly told the offended client, "What did you think you were getting for the low price? If you wanted perfection, you should have gone to one of those big expensive studios with the big chandeliers and thick carpeting."

The next day, a Sunday, Sid agreed to videotape a Bat Mitzvah for his friend in Oceanside. Sid was a childhood friend of Harold (Heshy) Adomovich, a fellow photography enthusiast he knew growing up in Brooklyn. Heshy Adomovich opened up his studio on Nostrand Avenue in Brooklyn. Heshy opened years before Sid opened his studio. Heshy opened up his studio in Oceanside in 1969, and he closed his Brooklyn studio in 1977, because it was a hardship to run two studios. Heshy was more observant than Sid. For several years, Heshy made it a point to call Sid and leave a message, "I just called to wish you a good *Shabbos*," on his answering machine. Heshy Adomovich knew his old buddy Sid did not observe the Jewish Sabbath. When they were kids, Sid boasted to Heshy that his uncle Gabriel told him that they have a very nice *Shabbat* service at Sing Sing.

Sid Weitz filmed and photographed and videotaped jobs for Heshy Adomovich throughout the years of their friendship. Being a true friend, Heshy reciprocated, only Heshy did not work on Saturday.

When he arrived home in the early evening from his job, the humidity and temperature had lowered. Sid and Norma slept with the air conditioner off and the bedroom window open. At five A.M., "Der Cubana Yid," without her dog, but with her girlfriend, took her power walk—walking by the Weitz house, talking very loudly about nothing that would concern a sleeping couple at five o'clock on a Sunday morning.

As he shaved, he saw an old man looking back at him in the mirror. *When did I get so old*, he wondered. *When did I age, I look like my father.*

He looked at his eyes, the eyes that had seen so much through a camera lens.

He was old because young men who parked his car at halls told him that he shot their Bar Mitzvahs. He was now photographing clients' *remarriages*, for the *second and third time*. He wondered how many of his brides and grooms have since divorced.

This is the way it went in the candid photography trade—studios folded, couples divorced, bride's shot their grooms while they slept, husbands beat their wives to death, and little children you photographed for a team picture were killed crossing a busy street. This was supposed to be a happy business.

Sid could not get an assistant to help him on this Bat Mitzvah. He asked Norma and she agreed. Norma occasionally assisted him on jobs. Sid used to joke taking Norma on a job, was a cheap night out. Video assistants help in setting up the constant lights, and audiotape recorder. Today, Sid would do the heavy work himself. Norma's job was to point a video light on a monopod where Sid directed her to point it. She also was to keep an eye on the equipment for him.

Driving to Temple Beth Israel of Cedarhurst, Sid had to swerve the big Chevy to avoid three women who were walking three abreast in the middle of the street. Those damn women took power walks in the middle of the street, when there was a perfectly good sidewalk. Further up Chesterfield Road, the same two women from last week were stopped in the middle of the street talking to each other, in their Mercedes Benzes. This time, Sid leaned on the horn for all he was worth; they got the message and moved.

This was another elaborate Five Towns Bat Mitzvah. The photographer Heshy sent was a young woman named Myra, whom Sid had never met. Her light man was a young man, Joe, who was being broken into the trade.

Sid set up two Tota lights, which were constant. He turned the lights off when not taping.

He had a Bogen tripod, which accommodated video cameras on a Bogen dolly cart. The video camera Sid used today was a Panasonic 450. The camera had Armato's Porta Light on top. Norma had an identical light on her monopod. They were double lighting for the video, however, the second light was a constant light not a strobe. Also on the dolly, was a Magnavox color monitor used to view the action and to monitor the color and batteries to power the camera light. The camcorder had its own batteries.

Nearby, on a luggage cart, were cases that contained a Panasonic 460 camcorder, an older version of the 450, as a backup. Both of these camcorders accommodated the super VHS format. The other cases contained extra lights, extension cords, batteries, microphones for interviews, shotgun microphones, lavaliere microphones, videotapes, tools, gaffer and duct tape, and weighted sandbags to steady the light stands—everything a good videographer needed on a job.

Sid was wearing a double-breasted black tuxedo. Norma wore a conservative black pants suit, with a white dress shirt open at the neck. A couple at one of the tables remarked that they looked like a nice old couple.

Cocktail hour was over and the reception began. The candle lighting ceremony was the first event, followed by a *hora*.

"I hope you're happy, Norma, I left the cigarettes home. I think I'm starting to shake."

"Sid, you'll do just fine."

The candle lighting ceremony began. Guests were called up to honor the Bat Mitzvah girl by lighting a candle on the huge cake. The disc jockey was playing lively Jewish music.

Sid hated disc jockeys, he always did. There was nothing like a live band to set the mood of an affair. Most of the disc jockeys he worked with, in his opinion, sucked. To be a musician you need talent, to be a disc jockey you don't. How much talent do you need to spin a record?

Sid Weitz was making some so-called retirement pocket money. He liked working; he believed he was the best at what he did. Although this job was not his, it was a good job, and he knew it was going well. He knew he was going to enjoy taping it.

As guests lit the candles on top of the cake, they smiled at the video camera.

Norma was right, as she always had been; he was going to do just fine.

Chapter Twenty-Three

June 1966

S teven Weitz, age three, sat on the rug in the den of his parents' house in Hewlett, Long Island. He looked adorable in his Bermuda shorts and short-sleeve, red and white vertical-striped polo shirt. Alongside of him on the floor was a large toy doctor's kit. The instruments rivaled any top specialist's office.

His father, Sidney Weitz, age thirty-five and owner of Montclair Studios, one of Long Island's busiest portrait and wedding studios, looked at him from time to time with paternal pride. He glanced only from time to time today, because he was preparing his equipment to photograph a Bar Mitzvah and reception at a large well-known synagogue hall located on Ocean Avenue in Brooklyn's Flatbush section.

Sid Weitz sat in the shirt and pants of a Nehru-style black tuxedo, which was in style this year. He lit both an unfiltered Pall Mall and a filtered Kool menthol cigarette at the same time, taking alternate drags on each.

Morgan, their sickly one-year-old Weimaraner dog sat at his feet, while Sid busied himself loading his Koni-Omega Rangefinder, 6x7 medium-format camera.

Steven Weitz, at three, was almost a carbon copy of his father—his dark brown hair, parted on the left and brushed to the side, his brown eyes, and charming smile.

"Daddy?"

"Yes, Champ, what can I do for you?" Sid looked at his son.

"I think I should examine you."

"I feel fine, Doc."

"You look tired, please?"

"Okay, a quick look, I gotta get to work."

First Steven looked in his father's ears with his toy light, then shook down his toy thermometer. "Turn over, Steven matter-of-factly told his daddy.

"Nothing doing, Steve-a-reno!" his father retorted. "Doctors don't take grownups' temperatures in their tushies, they use an oral thermometer, see in the mouth," Sid put the thermometer under his tongue, "See, like this."

Norma Weitz walked into the den. She was beautiful, and although she was 100 percent Jewish, she was often taken for Irish. Their seven–year-old daughter Linda took after her in looks. Norma's red hair was worn in a shoulder-length flip style. She was wearing a white blouse and black slacks.

"Honey, Daddy's very busy right now, why don't you examine Morgan?"

Obediently, Steven Weitz sat back down on the floor to examine his next patient.

Morgan thumped his tail on the floor and genially rolled over onto his back for a tummy rub.

Young Dr. Weitz placed his right hand between the un-neutered Weimaraner's legs to check for a hernia.

"YIPE! YIPE! YIEYEEEP!" the poor patient cried out.

"Oh Jesus, now what did you do?" his father demanded.

"Steeevieee!" Norma shouted, "The doggie doesn't like it when you squeeze his *gibbel*, how many times do I have to tell you that?"

His feelings hurt and somewhat frustrated, young Dr. Weitz walked away.

Morgan got to his feet and bit Steven on his rear end.

The little boy cried out in pain.

"Ahhh. See, that's what you get for doing that to him. Nice going, Steven!" Norma shook her right index finger as she scolded him.

"Alright, let me see," Sid walked over to them and he pulled the waistband of Steve's shorts down. Didn't even break the skin, Norma, look."

Norma looked.

"Good boy! Morgan, very good boy!" Sid praised the dog.

"Christ's sake, Sidney," Norma said, somewhat disgusted.

"Listen, every time a doctor does that to me, I feel like biting him on his ass!"

"How come Morgan doesn't like me?" Steve asked his parents tearfully.

"He doesn't like you because he thought you were the veterinarian. Doctors he hates, you he loves," Norma answered.

Sid looked down at his son, smiled, looked back across to Norma, and extended his left hand out, palm up.

"My son, the doctor!" he exclaimed.

Chapter Twenty-Four
May 1989

"My son, the doctor!" Sid Weitz called out with paternal pride. Today was one of the proudest days of his whole life and fuck the world.

Today was the day Jewish parents dreamed about—the day a child graduates from medical school. Sid and Norma Weitz were, thank God, alive to see this day. Today their son had officially earned his medical degree. Sid and Norma had earned their bragging rights.

Sid and Norma Weitz converged on the area in the center of an athletic field where all the graduates gathered after receiving their diplomas. Actually, they were not handed diplomas at all. The graduates were handed a rolled up piece of paper with a blue ribbon around it. The diplomas had to be picked up later.

The whole area was a sea of black caps and gowns. The graduates wore the green stole of medicine around their necks.

Norma hugged Steven first. She wore a conservative beige floral print summer dress and white straw garden party-style hat.

"I am so proud of you, honey," Norma said, her voice full of emotion. She sounded like she did on the day of her children's confirmation. She sounded that way on the day of her daughter Linda's wedding.

His father, Sid Weitz, wore a tan summer business suit with a white shirt and a green and beige patterned tie. He wore his distance glasses to see his son; he also needed them for when he videotaped the awarding of the diploma.

"My son, the doctor! You made it; you made the old man very happy."

"Thanks, Dad," replied Steve, "but you're not an old man."

At the age of fifty-eight and with two grandchildren, his father felt like an old man. Still, he had the stamina to photograph affairs. He wished that he had inherited his father's stamina for the grueling work, which lay ahead. He had no illusions; Steve Weitz knew a resident's life was not easy.

It was a hot day, and Steven roasted in the charcoal gray suit he wore under the black gown. He noticed his mother was perspiring lightly. His father's silver hair was moist-looking. The mustache that his father sported that year looked soggy.

"Let's go to the tent for the luncheon," Steven suggested.

"Doctor! Doctor! I need a doctor!" a gruff Brooklyn Jewish accent called out. It was Sid's father, Burton Weitz, eighty-three, a retired plumber. He was an older heavier version of Sid. He came running over with his wife, Nettie, in tow.

Steven cupped his right hand to his forehead. "Oh, no," he mumbled, "please, Grampa, behave today."

"Hey, Doctor," Burton Weitz extended his hand, "you learned about manipulation, so pull my finger!"

"Oh, Burt!" Nettie Weitz hit her husband across his upper arm with her purse.

"Listen, Doc, I got a pain down here," he tapped his fly, "I think I caught something from your grandma!"

"Holy shit, Dad, cool it!" Sid muttered, not quite under his breath.

"What! What? What did I do?" Burton asked gruffly, as he stepped back right onto a female faculty member's foot.

"Ow, sir!" the lady admonished. "My foot, ow! Please look where you are going, sir."

Burton gestured both hands toward the lady in the black cap and gown, palms up. She returned the gesture with a sneer.

"Beh, beh, behhh behhh behhhh!" he growled his reply to her.

The female faculty member nodded at Steven, then walked off.

Oh, well, at least the day started off nicely. He just wanted it to continue smoothly. Sadie and Aaron Levine, Norma's parents, came over. They were in their mid-seventies. Norma's mother, Sadie, did not care for Sid's parents or Sid either, for that matter. However, they were happy God let them live to see a grandchild graduate from medical school.

"We are both very proud of you, to have a grandson who is a doctor," Sadie said. Such an honor for the family, I gave a donation in *shul*." She hugged her grandson. Norma's parents, like Sid's, were born in America, so their accents were Brooklyn Jewish, not European.

"I'm glad you and Grandpa could come, Nana." Steve called Norma's parents Nana and Grandpa, to differentiate from Sid's parents, Grandma and Grampa.

Sid really did not like his in-laws all that much. His father-in-law, Aaron Levine, thought Sid was alright. His son-in-law was a good hardworking man. Sadie, his mother-in-law, thought he was common.

"Listen, Sid is a good father, a good husband, a wonderful person, and he takes nice pictures, but has a screw loose," was one of her compliments. She heard Sid's exasperations from time to time, which were toned down for his family. "You mustn't curse when you get angry, Steveleh," she warned her grandson, "you mustn't display your temper, otherwise people will look at you and say, 'Ooh, common!' You don't want to be common like your daddy!"

Sid thought his mother-in-law was a *ferbissen*, which means 'a nasty person' in Yiddish. Aaron, his father-in-law, was a nice emasculated man. He was a Jewish liberal masochist. In 1972, he not only voted for George McGovern for president in the general election, but in the New York primary, as well. His father-in-law made valid political arguments. He said he hated the Mayor of New York City Ed Koch, because he talked too much.

"Mayor Koch should keep his mouth shut!" Aaron Levine went around saying.

"Keep his mouth shut about what?" Sid asked. "Mayor Koch, who is Jewish and the mayor of a heavily Jewish populated city, should allow his people to be used as punching bags for the world's problems, just to please the Farrakhan supporters, who usually support his party? Bullshit! You tell 'em, Ed!"

Aaron said he did not vote for Koch in the last election and did not plan to vote for him in the upcoming election, because he did not like the way the mayor laughed. Sid thought that was the most valid argument he had ever heard…not voting for a candidate because you did not like his laugh.

"Aaron," Sid told his father-in-law, "you should be a panelist on the *McLaughlin Group*, or the *Brinkley Show*."

Both grandfathers were wearing light summer suits, both grandmothers wore summer dresses.

Their daughter Linda and husband, Mark Sossin, came over. Linda had just given birth to their second child Alec. Mark's parents were watching him, but would bring him to the party at the Weitz house in Hewlett this afternoon. Peter, their eldest, age six, looked both dapper and warm in his blue blazer and white slacks outfit. He warmly hugged his Uncle Steve.

"I'm not calling you Doctor, you know," Peter said.

"Steve will do just fine," Steve replied.

"I love my little buddy!" Sid placed his hand on Peter's shoulder.

Linda Weitz Sossin, thirty-one and an audiologist, congratulated her baby brother. They got along very well, for which their parents were thankful. Linda had Norma's features and reddish hair, which she wore parted on the left, and worn to the nape of her neck. Her hair was layered and brushed in an inverted flip at the neck. She wore a beige jacket and skirt ensemble. Mark Sossin, also thity-one, also hugged his brother-in-law. Mark was six foot one, well built, with wavy black hair, layered and parted on the right. He also wore a mustache. He looked more like a leading man than a foreign trade consultant. Sid liked his son-in-law very much. He usually sent them postcards when he traveled abroad. Sid, however, often referred to his son-in-law as a 'fuckin' academic,' because he liked to figure everything out.

Sid lit a Viceroy.

"Come on, Dad, not here."

"Whatsa matta, "Sid retorted, "nobody here is specializing in oncology?"

"Let's take a picture," Norma suggested. "I want a picture of everybody."

"Why not, we have a photographer," Aaron said.

"Bullshit!" Sid exclaimed. "Norma and Peter are gonna be the photographers today." Sid answered his father-in-law.

"Common, common," Sadie said.

Pictures were taken of Steve alone, with his sister and nephew, his parents, and grandparents; and then a classmate of Steve's took a large family picture for them.

After the pictures, they all walked to the large tent for the luncheon together.

When Steven was finished with his medical studies, Sid and Norma anticipated this day for weeks. So did Steven, even more so.

All the hard work and aggravation a medical student endures finally paid off. Steve could relax, for awhile. Soon the internship and residency was to begin. This was more taxing than medical school.

Sid announced the graduation a few weeks earlier in his photographer's association's newsletter, as he had when Linda became an audiologist. Two professionals for children was something to *kvell* about.

Two weeks ago, Sid ran into his long-time friend Abe Susskind at a Bat Mitzvah he was shooting. The affair was held at Lowey's of Great Neck, a famous landmark catering hall. Abe Susskind was photographing a wedding. They schmoozed during the dinner, while they took their break out in the second floor corridor.

Abe Susskind, sixty-one, a burly man with brown and grey hair, and a large nose congratulated his old friend warmly.

"*Mazel Tov*, Sid; a doctor…lots of luck to you both."

Sid thanked Abe for his good wishes.

"Well, listen, it's still an honorable profession; Steven worked hard and he made it, so thank God."

"Absolutely," answered Sid.

Norma's coworkers at the bank also congratulated her. Her girlfriends were also happy for her. She loved it when other ladies she was cordial with wished her well in the supermarket or library, or at the local diner, or at the dry cleaners.

Sid called a kosher off-premises caterer with whom he was friendly, to make a backyard party after the commencement party. The Weitzes opted not to set up a tent. If it rained, they would be fucked, Sid knew. So what, he reasoned, so the *chazzas* and *schnorrers* will go home hungry.

Rain was not in the forecast today.

The Weitzes invited only extended family—cousins, aunts, uncles—as well as close friends of theirs. Steve invited his small circle of close friends. The young lady Steve was seeing lived down the block. She was invited to the party, along with her parents. She did not come to the graduation today. Sid and

Norma liked Gayle Eysenberg, a year younger than Steven, and a business major. Gayle Eysenberg was a beautiful brunette who was well spoken and well to do, her father was a top criminal lawyer.

Steven and Gayle were seeing less of each other these days and this concerned Sid and Norma, as they really liked her. They would be very happy if Gayle turned out be the girl of Steven's dreams, because she was certainly the girl of theirs.

This was part of the reason Sid and Norma wanted their son to attend an American medical school. *Oy*, if their son had to go to school in the Caribbean, or Mexico, or Guatemala, God forbid, he could marry a girl down there. They were afraid of what could walk through their front door on his arm. Norma thought she might talk to Steven later and find out what the situation with Gayle was.

The day started out uneventfully. The graduation took place on the third Monday in May. Sid loaded their personal Hitachi VHS camcorder, which was somewhat smaller in size than his professional super VHS Panasonic camcorders. He had used this Hitachi camcorder a few times as a backup when his studio was still shooting with VHS. The camcorder was delegated to personal use. Norma bought a 'palm-sized' VHS camcorder, so they would be able to carry something small on trips. Sid liked it, but he thought the Hitachi was perfect for today, as he did not want to *schlep* his professional gear.

Early in the morning, Sid placed the invitation from the school against the flowers along the front exterior of the house and videotaped it, the way he did at receptions. Shortly after, Linda, Mark, and Peter pulled up in Mark's white late-model Toyota Supra hatchback. They drove in from the Brightwaters section of Bay Shore out in the south shore of Suffolk County. Sid was surprised they came in Mark's car, and did not bring the 1982 Buick LeSabre coupe he and Norma gave them, when he bought the '84 Chevy Caprice. He gave Steven Norma's '81 Lincoln Town Car, now starting to fall apart. Sid wore his cars out shooting jobs.

Sid embraced Mark, and kissed Linda. Peter ran up to him.

"How are you, big guy, how's the little guy?"

"*Oym foine*, baby!"

Since age three, Peter was able to do a reasonable impression of Sid's gravelly Brooklyn accent, which people said sounded like a cross between Humphrey Bogart and George Burns. Peter called Norma Gam, but never called his grandfather Grandpa, he always called him Sid. Sid loved his eldest grandchild very much and got a kick out of him.

"How's Alec, you didn't tell me?"

"He cries a lot; he gives me a headache."

"Uncle Saul, Uncle Seymour, and Aunt Helen gave me a headache when they were babies, too."

"My folks are bringing him over for the party, Dad," Mark said.

"Beautiful, I love my grandchildren!" Sid knelt down and gave Peter a bear hug.

"You smell like an ashtray, Sid," Peter pulled back.

"You don't smell like a lily either, kid."

"Better than you!"

"Let's go inside, the whole block doesn't have to know how I smell."

"You smell fine, Dad, just a little smoky; I'm used to it by now."

They went into the house.

Half an hour later, a late-model Mercury Marquis sedan pulled in front of 51 Chesterfield Lane. Four elderly people got out. Norma asked her father if he could give Sid's parents a lift out to the Island, he agreed. That was nice when you consider her parents did not like his parents very much. At eighty-three, Sid's father still drove. Ten years earlier, they sold their home in Midwood and moved into an apartment off Ocean Parkway in the same section. Burton Weitz always drove large Chryslers, Buicks, or Oldsmobiles. He was a successful plumber with a large staff under him. Since he no longer needed a large car, he recently bought a small Chevrolet Corsica. Norma's father had a big car, so he asked her if her father would mind driving his parents. After all, they did not need all the cars at the house. Norma said her mother would, but they would do it anyway. Norma's parents also owned a home in Midwood until seven years ago; they sold it and moved into an apartment off Shore Parkway in Bay Ridge. Both sets of parents spent three months in Florida during the winter months. They did not socialize when they vacationed in Florida; come to think of it, they hardly socialized at all.

Steven Weitz, five foot seven, slightly muscular, with dark brown hair parted on the left and brushed to the side, came down the stairs of the Weitz family split-level house. He wore a charcoal gray single-breasted suit, white shirt, and plum-colored solid tie with a gold clasp his father had given him. His black oxford wing-tipped shoes were polished to a high gloss.

"How do I look, Mom?"

"Good, very good, Doctor!" Norma smiled approvingly.

Steve took off the suit jacket and hung it on a hangar in the hall closet.

Sid opened the door for the grandparents, who hugged their physician grandson with pride. Sid excused himself to go out into the backyard to see how the caterers were setting up. Plucky, their four-year-old gray striped female pussycat followed him out. She wanted to get away from the company.

The caterers were busy setting up the guest tables; there were seven, and the smorgasbord tables and chafing dishes. Ruby Mermlestein of Rueben Caterers, a friend of Sid's for thirty years, supervised the operation.

"Okay, Ruby, listen," Sid lit a Viceroy. "If your serving staff has to use the toilet, use the one downstairs in the den, not in my office. Please don't let anyone go to the toilet upstairs. Don't let your people go through my house while we're at the graduation, or while we're here, for that matter."

"I'll watch, Sid, you hired me because you know my clean reputation."

"Don't let your people mess up my kitchen or dirty my house. Also, tell your guys to be careful setting up the tables and, shit, my gardener is expensive, so your guys better not fuck up my yard or my garden."

Sid had a feeling that he was being watched. He turned around and looked up at the kitchen window.

Norma's mother, Sadie, was watching the catering crew set up.

"Ooohhh, common!" Sadie sighed.

Sid turned back to the caterer and shrugged.

"Also, watch that you don't drop anything into my pool."

"Don't worry, Sid, I'll watch," the caterer assured him. "I'll take care of everything."

It was time to leave for the ceremony. Everyone was waiting in front of the house with the man of the hour, everyone except for Sid and his parents. They all had to urinate. Sid went into the large main bathroom in the hall, after his father.

"Shit, Dad!" he called out, "You peed all over the side of the bowl, and look at this! On the floor, too, give me a break!" Sid proceeded to wipe and disinfect the area.

"He didn't make in the toilet?" Nettie asked her son through the closed door.

"Not even close, Ma!" he answered.

"Burt, maybe you should sit down when you go?" Nettie suggested.

"Why don't you mind your own business, dummy?" Burton bellowed.

"I'm trying to help you, Burt!"

"Shaddap, dummy!"

After Sid locked the door and activated the burglar alarm, he made travel arrangements with his son-in-law Mark.

"Listen, what the hell do we need to take so many cars for? Take my Chevy, it's a four door; you and Linda take Norma's folks, I'll take Steven and my parents."

"I want to go with Sid," Peter said.

"You can have him, Dad!" Mark retorted.

"Yeah, okay, Peter rides with us, let's go."

"I was thinking, honey, my dad has a big car, we could take the others in the Chevy."

"I don't want your folks to get lost; Mark knows where the school is."

"Mark can direct Dad."

"I wanna take the Lincoln."

Sid opened the trunk of the maroon 1984 Lincoln Mark V. He placed the camcorder, a lightweight tripod, and his folded suit jacket inside. He folded over the front passenger seat for Norma, helped his mother in, and his father followed.

"Last time I buy a coupe. I didn't learn my lesson after the Buick, what a pain in the royal ass."

Peter stood in the driveway laughing.

"What's so funny, kid?" Sid asked him.

"You said royal ass!"

"So?"

"It's a royal pain in the ass, not a pain in the royal ass!"

"You sure?"

"I'm sure, Sid."

"How do you know?"

"That's what my mom calls me all the time, a royal pain in the ass!"

"I wonder why," Norma said.

"We gotta go, Pete, sit in the middle."

Sid started the Lincoln, and Mark pulled the Chevy out of the driveway, waiting to follow.

Sid eased the big Lincoln along Chesterfield Road, honking at two cars stopped in the middle of the street to talk.

"Sid, don't yell anything," Norma warned, "that's the rabbi."

"Screw him! The schmuck stops to talk in the middle of the street."

Peter laughed.

"Norma, you didn't invite him to the party, did you?"

"No, Sid, you asked me not to."

"Good, I can't stand the putz. I don't want him at my house. At Steve's Bar Mitzvah, he gave a sermon about Noah. He kept yelling, 'Was Noah a mediocre man? Was Noah a mediocre man?' Whatever the hell that meant."

Peter laughed.

"I still remember what he did when Linda and Mark got married, he said, 'Dr. Sossin is a well-respected dentist in our community, Mrs. Sossin has been a respected elementary schoolteacher in our community over twenty years. The bride's parents, Mr. and Mrs. Weitz, also live in the community,' the sonofabitch!"

Peter laughed.

"Shah, shah," Sid's mother said.

Upon arriving at the school, Sid and Mark parked next to each other. Together, they walked across the parking lot. Sid explained the Latin writing on a post in front translated into English read, It is either here or Guadalajara!

The United College of Osteopathic Medicine was an impressive medical school located on a major thorough fare on the North Shore of Long Island. It was a terrific school at which to learn medicine, Steven Weitz believed. There were some who, out of contempt or ignorance, referred to U.C.O.M. as the D.O. school. Students who graduated an Osteopathic college had the letters D.O. after their names, rather than M.D. Graduates of Allopathic medical schools used M.D.

D.O. and M.D. meant the same thing. A physician with D.O. on their certificate was not a chiropractor, was not a podiatrist. The graduate was a medical doctor; it really does not matter whether the person treating you is a D.O. or an M.D.

The graduates sat on bleachers on the perimeter of the athletic field, waiting to be photographed. The athletic field belonged to a large university, that shared the property with the medical school.

The school hired a photography company that specialized in commencements and proms. Sid had heard of the outfit, but did not know them personally. He watched the head photographer, a thirty-something, loud-mouthed young lady snapping directions. She was shooting with a Pentax 6x7 medium-format camera. Dressed in a short white skirt, blue blazer, and white nylon stockings, she caught Sid's attention. She had shoulder length reddish brown hair, Norma's color. She stood on a stepladder as her assistants set up the picture. Sid glanced up her skirt, he could not see anything. She had a throaty voice and a pretty face, with angry-looking eyes—beautiful, but angry looking. Sid figured she was German.

Sid aimed the Hitachi camcorder at his son. Norma had Sid's Canon AE-1 35 mm camera, with a zoom wide-angle lens and a Vivitar 283 strobe on top. Norma, a photographer's wife, knew about using flash outdoors as a fill for shadow areas. In her purse, was a standard 50 mm lens. She shot a few frames.

Steve waved at his father, then rolled his upper lip up and made a face, and then he playfully waved his father away. Sid changed angles a few times.

"ALRIGHT, GUYS, HERE WE GO!" the loud, attractive photographer hollered.

Sid panned the camera from the group to the photographer, then back to the group. Several more pictures were taken. Then one more picture just for fun of the group doing the 'wave.'

Sid observed the head photographer talking to her staff. One man was carrying a Pentax 645 medium-format camera. This was similar in design to Sid's Mamiya 645 medium-format. The camera was on a bracket without a strobe, and Sid thought this was a mistake. He observed several young men and women carrying Nikon F3 35 mm cameras with Vivitar 285 strobes. The 285 differed from the 283 because the head could contract or expand for wide-angle and telephoto pictures.

The photographers were young men and women. This outfit trained young, budding photographers. This was one way to get into the business. Some assistants carried tape recorders. Sid knew how the commencement photography operations worked. The company asked the school for some programs to identify the graduates, then taped descriptions of some students, with a portable tape recorder, held by an assistant.

He shot a series of portraits of Steven in his suit, as well as in cap and gown. They came out very well. Steve and Norma had just finished picking out the proofs for the finished portraits, and they were at the lab being enlarged and retouched.

"Whatever these schmucks want to charge us for these graduation pictures, I'll pay. I'll take a picture of everything they shoot of Steve, provided that their shit comes out. Today is a once in a lifetime event, so I'll take the pictures."

It was time for the commencement to commence.

The graduation ceremony was being held under a large tent on the campus. Sid positioned himself in front of the graduates' entrance. A security guard informed him that the graduates were going to enter there.

The school band, composed of physicians of the faculty, played the Grand March from the opera *Aida*. Sid thought this selection was classier than, Elgar's *Pomp and Circumstance*. *Pomp and Circumstance* was for high school.

The graduates entered. They followed the carriers of the banner. Sid had his earphones on to insure his microphone was functioning. Steve looked at his father as he walked past. The graduates were ushered to the reserved area in the front of the tent. Sid was beginning to *shvitz*. A powered tape recorder was set up on the stage, a cord was plugged from a jack in the speaker to the microphone jack in the tape recorder to record the entire ceremony; this also aided identification. After taking the group photograph, the photographers took some overview pictures of the school, later they would take overviews of the commencement itself. The photographers were to also take one picture of each graduate being hooded, one of receiving the diploma, and one final photo in front of the school flag holding up the diploma. If any photographer missed a graduate due to human or mechanical error, and there were always human and mechanical errors with those schmucks, the photographers were instructed to shoot the floor, on the empty frame to stay in sequence. If a camera stopped functioning, the photographer was instructed to reach up, press the test button on the strobe, and pretend they were actually taking a picture. Sid wondered if his son's photographs would turn out well today, if at all. That's why he brought his own camera with two lenses and a strobe. If Dad's a professional, then why rely on schmucks to do the job?

A week earlier, Steven put on a suit and tie, along with his cap and gown for a series of formal graduation pictures. Steve drove to his father's studio in Elmont.

"You and Lenny let the place go."

"Lenny works upstairs, most of the time I'm down here alone; I'm gonna move out soon, business is slowing down."

It was getting hotter. The faculty filed in, and the Grand Marshal declared the commencement ceremony open, banging the mace on the stage twice.

Steve Weitz roasted, nervously waiting with anticipation for when his name was to be called, as he sat among his fellow graduates.

After the *Star Spangled Banner*, Sid joined his family, placed the camcorder on the tripod, which Norma had opened for him to record the ceremony from where they sat, and satisfied, he sat down next to her.

First, a minister delivered the invocation, and the university president welcomed everyone. The guest speaker, a state senator, made a speech. Student awards were bestowed, and then an honorary degree in osteopathic medicine was awarded to the guest speaker.

Sid and Norma glanced at the program together. They noticed a lot of Patels and Chans. Norma commented about the twin brother and sister graduates from India.

"I wonder how people can tell them apart. I don't think I could from their first names."

"My son has a little penis," Sid said, doing a reasonable Indian accent.

The people in the front row giggled.

It was time for the awarding of the medical degrees. Sid ran back to the front. Outside of the tent he stood facing the stage in a side view.

Finally, the moment they had waited four years for, perhaps even since their son's birth. The dean called the name of Steven Andrew Weitz.

The Weitz, Sossin, and Levine families applauded.

The young man strode erect to the stage. Sid taped the hooding and the bestowing of the degree. When the young man turned around, he realized something was wrong.

"Fuck! That's not my son; he's not my kid, fuck, fuck, shit!"

Sid taped the graduate who was called up before Steven, Adam Lawrence Wein. The fucking kid looked like Steven.

He was not too late, thank God. Steven Andrew Weitz was just about to be hooded. Sid captured the whole wonderful event. He held up the ceremonial diploma, as he walked past his father returning to his seat.

The dean told the graduates they could now move their tassels from left to right.

The doctor who was the head of the New York State Osteopathic Society delivered greetings to the class. He said that he was honored to be the first doctor to address the graduates as colleagues. A huge burst of applause erupted.

Sid and Norma's eyes were tearing. They saw fathers, mothers, brothers, sisters, uncles, aunts, grandparents, even spouses who were themselves physicians, place the hood of medicine they worked so hard for lovingly on their loved ones…how moving. What a great day to be a parent.

A class address given by a student followed. The dean then asked all the graduates to rise to take the Osteopathic Oath, which is different than the Hippocratic Oath, yet cites the same principles.

"Please repeat after me," the dean spoke, "I, your name."

Some of the people replied aloud, "Your name." There were a few polite chuckles.

"Do hereby affirm my loyalty to the profession I am about to enter. I will be mindful always of my great responsibility, to preserve the health and the life of my patients, to retain their confidence, and respect both as a physician and a friend who will guard their secrets with scrupulous honor and fidelity, to perform faithfully my professional duties, to employ only those recognized methods of treatments consistent with good judgment and with my skill and ability, keeping in mind always, nature's laws and the body's inherent capacity for recovery.

"I will be ever vigilant in aiding the general welfare of the community, sustaining its laws and institutions, not engaging in those practices which will in any way bring shame or discredit upon myself or my profession. I will give no drugs with deadly intent to any, though it be asked of me.

"I will endeavor to work in accord with my colleagues in a spirit of progressive cooperation and never by word or by act cast imputations upon them or their rightful practices.

"I will look with respect and esteem upon all those who have taught me my art. To my college I will be loyal and strive always for its best interests and for the interests of the students who will come after me. I will ever be alert to adhere to and develop the principles and practice of Osteopathic medicine and surgery as taught in this college.

"In the presence of this gathering I bind my oath."

Steven Weitz felt choked up, and his eyes teared. *Could it be, finally, all the hard work paid off? I am a doctor!*

Sid Turned to Norma and kissed her softly on her lips. Their grandson Peter stared at them.

"What the hell you looking at, kid?" Sid asked him, "You're next!" He leaned across Norma and Linda to kiss him.

"*Mazel tov*, and *Siman tov*," Norma sung softly.

A three star army general, who was the army's top osteopathic physician, administered the military oath of office to those graduates who were serving in the armed forces.

The minister gave the closing benediction

The grand marshal declared the commencement ceremony closed, with one loud bang of his mace.

Right before the recessional began, Sid took the camcorder off of the tripod and ran back to the place he had taped the processional.

The new doctors walked back to the large field. They did not look like doctors, they were all so young. They looked like kids. They *were* kids, they had their medical degree and a title now, but they were kids.

Sid and Norma were surprised when several female students kissed their son; one young woman kissed him on the lips. Why not? Steven Weitz was good looking; he looked just like his father, only better. He was an attractive guy. He even played baseball and football for the local town leagues when he was younger. Good looking and a doctor, too! Quite a catch!

Together they walked to the large tent that was set up for the luncheon.

Peter was impressed; he had never seen a tent of that size. His grandfather told him that he had photographed several receptions in tents like this one. The tent did not have any fans, so the atmosphere grew stuffy.

The 'luncheon' was an assortment of finger sandwiches, soft drinks, cookies, hot coffee, and tea.

Burton Weitz was disappointed with the spread his grandson's medical school put on.

"Little sandwiches, a can of soda for lunch? What is this shit? What kind of shit is this?"

Sadie Levine, Norma's mother, gestured her thumb at her son-in-law.

"See, this is why, ahhh you see!"

"What is this shit?" Burton continued, "What is this shit? For all the money you pay the school they can't give you a better lunch?"

"Sid and Norma made a catered party, Burt, at the house," Sid's mother Nettie said, trying to quiet him down, "you'll have plenty to eat."

Burton shrugged.

Steve's face turned slightly red, as he laughed nervously.

"What's wrong?" Norma's father, Aaron, asked him knowingly.

"Nothing, Grandpa."

It was time to go. Steven could not believe it, four years of hard work, then just like that, it was over. Does everything in life end this way? Suddenly turn around and it's all over, then you wonder where the time went.

Steve picked up his real diploma, while his family took one final look at the campus.

Diploma in hand, he got back into his mother's Lincoln. The car proceeded toward the school's exit. His father was puffing a cigarette as he drove. His first mission as a physician was to try to convince his dad to quit smoking.

Steve picked up the camcorder and shot the college as they left. He aimed the camcorder at the school sign, as the powerful Lincoln glided out onto Northern Boulevard.

Chapter Twenty-Five

At twenty-six, Dr. Steven Weitz was an attractive young man. Layered dark hair, good complexion, average straight nose, and brown eyes; people commented, he looked just like his father. He did not mind, his father was a handsome man. He just did not want to sound like his father.

Dad is very verbose, he has his unique way of putting things. Steve knew his father was always right, because his dad's friends always said, "You're right, Sid, you're right, whatever you say, you're right."

He looked at himself in the mirror on his dresser. He looked the same; he did not yet have the serious face of a doctor.

"Hmmm, say ahhh, hmmm," Steve practiced his doctor's voice. "Hmmm, I have some bad news, Mr. Smith, I'm afraid we'll have to operate. You can't afford an operation, you say? Alright, we'll just touch up your x-rays."

His dad hooked up a speaker for the stereo unit on the patio, years ago, when he was still a legend in his business. Lively Latin dance music was playing. Not salsa or Latin-style jazz, but real, country club sounding Latin dance music. *Tea for Two* was playing in a cha-cha version.

He looked at a picture of himself with his parents and sister that was taken at his Bar Mitzvah. He loved his mother, she was his best friend. He loved his sister. When he was young, she put up with his childhood pranks. Although, he had an older sister, and no brothers, he could talk to her. He could tell her things. Linda felt the same way about him. He felt close to his brother-in-law. Mark was like an older brother to him. Sometimes he thought his father liked Mark better than him.

He looked at the bearded man in the family picture. *You could come across real cool some times*, he thought. *Dad wore a beard, he owned a few convertibles, he had a cool job, why weren't we ever that close?"*

"I wish, I knew you better as a person, Sid," he said out loud, alone in his empty room. "You're funny at times, other times I never knew what was going to come out of your mouth. I knew you as a photographer, not really my father. After I turned eight, Sid, it was like you didn't have time for me anymore. You didn't have time for Linda anymore. You didn't even have time for Mom. You took us on a lot of nice trips, so you could brag about that. You bought all those fancy cars—those Cadillacs, Lincolns, Buicks, and that clunky Chrysler mom hated, the convertibles—not for Mom's comfort, but to tell all your photographer friends about the car you drive.

"I never really spent much time knowing you. I don't agree with Nana, I'm not better off for that. I heard you are a funny guy at times, you're a good storyteller, and there are some who say you're a character. You're probably a fascinating man. Too bad we never really did anything together, I don't count the times I assisted you on jobs. You were either busy working or yelling at me.

"I know you love me, I love you, Dad, but I know your life has always been the studio. It isn't that you are at times neglectful to your family in the pursuit of your livelihood. The studio, the job, has always been you're first love. That's true, Sid, the studio is the love of your life, and Mom is your mistress."

Never on Sunday as a cha-cha was playing out in the backyard.

There was a soft knock on the door.

"Steve, are you talking to someone in there?"

"No, Mom, just thinking out loud; jitters, I guess."

"Well, come on out back, everybody's here; they're all asking for the guest of honor. Gayle's here with her folks."

"Be right out, Ma."

"Well, come on, your father says you better put in an appearance, he wants you to know this party is costing him a fortune."

"So, he'll raise his prices"

"Is that nice? Come on, everybody came to see you."

"Be right there."

Steve tightened his tie and looked out the window. *Gayle*, he thought, *she and I have grown apart. I don't think I love her, I don't really know if she loves me. I'm not comfortable with continuing a relationship with her.* He put on his jacket and left the room. As he walked downstairs, he figured his father probably would say he broke up with her just to spite him. Every time he showed independence, his father said he was being spiteful.

The doorbell rang and Norma and her mother walked over together. Steve walked behind them.

A short white-haired, thin woman of eighty stood on the doorstep.

"Mrs. Gothelf, how are you, everything alright?" Norma asked.

Mrs. Gothelf was a widow who moved in with her son and daughter-in-law next door. She wanted to know if anything was wrong.

"Everything is fine, Mrs. Gothelf. Steven graduated from medical school today; we made a party in the yard.

"Oh, *mazel tov*, young man," she shook his hand. "No, nothing wrong, I came over because when I saw food being delivered and all the cars parked in front, with the people all going in, I thought, something, God forbid, happened to your husband."

"From your mouth to God's ear," Sadie said gesturing upward.

"No, we're making a party; if something like that happened, we wouldn't be playing music, Mrs. Gothelf, listen."

"Well, listen, why not?" Sadie commented.

"You know, Mother!" Norma drew an angry breath and shot the elderly lady a dirty look.

"Oh, alright, well I guess I'll go home and sit all alone by myself in the house; maybe I'll sit out in the back in the sun and listen to your nice music."

"You sit alone?" Norma sounded concerned.

"My son works, my daughter-in-law, she goes to Loehmann's and the beauty parlor, my grandchildren, they live far, they don't want I should stay by them, and I don't like to go around by myself, so I sit all alone."

"You don't have any friends?" Norma felt sorry for the old lady; after all, she didn't think she was far off from old age herself.

"No, no, not out here on the Island. We used to live in Sheepshead Bay. When my husband passed away three years ago, my son said he wanted I should stay by him." She turned to Norma's mother, "We went to Miami for the winter, my husband passed away down there."

"Terrible," Norma said.

"Oh, you poor thing," Sadie said shaking her head.

"My husband," Mrs. Gothelf continued, "dropped dead crossing Collins Avenue; right in the middle of the street, he dropped dead."

"In the middle of the street?" Steven remarked.

"He had the light!"

"Come on in," Norma took the old lady by the hand, "you'll stay a while, come join the party," Norma led her into the house.

"You'll have a nosh," Sadie invited.

"Yeah, glad to have you," Steven mumbled.

This was a good crowd for a Monday afternoon, Steve assessed. He knew most of Dad's photographer friends were closed on Mondays, so they would not have any trouble attending. This was late May, so most of the relatives could take off and come over, at least for a while, anyway. The ones who couldn't make it would not be missed. Jees, now an old lady at the party, Christ, Dad's gonna love this.

Sadie took Mrs. Gothelf out back.

Sid ran into the house.

"Hey, yo, hey!" he cornered Norma in the kitchen. "What the hell is this? Why is the putz from next door's mother here?"

"I invited her."

"For what," he raised his voice, "for spite?"

"No, she came to the door; she thought people were coming over because I was sitting *shiva* for you."

"Him first!"

"She hasn't any place to go, love, so I told her come in for a nosh."

"If she hasn't any place to go, then why my place? I hate that goddamn weasel next door!"

Beautiful. Steven thought *beautiful, a house full of people and the old man is going to have one of his episodes.*

"Sidney, she's an old lady; don't get excited, she's all alone."

"Her son is a dirty sneak and weasel; I hate the sonofabitch and if that schmuck is a sonofabitch, then remember, she's his mother!"

Steve leaned against the refrigerator, this was all very true. His dad hated the man next door. The people who lived next door were nouveau rich shit heads, who thought the photographer and his bank teller wife, were beneath them. They wouldn't even consider such a working class moron to photograph their kid's affairs; they used David and David in East Rockaway.

There were run-ins. A few years ago, Mr. Gothelf asked Mr. Weitz if he could ask his gardener to cut the hedge on the left side of his lawn, which was round, to match the hedge on the Gothelf property, which was square; after all, it was closer to the Gothelf house, than it was to the Weitz house. Mr. Weitz told Mr. Gothelf to go fuck himself. Mr. Gothelf acted as if he had never heard that expression before. Upon arriving home from work the next day, Norma saw Mr. Gothelf finishing up his gardening, on her hedge. She informed her neighbor, that she thought he had a lot of *chutzpah*, that her husband told him that he could not accommodate his artistic whim, that he had no right to vandalize her property. Mr. Gothelf told Mrs. Weitz, if she didn't like it, she could call her lawyer.

Sid was enraged, he called his lawyer, his brother Seymour. Seymour didn't want to touch it, told his older brother to go next door, punch the guy in the mouth, then cop a plea for a lighter sentence. Sid decided to hell with it, the sonofabitch wants me to beat him up, so he can get me arrested, and then sue. For spite, I'll ignore it.

A few years later, another endearing incident occurred. It was the beginning of spring, the gardener had just seeded the front lawn, and a period of time had to pass before the lawn could be mowed. The grass was doing very well, growing high. Sid was loading his car up one Saturday afternoon to go shoot a job. It was a warm day, everybody was outside. Mrs. Gothelf rode by, sitting in the passenger seat of a car driven by her best friend, another neighborhood, darling "Der Cubana Yid." She was a Jewish woman from Cuba, and Sid could not stand that bitch, either. Mrs. Gothelf lowered the car window.

"CUT YOUR LAWN!" she yelled out right in front of the whole neighborhood.

The car went by too fast, so he did not have time to moon her. Now he's gonna feed the bastard's mother?

"This day is turning out well, alright, Doctor," he turned both to and on his son. "Everybody came to see you, go outside and circulate, come on, shake your ass!"

"You mean they didn't come to see you and hear your stories?"

"What stories?"

"About how you called some banquet manager or bandleader a schmuck."

"Don't start with your father, Steve," Norma sighed.

"Yeah, don't start with your father," Sid seconded, "especially after he paid for your medical degree, come on chop, chop, crack shit! Go receive your adoring public."

"I'll be right out, you go on ahead."

"Yeah, okay." They went out of the patio door.

"Well, baby, don't you think you should offer your guest something to eat?" Sid pointed at Mrs. Gothelf, who sat alone on a redwood chair on the grass.

"Can I fix you a plate, Mrs. Gothelf?"

"I'm not very hungry, I'll have a snack."

"Alright, honey," Norma smiled, "I'll bring you some sliced turkey, some chopped liver, and some potato salad."

"Maybe some roast beef, if it's not too much trouble, some sliced brisket with the gravy on the side, a piece of derma, some of that Italian-style eggplant, and the spinach and shells on a separate plate, please, darling."

Sid turned to Norma and shrugged.

"Would you like something to drink?" he asked her.

"A daiquiri."

"I'll have one with you," he sighed.

Steven stood on the back porch, watching his parents wait on their elderly guest. *Well*, he thought *time to see everybody*.

Steven stood on the patio, waved his hand to acknowledge the party guests

"Look who's here!" both sets of his grandparents called out.

"My special little boy!" Norma called out.

"Ahhh, ooohhh!" everybody sighed.

Steve noticed that everyone stood with their back to him. Everyone except the old lady sitting in the redwood chair, eating away.

Dr. Nathan and Ellen Sossin, Mark's parents, walked into the backyard with Alec, his sister and brother-in-law's new baby son.

His great-grandparents kissed him.

Sid placed his finger on Alec's tummy. "Pippy, pippy, pippy, pippy, it's grandpa, honey."

"Get your camera, Sid."

"You get my camera, Norma, I'm entertaining."

Steven felt crestfallen—two years for an associate's degree, two more years for a bachelor of science, four years of hard work in medical school, and I'm upstaged by my two-month-old nephew at my own graduation party.

Steven moved toward the crowd. He attempted to get their attention.

"Ahem!"

Chapter Twenty-Six

"**S** TEVEN!"

"THE DOCTOR!"

Everyone burst into applause. Sid announced the man of the hour. Steven felt the way the Benjamin Braddock character did in the movie *The Graduate*. His father, the guy who played the cardiac surgeon on *St. Elsewhere*, embarrassed the hell out of his son in front of all their guests. His father's partner's wife, Sherry Schecter, an overweight brunette who was squeezed into a pair of white slacks and a pink silk top was the first to hug him.

No way, Mrs. Robinson, he thought, *not even if we both put paper bags over our heads. If Lenny leaves without you, Sherry, you're taking a cab; I can't stand your stupid daughter either.*

A fifty-two-year-old elegant-looking man in a gray suit hugged him. He had graying brown hair and a neat mustache.

"My little nephew, *mazel tov*, a doctor."

"Thank you, Uncle Seymour."

"I hope I never have to defend you."

"Don't worry, Sy, I would hire a heavy hitter; you're not that good a lawyer."

"Listen, stick to the medicine kid, a comic, you're not."

An attractive woman with neatly coiffed brown hair hugged him. His Aunt Miriam, Seymour's wife.

"Our little Steven, a doctor. Here, this is from us," she handed him a thousand dollar check.

"Shit almighty," Seymour groaned, "Eysenberg is here, your girlfriend's father."

"*Oy*," Miriam moaned, "that was a million years ago; you were an assistant district attorney, he had to make a monkey out of you."

"I thought he was slime. He defended the worst killers, rapists, and murderers, still he believed in his clients."

"You're a lawyer, Uncle Sy; you haven't prosecuted in seventeen years."

"I'm a civil attorney, I don't defend killers."

"Steve, don't listen to your uncle, your girlfriend is a catch; don't louse it up, don't let her get away, you hear me? A good catch for a doctor!"

Steve's girlfriend came over. She flashed a white radiant smile at him. Uncle Sy and Aunt Miriam stepped back.

"Counselor," Seymour nodded to Gayle's father.

"Mr. Weitz," George Eysenberg acknowledged him.

Seymour leaned and whispered into Steve's ear. "He's in luck, my ex-convict Uncle Gabriel is here; maybe he's coming out of retirement to plan a heist, and he can defend him."

"Sy, my God!" Miriam reproved he husband. She grabbed hold of his upper arm, "Come, let's eat. Good to see you again, young lady," she nodded to Gayle as she led her husband to the smorgasbord table.

Sid hit the remote on the hi-fi system. The backyard filled with music. Perez Prado was playing his signature cha-cha selection, and some of the guests began to dance. Sid was happy with the spread he and Norma had made. A tall muscular, dark-haired man entered the yard accompanied by an attractive blonde woman.

"Hey, who called the cops?" Sid yelled out.

"*Mazel tov, bubie,*" replied Harry Lowenstein, who was not only one of Sid's top candid men, but he was also a New York City police officer. His wife, Rachel, hugged Sid, and then excused herself to find Norma.

"So, Detective, are you still on the job?" Sid asked as he hugged Harry.

"Officer, Sideleh, it's still officer; they wanted to put me up for detective a couple of years ago, but..." Harry shrugged.

"You didn't need it," Sid offered.

"I didn't need it," Harry repeated, "also, I have seventeen years on the job. I'm getting out in twenty. Already, I earn what a lieutenant earns by shooting for all the studios along with my cop salary, so I'm doing alright, that is, except for when my friend makes me shoot his daughter's wedding without pay..."

"You would charge me to shoot my daughter's wedding?" Sid asked in mock surprise, "Me, me, you would charge me?"

"You didn't even offer me a plate of food."

"Of course not, you were too busy working. We needed you to shoot the wedding, not to eat, but today you'll eat; look, we have tongue and pastrami, you'll take some on rye bread with potato salad and you'll eat."

"So, who's here from the trade?" Harry asked.

"Not a one, they couldn't make it, just Lenny and his fat ass significant other are here. Norma sent a card to my ex-partner Carl out in Arizona, I wonder if he'll send a gift..."

"He will, Sid," Harry assured him, "but I'm surprised I don't see Franklin Photographers here."

"I haven't spoken to him since we had that falling out in '73. He got angry at Carl and called me up to say Carl did something unethical to him, so I tell him to piss off. I stuck up for Carl, he was my partner, I had to stick up for him, and so at an association meeting, Frankie says to me, 'Fuck you where you breathe.' I never crossed paths with him after that."

"Jees," Harry shook his head.

"I know," Sid continued, "after many years of friendship, and sharing bungalows with our families together, boom, the end. But, who the fuck needs that ex-con's company anyway? Besides, I hear he only does portraits now, nobody books him for candids anymore."

"You still speak to your best friend Heshy Adomovich though, Sid?"

"Yeah, Harry, but they're in Israel for a relative's affair, a *bris* I think. We talk all the time. Once in a while, I shoot a job for him if he gets stuck, but when he doesn't get me in, he leaves a message on my machine, 'Good *shabbas*.'"

"Good *shabbas*?" asked Harry.

"Good *shabbas*; he knows I don't observe, so he calls. He and Ina sent Steven a check for two hundred last week. The damnedest thing is they still talk to Carl and Cindy out in Arizona. They go out to see them, but they don't stay by them, because they're Orthodox, so Carl gets them a place near a *shul* they can walk to."

"What about our friends Marion Studios, the Feinbergs."

"Shit, Harry, I never see Bobby Feinberg or his ex-wife, Roberta, anymore. She has her own studio now, in the house in Sheepshead Bay she won from him in the divorce. They're still the biggest in Brooklyn, I hear, them and that wop in Bensonhurst, Valentine Studios."

"Yeah," Harry agreed, "they're still big, I still shoot for Feinberg, and I used to shoot for Valentine."

"We all did, Harry baby, old man Valenti, the grandfather, hired us kids to shoot those Italian football weddings for twenty-five bucks a job. I was close to Bob Feinberg's old man when they had the studio on Pitkin Avenue, The Feinberg Brothers—me, Carl, Heshy, everybody shot for them. We all used to go up to the country with our wives and kids to stay by them. Old man Feinberg had a bungalow; we'd all go up for association weekends. A lotta fun, Franklin Malkin used to come when he wasn't in jail for pornography, and his son used to pee outside in front of my daughter."

Harry shook his head.

"I dunno," Sid went on, "after all these years we get older and drift apart; shit man, I'm winding it down, too. Do you still shoot for Mr. Orthodox, Dov Learner, Learner Studios on Thirteenth Avenue in Boro Park?"

"Sometimes, he's getting old..."

"We all are, *bubie*," Sid interrupted Harry.

"But, still he shoots," Harry finished.

"Mr. Pious," Sid lit a Viceroy, "with his big black Cadillacs."

"No more Cadys," Harry replied, "Dovie drives a Lexus now."

"A Lexus, God bless him, doesn't he know Hitler said the Japanese were yellow Aryans? Probably does, but doesn't give a fuck, because all the affluent Chassids drive Lexuses today."

Sid flicked an ash, "Eat, Harry, we'll bullshit later. Go say hello to the doctor, I've gotta circulate, and say hello to the rest of the *chazzas*."

Harry laughed, *chazza* was Yiddish for 'pig,' Sid would call his invited guests *chazzas*.

Steven Weitz was uncomfortable, but he was happy his Great Uncle Gabriel Weitz was there. What a character, Uncle Gabe was an ex-convict and career criminal and proud of it. Rumor had it that his father's first camera was given to him by Uncle Gabe, such a generous gift, but Gabe didn't pay a cent for it, he stole it out of somebody's apartment.

Steven loved hearing his uncle's war stories. He told Steven that there were three things he was proud of during his long career. He never hurt anybody, he never finked on anybody, and he never took it up the ass in jail.

"Ain't ya gonna kiss your great uncle, Doc?" Gabriel Weitz asked Steven.

Gabriel Weitz was a stocky bald man with thin dyed black hair around the sides of his head. He had a full black mustache, and the face of an amiable bulldog, which is what he was. Uncle Gabe was wearing a cheap light gray polyester suit, which he probably bought at Goodwill or a pawn shop. He wore dull gray leather loafers, which had fallen off a truck. His shirt, which was white, was a few shades lighter than his gray suit, and the necktie was an old clip on.

They firmly embraced, happy to see each other again, it had been a while. Gabe had not been in prison for a long time, but although semi-retired, Gabe was cautious, not reformed.

"When did you get out?" Steven asked his great uncle.

"Ha, ha, a wise ass," Gabe laughed.

The two sat on a redwood bench; the cushions for the back and bottom made that piece of wood comfortable.

"A doctor in the family, I'm proud; ya know, we had a couple of decent doctors in Sing Sing, but the guy we had up in Elmira that time was a quack."

"I've already worked with some prisoners on my rotation. Next month when I start my internship, I'll have emergency room rotations, so I know I be working with prisoners there, too.

"Well, listen," Gabe said smiling, "I know doctors make a hell of a lot of money, but for most of my adult life, I had free medical care. Here," Gabe took out two fresh one hundred dollar bills, "put this in your pocket, *mazel tov*."

Steven hesitated.

"Take, take," Gabe thrust the bills at him, "ya think I stole it?"

"The thought had occurred to me," Steven replied.

"The thought had occurred to me," Gabe mimicked, "talks like a college boy, then again you are one. Take my gift, it ain't stolen, it's my Social Security."

"You don't get Social Security, Uncle Gabe."

"Only because I didn't pay into the system; that, by the way, is discrimination because I'm old. In my profession we ain't got withholding taxes or pension plans," Gabe lamented in a melodic baritone, with a slight Vaudeville-sounding Jewish accent.

"I thank you, Uncle Gabe," Steven accepted the money.

"You're welcome. Be careful, I see in the papers, today doctors go to jail because of insurance fraud, dealing drugs, and fondling patients."

"Don't worry about me," Steven assured his great uncle, "I am going to be honest and ethical, and I can't imagine taking a dump out in the open."

"It ain't so bad, Steve, ya get used to it, sometimes real fast, especially if ya gotta go. It ain't so bad if ya got a single man cell. Nobody sits and watches you crap, feh! Alright, some weirdos do, but that's the life we have."

"I'm straight, there's another reason to be law abiding."

"Well listen, Steve, ya just gotta watch yourself, and handle yourself, stay away from the queer punks, you'll be alright."

"I see."

"I'll tell you another thing, we got guys inside who act like girls, they even look like girls, they do it for compensation, and some of those darlings will do it for free. The key to surviving on the inside is knowing how to take care of yourself. You keep away from queers and inmates who need relief. If you need relief, you wait until lights out when you're in your cell alone, then you masturbate into some toilet paper, but not too much; I knew a guy, a forger, doin' a five-year stretch, he had this sweet beautiful wife on the outside who he missed. So, he jerked off so frequently he didn't have any toilet paper left to wipe his ass with. That's why I believe that Dr. Ruth radio therapist lady, when she says too much masturbation is not a good thing."

"Where do you live now, Uncle Gabe?"

"I live in a nice part of the lower east side in the city, in a furnished studio apartment, really like a small room, but what the hell, it's Manhattan."

"You got it made."

"Always have, kiddo, the easy life for me. Ya know, that time your pop's studio was broken into, he thought I did it."

"Did you?"

"No, I wouldn't steal from a nephew, besides that alarm his partner Carl installed years ago was very hard to figure out. I asked around, but never found out who did it, not professional thieves. Probably junkies, I bet."

Gayle Eysenberg came up behind them and put her arms around Steven.

"Aren't you going to spend any time with me?" she asked him.

"Sure, Gayle, I'm sorry for neglecting you."

"As well you should be," she answered.

Gayle Eysenberg was five foot eight inches, the same height as Steven. She had jet black hair worn shoulder length and swept back, she had a widow's peak. Her eyes were violet, her nose a prominent beautiful Semitic nose, but not overly Jewish. She had medium-sized breasts and slim hips with a shapely rear end. She was trim, because she took care of herself by exercising and jogging, but she was not on a permanent diet like her mother and many other ladies in their Hewlett neighborhood.

"Go, go, circulate, join the party, you're neglecting your guests." Gabe helped Steve to his feet.

Gayle took his arm. Steve said, "Alright, let's go."

"Besides," Gabe went on, "it's not a good thing for a young Jewish doctor to be associating with the criminal element. Look, your mom and pop are doing the cha-cha-cha; go on and enjoy, you earned it, kiddo."

Steven and Gayle walked arm in arm from the side yard to the patio to join his party. The music grew louder, Steven felt somewhat anxious and nauseous.

Chapter Twenty-Seven

The graduation party was winding down, which was fine with the graduate, he had had enough. He was lucky today, in the sense that he had successfully evaded his Uncle Simon. Norma's older brother Simon, or 'Simple Simon' as he was known, was not known for his intellect on either side of the family. Although he was Norma's brother and she loved him, she agreed with her husband that her brother was blessed with an I.Q. of one.

Simple Simon had trouble putting two words together, and the words he did use were never used in the proper context. His conversation was full of, "I uhhh, uhhh, errr, that is, in other woids, uhhh uhhh iiihhh ihh, ihh...."

Simple Simon was a carpet cleaner for a large company. He and his wife, Sybil, lived in a dingy old building in the Brighton Beach section of Brooklyn.

During the day, Steven and Uncle Simpleton spoke briefly.

"Well, uhhh, I ah, ahhh, see uhh, that we got a doctor in the family, that's nice, that's nice, very nice." Simon, a tall man with thin reddish hair around the sides of his head, wore tinted metal-framed glasses and had the face of a man who was perpetually bewildered. He wore an out-of-style gray Glen plaid suit.

"Well, now that you graduated from medical school, you've come to the point of no return. In uhhh, in other words, prior to, to, uhhh, becoming a physician, you could change your career plans, now you must pursue your chosen field of endeavor. You ahhh, ahhh, iihhh, have invested a lot of time and monetary capital into your training, you can't turn back now."

"Well, I graduated, Uncle Simon."

"I uhhh, know, I know you did, you excelled in you course of study. Too bad your cousins could not attend this most magnificent event today."

Steven did not miss his first cousins at all. Their son Gary was an arrogant prick, who did not want his Uncle Sid's studio to photograph his wedding, because Helaine, that stuck-up Jewish princess whom he married, didn't think

Uncle Sid was quite good enough for them. The same was true of 'Simple Simon' and 'Surly Sybil's' daughter Leonore, who married that Israeli physical education teacher, who only wanted to brag about what a great basketball player he was. Leonore had a big nose, her husband, Danny, had broken front teeth, so they looked well-suited for each other.

"How are you coming with your college degree, Uncle Simon?"

"Well, I'm working on it. I, uhhh, take a few credits at night, then there is a lot to learn."

"Well, you'll get there, don't worry." Steven did not really think Simple Simon would ever graduate.

Finally, Steven was able to tear himself away from Simple Simon. Mixing with the other invited guests was not any less taxing on his nerves. Thinking about the graduation party scene in the film *The Graduate*, Steven longed for the sounds of silence. He spent the remainder of the party alone with Gayle, not necking, just talking. Gayle couldn't make the graduation, her college was on a different schedule, and she was not finished for the semester. A business major, Gayle had an economics final today.

"So how does it feel to be a doctor?" was one of the questions she asked Steven.

"Exhausting," was the only answer he could think of.

"Wanna go over to my house and make love?" she asked.

"Too tired," he truthfully replied.

"Okay," she shrugged.

It was getting dark, and many of the invited guests were leaving, pausing for that long, never-ending Jewish goodbye, where the most important discussions are saved for this time.

The same question was asked that is always asked at the end of a Jewish family gathering at a relative's house on Long Island, "Who needs a ride back to Brooklyn?"

The grandparents, the aunts and uncles, and the cousins all left. Uncle Gabriel escorted Mrs. Gothelf home, before catching a ride back home with Sid's parents. Burton Weitz, Sid's father, and Gabriel were brothers. Gabe wasn't interested in his brother's trade. Burt was a crook as a plumber, he just appeared to make an honest living, and Gabe thought Burt was a bigger crook than he was. Gabe's offer to escort old Mrs. Gothelf home was not an act of chivalry, this was the Five Towns, and he wanted to case the house.

Gayle's parents had also gone home, Mark, Linda, their sons, Harry and his wife, and Lenny and his wife remained.

They all sat at the patio tables winding it down. Sid had long ago removed his jacket and tie, his shirt sleeves were rolled up. The photographers were telling stories. Dad was being charming, Steven observed…well, maybe not charming, but entertaining, his war stories always were.

There were two tables pushed together, a white round resin table with a glass top and an open red striped umbrella and a long rectangular redwood picnic table without an umbrella, which was pushed onto the patio when company came.

The coffee was being sipped, pastries munched, and the caterer's illegal 'Ricans' were clearing the setups away.

"What about Saul Pechevski?" Harry Lowenstein asked.

"Dead," both Sid and Lenny answered at the same time.

"What?" Harry asked in disbelief, "He was in good shape."

"His shape had nothing to do with it, Saulie was murdered."

"Whaaat?" Harry cried out.

"I'm surprised you didn't know about it 'cause you're a cop."

"What happened, Lenny?"

Sid took over. "Saulie, who was always a lousy shooter, gave up candids and went into pornography. He shot the same shit as Franklin Malkin used to shoot, but at least he didn't work in his studio. Saul got rid of the studio and took a loft somewhere in Soho. Anyways, one day there's a knock at the door; it's two guys in dark suits, and they say, 'Hi, how ya doin'? We're your new partners, and they explain what the new setup is to him, 'cause everybody goes along with these guys." Sid bent his left ear forward with his left index finger and moved the right side of his nose over with his right index finger. Gayle listened intently, as this sounded like a good one. "So Saulie, a bruiser himself, let loose on those two guys, chung, chung." Sid swung his fists carefully, because Harry's wife sat across from him, chung, chung. "Then he throws the both of them down the flight of steps." Sid mimicked a person picking someone else up by the collar, "Bloom, bloom, bloom, bloooom, right down. A couple of weeks later, he's eating with his wife in a restaurant on Nostrand Avenue in Brooklyn near their house. His wife goes to the store next door to pick up something, a man comes in, and 'bang, bang, bang,' puts a couple of bullets into Saulie's head, the end!"

"Jesus," everyone at the table said.

"Tell about Larry Kessler," Harry implored of Sid.

"Yeah, my son's girlfriend doesn't know this one. Okay, Larry is a putz who had a high-volume studio in Riverdale, the Bronx; only, by the people who live in Riverdale, Riverdale ain't the Bronx, *Fort Apache* with Paul Newman is the Bronx, Riverdale is Riverdale. So, putz Larry over-extends himself, gets himself into debt, over-extends his legitimate loans, and goes to the mob. Well, he has trouble paying back the mob. You see, Gayle, the mob charges you something like 50 percent interest on top of what they loan you."

Gayle shook her head, "I know."

"That's right, your daddy defends those people. So, one day they visit Larry, since he's into them, they say, 'Okay, now you're in the cocaine business,' so putz Larry is dealing for them. Now one thing leads to another, buh, buh, buh, and there's a bust, Larry gets pinched. Larry's in trouble, and being smart, he makes a deal, he gets probation, but in return he has to wear a wire. Okay, so he tries to get people to incriminate themselves, but they find out about what he's up to right away. One night, he's working alone, the guineas come into his studio and beat the cum outta him." Everyone laughed; Sid was getting into his story, so he forgot to tone down the material for Gayle's benefit. "He lived, went bankrupt, completed probation, but he's still alive."

"Our buddy, Howie Loeb, was like that," Lenny offered.

"Tell me about him, Mr. Weitz," Gayle requested.

"Listen, beautiful, you've been going with my son for a while, and you call my wife Norma. Call me Sid, I'd Like that.

"Okay, Sid."

"Much better. Well, Howie is nothing to tell about. He loved going to the racetrack, he wanted Carl and I to take him in as a partner, but who needed such a gambler? He had a busy place, Simcha Photographers on Fort Hamilton Parkway right on the Boro Park border. He was open on Saturday, so the pious ones used to spit on his windows—religion is what's right for them, the same with the 'right to lifers.'"

"It's getting late, my friends," Lenny and Sherry stood up.

"Speaking about photographers and their studios, when am I going to have a picture of you two in my studio window?" Sid asked Steven and Gayle.

"Damn it, Dad! We're not even thinking about that," Steven said angrily.

"I am," answered Gayle.

"Good girl," Sid shot back.

"Christ's sake, Sidney," said Norma.

"Don't think about it," added Steven.

"See, Norma, from Linda we get grandchildren, from Steven, we get aggravation."

"Oh, Sidney," Norma paused, sounding exasperated. "Oh, go blow it out of your ass, will you please?"

Everyone present laughed at Norma's uncharacteristic sailor-ish remark.

"Dad, I am not ready for marriage, isn't it enough for you I graduated medical school?"

"No," Sid's gravelly sounding voice sounded firmly blunt.

"What your father is saying, Steven..." Norma tried to explain.

"What your father is saying," Sid cut her off, is that I'm almost sixty years old, I still go to work every day and bust my ass, so I'd like to enjoy grandchildren at this stage of the game."

Gayle stifled a giggle; because of Sid's Brooklyn accent, the word enjoy came out "enjur."

"Go now, Sidney," Norma pointed to the sliding glass kitchen door, "go now, enjoy the two grandchildren you have sitting in the den."

Sid walked to the den, calling over his shoulder, "I'm a good father, believe me, I made everyone happy. Now I want some *nachus*, you know it's Yiddish for "joy"; it isn't much to ask for, I'm entitled!"

Sid slid open the heavy glass door, and walked through the kitchen into the den. Baby Alec was sleeping in his carriage. The adults in the Weitz house were not advocates of leaving small children unattended, but his older brother Peter was deputized to watch his little brother. The only problem was, young

Peter had fallen asleep on the job, no big deal, as the den was just a holler away from the patio, and they couldn't have access to the pool without getting past the adults.

"Ten hut!" Sid called out, and Peter sat up on the couch.

"You know, when I was in the army, men used to get shot for falling asleep on guard duty."

"I wasn't sleeping, Sid."

"Sure, you just think better with your eyes closed. *Oyyyy*," Sid sighed. "When Grandpa wants you to be quiet, you scream and run around; when Grandpa wants to make koochie koo," he paused to look adoringly into the carriage at Alec, "everybody is sleeping. Well, I'm glad you're awake, you'll be going home shortly, so I wanna finish spoiling you rotten."

"What's 'speral,' Sid?"

"Spoil, you know what a grandfather does to his grandchildren, what happens when you leave milk in the 'fridge' too long, spoil."

"Oh, spoil."

"Isn't that what I said?"

"I guess."

Steven Weitz walked Gayle Eysenberg home. She lived around the corner from the Weitz house. They walked onto Peninsula Boulevard, turned right, then walked to Marlboro Road, turned right again, and then right into Parliament Court, the cul de sac where Gayle lived. They walked arm and arm in silence.

"Your father wants me to call him Sid, that's a good sign."

"The mail lady calls him Sid, too."

"That's because he's in love with her."

"He and all the men on the block," Steven said.

"Well, with the way she's squeezed into a uniform that's a couple of sizes too small, I'm not surprised. I'm a woman, we pick up on those things; I'd like to slap her."

"You can't, it's a federal offense."

"Her uniform pants and sweater should be a federal offense."

"She just wants to be noticed, that's all, she's a cute kid."

"I hope her pants split when she's making her rounds, that would be real cute, then she'd get noticed."

"Somehow, Gayle, I don't think your dad will leave your mom for her."

"Of course not, she's probably uneducated; besides, she's not Jewish."

"I thought you wanted me to walk you home, now we're discussing our postal service?"

"Steve, you have your father's sense of humor."

"I'm very sorry to hear that, because he's an obnoxious asshole."

"Do you want to come inside for a while?" she asked.

"No, I'm bushed. I want to go to bed already, too many people today!"

"Well, goodnight then."

Steven and Gayle kissed—it was not a passionate kiss, it was a light kiss on the lips. He sensed Gayle was not satisfied, and at the moment, he really did not care.

"See you tomorrow, Steven?" she asked.

"Sure," he shrugged, sounding non-committal. He left her standing at her front door and walked home.

Chapter Twenty-Eight

When Steven Weitz returned home, his parents were sitting on the floor of their den, playing with their grandchildren, and they barely noticed him.

Steven's sister Linda Weitz Sossin sat with her husband, Mark, on the couch, watching with maternal pride. When Steven walked into the den, Linda turned to her husband, "Mark, hang out here for awhile, I want to talk with Steve."

"Okay, I'll watch your parents get down on the kid's level, it's kind of cute, yet at the same time quite sickening."

"That's because your parents don't play with their little grandchildren. I'll be right back."

Linda walked out into the hallway, and placing her right arm around Steve's shoulders, she led him to their father's home office/studio.

"I want to talk to you for a while," she told him, "let's talk in Daddy's office; lock the door."

"How *are* you?" she asked.

"I'm okay."

"How *are* you, I mean *really*?" Linda asked her brother once again, this time sounding very concerned.

"I think I'm all fucked up," he answered.

"I think you're feeling kind of fucked up, too, which is why I wanted to talk to you. What's eating you, Steve."

"I don't want to get married right now, Lin.'"

"Tell him that."

"Uhh, huhh, huhh," Steve laughed in a deep sarcastic tone of voice.

"No, really," Linda smiled, "be firm, tell him you're not ready to get married, yet, you've not told Gayle your intentions."

"It doesn't matter, Lin, Dad announced his intentions to Gayle; he intends to make her his daughter-in-law."

"No, really, Steven," she moaned, "tell him you're not ready for that, yet."

"You know what his answer will be."

"His answer will be, 'You've just graduated medical school, you're starting your career, you're young, yet, and you have time.'"

"His answer will be, 'Schmuck, schmuck, she's a good catch; she's a nice Jewish girl, you schmuck!'" Steven did a respectable impression of his father.

Linda laughed hard.

"Putz, when I was your age I was married. I went out every day and shot in-home baby pictures for a dollar and a quarter a sitting, then on the weekend I'd go out and shoot candids—three weddings on Saturday, two on Sunday."

"Steve, he loves you, he'll understand."

"Mom will understand; Dad only understands what's good for him."

"But," Linda shifted crossing her legs, "what was good for him was not bad for us. We were comfortable kids, we had it better than a lot of his colleagues, some of them really struggled. Mom always had nice things, so did we. Don't forget we went to Europe not once, but twice, a lot of our friends never went. He gave us cars when we started to drive, and sent us to college, don't forget that. His being who *he* is," Linda emphasized, "his being a hustler, is what made our lives very nice as kids, remember that."

"He's just, just, so…"

"Let's see," Linda helped her brother, "crude, crass, vulgar, a pain in the ass, a prick, and a lowlife. Yes, I know, his colleagues all say that about him; I know, I have heard it, believe me. But, *he's* a good husband, father, and grandpa," Linda emphasized, the word *he* again, "he's also a very good son, and brother, and he's not a bad photographer, either."

"I know," Steven admitted, "I love him, but he is a pain in the ass."

"And he always will be," she affirmed, "but so what? He's our dad, if that's the way his friends see him, so be it. We love him, he's good to us."

"He did manage to drive Carl out to Arizona."

"Partnerships are the same as marriages, Steve, sometimes you can't work things out, and it's over. But, I'm sure Carl did things to upset him, too."

"I'm just afraid that I'm going to fuck up."

"Steven, you are not going to fuck up! If you walk around with that attitude and keep on saying, 'I'm going to fuck up,' then you'll fuck up! Think positive!"

"I'm positive that I'm going to fuck up."

"Oh, my God, Steve, you're hopeless. You'll be alright, you're going to have reinforcement of what you've already learned in medical school, and you'll learn and grow over the next couple of years, as you go along."

"You know, Lin, you sound a lot like Mom."

"Of course I do; Mom was always intellectually smarter than Dad, she just never let him know that."

"You really think I'm going to be alright?"

Why wouldn't I think that, Steve? You're my brother!"

They both stood up at the same time and hugged; this was both the hardest and the longest they had hugged in a long time.

"You know what Dad always said, Lin, whenever I told him I was worried about something, whenever I had a problem? He'd say life is good."

"Steven," Linda said hugging very, very hard now, "Life is good!"

Chapter Twenty-Nine

L ife was good.
Life was good, that's what Sid Weitz was thinking as he stepped out of the bathroom, life was good. With all the bullshit, things turned out nicely. When Sid married Norma and started a family, they worried about how things were going to turn out; every photographer is concerned about what develops, so far everything came out good, although the journey of life was not over, yet, he hoped not for a very long time to come.

Sid stood in front of the queen-size double bed, clad in gray Kmart pajama bottoms, bare-chested. He smoothed out the matching long sleeve, collared shirt before putting it on.

"We have a married daughter with two children and a son who's a doctor about to be engaged to a nice Jewish girl."

"He's not engaged to her, Sid," Norma was already in bed propped up on the pillows.

"He will be, they're in love; it's a good match, you'll see."

"Oh, Sid, stop."

Sid stood at the foot of the bed, "Listen, they're in love, they've been going together for a long time, they're right for each other."

"Keep it up, Sid, just keep it up, and he'll walk in the door with a black girl."

"Like Moskowitz's kid down the street? Remember he sat with her in the booth in the diner, showing her off to the world. She wasn't anything like that cute anchor woman on Channel Two."

"Whadda ya mean?" she asked.

"Not a cutie, not light skinned, or even well spoken."

"Let his parents worry, Sid."

"That's the point, today Jewish parents, I dunno, they, they take too much shit from their kids. Listen, if that punk down the street was Italian, his father and brothers would go into that lousy kid's room with baseball bats and make their feelings known to him."

"Did you check the locks?"

"Yeah, I gotta go downstairs for a minute."

As Sid opened the bedroom door to leave, the Weitz's four-and-a-half year-old gray-striped cat Plucky came in.

"Meeeew," Plucky moaned.

"Plucky's cute," Sid said, looking down at her, "Plucky's cute, Plucky's very cute! Go to Mommy."

Norma went back to her peaceful reflecting after Sid left the bedroom.

Norma had to agree with Sid, things turned out well; they were lucky. They weren't Jewish society people with a mansion up in Muttontown, but they were, well, lucky.

Life was not without trials, tribulation, and heartache. Norma, as a young wife in a walk-up apartment in Flatbush, didn't think they were ever going to be comfortable, but with her bank job and Sidney out shooting, they got by. Things came together when Sid went on his own and hooked up with Lenny Schecter, who had access to lists of newborn babies. Sid sat in the apartment and made cold calls, using the reverse directory. Between that and his being a top candid man in demand by so many studios, they were able to move into an apartment in Gravesend, with an elevator before Steven was born.

Sid and Carl moved into an office and had their own processing lab to turn out the baby photos; they took in outside work and made a lot of money. Then, they found a store run by two candid photographers who also operated a processing lab, but did not know what they were doing. Sid and Lenny bought them out a couple of years later and Carl, who was already a renowned master portrait and candid photographer, became a third partner. He was a studio manager with big following, and the rest was history.

Linda was a good girl; sure there were a few infractions along the way which were punished, but nothing too terrible.

Once when Linda was in her first year of college, they got a phone call every parent dreads. It was about twelve o'clock on a Saturday night; Sid had shot a big Irish wedding that afternoon, and he and Norma were both getting ready for bed, when the phone rang. A policeman informed Norma that her daughter had been injured in a car accident and she was at the Nassau County Medical Center in East Meadow. Norma and Sid dressed, and were about to leave, when they paused at Linda's bedroom door. In shock and disbelief that anything terrible could have happened to one of their children, they opened the door. They saw a figure on the bed. Turning on the light switch, they found their daughter asleep, snug as a bug in the rug. They shook her awake to find out what the hell had happened, and Linda told them she loaned her license to a friend who was a year younger, so she could go to a bar that night with some friends.

How the hell could someone as smart as her be conned into doing a stupid thing like that, her parents wanted to know. Thank God she was alright, but things were not over, yet.

Norma asked who the girl was, and Sid called the girl's parents to inform them. He did not want to call the cop back at the hospital, as he was afraid Linda could be subject to arrest. The girl had her own Identification with her, so the cop believed her when she told him her friend left her wallet at her house. Being a Nassau County cop, he did not want to tax himself figuring out the facts. They grounded Linda anyway.

It was a fender bender accident; the girl's injuries were very minor, if present at all. She was hit in the back, so she wanted to get rich from the other driver's insurance money.

Steven was another story, a good boy, yes, but he did nutty things sometimes. Things which Norma did not want to think about right now; thinking about those antics would ruin the mood of the day.

There was one thing, which came to mind—Steven's budding curiosity one early summer when he was eleven, going on twelve. He had spent the day reading Norma's *Woman's Day* magazines, and spent the remainder of that day asking her questions about sexual functions and parts of the female anatomy.

When Sid came home at six, she filled him in on their son's new interests.

"All day long it was, 'Hey, Ma!' she told him, 'Hey, Ma! Hey, Ma! and Hey, Ma!"

"Hey, Ma! What's a douche?"

"Hey, Ma! What's vaginitis?"

"Hey, Ma! Does your uterus give you any problems?"

"Hey, Ma! I thought a vulva was a Swedish car."

"Oh, and hey, Ma! You got a hymen?"

"Oh, and you'll love this, Sid, 'Hey, Ma! I got a prick!'"

"He got that from your *Women's Day*?" he asked her.

"No, not from *Woman's Day*, but he picked it up and knows what it means."

"So what? Norma, it doesn't bother me, he's a boy; sooner or later he's going to want to know about all that fun stuff, a lot of boys find out about it at this age, I did. What I didn't learn in the street, I learned when I went into the service."

Maybe this is what sparked Steven's interest in medicine, who knows?

Steven was a good boy, he just marched to the beat of his own drum, not his father's.

Sid came back into the bedroom, and he walked over to the portable color Quasar television set. Plucky was sitting on top of it, like a statue, "Good night, old cat," he said and extended his left hand to pet her.

"Mrroww!" Plucky said, as she swiped her paw at Sid's outstretched hand.

"Ow, you little bastard!"

"What happened, Sid, she get you?"

Sid swung his right fist at Plucky, but she was too fast for him, and leapt off the television and out of the room before Sid's fist came around.

"Don't hurt my cat!" Norma admonished him.

"Tell her not to hurt your husband!" he shot back.

Norma laughed as Sid went into the bathroom to wash his hand and apply some wintergreen rubbing alcohol to the scratch.

When he came out, he got into bed on the left side, which had been his side since they were first married, and turned out the light.

Side spoke, "I just don't want Steven to ruin things for himself. Gayle is a good *Yiddishe* girl, a *haimish* girl, an intelligent girl, that's all; she would be good for him. He's a doctor now, he has everything, so why not? She loves him, he's going to start his internship next week, we can help them out, her parents have *gelt*, so let them set the date."

"But does her love her, Sidney, damn it?"

"Love shmove, what's not to love about her? She's a beautiful girl, a good catch."

"From you he'll catch a breakdown. Sidney, really, I don't want to discuss this shit any more. Let Steven handle this, if he loves her, they'll get married—if not, then not. What will be, will be."

"What will be will have to be what's right, what's right for him."

"And what's right for you."

"What the hell is so wrong with that?" he answered back.

They lay in silence for a few minutes.

"Want to make love?" Norma asked.

"With you?"

"Who else?" Norma sounded annoyed.

"No," Sid rolled over on to his left side his back to Norma.

"Christ's sake!" Norma rolled over on to her right side back to back with Sid.

Chapter Thirty

S teven Weitz rolled his eyes open.

The digital clock on the night table read one-thirty. It was a mild night, the windows were open, and a gentle breeze rattled the papers on his desk.

He was up, wide awake and couldn't sleep, anxiety.

There was a scratching at the door. He got up, opened the bedroom door, and left it ajar, so his visitor could leave if she wanted to.

"Plucky, what are you doing here; did you go after the old man again?"

"Meeeow."

"Good cat."

Plucky rubbed her head against his chest, then she kneaded the sheets and lay down beside him. Steven leaned over and kissed the cat on top of her round head.

He couldn't get back to sleep, so he passed the time reflecting; he remembered one of the few times he helped assist his father on one of his jobs. A terrible thing happened on this job, actually it was very funny, very embarrassing. It was Steven's fault; he was just at the wrong place at the wrong time. He started to laugh as he thought about what will forever be known as the 'horsey back incident.'

It was August 1978; Sid was shooting this huge Jewish wedding up in Larchmont. The temple had a very rich congregation, and certainly these clients, who were recommended to Montclair Studios, were very rich. Steven recalled that was a busy weekend for his father, it was the weekend before Labor Day. Sid had booked a lot of jobs for that weekend, and he was short of help. Steven agreed to help his father and light for him for fifty dollars.

The ride up to the temple in Larchmont was pleasant, traffic was light, the car, a 1977 Chrysler New Yorker, glided along the parkway. The car was a white four-door with a vinyl landau roof and side vents in the windows of the front doors, reminiscent of the cars his family had in the '60s. It was a huge car and Norma hated it, she said it was clunky. They had another huge car, a '76 Mercury Grand Marquis red convertible with a white top, which was the last convertible the Weitz family owned. Sid opted for the four-door that night.

Sid hollered at Steven a bit that night about his aiming of the second strobe light, which was his job to hold throughout the affair. Sid was in top form that night, he knew the importance of this job, and he worked his ass off to impress those clients. He set up a background along with studio lights for the formal portraits before the ceremony. Sid even used his 6x7 Mamiya RB-67 camera, which he seldom took out of the studio for the portraits and formals.

Steven thought his father looked good that night, too. Sid wore a black single-breasted tuxedo without a bow-tie, and the white dress shirt without ruffles over the lapel of the jacket. Several actors, including Sylvester Stallone, were wearing the style at awards ceremonies that year. Photographing the ceremony was not permitted at this conservative synagogue, so Sid did not need to put on the bow-tie, in fact, he shot the reenactment with his jacket off. Everything was going smoothly until the *hora*.

Sid shot the candids with his Mamiya 645 medium-format camera; it was on a Mamyia deluxe 'L' grip, with a customized arm attachment. The attachment allowed the flash to be swiveled at a forty-five degree angle for vertical photographs. The strobe on the bracket was an old Multiblitz manual unit. It was powered by a large battery in a leather case, which Sid wore over his left shoulder. He wore a small black case over his right shoulder. This case held the film cassettes for the 645. The cases were at times cumbersome, but Sid was used to it, he wore heavy cases back in the '50s and early '60s, when he shot candids with Speed Graphics and Crown Graphics.

Usually, Sid did not bring ladders on his jobs; he pre-focused his camera and held it up when people were lifted up in the chair. Tonight he brought along a tall aluminum photographer's ladder from his studio.

Sid stood above the people during *Hava Nagila*; after the bride, groom, and their parents were lifted up in the chair, he shot down at the dancers in the circle.

That's when it happened.

A large bald man clowning around, acting like an asshole, lost his footing and tripped sideways onto Steven, his heavy foot landing on top of Steven's. Steven yanked his foot out from under the fat man's foot very hard; he flew hard sideways to his right into his father's ladder. The aluminum ladder flew out from under Sid's feet, falling sideways onto a short woman, knocking her over.

"Shyyyyiiit!" Steven heard his father yell, as he looked up.

Sid felt the ladder fall from under him, and he quickly jumped up and grabbed hold of the large brass and crystal chandelier, swinging like a cowboy in a saloon fight. The camera strap was around his neck, so he was able to let go of the grip, which he would have done anyway. Sid felt his grip loosening, and knew he could not hold on much longer. He thought about the orange striped cat they had at the time, Weanus, and how he always landed on his feet; Sid thought maybe he could do the same. He bent his knees slightly for impact, while releasing his grip and braced himself.

The bride was standing right under him now. Sid landed squarely on the bride's shoulders with an audible 'whump.'

"AYYYYIOAHH!" the bride screamed as she grabbed both Sid's legs and held on.

To keep his balance, Sid grabbed both sides of the bride's head.

The bride hopped back and forth, then twirled around and around and around, giving her photographer the horsey back ride of his life.

A roar went up from the guests.

"AHHHHHH!" some women screamed.

Some men who were a bit spirited yelled other things.

"YIPPPEE!"

"YEEEHAAH!"

"WHEEEEE!"

"YAHOOO!"

One Jewish accent cried out, "RIDE 'EM COWBOY!"

"GET OFF HER, SCHMUCK!" another man yelled.

The bride collapsed to the floor, the photographer going down with her.

THUD!

Actually, Steven heard two thuds.

The band stopped playing, a crowd gathered, and an eerie hush descended on the hall. You could hear a pin drop.

A sixty-ish woman in a blue beaded gown with tinted blonde hair broke the silence. "I DON'T THINK THAT'S FUNNY!" she yelled.

Neither did Sid.

The bride's father helped him up, while the bride's mother and the groom attended to the bride.

"Sid, oh, dear God," the bride's father said, "dear, dear, are you alright?"

Sid did not know what to say.

"Stephanie, are you alright?" the bride's mother asked, "Are you alright?"

"Mimm mummm mim mim mim," the bride answered.

"WHAT, WHAAAT?" the bride's mother asked.

"Mum thhp mimmm moom blah," the bride answered.

"WHAT? Stephanie, what? Are you alright?"

"No oh ohhhhhh ow, no oh ho ho oh!" The bride shook her head, "Why did that terrible man do this to meeee?" she wailed.

A guest handed the bride her veil, which had fallen off, and she sobbed into it. Some of the guests helped her to her feet. The maid of honor helped her sister to the ladies' room; the groom reached out for her hand, but she pushed him away.

"What, what did I do?" he asked bewildered.

The bride's mother stood on the dance floor; she did not move, as she began to cry.

"Oh, dear, what's wrong?" The bride's father placed his hand on her arm, "What's wrong with you now?"

The bride's mother just stared down at the hem of gown and cried.

"WHAT'S WRONG?" her husband asked again.

"I PEED IN MY PAAAAANTS!"

Sid got to his feet and grabbed his son by the right arm as he faced him. He shook the boy's arm violently.

"WHY, WHY, FOR WHAT?"

"It was an accident, Dad!" Steven explained near to tears.

"ACCIDENT? ACCIDENT? YOU WERE AN ACCIDENT!" his father yelled.

Steven then explained what happened. His father seemed more concerned for his reputation, than about his son's well being. He was also too busy thinking about the bride.

Father and son both walked off the dance floor, "Did you see what that crazy bastard did?' someone muttered.

"What can I tell you, he needed to get his shot," someone else replied.

"Find out who the photographer is, I won't use him," said another.

They finished the job, the clients did not sue, and the whole ride home was passed in silence.

Norma laughed so hard when Sid recounted the story for her, tears rolled down her cheeks.

Sid had just started to offer video coverage; that year, they filmed the affair with a professional movie camera, then transferred the film to videotape and edited it. A dopey looking movie photographer, who Steven could not remember, captured the incident. The clients were told the movie photographer did not record that spectacle, but the footage was on a film reel, and also a video transfer tape in Norma's drawer. Sid did show it once to Linda and Mark, before the grandchildren were born. "Someday, the grandkids have to see this," Norma always said. This event did go down in the annals of the industry, because Sid's colleagues knew the story, probably heard it from the band or the guests. They knew better than to remind Sid about it.

Steven knew his father had a sense of humor, "After all, he didn't kill me," he reasoned.

Steven laughed himself to sleep.

Chapter Thirty-One

S aturday morning was a good time for sleeping late, unless you made your
living photographing weddings. Sid Weitz earned a living from that for
almost four decades. When he was not shooting Christian weddings on
Saturdays, he shot Bar or Bat Mitzvah ceremonies in reform synagogues. When
he was not doing that, he was up getting ready for work. Not an observant
Jew, his studio was open on Saturday from eleven a.m. until four p.m.

A young doctor having some sort of an anxiety attack might be up early
on a Saturday morning, as well.

A very nice woman, who was a photographer's wife, might also be an
early Saturday riser to help see her husband off on his job, even though she did
not have to. Even though he did need her to do things for him, Norma did
sleep late on some Saturdays, however, but not today. The whole Weitz
household was up, except for Plucky the cat.

Sid woke up very early, moved his bowels, showered and shaved, sprayed
on deodorant, splashed on some cologne, and then ate a light breakfast.

After breakfast, Sid dressed, placed his camera case and second strobe
light, which his assistant carried, in the trunk of the blue Chevy.

Both Steven and Norma were up by then. Steven sat at the round wood-
tone Formica kitchen table; he stared glumly into his coffee.

Norma puttered about at the counter near the stove; she knew her son was
troubled about something, mothers just know.

Sid walked into the kitchen, wearing the pants of his charcoal gray Pierre
Cardin suit and a light blue, long-sleeve dress shirt. He folded the single-
breasted jacket over the chair, then placed a blue tie with light gray and
burgundy, slanted vertical stripes in the jacket pocket. He always put his tie on
when he left the bride's house for church. He was wearing a suit today, instead
of a tuxedo, because he wanted to.

"It's not that warm today," he commented, "the kid should be here soon."

"The kid," was Sid's assistant, Jeffery Glassman. He had been working with Sid for a while now, as they had developed a good working relationship. Steven thought his father had a better relationship with his assistant than with him.

"It's going to be in the mid-seventies, love," Norma volunteered.

"What's eating our son the doctor, doctor, doctor? What's bothering you?"

"Nothing, Dad, just have some things on my mind."

"If you got something on your mind, then something is bothering you."

"Just nervous about things."

"What things? You're gonna start out life with more breaks than I had, believe me."

"Leave him alone, Sid," Norma pleaded, "all graduates get some anxiety."

"What do I know?" he said, "I didn't graduate college, because I didn't go. I graduated New Utrecht High School. Only thing that made me nervous was when I shipped out to Korea."

"Steve," Norma placed her hand on her son's shoulder, "your father wasn't nervous, he won that war for us."

"It wasn't a war, Mom, it was a police action."

"Tell that to the gook who shot me."

"And that guy didn't even know you, Dad."

"I meant to ask you something, Steve, what's going on with you and Gayle?" Sid sounded concerned.

"Nothing."

"That's what I'm afraid of, why don't you see her today? It's a nice day, take her to lunch."

"I can't, Dad, I'm busy."

"You're busy not seeing her, is what I think."

"Dad, right now I'm not innerested in what you tink."

"Oh, pardon me, my Brooklyn accent. I didn't have the advantage of growing up in the sub'boibs like you did."

"Now stop it, you two," Norma scolded, "stop it, let's not get on each other's nerves."

"Yeah," he sighed. "I gotta a big job, a big Greek wedding; we start at the house in Garden City, then we go to the church in Hempstead, then to the park in Garden City, and then to the caterer in Astoria, you know, the big one."

"Who's getting married again, Sid?" she asked him.

"The daughter of the biggest siding installer on the Island is marrying the son of a man who owns a chain of diners in the greater New York area. That's one thing about the Greeks, they have the money to spend like Jewish clients; these Greeks, they'll spent the money, all you need to be is a photographer with a known name, like me," Sid flashed his trademark toothy leery grin, which he used to get subjects to smile.

"You'll do alright, then," she assured

"Sure, when she came into the studio with her parents to make the arrangements, her father told me how well he was doing. 'We are veeerrryy beeeezzzee,' Sid did a very convincing Greek accent, gesturing his hands expansively, 'weeee are veeeerrryy beeeezzzzeeee, we put up theee siding all over the Island.'"

"Is that the man you said who owns all those Mercedes?" she asked.

"Uhh, huh, also, he's a funny guy, he asks me, 'Tell me sometheeng, when you photo-oh-graph a job, do you ever say bad worrud to make peeple to laugh? You tell them to say, *scatta*?'"

What's *scatta*?" Norma asked, sitting down with her coffee at the table.

"*Scatta*," Sid still doing the Greek accent, continued, "means, sheeet, I went to wedding, where photo-oh-grapher saya to teee peeeple say *scatta*, I laugh when he take thee peecture."

Sid sat down.

"These people are really big, because the guy who played Kojak is going to be a guest."

"Really, Dad?"

"Yep, ya wanna meet him, you can light for me; I'll give you another opportunity to throw me off a ladder."

"That was accident, Dad, you know that."

"Yeah, yeah, what about when you were eleven? Was throwing the yogurt out of the car window at a man an accident too?"

"*Oy*, Sidney," Norma held her right hand up, "that was a long time ago."

"I'll try to get a picture of Kojak for the studio; I have some paper, when he's not eating, I'll try to get an autograph."

The door bell rang, Sid went to answer it.

Sid walked into the kitchen with his young assistant, Jeffery Glassman.

Steven and Jeffery exchanged greetings, and Jeffery congratulated Steven on his graduation.

"Can I offer you something to eat, Jeff?" Norma asked.

"He doesn't have the time," Sid replied before Jeff could answer, "we have to go."

"Thank you, Mrs. Weitz," Jeff said.

"Please, Jeff, call me Norma."

"Just don't call her, I'm a jealous husband."

Jeff laughed politely at his boss's quip.

"Let's go, c'mon, we got Greeks to shoot. The cameras are in the dining room; you grab the backup, the rest is in the car. This bride is a pretty girl, but she has a Greek nose; her mother is pretty, too, but she as a big Greek ass."

Norma shook her head.

Sid and Jeff left the kitchen together.

Norma and Steven sat at the table in silence, drinking their coffee.

"Mom?" Steven asked, "The house always seems quiet when Dad isn't home."

"That's because it is," she answered.

They both laughed.

Chapter Thirty-Two

Norma Weitz sat at the kitchen table alone, Steven went out back to take a swim. Going on fifty-three, she looked a lot younger. She looked around the kitchen at all the conveniences, being married to Sidney Weitz was not always easy, but it was a lot of fun, never a dull moment.

Norma married Sid before he went into the army. It was his earthiness, or as her mother put it, his commonness, she found attractive, along with the rest of him. Sid was Norma's first real love; in fact, she had never seen a penis up close before, not even her father's.

Norma lived with her parents while Sid was in the service; living on a military base was not her cup of tea.

Then came the telegram that he had been wounded, and she flew to the hospital in Seoul, South Korea, as he recovered. She looked over his purple heart and told him how proud she was of him.

"You're proud I got shot? Thanks a lot."

She did not mean it that way, she explained, he told her he knew what she meant.

When he returned, they moved into a small basement apartment in Brooklyn. The apartment was crowded with their meager furnishings, their clothing, and Sid's equipment.

Sid resumed his photographic career; before he went into the service, he processed film and printed photographs for a large studio that photographed school pictures and affairs. Sid was a legend at that place, for knocking out black and white school portraits quickly. He devised a way to secure the paper in the enlarging easel by vacuum suction. He had a red filter, set for focusing the image, as the red did not affect the photographic paper, then he would hit the white light and print. He was able to produce so many pictures in such little time, and that made the boss very happy.

Sid was also a legend at the high volume in-home baby photography studio he was working for. He and his friend Carl Resnick were the fastest shooters, with the biggest grossing sales. People in the studio used to ask, "Weitz, Resnick, how do you do it so fast?"

Norma remembered Sid's method; he got two heavy leather straps from the post office to secure his equipment. He used an inexpensive Ricoh flex camera with a strobe, which had a cheap dish reflector that cost about five dollars. The camera was placed on a cheap tripod. The background Sid used was a window shade on a stand. In a case he carried props, film, and accessories. The leather straps held the camera tripod and background together, while the case went over the shoulder. All the equipment was always set up ready to go.

Sid had bought an old Volkswagen, in spite of his hatred of Germans, because it was the only car he could afford at the time. He removed the front seat, which served as a reading chair in the living room, when not in the car. Without the front seat, Sid could slide the equipment in and out, moving fast through his appointments. While at one baby's house, Sid called his next several appointments, telling the mothers to have the babies ready. The commissions rolled in, so along with Norma's job, they did well, even after Linda was born.

Sid and Carl decided to start their own baby studio, rather than making someone else rich. In addition to shooting weddings for the other studios, they could earn big bucks. Then they met up with Lenny Schecter, a baby photographer and top salesman, who told them he had access to lists of households with babies and children.

Norma remembered the telephone calls Sid made selling in-home portraits sessions, often using a reverse directory. If he saw several names at one location, he knew it was an apartment house. Often, young mothers had to take their calls in a neighbor's apartment, as a lot of people in those days did not have their own phones. Sid put the playpen on top of Steven while he cold called to restrict his movements.

Norma kept a tight household budget, along with the baby money, and her salary, Sid got twenty-five dollars to shoot a wedding or Bar Mitzvah, which later went to thirty, then to thirty-five. They spent wisely on essentials.

By a fluke, the three partners began to process and print their own photographs. They had been using a lab in Laurelton, but in the summer the owner closed and went on vacation for two weeks. In the baby photography business, it was 'catch-as-catch-can,' so there was no way a busy company could be shut down for two weeks, so the partners decided to look for another lab to do their processing. This was the beginning of Baby Craft Photographers, Montclair Studios, and Sid and Norma's life in the Five Towns section of Long Island.

Sid, Carl, and Lenny found a studio in Elmont that did processing and printing for the trade. The studio owners agreed to print for their fledgling Happy Time Photography. The partners were greatly disappointed. When they returned to pick up they were mortified. The first time, when they came to pick up the finished work, it was atrocious, and needed to be done over, which was a fate worse than being laid up for two weeks while the printer was on vacation, as do-overs were more time consuming. The studio owners assured the partners that they would do the whole thing over, there would be no problems.

The second week, when Sid drove over to pick up the work, it was as bad as it was the first time—it was stained, it was rusty, some pictures were overexposed, while others were underexposed. They offered to do it all over again, but by this time, their regular photofinisher was back from vacation.

The studio owner told Sid that this business was really not for them, which Sid thought was the understatement of the decade. "We'd like to get out," they told him, "would you like to buy it?" they asked.

Sid, Carl, and Lenny, decided that: A) It was not a bad idea, and B) they'd go into the wedding and portrait business for themselves and have their own lab. They could wholesale lab work to the trade, making even more money. The lab downstairs in the store was too small for the scale they wanted to work on, so they rented upstairs for the baby studio's offices, and expanded the downstairs for the lab and the studio, combining it into the newly-formed Montclair Studios. That was the birth of an industry legend.

Then everything for Sid, Carl, and Lenny came together, not gradually, but all at once. Happy Time Photographers became one of the biggest in-home baby photography studios in the Greater New York region. Montclair not only became one of the biggest portrait, wedding, and bar mitzvah studios in Greater New York, it became legendary, due mostly to Carl's innovative shooting style. The three partners shot stills and movies, and also hired top notch candid photographers and movie photographers. They sent the movies out to a skilled movie lab that did editing. They hired highly-skilled processors, printers, retouchers, spotters, and a young lady who was a photo colorist. Coloring black and white photographs was a popular process in the 1960s. They also did photo finishing as subcontractors for other studios. Montclair also had some publicity and commercial photography accounts. Sid's brother Saul 'Sol' Weitz was a renowned commercial and fashion photographer, who had a studio in Greenwich Village, and he sent Sid the commercial jobs that were too small for him.

Sid remembered his successful plumber father telling him, "If you want to make it in business, you need good connections." So, Sid got connected with the right people. *More like the wrong people*, Norma thought.

Sid met three brothers who said they were in the catering business. The truth was, the three brothers were members of a mafia family, whose family did own a few catering establishments.

Norma shuddered in the chair when she recalled these men, and what was crazy about this was her husband actually became friends with them. Norma remembered the three brothers, Rocky, Punchie, and Geppie. Sid paid them well for the privilege of being their hall's official house photographer. Carl was too classy to deal with them, Lenny was too busy running the baby studio, so those so-called men of respect dealt with Sid. Norma feared for her husband.

She hated when they had to attend Geppie's annual Christmas party. Each brother also took turns 'going away,' which meant doing time.

"Hi, how are you, Norma?"

"Where's Punchie?"

"Oh, he went away for a while."

One incident frightened Norma so much, she begged Sid to sever ties with those brothers, which he refused, saying they were good for business.

What happened was, the uncle of the three brothers was the number three man in their family. His daughter was getting married, so the uncle arranged to meet alone with Sid at the studio one evening, but his three nephews also were there. Norma had the urge to vomit, when Sid later told her the whole story.

The uncle sat across from Sid.

"My daughter getting a married."

"Where's the reception?"

"My nev'ayoos will pick a you up, we can't a tella you that."

"What's the groom's name?"

"We can't tella you that."

"Where's the church?"

"We can't tella you that."

"Well, what is the date and the time me and my crew should be ready to be picked up?"

The uncle looked at his three nephews.

They nodded.

"Okay, we can tella you that!"

"So, for a the pictures an' a the movies, we wanna three albums, one a for a the bride, two for the mammas, how much?"

Sid told him how much including the sales tax, because he knew they were law abiding businessmen.

The uncle snapped his fingers, Punchie handed his uncle a roll of bills, and the uncle handed the bills over to Sid.

Sid thanked the uncle and counted the bills, then entered the date of the wedding in his appointment book.

At nine o'clock that night at home, Sid received a phone call from an enraged Geppie.

"YOU DUMB FUCKIN' JEW!" Geppie did not even say hello, Sid had made the mistake of counting the money in front of the uncle.

Things were bustling at the studio with thirty people working under the partners, which included full-time sales people, receptionists, and a part-time bookkeeper. The money just kept on pouring in.

Then Sid, Carl, and Lenny bought beautiful homes on Long Island. Sid and Norma got a hell of a good deal on the house they bought in Hewlett. It was ordered sold by a divorce court judge, and the estranged couple was desperate. Sid paid a couple of thousand dollars, and had a monthly mortgage of fifty-six dollars, which he worried about not being able to pay. They added on extensions and put in a pool…in those days, studios were able to hide cash payments from clients.

Then Sid bought fancy cars. Norma tooled around in Cadillacs, Buicks, Oldsmobiles, Lincolns, and that Chrysler that she hated. Sid drove convertibles, Norma had jewelry, and the children had toys, bicycles, and nice clothing. Sid was a good provider, she told friends and family; a good husband and father, too.

In the summer, they took some great vacations—usually two during summer months—one with the children and one without. They took the kids to Europe with them not once, but twice. They also got along well; it helps when two married people actually like each other and enjoy one another's company. Norma always let Sid think he was in the right, she knew he needed that. Sid was capable of saying terrible things about others, but not Norma; she just could not do that.

Every so often, Norma helped Sid out on jobs, but she stopped after a while, because she did not like his professional side.

While she was assisting on a job in Brooklyn, in 1969, she actually hollered at him for an action of which she did not approve. Sid often shot in Brooklyn; his studio based on Long Island had a big Brooklyn following, so big that they had a small office there until 1974.

During a *hora* at a wedding, Sid elbowed a man very hard in the jaw to get him out of his way. As soon as the *hora* had ended, Norma went over to Sid and yelled at him.

"You go over and apologize to that man!" She ordered him on the dance floor, "Go, go now say you're sorry!"

"Ohhh, awright," Sid gave in, walking over to the man, his head down, his face red, embarrassed like a small child being reproved by a parent in public. "My wife says I have to apologize. Look, I don't want her to be mad at me, so I'm sorry, mister."

Things just seemed to happen when Norma assisted him on jobs. Later on that hot late spring Sunday afternoon, as they were walking to their car on Avenue P to East Fourteenth Street, where their 1969 Buick Electra was parked in the municipal lot next to the fire house, the Weitz's witnessed a terrible automobile accident. One car heading down East Fourteenth Street was hit at high speed by a car heading toward Coney Island Avenue. An elderly man in the front passenger seat in the first car was ejected.

"AIRBORNE!" Norma heard her husband shout. She couldn't believe it.

Another car slammed into a car parked on Avenue P to avoid the pile of blood and guts in the street.

An elderly couple who were guests at the wedding cried out, "OY, MEINE BEAUTIFUL CAR," which was an old Plymouth with rust spots.

"DO YOU VANT EN EMBULENCE?" the owner of the parked car called out.

"YEEEEYESSSS!" cried the driver of the first car.

"Ambulance?" Sid hollered. "You're gonna need a water truck and a street sweeper!"

That did it! Norma walked away from him.

"YOU'RE A LOUSY DRIVER!" the old man hollered to the woman who hit his parked car.

"I KNOOOOWWW!" she answered.

"I'd call for help," Norma heard Sid yell as he walked away, "but I have a long trip out to Long Island!"

"You know, Sidney, I can't take it from you anymore," she told him. "I thought you were going to take a picture to sell to the newspaper."

"I could have," he said as he drove to the Belt Parkway, pulling over to let a police car race to the scene. "I know a few fellows who would have. Why are you mad at me, I pushed you out of the way when that man's shoes went flying, you could have been hit with one."

That was the way it was with him. Her mother said Sid was common, Norma did not think so, just rough around the edges. Still, she loved him and after over thirty years they had a great marriage.

Their daughter Linda was planned, their son Steven was an accident. He was conceived during a photography association convention at a kosher resort in the Catskills. Since the money was pouring in they could afford another child. Norma jokingly thanked Sid for being a good sport about having it.

A good marriage, two wonderful healthy children, a nice son-in-law, two healthy grandsons, a home, security, and comfort—they had it made.

Norma remembered back in 1969, they had driven to the movie theater in Elmont to see *Goodbye, Columbus*. They had both read the Philip Roth book years earlier. During the drive home, Sid commented on how he objected to the scene at the smorgasbord table, which showed the photographer eating next to the guests like a pig, plate in one hand, camera in the other.

"I don't eat like that on the job."

Norma, who had assisted him on some jobs said, "Oh, yes, you do!"

"Well, anyway, I shoot those big lavish Jewish weddings; that's the way the nouveau riché act at affairs, and I work for those people."

Norma, who was well aware of her suburban surroundings, told him, "Work for those people? Sidney darling, we are those people!"

"What's so bad about that?" he asked her.

"Nothing," she told him, "nothing at all."

"Goddamn right," he answered, "our kids will have better and will do better than us."

Sid was right about that, so far.

Norma got up and walked to the sliding glass kitchen door that led to the pool, and she watched Steven swim. Life was good, she was thankful to God for that.

She was content; she just wanted Steven to be content. He worked very hard for his medical degree, he earned and deserved it.

Steven also deserved to be content.

Chapter Thirty-Three

On this Saturday morning, Linda Weitz Sossin sat in her kitchen in her Suffolk, Long Island, home watching her husband play with their two boys. At age twenty–nine, her life was coming together. In fact, it was pretty much together. She was a career woman, an audiologist, with two beautiful sons. He husband, Mark, was a foreign trade consultant for a prominent firm.

Mark Sossin, thirty-two, ran into the kitchen to get a Frisbee. He was tall, with curly black hair and a mustache; he looked like a Jewish Tom Selleck. Linda's father, Sid Weitz, thought he looked like the guy who played Rhoda Morgenstern's husband, with a mustache.

"We're gonna play Frisbee now," he said as he dashed back out. Non-observant Jewish families played games on Saturdays, while the aging patriarch of the family was out photographing a wedding.

Sid and Norma took to Mark right away, and he liked them immediately. They thought he was a nice, handsome, professional, educated Jewish boy, in other words, a good catch. Sid often referred to Mark when talking to his friends, as "My son-in-law the fuckin' academic." True, Mark was educated, he had a masters degree, but Linda loved him, was happy, and he made a nice dollar, so he was an ideal son-in-law.

Linda walked up the stairs to the master bedroom, undressed, and took a shower. She was a carbon copy of her mother in every way, looks (although her hair was longer), tolerance, and positive attitude. Mark was not a pain-in-the-ass husband like her father, whom she adored.

As she washed she thought about her brother. She prayed that Daddy would not make him crazy over his girlfriend or anything else.

"What does he want from the poor kid," she wondered out loud. "He wants him to get married now? Steven has time; Gayle isn't running away, she isn't even the best girl in the world. Why rush Steve, Dad, let him be happy."

Linda remembered how her father made her crazy when she and Mark announced their engagement. Daddy had an episode at the reception with his videographer and almost ruined the affair. Linda knew Daddy wanted to make her happy, even if it meant ruining her wedding to do it.

Traditionally, the bride's parents pay for the wedding; Mark's parents chipped in a large sum of money, but Sid ran the show. Norma suggested things to him, letting Sid think he was right about everything.

They used the florist Sid knew, they booked at the best catering hall on the north shore of Long Island, and Sid told Linda, the outside garden was great for ceremonies and pictures.

When it came time to meet with the banquet manager, Sid told Linda, Mark, and his parents he would do all the talking.

"Absolutely, Sid," Marks father said, "whatever you say." Mark's parents had two boys, the older one was already married with a child, but they knew Sid knew the business.

"Daddy always does all the talking," Linda told her in-laws-to-be.

Sid sat across from the banquet manager dictating the terms for his daughter's wedding. The poor man could not get a word in edgewise, nobody could with Daddy.

"Listen, this is a Jewish wedding so first off, don't serve the beer in bottles, have the bartender pour it into glasses. We ain't gonna have people drinking it, reh, reh, glug out of the bottle like at a *goyish* wedding. Also, I don't want the bartender to put a brandy snifter on the bar with the dollar bills, so help me, I mean it! All gratuities included, so I better not see that shit, or I'll come into your office and drag your ass out into the parking lot for bothering my guests."

The banquet manager silently nodded; he had dealt with this putz before, he did not need aggravation from him now.

"Also, on the table I want big salt and pepper shakers with good holes; I want everybody to get a fair shake. Now, for coffee, you better put that non-dairy creamer into large pitchers; I don't want any of your piss pot creamers, so my guests don't have to beg the waiters for more cream for that second or even third cup of coffee."

"Piss pot creamers, Sid?" the banquet manager asked stunned.

"Yeah, those tiny pitchers you use so you can save money on your precious non-dairy creamer."

"Oh."

"And another thing, we want a decent salad. Don't put the goddamn salad on a tiny butter plate; you ain't cheating me out of a salad. Put the salad into a good-size salad bowl."

On and on like that, it went. Linda was afraid her father was going to scare Mark off.

Linda loved her father very much. She remembered that as tired as he was when they were not as comfortable, he always played with her. She loved to sneak up on him in the apartment and yell boo! One day Linda, at age three, ran into the kitchen scared to tell Norma about what she saw.

"Mommy, Daddy should go to the doctor!"

"Why, honey?" Norma asked.

"Because he has hair all over his sissy."

"That's normal, Linda."

"Noooo," Linda protested, "Neal doesn't have hair on his sissy!"

Neal was Norma's sister's two-year-old son, who Linda saw being changed on many occasions.

"Honey, big men have big hairy sissies; it's alright, believe me."

"Because Daddy's sissy is so hairy, does it tickle when he puts it in your tushie at night?"

"Who told you that?"

"At nursie school, Sandy Kaplan my best friend said so."

"Whaatt?"

"Sandy Kaplan says her daddy put his sissy in her mommy's tushie, then she got fat and constipated, then she had to go to the hospital to make a big doody, and her brother came out."

"Your little friend from nursery school told you that?"

"Yup," little Linda nodded cutely.

"Well, she's right, just don't tell Daddy you know, because he's supposed to tell you when you're older. Let's keep this our secret, okay?"

"Okay."

"Linda, just don't let any little boy ever put his sissy in your tushie, or anywhere else, promise?"

"I promise, Mommy, I don't want to go to the hospital to make doody and have a baby."

"Good girl."

"Does Daddy's hairy sissy tickle?"

"A little."

"Oh."

"Go play."

"The mommy has to want the baby, Sandy says; she says, she says, the mommy has to say, 'Come on baby! Come on baby!' so they can make a baby."

"That's right, darling, please go play now."

Years later, Linda learned that her friend's information was not very far off. She turned out alright because of her mother and in spite of her father.

Linda's wedding day arrived, and, of course, Daddy was being a pain in the ass, driving everyone crazy. Linda understood why. This wedding was very important to her parents, her father especially. Not only was it the wedding of their first child, Sid wanted this wedding to rival weddings he shot for those bastard clients of his over the last thirty years. It was his turn to put on a show.

"Daddy might have made a good Broadway producer," she told Steven. "He can really put it together."

"All the actors in the cast would tell Dad where to put it."

The rabbi talked too much, Sid thought.

"Please," he told the rabbi, "don't talk so much, just perform the ceremony. No buh, buh, buh, Noah was a mediocre man. Just stick to the point, perform the ceremony, and then let's eat."

The wedding was beautiful, Daddy saw to that, God bless him, but all night long he ran around fighting with all the vendors.

The photographer, Harry Lowenstein, one of Sid's top candid men and a New York City cop, was doing an excellent job. Sid kept bugging him nonetheless.

"Harry, take a picture of this, shoot that, pose them this way."

Harry turned to Sid during a large group picture, "Siiiiid, leeeeeave meeeeee aloooone." He soothingly told Daddy. Daddy knew it was time to cool it.

Sometime later Linda heard a story, which became industry legend. At the end of the evening, Harry went over to Sid and asked him for his wages.

"What, you don't shoot my daughter's wedding for me out of friendship? You would charge me to shoot my daughter's wedding? Me? Me? You would charge me? You should be ashamed, Harry; I'm disappointed in you."

"Sid didn't pay me for shooting his daughter's wedding," Harry told people in the trade, "I understand, that's Sid! But the sonofabitch, I've known him thirty years, he could have at least given me a plate of food!"

The videographer was another story.

Sid had called this know-it-all Irish kid, who he had subcontracted before. Tonight he did nothing right. Sid followed that man around all night long hollering.

"Can't you light the job properly? Tell your assistant to hold the fuckin' light higher!"

"Your lights are too goddamn low for that room! Now they're too goddamn high for this room."

"Put you're fuckin' earphones back on, monitor the fuckin' sound; don't you know how to do anything?"

Then at some point during the reception, Sid wanted something to be done his way, but the videographer couldn't quite get it.

Annoyed at Sid, the videographer testily explained that his was the right way and for that matter, the professional way.

That did not go over with Linda's daddy.

"THAT'S IT!" Sid hollered in the middle of the banquet hall, taking off his tuxedo jacket, "I'M THE FATHER OF THE BRIDE AND I'M GONNA BEAT THE SHIT OUTTA YOU!"

Sid charged toward the young man, who held his ground, when Harry and Sid's commercial photographer brother Saul, grabbed and held onto him.

Linda's Nana Sadie, Norma's mother, exclaimed, "Ooooohhhh, common!"

"Sid, you throw one punch, so help me God, I'll book you!" Harry the cop warned.

"Lock him up," Sadie encouraged Harry, "put him in his place, a *shtarke* (in Yiddish, that meant a strongman or brute), go take him away to jail."

"Give 'im a bullet!" Sadie's sister Hannah yelled; she didn't like Sid either. Sid finally calmed down and enjoyed the wedding.

Linda couldn't believe how long ago it was. After toweling off, she opened her leather bound reversible bridal album. It was ivory colored and gold lettering on the front read, "Our Wedding" in script. On the lower right-hand corner, "Linda & Mark" and the date. Inside the front cover the gold letters read "Montclair Studios," with the phone number.

Linda leafed through the book. She stopped at one picture of her and Daddy dancing an ethnic dance, taken from the side, "He looked good with that beard."

"Who did?" Mark stood in the doorway.

"My father, remember he had a nice beard when we got married."

"You're right; he did look good with it. Looked more like a photographer," Mark mimicked Sid's voice.

"Oh, Mark, you better not let him hear you do that, he thinks he's charming."

"He is charming, Lin, in his own crude way."

"My daddy loves you, Mark."

"I love him, too," they both sat on the foot of their bed, as Mark fondled Linda's right breast. "He calls me a fuckin' academic."

"You are a fuckin' academic, that's one thing about you he likes."

"What are the other things?"

"You're Jewish, have money, a good job, you gave him grandchildren, oh, and you've made me very happy."

"In short, a good husband."

"A very good husband."

They kissed.

Mark looked into Linda's eyes, "What's wrong, tell me."

"Steve, he's worried about his future, about being a doctor. Daddy wants him to marry Gayle; he's not ready for that. Also, I don't like Gayle all that much, she's a spoiled J.A.P."

"Aha, your father again!"

"No, my father still."

"Because of that young lady's background and station in life, she's good for your father, but perhaps not right for Steve."

"Correct. Which is why I'm worried about him. Look, I love my father very much, he's given us the world, even when he couldn't, and I want Daddy to be happy, too."

"He is happy and soon he'll retire."

"He says fifty-eight is too young, also he has to dissolve the corporation to get his Social Security."

"Lin, everything is going to work out for your brother and for your father."

"Still, I'm worried."

"Don't be."

"Where are the kids?"

"Alec is napping in his room, Pete is playing outside,"

"Good, I think I'll call Steve now, I'm worried."

Mark eased Linda down on the mattress, and opened her robe, "Don't be worried about anybody." He pressed his lips to her vulva.

Chapter Thirty-Four

"Hello?" Linda Weitz Sossin answered her kitchen phone.

"Darling, how are you?"

"Mommy, I'm fine, how's Daddy?"

"He's alright, he's shooting a Greek wedding; everybody there will be named Georgie, Gus, Nicky, Pete, and Alex."

"Who are they, do you know?"

"Loaded people—one father owns a siding business, the other father owns several diners."

"Sounds like a lot of baklava. Is he smoking?"

"Not so much, I keep after him."

"Not so much is still a lot, Mommy."

"We'll keep on it. How are the boys?"

"They're fine, I'm making them lunch. I just gave Mark something to eat."

"Steven is fine, too, just a little mopey."

"Mopey?"

"Well, he's anxious right now, Daddy wants him to get married. He has time, yet."

"He certainly does, Mommy; besides, I don't care for Gayle all that much."

"She's a nice girl, Linda; just a little 'jappy' is all. Your father *loves* her."

"But does *Steve* love her?"

"I don't know, I want Daddy to stop hochking him. Steve's a good boy, though he wasn't exactly the Beaver."

"True, he had some problems along the road of growing, but his father wasn't exactly Ward Cleaver, either."

"Listen, Linda, if Steve wants to see other girls, Jewish or not Jewish, then he should go out with others. He's a grown man now, a doctor; he can make his own life."

"You wanna tell Daddy that?"

"Not today."

"So, Mommy, do you want us to come over tomorrow?"

"Sure, Daddy won't be back until after four-thirty, he's shooting a Bat Mitzvah."

"I wish he'd work out of the house now, instead of going to that area."

"Linda," Norma sounding firm. "Listen to me, Daddy is still too young to retire just yet. Besides, he's not ready to close the studio; there is still some business left. He talks about closing and working from the house, but he says two more years, he says working at home right now would be very boring for him."

"Boring would be safer for him. That area is not a great place to be anymore; I worry about those licensed guns he wears."

"Don't worry, Linda, he hasn't shot anyone, yet; he says the *shvartzes* don't bother him."

"Yeah, just the other merchants."

They both laughed.

"Do you and Daddy ever speak to Cynthia or Carl, Daddy's ex-partner?"

"No, not since Carl's mother's funeral. I think Carl wrote daddy after the funeral. I sent Carl an announcement about Steve's graduation, but there is no contact."

"They have nothing to do with each other, then."

"No, not really, pity too, they were friends before they were partners."

"But, Daddy has nothing to do with him?"

"Well, your Daddy tells me Carl is senile—he sits around the house all day, he doesn't recognize anybody, and he doesn't know where he's at. But, that is not exactly true; Heshy Adomovich tells me Carl and Cynthia are doing rather well."

"Are they really?"

"Yes, they have their own Montclair Studios, because, when they moved out to Arizona, they had the right to the name. Cynthia isn't just a manager, she shoots now."

"She became a photographer late in life, then. What about you, Mother?"

"Oh sure, go out on jobs and get the aggravation your father gets this late in my life."

"I was joking."

"But they are doing well—they have their own finishing lab, corporate accounts, they do publicity work, and Heshy said Carl finally got into video."

"Oh, Daddy would love to hear that," Linda said with mock sarcasm. "That would make his day, to know Carl agreed with him, finally."

"Heshy says that Arizona agrees with them, but they're going to retire in a few years."

"Everybody from Daddy's generation is leaving the business."

"Well, Daddy says at association dinners, the talk is who retired, who moved to Florida, who died, and who's sick. All the old candid men are dropping off like flies, your Daddy said."

"Just as long as it isn't him, Mommy."

"Listen, he's in good health; God willing, if he gave up the cigarettes, he'd be fine. Those old *altacockers* from your father's time, they're tough as nails, they can do the job."

"Alright then, Mommy, we'll see you tomorrow."

"Yes, let's barbeque; okay, love, take care, goodbye."

"Bye, Mommy."

Chapter Thirty-Five

Meanwhile, out in Phoenix Arizona…
Business was brisk at Montclair Studios of Phoenix.

Carl and Cynthia Resnick just took in a quarter of a million dollars. The money came from portraits, weddings, Bar Mitzvahs, communions, confirmations, christenings, sweet sixteens, quincés, anniversaries, passport/ID, commercial and publicity work—everything Carl used to do back in New York.

Life was good.

Carl Resnick, five foot nine with neatly coiffed gray hair and a thin mustache, and his wife, Cynthia, who had black hair worn up, sat in the showroom of their studio reading the announcement Norma Weitz had sent them. Carl wore a tan summer suit, while Cynthia wore a white pants suit that flattered her. She was a fifty-three year-old grandmother, but looked a decade younger.

Carl was born and reared in the Bronx, but studied elocution as a young man, because he did not want to sound like he came from the Bronx, even if the accent did work for the actor, Tony Curtis, who was known in Carl's old neighborhood as Bernie Schwartz.

Cynthia, whose first name was originally Henrietta, was from Brooklyn, and she had traces of an elegant New York accent. Cynthia pronounced New York, 'New Yahhk,' she said see you 'latahr,' and once threatened to throw a photographer out of her studio on to his 'ahhhss.'

"I'll be damned, the wolverine's son became a doctor. I hope the boy's bedside manner is better than his father's."

"Well, Carl," Cynthia spoke, "we ought to send a check."

"But what, Cynthia, how much? Sid never calls, he never wrote back to me. We haven't spoken since my mother's funeral, and as usual, he didn't have anything nice to say about anyone."

"Well, it's what I always said when we lived in New York—Sid has class it all tends to be low; Carl has a lot of class, which tends to be high."

"Cynthia, that man was a character. We were the opposites"

"As different as night and day, Carl, that's what made the business work all those years, you were like the odd couple."

"Exactly like the odd couple."

Cynthia sat on the plush felt couch in the showroom, "Or, even like the Sunshine Boys. Sid is a character, yes, but he was always honorable with you, albeit a pain in the ass."

Sid Weitz being a pain in the ass is part of the reason Carl Resnick moved to Arizona. He believed Sid was going to bankrupt the business with his new video fetish. Beginning in 1976, Sid started incorporating video coverage. It did not really get off the ground until 1978. By 1983, after Carl had left, the video production department was in full swing.

Sid even had a separate business name and phone number in the *Yellow Pages*. Montage Video Productions booked weddings independently from Montclair Studios for ten years. In the '60s, Sid and Carl had a separate movie production company, Clairmont Film Productions, so this business was familiar to Sid.

However, Carl was an artist and a purist, who saw video as a fad that would detract from the photography. To him, it was nothing more than whimsical amateurish imagery.

Sid, as a businessman, always saw the big picture; he knew in the 1980s video would be the way to go. There was money to make in this new market. Sid also knew that video, like movies, involved less bending than still photography. In 1976, Sid was aware that fifty loomed on the horizon of his life. He felt good, but he was not in his twenties anymore. If video was a way of doing the job, but with more ease, then why not?

After a family vacation, Carl and Cynthia decided to relocate to Phoenix, Arizona.

It was a late fall day, cold and damp, when Carl told Sid of his decision.

"Sid, I'd like to sell my share of the business," Carl gently said in the studio's production room. Sid was spotting a print; he did not usually spot prints, but he saw something he wanted to correct himself. "I can sell my share to someone else, if you like, but Cynthia and I want to leave New York."

"Why, where are you running?"

"Arizona, Sid."

"Carl, you're a putz!" Sid leaned back in the swivel secretarial chair. "What? You're gonna start out again at your age? You read the fuckin' papers; you know today nobody hires anyone close to fifty. Besides, what the fuck are you gonna do in Arizona?"

"Well, Sid," Carl calmly continued, "I'm going to open a studio. Cynthia and I have a suite picked out. It's a Jewish area; we think this could work out."

"But fuckin' Arizona, what do they have out there? They have rattlesnakes, scorpions, a hot as fuckin' hell desert, and Barry Goldwater. What's the attraction? 'Cause if there is one, frankly, I don't see it."

"It's a beautiful place, Sid," Carl replied holding his voice at a calm level. "We're putting the house on the market, we found a house out there, the kids like it, and my parents want to come out with us, so that's it."

"So that's it?" Sid got up and gestured to the seat cushion, "That's it, kiss my ass, that's it!"

Carl turned around and bent over, "Kiss mine!" Then Carl turned to Sid again, grabbing his scrotum, "And my balls."

Carl has balls? Sid stood up raising his voice, "Shtoomie, milquetoast has a pair of balls! You got balls from working with me; you never could stand up to anybody. I'm shocked that you survived the Navy."

"Sidney, let's not have any rancor," Carl said still speaking calmly, "we were always friends, let's part friends. Look, tomorrow, we'll sit down and discuss the dissolution of our partnership."

"Okay, Carl, don't cry. We're still friends, we're just not partners."

"You'll get used to it."

"I have to go home for a while, Sid. It was a great eleven-year run; this will work out for the both of us."

"Of course, you've learned a lot from me."

Carl knew this was the other way around, still he held his tongue.

"If that's what you want, then *zie gezundt*, go in good health. We'll be friends, just not partners; fine, whatever you want."

"You'll get used to it, I know I will. See you later, Sid."

Carl left the production room and as he closed the door, he heard a hard object slam into it.

"How did Sid take the news?" Cynthia asked when Carl got home.

"Better than I expected, he threw something at me, but this time, he waited until I was out of the door. I tell you he's a changed man."

Sid paid Carl weekly. The checks always arrived on time. Sid took credit for the fact that Carl drove out to Arizona with a '76 Lincoln Town Car.

"From me he made money, even more money than when his father had a studio." That's what Sid told everybody who knew them.

When Carl and his family moved out to Arizona, they operated Montclair Studios, Montclair West as they called it, as Carl still owned part of that name. They told people there was a Montclair East in New York, run by a former partner; God only knew what Sid told people.

Carl tried to make the buyout as easy as possible for Sid; he asked Sid if he wanted to send a weekly check like a salary check, or a monthly check. Business costs were taken care of; hope sprang eternal, and every month a check a arrived. It was not Sid's honesty, Carl and Cynthia questioned, they were not sure how long the business would survive, especially without Carl. They honestly did not know if they would get all of their dollars from the buyout, but they did.

"Sid is still in business, still over there," Cynthia snuggled closer to Carl, "the neighborhood is bad, but Heshy Adomovich says he's working. He shoots a lot for Heshy now, he doesn't get a lot of work from the street, and he's already had a theft. But Sid's a survivor, he can manage money, and he's a good candid man, not an artist like you."

"Nobody's like me," Carl paused, shook his head. "Oh God, I sound like Sid."

Cynthia laughed. She told people that Carl and Sid being total opposites and playing off each other, is what made the business work. She always said, Sid's a character, yes, but in the business, they kind of complimented each other—Carl is very personable and talented, Sid was personable, but not with the same elegance as Carl. Sid had good business sense, not that Carl didn't, because he certainly did, but he allowed Sid to do the business part, while he did the creative part, because Carl was the talented photographer. At the studio, Carl was the portrait man, the creative man, Sid was the hustler.

Sid was the business head; he was good at managing money. Carl was good at photographic creativity. Sid ran the office and Carl ran the camera room, that was how they complimented each other and how they became legends.

It was also known that Sid was a very good salesman, but Carl was a softer sell, much less intimidating.

Carl spoke differently than Sid, Sid cursed, although he was careful around women and clients, he used the 'F' word with aplomb. Carl did not speak like that, he never did, which is why his marriage to Cynthia lasted almost forty years.

"He's still in business; I hope he uses the techniques I taught him."

Early in their partnership, Carl told Sid he would work with him and teach him his award-winning techniques. Sid agreed and was a fast learner, but soon grew tired of using Carl's artistry. He said it was gravy; the real money was in the standard bread and butter candid pictures. He did not need to be a fucking artist, he shot for money, not awards; an award could not buy you a Cadillac. The trade that he was interested in were green ribbons, meaning money, not blue ribbons.

Sid wanted to shoot candids, he argued that the artsy bullshit was too time consuming on a job; true, that fancy pose by columns or those available lights, or multiple lit portraits looked great in the showroom window, but who the fuck is going to put fifty of those pictures in their album.

Carl knew in his heart Sid was wrong, people wanted artistic photographs taken by a talented artist, in addition to the standard posed and unposed event photos Sid favored.

Fortunately, clients agreed with Carl. He was always in demand. Carl started charging a hundred dollars, then later on, two hundred dollars for clients who requested him. More people requested Carl than Sid.

"Send us the man who shot my son's Bar Mitzvah, the very nice one, not the man who shot my other daughter's wedding, he was so obnoxious, my daughter wanted to kick him."

Day after day, night after night, Carl taught Sid, shared his knowledge with him, and Sid rewarded Carl by hollering at him in the studio, cursing him whenever he lost his temper, and dismissing his craft as bullshit.

"We were all young and beautiful in those days," Cynthia said, nuzzling Carl.

"Yeah, even Sid was young and beautiful then; we were something back then," Carl remembered the studio.

The studio, was located in a bustling business district in Elmont, Long Island. The town was somewhat integrated, and the studio was in a visible location, a couple of doors away from a huge movie theater, a travel agency, and a print shop. There was a pizzeria on the corner, so the staff never went hungry.

Upstairs, the baby studio was busy with in-home baby pictures.

Mona Sherman was the studio's colorist/retoucher. She was a pretty blonde young lady, who told her friends that she was raised a nice Orthodox Jewish girl, but from her boss she picked up a new language. Sid never swore in front of her, but the walls of that studio's office were paper thin. Mona was always a witness to Sid hollering at Carl.

Carl started recalling the days when they were young and beautiful. Mona watched Sid one morning as he lay in wait for Carl in the private office they shared. The veins were bulging in Sid's neck.

Carl walked in, and he had not closed the door.

"Good morning, Sid, I heard on the radio President Johnson says he'll sign this Medicare."

"CLEAN UP YOUR FUCKIN' DESK!" Sid greeted him.

"It's a bit disorganized, I'll get to it."

"IT'S A FUCKIN' MESS, LOOK AT IT! CLEAN IT UP, YOU FUCKIN' SLOB. I NEVER HAVE TO LOOK FOR ANYTHING!"

It went like that for eleven years of partnership.

"Yeah, young and beautiful," Carl said.

"What's wrong, dear?"

"Nothing, hon, I guess we have to send him something."

"Well, I guess fifty, maybe a hundred, we'll see."

"Yeah," he said, "send it to Norma. Sid never answers my correspondence."

"Because he can't write, dear."

Carl laughed.

"He made you nervous during the day at the studio; when you were dealing with clients, you used to be so afraid that he was going to make a snide comment, for which he was famous."

"Because he always did. Once a lady asked him how she was going to get that heavy frame she bought up on her wall. She wanted to know if we came over to hang it. Sid said, "Yeah, we keep a *shvartze* chained in the basement for that kind of work," and he didn't stop. I pushed him into the other room, I had to; I couldn't risk offending that lady any further. Motor mouth was shocked at my actions, but he didn't go after me, because he would have beaten the crap out of me. He stayed in the camera room. I guess I can laugh now, but in those days I shook."

"Well, listen, Carl, whatever you both did, it worked. You both needed each other back then. I loved it when you called him a wolverine."

"Cynthia, you know I don't use bad language, wolverine is as coarse as I get, and sometimes I called him a sloth."

"Yeah, when you were really angry. I'll send out a card with a check. Sometimes I miss him."

"Sometimes I do, too," agreed Carl, "just not when I have peace and quiet in the studio."

Chapter Thirty-Six

One o'clock Tuesday afternoon Sid was sitting at a desk in the reception area of his studio finishing paperwork. Business was good, could be better, but money was coming in, for now, anyway. George Bush had been President for half a year now; the economy was not the same as it was under Reagan. Things had to change, for the worse not better. Sid was still reeling from the September '87 stock market crash, then the following September, more market troubles. Sid had voted for Dukakis, he thought that Greek had a fair chance of winning in '88. He wanted the winner to give the businessmen, who were the backbone of the American economy, a good year financially. So far, so good

Sid sat at a black metal desk with a simulated wooden top, at the left side of the reception area. Years ago, in the heyday, a receptionist sat at that desk answering the phones, greeting the people, and doing the paperwork. Sid had a private office in the back, now seldom used, because he had to monitor the front of the studio. A loaded two-inch, .38-caliber, five-shot stainless steel Smith & Wesson Model 60, loaded with hollow point bullets was in a brown leather clip-on holster in the top drawer. Sid had a business permit for this firearm. This firearm was often favored by N.Y.P.D. officers as an off-duty weapon; detectives also used it. He also had a six-shot, blue steel, .38-caliber Colt Cobra with a two-inch barrel. This six-shot short barrel .38 was the choice of working detectives. Sid also recently purchased and registered a plastic Glock 26, 9 mm, semi-automatic pistol. The Glock's barrel was longer than his revolver's. This was what off-duty officers now carried. The N.Y.P.D. had started to incorporate the 9 mm into their department. The Nassau County police also were phasing them in, so Sid decided to afford himself the same protection. He practiced firing his weapons when he could. As of yet, he had not fired any of the guns *at* anybody, God willing, he would never have to. He felt safer knowing that they were there, just in case. The other two weapons remained locked in his house. He preferred the stainless steel .38 for the studio.

Sid wore a royal blue cotton short-sleeve shirt, beige polyester pants, and beige moccasin loafers with dark blue socks.

It was a warm day and the air conditioner was on medium. Upstairs, the baby studio in which Sid still had a business interest, bustled. The phone on Sid's desk—a black button dial office phone, which was standard throughout the studio, except for the production room, which had a white standard pushbutton phone—had not rung all morning. There was a time at this studio when it seemed that the phone never stopped ringing. That was due to reputation, because they only ran a large advertisement in the *Yellow Pages* 1968. Some said the reason why the phone did not ring so much anymore was because Carl was not there anymore.

The walls of the studio were adorned with photographs, mostly color, taken by Sid and by some of his top candid people, who no longer worked there. Some of Carl's portraits were still on the wall. Too many of the wedding formals looked outdated and were faded, especially the pictures taken outdoors that had turned green. The bookcases and the round kitchen table in the reception area where clients sat, had albums of all sizes near and on them. Weddings, Bar and Bat Mitzvahs, and anniversaries—memories were preserved in bound leather.

There was a faded plush couch with a scratched coffee table with albums and folios near the front entrance.

Sid took a quick look around, he guessed everything he had broke his ass for over the years had paid off. He lit a Viceroy.

Soft jazz was playing through the studio. He loved Jazz Blues, Jazz Rock fusion, and some Rock that evolved from Jazz.

Sid was also into stereo systems. The music was played on an old system, with a turntable, an AM/FM radio, a cassette deck, and an eight-track deck. A few years ago when the studio was broken into, the stereo was not taken, probably the thieves could not fence a unit with an eight track, nobody wanted it.

Sid wrote a business deduction for this unit. In the mid-'70s, Carl needed a new hi-fi for his house. Sid offered to go because the studio needed a new system, too. He told Carl that he would do all the talking.

"Sid always does all the talking," Carl told the receptionist.

They went into a major appliance retailer. After a short while, Sid knew what he wanted for the studio. He told Carl, the unit would be great for his home, too. He would see if the salesman would give him a deal for two units.

What the salesman tried to do, was sell him an inferior unit at a higher price.

"Sir, these two smaller units have better sound; true, they cost more, but the quality is much better."

"Sir," Sid answered, "the model I want has more features, better speakers, and is made better. I'm going to go down the block to your competition, because maybe he'll give me a better price than what's written on this tag, because I want to buy two."

"I can see your a discriminating gentleman," the salesman replied. "I'll box two of these units for you, and I'll give you a price lower than the guy down the block."

It always went like that for Sid, always—photographic and video equipment, furniture, jewelry, cars, everything. On the bookshelf, there was a small CD player with speakers, because hi-fi aficionado that he was, he was not behind the times. He also had a CD player plugged into a more modern hi-fi unit at his house. Somehow, with all its hi-technology, it just was not the same as the old vinyl.

The door opened and a young Puerto Rican man in work clothes carrying a clipboard walked in. Time for pickup for the lab. Sid still had the processing lab pickup and deliver his work.

"*Buenos dios, señor, comésta?*" Sid called out.

"*Muy béin*, Mr. Weitz, *qué pasa?*"

"*Mucho mierda, amigo.*" Sid rose.

"Les' esee, jou gotta some proofs ready, some finished work, jes, here, 'leven by seextin, sixtin by twenny, all kinds o good estuff."

"Okay, kid, I have these bags with rolls of film for proofing, portraits, and candids; this is the cut work," Sid handed the young man lab envelopes of work.

The delivery man paused to listen to the music.

"Jou like a Jazz, eh? I like a Jazz tu, I like a blues. I like a Latin Jazz, jou know, Tito Puente; jou like a Tito Puente?"

"Si, Tito Puente isn't all that much older than me."

"I guess not. Jou like a Gloria Estefan? Che's a Cubano, che hab a bery bad accident a couple months ago, che almos' die. They a say che was a goin' be a cripple, now che goin' be arigh', they give her thee beeg operation, now che walk again' das good, I like when che stan' up and chake."

"No hope, son, forget it." Sid sat back down at the desk.

"Wha?"

"She's married, and the guy she's married to doesn't sound like he just stepped off of the banana boat. You're a nice looking kid, but you're too poor and common for her. Gloria Estefan does not live in the barrio, amigo. Che hab a berry nize' chouse, on a lot of lan.'"

"I know da," the deliveryman said, softly, sounding crestfallen.

"But, in answer to your question, yes, I like Latin Jazz, Latin music, and some Gloria Estefan; they play her songs at affairs. I have this new tape, Cuban Music, see?"

The delivery man looked across the desk.

"Cuban hits?" he asked.

"Good stuff. Let's see, we no like a Castro. We can no afford good leevin' conditions. Things no so great in Cuba seence Desi die."

"No, jou make a da' up, 'cause jou funny, but da' looks like good music. Wanna play esome?"

"Are you normal?" Sid bellowed, "I got time to entertain you? You're gonna get in mucho trouble with jour boss, go."

The delivery man bid Sid a good day and left with the work envelopes. There was no cash exchange as Sid had an open account with the lab, which was paid on the first of each month.

Sid looked out of the window; the neighborhood had changed over the years. All the white merchants were leaving or had already left; he wondered how much longer he was going to last here.

An hour later, a good-looking fifty-something *zaftig* blond woman came into the studio. Mona Sherman had finished photos that she had airbrushed to Sid and Lenny's specification.

She was wearing a form-fitting, light blue pin-feather jump suit that accentuated her round buttocks and lower tummy bulge. When he was in the service, Sid picked up women with lower tummy bulges, because he liked cumming on them. Norma did not have a tummy bulge, but he came on her tummy a few times during the early stages of her pregnancies.

"See if you can get it in my belly button," she told him, "maybe we'll have twins."

"Hi, Sid, *Mazel tov* on Steve's graduation."

"Thank you," he replied. Mona had two sons who were both doctors, so she knew what having a child who was going through medical school was all about. "I told Steven, that this is not quite the end of your labor, now you have many more years of hard work ahead, all before you get to hang out your shingle."

"Don't I know it," she sat at Sid's desk, her bosom looking as supple as it did three decades earlier. "My boys are still in their residencies, a lot of hard work for years to come yet, I know."

"What ya got for me, Mona?" he asked.

Mona handed over several work envelopes; she used to work full time at the studio, years ago, back in the days when they had a staff. She spotted, retouched, colored, and framed photographs for Sid, Carl, and Lenny for years. Currently, she worked for the processing lab which Sid used, but she also did freelance work for several photography studios from her home. She was tops in her field, so photographers did not mind paying for her services.

"I have these candids I spotted for you, some Bar Mitzvah portraits, and these studio portraits you needed some airbrush work on."

Sid looked over Mona's work, it was beautiful as always, and he told her so.

"Would you like to write me a check? It's the first of the month."

"Shit, I forgot, I owe you for the month; wait here, babe, I gotta get the check book and it's in my office."

When Sid returned, he saw Mona looking at the worn blue carpeting.

"I know, I let the goddamn place go but, I'm gonna leave in another year or so."

"How much is rent now, Sid?" She asked.

"Sixteen hundred a month, but the Chinaman who bought the property says he's gonna raise the rent next year, so screw him. I'll either work from my house or rent an office, and let that Chinaman pay to take my sign down…up his."

"But really, Sid, tell me how you really feel about the landlord."

They both laughed.

"Tell me, do you still see the other Chinaman? she asked.

"What other Chinaman?" he answered. "How many 'chinks' do you think I have on my social register? I just know the laundryman and the restaurant in Woodmere."

"The fellow who did your frames," she said.

"Oh, that Chinaman! Yeah, Mona, I still use him, he's as cagey as ever because he grew up in America; his son is in the business now, too."

"I remember you and Carl used two housewives in Canarsie for your plaques and you had a run in with that moron Franklin Malkin."

"Right, right," Sid sat facing Mona across the desk, "somebody had one of Franklin's pictures he wanted put on a plaque. Franklin wouldn't do it or was too over-priced, I don't know what."

"So, the man came in here and Carl does it for him. He got the plaque from your suppliers, those two women," Mona recalled.

"Yes, but then according to Franklin, Carl put our name on the plaque with Franklin's picture and showed it to him, because, Franklin said, Carl knew that it would annoy him, remember Mona?"

"Yes, Sid, and Malkin called you up yelling and cursing."

"I was busy in those days," Sid continued, "I didn't have the time for his bullshit. Carl was my partner, so I stuck up for him right or wrong."

"Remember," Mona said, "you told me he confronted you at an association meeting and yelled at you some more in front of everybody."

"Yeah," he said, "yeah, the schmuck with all our wives present says to me, 'Fuck you where you breathe.' I shouldda flattened him."

Mona nodded.

"*Pardon mon Francaiçé,*" Sid added, remembering what he just said.

"He said that you didn't," Mona replied, "pardon his."

"I haven't seen that schmuck in years."

"How are things here now, Sid, any trouble?"

"No, not since that burglary. I told Norma some studio and office supplies were taken, I didn't want to upset her; but they took a lot of stuff—old candid equipment I had for studio use, some studio cameras, electronic strobes, radio slave units."

"You don't worry?"

"Sure, I worry," Sid replied, opening the top drawer to show Mona his holstered gun. "Why do you think I have this?"

"Oh, put it away."

"Don't worry, Mona, I have a permit; damnedest thing was Norma was glad I bought them."

"Them? Them?" Mona asked in disbelief, "How many you have?"

"Four, two revolvers and one automatic."

"That's three," she corrected him.

I have a twelve-gauge shotgun like the cops use in that old wardrobe closet in the hallway back there. It would blow someone in half."

"You're kidding, Sid."

Sid put his lower lip over his upper lip, one of his trademark facial expressions, and shook his head 'no.'

"Aren't you afraid of the guns ever going off by accident?" Mona asked.

"Mona, baby, if any of my guns ever go off, it won't be by accident."

"What does Lenny say?"

"He doesn't know; I don't give a shit about what he'd say, screw him."

"Do you practice, Sid? I mean, you have to know how to shoot."

"Sure, I practice. I shoot can."

"Can, what kind of can?"

"Afri-can, Puerto Ri-can, Mexi-can, and Domini-can."

"Oh Sid, oh shit, I walked right into that one," she laughed.

"Well, anyway," Sid said.

"Anyway," Mona answered, "I have to go upstairs and see Lenny, then be on my merry way."

"Before you go, sweetheart," Sid rose, handing Mona some envelopes, "spot these prints, airbrush the background in this bridal portrait, retouch this negative for the bride's double chin. She wanted to know what could be done for a double chin, so I told her, for openers, try twenty push-ups each morning."

"Oh, God," Mona laughed.

"Anyway, I have a two-year-old *shvartze* baby girl coming in for a studio portrait soon and I have some busy work to do, yet."

The phone rang.

"Good afternoon, Montclair," Sid answered in his gravelly Brooklyn accent.

Not wanting to interrupt him, Mona waved goodbye, and Sid waved back.

"I'm getting married in a couple a months," the young female voice on the other end of the line said, "but I'm not lookin' to spend a lotta money on pictures; ya know what I'm sayin'?"

Sid knew what she was sayin'.

This was going to be a hard pitch; he momentarily looked out the studio window to watch traffic go by. Yes, this was going to be a hard pitch, but Sid wanted to try to score a home run.

Chapter Thirty-Seven

S id could not get that woman to come into the studio for a presentation. She just had to know everything up front. How much for this, how much for that, how much for an 8x10, how much for a 5x7, how much, how much, how much? What's your package? What's your price? That's the way it was in photography today.

Sid knew it was going to get worse, not better. His industry was on the cusp—the cusp of extinction. Now coming into the 1990s, digital imaging was on its way and here to stay. This was the beginning of the end of photography. At fifty-eight, Sid Weitz had his success, but he wanted a few more good years; however, it was going to be hard to achieve that goal. Too bad for the young fellows coming into this business today, especially full time. Clients wanted to know what's your package, what's your price?—in order just to walk in the door of your studio. Meanwhile, it costs a hundred thousand dollars today just to open up a business, any kind of a business, those poor bastards.

Some people would do well—some who knew how to handle this new computer age of digital imaging. Now there are going to be imagers, no more candid men.

Today, Sid had that in mind when he tried to get that young bride to come in.

"How much if I want parent albums along with my bridal album?"

Sid tried his example about going to a restaurant, to have 'serlern' steak; if you want soup and dessert, it's two dollars more.

The young lady was not having any of that.

"We don't want to spend money on pictures; we have the hall, the DJ, limos, and my gown."

Sure, everything was important, but us. He tried to explain, after the affair, when everything is over, and all that great food is floating in the toilet bowl, all she was going to have left were her videos and pictures.

It did not work. Thirty years ago, twenty years ago, even ten, it worked. Sure, there were always low-end package deal 'shlocktography' places. Sure, studios always had calls from the price shoppers, the deadbeats, the moochers, but you could sell people—they needed your service—not like today.

Today everything in this industry is an exact science—lighting, metering, imaging, and video editing.

Everything today is an exact science—computers in cars, word processors, even sex therapist Dr. Ruth, Dr. Judy—an exact science. In the old days, people just fucked. People fucked, made babies, had pleasure for centuries; today it's a science.

Sid got up and took a pee…without science.

A pretty black woman in her twenties came in carrying a one-year-old baby girl. Sid assumed she was married and knew who the girl's father was.

The girl's mother wore light blue jeans and a simple white pullover blouse. Sid assumed the ring in her right ring finger was a wedding band.

The baby was an adorable bright-eyed little girl. She wore a silver bracelet on her left wrist. Sid did not think it was a good idea to put jewelry on small children for safety reasons. Last week he shot a portrait of a six-month-old black baby. The little boy had rings on his fingers. Weren't his parents worried about him choking on them? A few weeks earlier, he and Norma were shopping in a large Long Island mall. They observed a young mother having her three-year-old daughter's ears pierced at a jewelry kiosk. The poor kid was crying. Norma commented that the mother should be arrested for child abuse. Sid agreed, they both believed piercing should be a decision made by adults, who wish to have themselves pierced, rather than piercing small children. Thank God their daughter did not have her boys pierced. That was another thing that bothered Sid, today so many Bar Mitzvah boys had their ears pierced.

This kid was a cutie; she was smiling before they began.

"You're Sid?" the mother asked. She spoke well, probably a college grad.

"Yes, that's me! I'm the one you spoke to. I guess this is Leslie."

"That's her, little Cinderella. Okay, do I pay now?"

"No, Sharon," Sid remembering her name, from the phone, "first I take the pictures, and then you can leave a deposit. Shall we adjourn to the camera room?"

The camera room in Montclair Studios was a blend of old and new. The wall had a large affixed background. There was also a motorized roller system, attached to the other wall, which held different color backgrounds, including one for Christmas and one for Easter. There were also some portable backgrounds rolled up, which were mainly used for location shoots.

The lights used were powerful eighteen hundred-watt second studio strobes, with modeling lights. Modeling lights were light bulbs inside the strobe head, to indicate to the photographer how the shadows would fall; they were also useful for focusing.

Sid had older tungsten and quartz flood lights, which because were on constantly, were a potential safety problem. They now sat in Sid's attic. *I have to get rid of that shit one day* he reminded himself.

There were white forty-five-inch reflective umbrellas on each strobe head. They provide a soft even light. He also had silver and gold lined umbrellas for when 'oomph' was needed. There were also white soft box attachments that were seldom used these days.

Sid set cute little Leslie on his 'baby posey,' then placed a smaller less powerful strobe light behind her pointed to the background.

There was an interesting assortment of cameras in that room. Sid had an old Century Studio Master, which used 8x10 sheet film. Once it was used for portraits, formals, and group shots, now it was just for show. Only the commercial photographers used 8x10 sheet film nowadays. This camera was versatile when Sid and Carl used it, because it had backs for 5x7 and 4x5 sheet film. There was also an old Beattie Portronic 4x5 portrait camera and an old Speed Graphic camera with a 135 lens and a 4x5 back for portraits. On a stand was a Mamiya RB67 camera, which in addition to using roll film, which produced 6x7 and 6x9 images, it also took 4x5 backs. On a table beside it, rested an older Mamiya 645, which Sid favored for portraits as he got older.

There was a Mamiya C2, Mamiya C330, and a Koniflex in the metal cabinet. These were all old twin lens reflex 6x6 cameras for portrait use. Also in the cabinet, was a Bronica SQ 6x6. These cameras were square formats, sometimes used for portrait work. Heshy Adomovich, Sid's friend, swore by a square camera for studio portraits, while Sid liked working in rectangle, but every now and then, he shot square.

Sid decided on the RB67 today. He held up a toy bunny to get Leslie's attention; the baby squealed with delight.

"See the bunny, honey? You have a bunny nose, I'm going to take your little bunny nose." Sid pretended to pull the little girl's nose off.

She laughed.

"Oh, you're into this, Leslie, aren't you? Yes, you are," he snapped a picture. "Yes, you are, she's into this," he turned to her mother.

"She's a good girl today. She thinks you're entertaining."

"Okay, angel, big smile here. Look who I have," Sid held up a President Ronald Reagan hand puppet he bought from a photographic supply company. "Look cutie."

The baby clapped her little hands in delight.

"Mr. Gorbachev," Sid said doing a fair Ronald Reagan impression, *Ich hub mached en mein hoisen,*" which in Yiddish or German meant, 'I have made in my pants.' Leslie somehow understood what that meant and laughed.

"*Oy, Ich hub gayn pishen.*"

More laughter.

"You have a great way with her, Sid."

"Been doin' it for forty years, darling," he answered Sharon while snapping a picture.

"Do you have children?"

"We have two, girl and boy. I'm a grandpa, my daughter has two little boys, maybe they'll have more."

"How old, Sid?"

"Fifty-eight, but I look fifty-seven, I'm told."

"I meant your grandsons."

"The eldest is four; the little guy is not much younger than this little cutie pie."

"He talk, yet?"

"Nah, but I can't get the older one to shut up."

"You take their pictures?"

"Oh sure, they been here a lot. I have a picture of them on the wall in the front, I'll show you. When Peter, he's the eldest, first started to talk, he told people his grandpa was a picture man."

"He meant photographer," Sharon sounded charmed.

"Yeah, people said, 'you mean grandpa is a photographer?' He'd say, 'Noooo, a picture man!'"

"That's sweet."

"So's your little angel." He changed Leslie's pose.

"What about your son?"

"I have a nice girl picked out for him, I just need him to meet me half way and marry her. Incidentally, Sharon, I happen to like being a grandpa."

"So do my parents; my husband's parents say they're way too young."

So the baby had a father, thank God.

"What, are you kidding? Young grandparents are the best, they have more energy, because they're young, and the grandkids will know them for a long time."

"Very true," she answered.

The portrait session had ended, and both subject and photographer had a good time.

Sid and Sharon sat at the desk in the reception area in the front of the studio. After complimenting him on his beautiful grandsons, Sharon wrote Sid a deposit check. He explained an 8x10 and the previews were included; she could order additional pictures and folio frames when she picked out poses from the proofs. He also showed her the brushstroke picture on canvas. She might be an easy sell.

She left, and Sid sat alone in the studio.

He realized he had not eaten. He turned on the answering machine, locked the door, and walked a few stores down to the pizzeria.

The pizzeria was there longer than Sid. It was run by a husband and wife team, Carmine and Carmela.

A short stout, pugnacious-looking, ape-like creature stood at the counter. This person had the face of a boxer. Her husband was somewhat better looking. He stood next to her; he was short and muscular with dark hair and a mustache.

"Hi," Carmela growled, it was hard to tell if she was angry, because she often growled. Carmine nodded and belched.

"I would like a veal…"

"Ain't got no veal today," Carmela cut him off.

"Okay, chicken marsala hero sandwich."

"Yeah," she answered.

A young, thin, but muscular dark-haired man sat at one of the tables alone, he wore jeans and an F.D.N.Y. tee shirt. Sid knew it was Ronnie, the couple's son.

"How are you?" Sid asked.

"Hey," Ronnie looked up and nodded.

"Ronnie's on the job, he's not a probie anymore," Carmine called out tossing dough.

"Where do you work?" Sid asked.

"Staten Island, I'm movin' there. I'm gonna be able to walk to the firehouse."

"Ronnie's gettin' married," Carmine said.

"Yeah, but we got a photog-a-fer," Carmela growled, "the bride wants to use this bridal center in Brooklyn; they got better prices than you photog-a-fers."

"Yeah, they don't ax too much money," Ronnie said.

They told Sid the name of the bridal center, and Sid knew of the place. He heard it was mob-connected and that the work sucked.

Carmela stared out of the window, as a black man walking past, paused.

"What does that nigger want?" she growled.

"Maybe he's hungry," Sid suggested.

"Then let him go to the sal'avation army for soup with his ripple. That's why we sold the place, too many *moulinyans* around here."

Moulinyan was Italian for 'eggplant,' but the word was also used to slur black people.

"*Moulinyan*, ya know what that is? You people say *shvartze*."

"I don't say anything like that," Sid lied not wanting to give that ape the satisfaction.

"*Moulinyans*," Carmela said.

"*Moulinyans*," Carmine called out.

"The niggers," Ronnie piped up.

"Who'd you sell to?" Sid asked.

"A spic," Carmela answered.

"He knows how to make pizza and Italian specialties, but he's gonna make Spanish shit for the neighborhood spics," Carmine spoke.

"And the *moulinyans*," Carmela added.

"Ya know, Sid," Carmine said, "Ronnie worked up in the South Bronx, and they had some type of riot up there. Right, Ronnie? You told me they overturned a deputy chief's car."

"Shouldda been shot," Ronnie shook his head, "Shouldda been shot."

"They kept setting the vacant buildings on fire," Carmine continued.

"They shouldda been shot," Ronnie said.

"Ronnie, why didn't you become a cop, then you could shoot people," Sid asked.

"Because," Ronnie explained, "the fire department is a better job, fah Chris' sake! Today, if you're a cop, you can get jammed up. Everybody loves us; we don't have to shoot the *moulies*. In the old days, it was better; my uncle was a cop, he'd beat up a nigger for causing problems...probable cause or not."

"If they didn't cause problems?" Sid asked.

"Preventative medicine, Bro," was Ronnie's answer.

"They earned their pay from the city, in the old days," Carmine said.

"We had a run in Staten Island," Ronnie went on, "near the fire house, some Jewish guy sold to jigs. So that house burned; he shouldda been shot."

"Bullshit," Carmela barked, "my son don't get paid enough to risk his life for them animals."

"So most of the guys in my company knew the situation, so we held back a while, let the house burn, before we went in. That guy shouldda been shot."

"Ya know how we can solve problems of the welfare people and all them illegal immigrants," said Carmine, it was not a question.

"I'm sure you've given it some thought, Carmine," Sid responded.

"We can build camps, you know, like out in the desert. We can make them manufacture things for the government. We wouldn't even have to pay them, just give 'em some food and bunks to sleep on."

"Damn right!" Carmela said.

"Also," Carmine continued, "we could solve the over population by sterilizing them, so they can't burden us with their babies, while they're doing their work for us."

Sid shuddered. This sounded like a terrible blast from the past.

"That was tried once before, you know?" Sid said angrily.

"I know," Carmine said, "and it worked. I bet we could make it work again, 'cause alls through history good ideas were tried over again."

"That's why we're moving away, too many *moulinyans*."

"*Moulinyans*," Carmine seconded.

"The niggers," Ronnie made it unanimous.

"Ya lunch is ready," Carmela growled.

Sid now remembered why he seldom ate here. He paid for his sandwich.

"Thank you," Carmela grunted.

"Have a nice day," Carmine said cheerfully.

"How can I?" Sid called out as he left the pizzeria.

He walked back to the studio. He had heard everything old is new again. Truly, there was nothing new under the sun. He had been hearing a lot about all that retro shit. It was being said in the photographic industry that big weddings were in again. From their mouths to God's ears.

But for a fifty-eight year-old Jewish father and grandpa, it was not a comforting thought to know concentration camps were in again.

Sid sat down in the stockroom at the small card table he used for lunch.

With those bastards gone, maybe the neighborhood will improve.

He looked at his watch. A couple of hours to go. Another day, a couple of dollars.

Chapter Thirty-Eight

W hile Sid Weitz was hearing his fellow merchants' suggestions for the new world order, his son Dr. Steven Weitz was breaking up with his girlfriend.

He called Gayle and made a date to meet her at her house. They met on the patio; she had prepared iced tea for them. He was not specific on what he wanted to see her about. She was excited; she styled her hair and put on a white cotton summer dress with a flowing skirt.

Together they sat on a white resin patio loveseat. Gayle moved close to Steven and slipped her hand into his.

"What were you so mysterious on the phone for, Steve?" she asked him.

"I've something very important to say to you."

"Haaahhh," Gayle let out on of her breathy sighs, which Steven no longer found seductive as she placed her head on his shoulder. The day she dreamt about was finally here.

Or, so she thought.

"Gayle, uh, well this is kind of awkward."

"Oh, Steve, just relax; I'm listening, and I really do love you."

"Well," he said.

"Relax, I want this to be special for you, don't rush."

"Gayle…"

"Yes, Steve?"

"I don't think we should see each other anymore, Gayle."

"What the fuuuccckkk?" Gayle's voice went up several octaves as she jerked her head off of Steven's shoulder.

"Oh," she giggled, "it's a joke, good one."

"No joke, Gayle, I'm not ready for commitment and I think I would like to see other women. I just can't marry right now."

"It will be alright, I'll see to that. Both of our fathers will see to that."

"I can't marry you, Gayle." Steven got up off the loveseat.

"Why? Was I mean to you? I gave you my love, I don't understand."

"Gayle, I just can't stand you anymore."

"Oh, my God," her voice high pitched now, with emotion, "oh, my Go-uhhd, oh, my God, oh. My Go-uhhd, he's dumping me. After a long time together, he's dumping me!"

"Sorry, Gayle, that's my fault. I should have dumped you sooner, I was waiting for the right time."

"Oh, my Go-uhhd! This is the right time?"

"For me it is, Gayle," he explained firmly, but calmly. "I just can't stomach you, frankly."

"What about me is not to stomach?" Gayle whined.

"Just that, you're conceited, ill tempered, spoiled, and a real racist."

"Why, because I don't have any black friends? I have a goyish girlfriend; she's not that close with me, because I just can't relate to a Catholic."

"Gayle, you're snottier than a used tissue. I just don't *love* you."

"When did you find that out, fuck face?" She was standing and very distraught.

"Lately, every moment I have spent with you."

"So that's it, shit face, you don't love me anymore?"

"I didn't say anymore."

"You never loved me, cockhead; you fucked me, that you liked!"

"You were the first girl I fucked, of course, I liked it."

"OH, MY GO-UHHD!"

"Gayle, I'm sorry," he said, "I have to go."

"What will your parents say? Your father, what will he say?"

Steven shrugged. He looked like Sid when he shrugged.

"He'll call you a schmuck!"

"Gayle, my father calls everybody a schmuck!" Steven retorted.

"OH, MY GOD, OH, MY GO-UHHHD, OH, MY GOD, OH, MY GO-UHHD! I CAN'T BELIEVE IT. I CAN'T FUCKIN' BELIEVE IT."

"Gayle! Stop you're outside," Steven snapped. "It's bad enough I know how common you are, but do the neighbors need to know?"

"COMMON? I AM NOT FUCKIN' COMMON, DICKHEAD!" she roared.

"My grandmother told me when I was a little boy, that when someone curses, people look at that person and say, OOOIIII! COMMON! Evidently she was right."

"You're rebelling against your parents, because they like me! They want you to settle down with a proper Jewish girl. Your father thinks it would kill you to do that for him."

"Then let my father marry you, it wouldn't last. You're not a saint like my mother," Steven walked to the driveway, "and you're not a proper Jewish girl, you're a stuck-up little J.A.P.!"

"FUCK OUTTA HERE!" she bellowed after him, "I don't ever want to see you again."

"Isn't that what I just got through saying to you?" Steven turned as he walked through the gate, "I said we weren't going to see each other anymore."

"NOW, I WOULD NEVER MARRY YOU, ASSHOLE!"

"You need not worry about that. By the way, dear, do you actually eat with that mouth?"

"OOOOHHHH! OOOOOHHHHH!" Gayle yelled after Steven.

"OOOOHHHH! and to think, I thought you loved me, to think," screaming violently down the block now, "I LET YOU GO DOWN ON ME, WE WEREN'T EVEN MARRIED!"

"Common, common." Steven Weitz shook his head as he walked away.

"I HOPE YOUR SISTER'S CHILDREN GET KILLED." She could be heard as he rounded the corner. "YOU HEAR ME? I HOPE THEY BOTH RUN INTO THE STREET AND GET HIT BY CARS!"

Chapter Thirty-Nine

When Steven Weitz walked into his house, he felt a sense of accomplishment. That was all he felt, accomplishment. He felt neither sad, nor happy. He had a feeling of finality. He had something to do and it got done.

Steve walked into his father's office, opened his top desk drawer, took a cigarette out of an opened pack, and lit it. He stepped into the small bathroom in that office and puffed without inhaling.

Steven never advocated smoking, especially now, as a doctor. Pleasurable as it was, smoking had too many health risks involved. He was happy his mother quit years ago, he wished his father would.

He puffed slowly. It was a full flavor cigarette, it tasted good. He puffed some more, then threw the cigarette into the toilet, peed, then flushed.

He went into the main bathroom upstairs, brushed his teeth, rinsed with mouthwash, and then washed his face.

Norma walked in the front door with groceries.

"Let me help you, Mom."

"Thanks, Doc." She handed him the bags.

"How was your date today?"

"Mom, it wasn't a date, I broke it off with Gayle."

Norma patted Steven's shoulder as they walked to the kitchen.

"You're not surprised?" he asked.

Norma shrugged. "I saw it coming, Steve, it's your life. You should never rush into anything you aren't ready for."

"Dad will be surprised." He sat down at the table.

"Leave him to me," Norma filled a tea kettle with water for instant coffee. "He's a nudnik, but I can handle him."

"How do you handle him?"

"I'll tell him you weren't ready for that kind of a commitment. He's your father, he will understand."

"This is not temporary, Mom, we're finished. We have to go our separate ways."

"Then, Steve, it's for the best. Sometimes that has to happen in a relationship; you move on."

Norma poured water into the cup, stirred in coffee, and sat down at the table facing her son.

"How did Gayle take it?"

"Badly, Mom, worse than I had expected. She called me names."

"Oh, my."

"She sounded like Dad when he gets going with his buddies. F, F, F, every other word was F."

"Oh, my, my."

"Then she yelled, among other things, that my sister's children should get killed. They should get hit by a car."

"My, my, my."

"Then I told her she was common."

"Yes, she is," Norma agreed with her son. "Well, I guess it's better things came out now. There is an old saying, 'You never know a person until you live with one.' I guess that's why all the young couples live together now before they get married. Your father told me, his unmarried clients have both their names on the checks when they give him the deposit. Boy, you couldn't do that in my day," Norma sipped her coffee, "unless you were in show business, a writer, or an artist living in Greenwich Village. Maybe it's better this way, to live together first, who knows."

"Well, Nana always said Dad was common. I love my father, but I can't disagree with her. Did it come as a shock, I mean when you saw how abrasive Dad can be with his snide remarks?"

"Well, I want you to know, young man, in spite of what your father is, he's a good father and husband, remember that! As for the other stuff, well, I knew he was rough around the edges when I married him, but common? No I wouldn't say that about him."

"Nana did," Steven reminded Norma.

"Well, sometimes Nana is a pain in the ass. She perceived that about him, because there are times he won't let her boss him around. He told her, when we were first married, 'I'm not your husband, see, I have a pair! I am not going to take any shit from you, so don't come into my home, and tell me what to do!'"

"Dad said that to Nana, the whole thing, just like that?"

"Yes."

"What did Nana have to say?"

"She said, 'Oooohhh common!'" Norma flashed her radiant smile.

"So, you kind of knew Dad's personality before you said I do."

"Yes, I knew he was a character, alright. We played off each other with our personalities. That's how this marriage worked. Much like at the studio, when Carl was your father's partner. If we had the same personality, the marriage would never have lasted. You know, Steve, Dad always says, 'My wife never has a bad thing to say about anyone, not like me.' People knowingly agree with him when he says that, too."

"I know he says that, Mom, I've heard him."

"See, he's not a bad guy after all. Okay, you sort out your own life and personal affairs; I'll handle the old coot."

That would be easier said than done, because Gayle Eysenberg was home, sobbing her eyes out. She also claimed that although the relationship was consentual between two legal age adults, young Dr. Weitz had nonetheless violated her virtue.

Nathan Eysenberg and Marianne Eysenberg were both in their forties, attractive, well-spoken, educated, and very wealthy. In addition to their domicile in Hewlett, they had a condo in Boca Raton, a house in East Hampton, and a duplex apartment on Park Avenue in Manhattan. Their driveway had Nathan's Cadillac Sedan de Ville for work, Marianne's Lincoln Town Car for her use, Gayle's Toyota Celica, her brother's Honda Civic coupe, and her father's Mercedes 450 SL for weekend pleasure. There was also a large classic Mercedes convertible coupe in the garage, which was given to Gayle's father by a grateful Mafia client. Nathan Eysenberg helped to get that fine upstanding businessman acquitted on drug trafficking charges.

"Gayle," Marianne sat on the bed next to her daughter, "Gayle, you're young, that happens in romance; sometimes it ends abruptly."

"I hate him, I hate him for what he did to me!" she sobbed.

"What did he do?" Her father asked as he stood by her bed, "Tell us."

Nathan Eysenberg had gray eyes, Marianne Eysenberg had blue eyes, the result was Gayle had violet eyes. They both had raven hair, as did Gayle.

"He talked me into having sex."

"Alright," Nathan placed his hand on her shoulder, "did he force you?"

"Well, he said he loved me, this was when he was acting like we were already engaged to be married."

"Creep," said Nathan

"Go on, dear," said Marianne.

"He put his mouth on me," she cried softly.

"He kissed you?" her mother asked.

"No mother, it was a sex act. He put his mouth down on my, you know."

"Schmuck kid, I'm gonna chew his parents out, but good!" Nathan raged.

"Front and back," Gayle added.

"Well, Gayle, you're an adult, but I'll look into this," her father assured. "You're better off without that young punk. You're better than he is."

"Dad's right, Gayle," Marianne spoke, "they're beneath us, they are so *trés un classé*. You hear the way his father speaks, 'Deese, dem, dose, foist, thoid, let's have serlern steak.'"

"Yeah, he acts like a big shot, but he's just a photographer, he shoots Bar Mitzvahs. He doesn't even get jobs from the blue bloods in the society page. Personally, I never thought much of him. That Sid's a real low moron," Nathan expressed his opinion.

"She works in a bank, she's nothing special, his mother," Marianne tried to comfort Gayle. Look who she married, she couldn't do any better. Look what your father-in-law would be, a cigarette-smoking, candid man. That's all he is, a paid servant. Frankly, Gayle, I never thought his work was that good."

"Yeah," retorted Nathan, "what is that asshole anyway? Sid is a *schleper* from Brooklyn. He has no class, even with all those Cadillacs and Lincolns he drives. He likes to show how great he is. He shows how much of a windbag he is. You can take the *schleper* out of Brooklyn, Gayle, but you can't take Brooklyn out of the *schleper*."

"Steven is a *schleper*, too!" Gayle whined. "Ohhh, my God, oh my Go-uud! I can't believe he hurt me like that."

"Gayle, it's over," Marianne said.

"Oh, my Go-uhhhd, I loved him! We were going to get marrie-hee-hee-ed."

"Gayle, come, you've been through enough; I want to buy you a new BMW convertible."

"Can I have a Corvette, Daddy? A yellow convertible, with an automatic transmission?"

"Sure, darling, whatever you want, you know that, always whatever you want. You'll drive it past his house, show him you're back in the market for an a real *mensch* this time, from a good family"

"Let's take Gayle out for lobster, before we go to the car dealer. Let her celebrate her dumping him, which is what she would have done, anyway."

"Alright, let's go," Nathan opened Gayle's bedroom door, "I want to talk to that photographer about his son. Maybe we can prosecute."

"Dad and I only want you to be happy, Gayle, we always have. You're a good girl. Whatever you want, that's what we want, too." Her mother hugged her daughter.

Later on that night after Nathan Eysenberg picked out his daughter's new Corvette, he called Sid Weitz.

By this time, Sid had been informed of his son's breakup. He was not happy.

The phone conversation between the two dads was hostile and did not go well.

"WHAT DO YOU MEAN MY SON VIOLATED YOUR DAUGHTER? THEY WERE IN A RELATIONSHIP."

"THEY WERE NEVER ENGAGED, SID! STEVEN TOLD HER HE LOVED HER, THEN VIOLATED HER!"

"FUCK YOU! IT WAS CONSENTUAL, SCHMUCK! YOUR DAUGHTER WASN'T VIOLATED; SHE LOST HER VIRGINITY IN NURSERY SCHOOL, PUTZ!"

That hurt Sid to say that, he liked Gayle and was looking forward to her being his daughter-in-law.

"FUCK YOU BACK, PRICK SON OF A LOWLIFE BITCH. I'M GONNA BRING CHARGES AGAINST YOUR SON!"

"YEAH, YEAH, AND FUCK YOU!" It hurt Sid that he had to stick up for his son, but a son was a son.

"I'M GONNA COME OVER AND SEE YOU BEFORE I SUE."

"YOU GOT NO FUCKIN' CASE, AND IF YOU COME OVER HERE, I'LL BEAT THE LIVING SHIT DAYLIGHTS OUTTA YOU, THEN THROW YOUR ASS INTO THE MIDDLE OF THE STREET."

Sid hung up the phone. Yeah, sure, there is no case, no criminality, just *schmuckiness*.

The phone rang, Sid picked it up.

"FUUUUCCCCKKKK YOOOOUUU!" he yelled into the mouthpiece.

"OOOHHHH, COMMON!" the voice on the other end said.

"Hey Norma," Sid called out, "your mother's on the phone."

Sid called Steven into his office to ream him out.

"*Putz fettig!*" Sid called Steven, which in Yiddish means 'pain in the balls.'

"YOU SHOULDN'T BE FUCKING A LAWYER'S DAUGHTER WITHOUT AN ENGAGEMENT RING, BETTER, YET, A WEDDING RING, PUTZ FETTIG!"

"Dad, we're adults, I think you're mad because I broke it off. Besides, THIS IS NONE OF YOUR FUCKING BUSINESS, NOT YOURS OR ANYBODY'S!" Steven yelled, using that word to his father for the very first time.

"THE FUCK IT AIN'T. THE PRICK WANTS TO SUE OR BRING CHARGES. HE CAN'T AND WONT! BUT, I DON'T NEED THE FUCKIN'AGGRAVATION!"

"Dad, she's twisting everything around."

"I'm sure she is, I know, but still…" he shrugged, pacing as Steven sat on the couch. "Still, you should have kept your dick in your pants. I'll tell you an old Yiddish expression, my son. When you think with your *putz*, your brain goes into your *tokus*, remember that!"

"Dad it was consentual. I just couldn't marry her."

"Listen, in Yiddish we say, '*No chuppah, no shtuppa*'! In my day, you had to wait for pussy until you were married. Listen to me, you couldn't get pussy until you were married. If you needed ass or pussy or a good fuck because your balls were turning blue, you went to a hooker, or if you were in the service, you went to Tijuana for action. That's how you did it in those days. That's how you got laid. Shit, man, I didn't attack your mother; I fucked gook whores in Korea."

"Dad, leave me alone, I don't need this right now."

"Neither do we," Sid answered his son.

The Eysenbergs never took legal action against the Weitzes

Steven knew his father meant well about everything—the lecture on premarital sex, and Dad's desire to see him settled down and married to a rich Jewish girl.

Steven sat at a desk in his room that was long outgrown. He pondered everything from his past. Too much from the past.

"I bet your daddy hollers on you a lot." Nana Sadie said while he was visiting her house when he was about five.

"He only hollers when he's angry," Steven told his nana.

"I hear different," she informed him. "He yells and curses all the time at work."

"Who says?" Steven wanted to know.

"I hear things," Nana Sadie answered him, nodding her head knowingly, "I get reports. He always screams at that poor man, Carl. One day your daddy's partner is going to give it to him good. He's going to say why you...and give it to your daddy in the eyes."

"My father is good," Steven defended Sid.

"Sure, he's a good man, a good husband, a wonderful father, but look and listen, a screw is loose," she tapped her head.

"You know Daddy yells at Carl?"

"I hear things, I get reports. Steveeleh, remember, it's not good to get angry and yell and curse. People will look on you and say, 'Ooooohhhhh, common!' like they do with your father. If you curse people, one day you will hear a knock at the door, and it will be the authorities. They'll come to wash your mouth out with soap."

Steven felt guilty that he put his parents through this. Now it was their business. Even though he was now a responsible adult, he was embarrassed.

Maybe that no pussy until you're married business was the best advice Dad had ever given him. He was not in love with Gayle, he knew that. She was not right for him, he knew that, too.

Mom had supported his decision. She was always supportive of him. At this point, Dad supported him, too, since that phone confrontation with Gayle's father.

It was time for him to move on; everybody in the Weitz house knew that.

He also wanted to get his own place, now that he was going to earn money.

Sid had told him he was going to start charging rent, Norma said, "We'll take the money, and save it for Steven."

Sid said 'no,' they would take the money and spend it.

Steven knew his life was just beginning; it was time for him to go and live it.

Chapter Forty

Steven Weitz was getting along just fine living his life. He started his internship, working at a private hospital in Brooklyn. The hospital was still kosher, as it was a Jewish hospital. Steven and his sister Linda were born there years ago.

Steven had a small apartment all to himself in Bay Ridge, Brooklyn. He was independent, except for the small second-hand Volkswagen Dasher his father helped him buy.

"A Joiman car, I hate Joimans," his father told the salesman. But, Dad helped him pay.

Steven liked living alone in Brooklyn, where he studied in peace and quiet. If he had to pay rent, he wanted to give it to a landlord, rather than to his father. At least that Greek did not live with him. His parents visited when they could, his mother brought him food and things for the apartment, which was appreciated. His father stopped by on the way home from a Brooklyn affair, if he was not too tired.

His rotations were not uneventful. As an intern on his first day at one large public hospital in Brooklyn, he wondered if he had selected the right career. As he walked through the corridor, he heard cries of desperation. It made him retch.

"OY, OY, OY, OY YOY YOY!"

"AY, AY, AY, AY, YI, YI, YIYYYY!"

"ALLAH, ALLAH, ALLAHH!"

A very old frail woman ran out into the hall crying out, "I AM IN AGONY! AGONY! AGONY! AGONYYYY!"

An elderly man on a ventilator got out of his bed to call for help, when his buzzer was not answered.

"Please," he called out, "it hoits, noiss! noiss! It hoits!"

Steven helped him into bed, and a nurse called the code, causing a chain reaction of utter chaos.

"EEE EYYYYY! the man cried out. Steven never heard a human make such noises in his life.

A team of clueless residents in surgical scrubs and white coats converged on the man's bed.

"ANESTHESIA!" A woman in scrubs, wearing a shower cap-type of cap called out. It was her job to insert a breathing tube.

An Indian resident, who did not know what was going on, stood in back of the residents, jumping up and down to get a view of the patient. The team saved the man, for now.

In the emergency room, a Haitian woman brought her teenage son in for stitches. She told Steven her tale of woe.

"De cups, de cups did eet to heem."

"The cups?" Steven asked.

"Dee poleeece! Dey beat my son up."

"Why?"

"Dey say he stole sometheeng and he holding weapons in hees poket. So de cup beat heem up, an' I tell dee cup I'm hees mother, he tell me mind my own fuckin' beesness, an' he pushed my son into de cup car, an' when de cup pushed my son into de car, he call heem a jeegabooo!"

"I was only arrested once, Doc." The patient volunteered, "I cut a man because he danced weeth my girl."

A Chassidic man brought his young son in for stitches in his chin after the boy fell. Steven told the father there might be a scar. The man told him not to worry, because his beard would hide it.

The psych patients were the most fun.

One night, Steven saw an Orthodox Jewish man handcuffed to a gurney. He had suffered a psychotic break of some sort.

"I VANT TO SEE A LAWYER! I VANT TO SEE A LAWYER! I VANT TO SEE A FUCKIN' LAWYER!" he said repeatedly.

"Hold on, hold on, we'll get you a fuckin' lawyer," one cop said.

"Yeah, first you'll see a fuckin' doctor, then you'll see a fuckin' lawyer," the second cop said, "and, mister, you're gonna need one."

"I VANT TO SEE A LAWYER, I WANT TO SEE A LAWYER, I VANT TO SEE A FUCKIN' LAWYER!" The man had a rhythm. Within an hour, every doctor, nurse, technician, orderly, cop, and patient in the emergency room was chanting, "I VANT TO SEE A LAWYER, I WANT TO SEE A LAWYER, I VANT TO SEE A FUCKIN' LAWYER!" along with the Orthodox man.

Nearby, a Chinese man was handcuffed to a chair. He stood on the street disoriented, when a police officer asked if he could help, the man attacked the officer.

The Chinese man saluted the police officer who was sitting in a chair across from him with his free hand. The cop returned the salute. This went on for over an hour. When an attending psychiatrist came to make an evaluation, he asked Steven which one was the psych patient.

For an intern in the emergency room, it was never a dull moment.

Steven went into a cubicle occupied by a pretty middle-aged Puerto Rican woman.

"What can I do for you today?" he asked her.

"My baginy eetches," she replied.

Steven had his ass groped by a drunken young woman he was stitching up after a fall.

He stitched up a drunken man the police brought in after he was mugged on the subway.

"Ya think he's inebriated, Doc?" the detective asked.

"Nah," the other detective replied, "he's Caucasian."

Another drunk required assistance. As he waited, a powerfully-built orthopedist walked by and snapped his finger hard across the poor old drunkard's nose. This stunned Steven. The drunk also was angered by the action of the orthopedist.

"Hey, ya shunuvfabish, ya ain't got no right ta do that."

The orthopedist flexed his rippling muscles at the drunk.

The man sat down and said nothing further.

An elderly black man gave Steven his medical history.

"Do you use drugs?" Steven inquired.

"No, I don't use no drugs, I'm an alcoholic."

The man really needed a place to sleep.

A young fireman held his index finger up to Steven.

"Hey, Doc, it's bad, right? It's pretty bad? Can you get me a disability?"

"Nope, I'm only an intern."

"C'mon, Doc, you can get me a disability."

"Interns can't do that. It's only a sprain, try the fire department doctor."

"Nah, dem bastards won't give me a disability."

An old man who fell and cut his chin in his apartment was brought in by his adult children, and emergency rooms prioritize cases, so the man was angry about the wait.

"I'm leavin!" he growled. The admitting nurse asked his name, "Bunoventena, and I'm gonna tell everybody ya didn't do a thing for me, yez rat bastards!"

Prisoners made Steven nervous. Often police officers brought people in custody to the hospital for treatment. Some prisoners were injured before their arrest, some were physically sick to begin with. Others had injuries caused by the cops themselves. Many of the cops often joked with the doctors about giving a prisoner a wood shampoo, which was a crack on the head with the baton.

The one good thing was police officers who worked near a hospital, seldom wrote doctors summonses for traffic violations. It was not a good idea to offend a doctor who might be working on you someday. Usually, doctors were given a warning and asked to be more careful. In exchange, the officers wanted the doctors to save their lives if they were ever brought into that hospital.

During that time, Steven also worked in the pediatric clinic. He thought the little black boys with shaved heads were very cute. One cute little boy climbed all over Steven, he even held Steven's hand as he skipped down the hall after the check up. Kids were supposed to be afraid of the doctor. Most of those kids liked Steven; he knew pediatrics was the right specialty for him. Some of the older attending doctors said he was a natural.

Steven had concerns for the Chassidic kids, though. Due to cousins marrying each other, many of those kids suffered birth defects, heart disease, bone disease, and even mental disorders. Their eyeglasses were thick as bottles; it was terrible what those people were causing their children to go through in life.

Most of those children were born in America, yet they spoke like old *mockies*. It was terrible; those kids sounded like greenhorns just off the boat at Ellis Island.

"Doctor, you got medicine for my ache, maybe?" a ten-year-old-child, yet.

Steven was not sleeping that much during his internship, or that well, and it showed.

His parents were worried; there were times Steven seemed irritable, on edge, and very nervous.

"His hands shake," Norma told Sid. "His hands shake. I think he's taking pills."

"They do drive young doctors crazy, that is true, but that is only because they want doctors to know what they're doing."

"Sid, they have reports on TV saying young doctors are overworked, under rested, and underpaid."

"Well," Sid, agreed with her, "but all of our doctors went through this, so he'll get through this, too."

"I just want our son to get through it alive."

"So do I, babe, it would be a terrible waste of money if he didn't."

"Sidney, goddamn it, you're a nudnik. You're being a real, oh, what do you always say at work, a real fuckin' putz."

"Don't curse, dear," Sid laughed.

"I learned it from you, common."

"You're mother calls me that, common."

"She's right, honey," Norma said sweetly.

Interns don't make the money full-fledged doctors make. They need to borrow money from their parents from time to time. Sid caught Norma lending Steven money. He was pissed. The boy is on his own, an adult, a doctor, what's this giving money shit?

"What the hell are you giving him money for? He works!" Sid asked Norma in the kitchen one day.

"He's short, Sidney, he doesn't make that much."

"Listen, I don't make that much anymore, do I ask him?"

"I'm not making real money yet, Dad. Everything is so goddamned expensive. Do you know how much toilet paper costs?"

"I know how much toilet paper costs," Sid informed his son. "Do you know how much toilet paper costs? I can afford toilet paper. When I was your age, I had a job, a wife, two kids, a car, an apartment, and toilet paper!"

"Dad, I can't afford toilet paper."

"So don't wipe your ass!"

"Daddy isn't kidding," Norma said. She gave Steven the money for toilet paper.

Steven had a meal ticket for the hospital cafeteria; that slop was a tad better than the takeout food he ate.

He found a homeless woman asleep in the front seat of his car, she said she was sorry. Now he needed the money to have the car's interior cleaned, deodorized, and deloused.

His ER rotation was up; he was to start his psychiatric rotation now. This was going to be fun. If he could understand his father, he could understand the patients, he reasoned.

Chapter Forty-One

During young Dr. Steven A. Weitz's psychiatric rotation, it dawned on him that psychiatrists were crazy. He knew from his experience in his surgical rotation, that surgeons were crazy. Psychiatrists were crazier.

When Steven stepped into an operating room for the first time with other medical school students, he was amazed at the skilled procedures. So were the other students, one young man put his finger into the open cavity in the patient's stomach and poked about.

"Take your finger and stick it up your ass," the surgeon instructed matter-of-factly. Before long, Steven saw that many of the surgeons were arrogant, cut, happy, cavalier cowboys.

Psychiatrists were another story.

Dr. Stanley Blaumauer, M.D., PhD. was the hospital's director of psychiatry. Dr. Blaumauer looked, sounded, and acted like Steven's father. He had his own method of therapy; he got down on his patient's level. He was just as crazy as they were.

"What are you, fucked up? He would scream at a patient. Act normal! Ya wanna spend the rest of your life in a fuckin' mental institution?"

A young woman suffering depression because of her being overweight was a victim of Dr. Blaumauer's so-called tough love.

"YA WANT FUCKIN' PROZAC?" he yelled at her during rounds, "I'LL GIVE YA FUCKIN' PROZAC, YA WANNA HELP YOURSELF LOOSE WEIGHT? DO EXERCISE! FOR CHRIST'S SAKE, DO DEEP KNEE BENDS!" Dr. Blaumauer hollered, "YOUR ONLY PROBLEM IS YOU HAVE A FAT ASS AND YOU DON'T TRY! YOU DON'T TRY TO LOOSE WEIGHT! YOU DON'T TRY TO HELP YOURSELF, YOU FEEL REJECTED, SO YOU SWALLOW SLEEPING PILLS, FOR FUCKIN' CHRIST SAKE, SWALLOWING SOME DIET PILLS WOULD BE

BETTER! IF YOU DON'T HELP YOURSELF, HOW CAN I FUCKIN' HELP YOU!"

It worked, as unorthodox as his treatment was, the young woman recovered. Dr. Blaumauer explained to Steven that if a patient was not willing to help themselves out of a problem they created, then that person was not entitled to any sympathy.

The other doctors on that service did not disagree openly with Dr. Blaumauer, as they were afraid of him. He was not above calling a colleague a schmuck in front of the entire staff.

The psych ward was not uneventful.

Every day a large black woman, who was totally bald, waved and called out, "Happy Halloween!" although it was still summer. When she was not doing that, she called out, "YABBA DABBA DOOO!"

A black female patient in her middle twenties approached Steven in the dayroom.

"Hey, Weitz!" she called out, "are you Jewish?"

"Yes, I am, Yvonne."

"I'm Jewish, too," she replied, "I answer to a higher authority!"

Steven doubted she was actually Jewish, he knew she got that higher authority line from an old Hebrew National hot dog commercial.

"Let's make Dr. Blaumauer happy and take our meds."

"I spoke Yiddish to Blaumauer, Weitz," she told him. "He speaks Yiddish to you, you know what *schmuck* is, don't you?"

"Yes, Yvonne," he answered.

"Then why did he call you that?" she laughed.

"Vell, listen," Steven said with a Yiddish accent, "It takes vun to know vun."

Yvonne laughed and took her medication.

As if on cue, Dr. Blaumauer appeared. "Did Yvonne take her happy pills?" he asked condescendingly.

"Yes, sir," Steven answered.

"*Sie goonisht eh helffen!*" Dr. Blaumauer said. In Yiddish that means 'nothing will help.' Many psychiatrists have faith in their patients. Blaumauer had faith in the fact that most of his patients would remain abnormal.

"Remember, young Steven," Dr. Blaumauer advised him, "as keepers of the asylum, it is not always our job to cure, but rather to contain."

Steven knew, for some of the mental patients there was no hope of a cure, this was the end of the line.

One rule for the psych ward was all doctors had to remove their white coats, as the white coats disturbed the patients, and they were already disturbed enough as it was.

Tyrone was an interesting patient. Steven worked with him frequently during his rotation.

"Shit, man," Tyrone, told Steven, "I had me a good business before I came in here, I was an entrepreneur. I wanted to incorporate. I was going to go public and offer shares of stock in my company."

"What kind of business did you have, Tyrone?" Steven asked.

"I sold drugs and needles."

During Steven's evaluation of Tyrone, he learned that Tyrone had several pets.

"Oh, sure, Doc, I love animals; let's see, I got dogs, a cat, a snake, a grizzly bear, a lion, an elephant, and Woody Woodpecker!"

Contain rather than cure. Dr. Blaumauer's statement, although it would not win a Nobel Prize, rang true.

Steven learned that Tyrone's goal when he was to be released was to kill the president. *Screw ethics and confidentiality*, Steven thought *if they ever let this guy out, someone better call the Secret Service.*

There was another floor with mental patients who were Jewish, mostly Chassidic. Sid and Norma were surprised when Steven told them there were mental patients running about in payis and yarmulkules. This was not widely known, Steven told his parents, but the Orthodox and Chassidic sects of Judaism had a great deal of mental illness. It just was not talked about.

"I guess it's because of all that intermarriage," Sid said

"They marry cousins," Norma replied. "That's what happens when cousins marry, the kids turn out to be crazy."

"All the intermarriage," Steven said, "causes other problems, heart problems. They have eye problems, too; those kids are so nearsighted, you ever see the thick glasses they wear?"

Norma and Sid nodded.

"The parents themselves make those poor kids crazy," Sid interjected. He shot many Chassidic affairs throughout his career; Steven thought his father knew what he was talking about on this subject. "They dress those kids up, they don't play like normal children, shit, they aren't normal children, and as soon as they turn three years old, it's off to *Yeshiva.*"

Steven nodded.

The Chassidic mental patients acted the same as the Christian mental patients.

Steven looked forward to another emergency room rotation and an upcoming internal medicine rotation. The patients were not always sane, but for the most part treatable.

On the last day of his rotation, Steven swiped a blue sign with white lettering, stating ALL POLICE OFFICERS MUST UNLOAD THEIR WEAPONS BEFORE ENTERING. He wanted a souvenir.

As Steven left the psych building, a group of mental patients were gathered on a yellow school bus, for some kind of outing; it looked like a scene from *One Flew over the Cuckoo's Nest.*

They sat on the bus, their faces expressionless, their eyes blank.

As the bus left the curb, Steven waved at the mental patients. They waved back, wildly, maniacally, with their vacant eyes unchanged, their faces expressionless.

For young Dr. Steven Weitz, it was back to the land of the sane. If not the sane, then the living.

Chapter Forty-Two

Early Winter 1990

Steven Weitz was tired, nervous, and edgy throughout the last few weeks of his ER rotation. He just wanted to get this bullshit over with and be a full-fledged doctor, but he knew he had a long way to go. Last fall, he was working an all night shift through the Rosh Hashanah holiday. His father had called to wish him a healthy, happy New Year. The switchboard located Steven and put Sid through. Sid heard a loud commotion of activity and a clatter of instruments.

"Steve, I just called to say Mom and I wish you a healthy, happy New Year, a *shanna tova!*"

"Dad! I can't talk now, my patient just went into cardiac arrest, I'll call you back!" With that, Steven hung up.

As he worked on the patient, along with the residents and nurses, Steven reasoned that, if his father called to wish him a happy New Year, he probably forgave him for breaking up with Gayle.

At ten-thirty that evening, Sid Weitz answered his home phone.

"Sorry I had to rush you off, Dad, but I was right in the middle of a full arrest."

"No problem, Steve," Sid assured him, "I understand. How did the patient make out?"

"Oh, he died."

"So you have some time to talk now?"

"Sure, put Mom on."

Now young Dr. Weitz had to struggle with a heavyset ninety-year-old woman. She was senile and spoke an incoherent mixture of Yiddish and English. The medical staff had a hard time telling which language was which.

Steven had the dubious task of drawing the old woman's blood, a task awarded to interns. He swabbed her arm with alcohol and attempted to insert the needle.

"BUM!" she snapped and pulled away.

Steven tried again.

"BUM!" she pulled away, with nurses and orderlies holding her down on the table.

Then the old woman tried to bite Steven, every time he prepped her arm.

"BUM!" (Chomp!) "BUM!" (Chomp!) "BUM!" (Chomp!) "BUM!" (Chomp!)

Steven turned to the old woman's daughter and son-in-law, "We are going to have to tie her down!" he shouted without compassion. It is hard for a person to be compassionate, while avoiding being bitten.

"Get the restraints!" a nurse ordered.

The old woman grabbed Steven's right hand firmly, taking it up to her mouth, and snapping her teeth angrily.

Steven did not let the woman's teeth strike his flesh, she was finally placed in restraints, and her hands tied to the examining table. She let out one final, "BUM!"

Steven was given the job of inserting a stomach tube through the old woman's nose.

"Not in nose! Take out!" the old woman ordered.

"Mama, you're sick and you fell down!" her daughter said.

"No, oh, oh," the old woman replied, "vhy should I fall?"

With that over with, Steven had to examine an elderly man. After asking him some questions, Steven donned a latex glove.

"Aha!" the old man sung out sweetly, "I know-oh, vhat you are going to do-ooh! A rectal!"

"Don't worry, sir," Steven told his patient, "this will be more of an indignity for me than it will for you."

"Yee hee hee!" the old man laughed.

Then he met her—the love of his life. When Steven met Christine, he just knew she was to be his soul mate.

He didn't know if there was such a thing as love at first sight, until he met Christine.

A very pretty twenty-two year-old woman sat on the edge of a hospital gurney in a great deal of pain, yet, somehow managed to stay in good spirits. Steven went over to her.

"You look young," she said, she had auburn shoulder-length wavy hair, green eyes, and a small nose. She had a melodic voice.

"So do you," Steven smiled.

He heard bells.

So did she.

Her name was Christine A. Copobianco. She was a substitute teacher, supplementing her paltry salary by working in a hamburger restaurant. Between two paltry salaries, Christine was able to survive.

"I have some insurance, but probably not enough," Christine told the young intern.

"Nobody has enough; don't worry about anything right now, Christine." Steven paused, then courtly added, "If I may?"

She nodded.

"Let's get you fixed up. We'll worry about paperwork later."

"It hurts like hell, Doctor."

"Steve," he offered.

"Hmmm, I don't like nicknames, I think I shall call you Steven. You look more like a Steven than a Steve."

"I like the way you say Steven." He caught himself leaning against her, as enjoyable as it was, he knew it was unprofessional.

"Hmmm," Steven said, sounding every bit the doctor. "Hmm, it's not all that bad; we'll get you over to X-ray. I think it's just a sprain, nothing seems to be broken."

"I went skiing with a friend, I guess I was careless. Do you ski, Steven?"

"No, I like tennis and golf."

"I don't play golf, but I like tennis, too."

"You're not going to be playing for a while, I guess you're friend is, is, is he waiting outside?"

"She, a friend I work with, she's a substitute teacher, too. We went up to the Catskills together. I don't have boyfriend, not at the present."

"Would you like one?" Steven asked.

She threw her lovely head back and laughed a throaty laugh, which was a trait of hers he would come to adore. Steven felt his penis beginning to stiffen.

After the x-ray, Steven went back to talk to Ms. Copobianco again.

"Cheer up, radiology told me it's a sprain. I'm waiting for the film now. Here," he offered her some red striped peppermint sucking candies, "this will make you feel better."

She took all the candies out of his palm.

Great, Steven thought to himself, *great, now I don't have any mints left.*

She unwrapped the cellophane and popped them into her mouth.

"You live here in Brooklyn," Steven commented, looking at her chart.

"Yes, in Park Slope, a very small apartment. But, I'm really from Long Island, out east in Suffolk, Port Jefferson."

"I'm from Long Island, too," he told her. "I live in Hewlett, in Nassau County. I was born here in Brooklyn, though."

"Well, I wanted to live in New York City, to be cosmopolitan," she said.

"Well," Steven observed, "you live across the river in Brooklyn."

"Brooklyn is about as cosmopolitan as I can afford," Christine laughed.

After Steven showed Christine the x-ray, a resident supervisor gave her instructions on how to alleviate her pain. She would be fine in no time at all.

"It has been nice meeting you, Christine."

"Same here, Steven, I hope we meet again some time."

"So do I," he said glumly. Steven wanted to ask if she wanted to exchange phone numbers with him, but he knew that was considered unprofessional conduct. Another missed opportunity, goddamn!

"I guess I will see you if I have any more mishaps."

"Well, I'm almost finished here in emergency, Christine, soon I start a rotation in internal medicine."

"Oh," she said sort of disappointed. "Oh, we'll see each other again, I'm accident prone."

Doctor and patient exchanged farewells.

Then she left the emergency room.

It was over.

A half-hour later Steven, while on a break, Steven Weitz, observed Christine Copobianco waiting, he assumed, for her friend to get the car. She sat on a cloth couch in the hospital's main lobby. She was beautiful, he thought. He watched as she opened a small bag of potato chips she got from a vending machine and proceeded to stuff her face.

Once again Steven heard bells. *This is the one*, he told himself, *I have found her*.

Chapter Forty-Three

Christine Copobianco stayed on Steven's mind. He thought about her frequently. That weekend, his parents came to visit at his Sheepshead Bay apartment, with his little nephew Peter in tow. They were babysitting him for the day, so they were able to watch their grandson and visit their son. It was a winter Sunday, when Sid did not have any affairs to shoot.

"Meet any new girls, yet?" Norma asked him.

"No, Mom, not really."

"Well, don't worry," Norma touched his hand, "it takes time; it's better not to rush." She looked at Sid when she said that.

"He's tired," Sid said during the drive home, "and nervous, see how his hands shake?"

"Yes, I noticed," Norma said, "he wanted us to just get the hell out of there, I could tell he was very tired."

"Well, listen, Norma," Sid shrugged as he drove the Lincoln onto the Belt Parkway, heading east, "they work those young interns and residents hard. That's why they deserve to own the big Cadillacs and house, they've earned it. They worked hard for it."

"Here, here!" Norma agreed. This was kind of funny, because years ago, before their son was a doctor, they used to discuss how their doctors were overpriced, overrated crooks.

On a Monday afternoon, Steven walked into the hospital cafeteria for lunch. He heard a familiar female voice.

"Steven, I've waited over two hours for you, dear; don't you ever eat?"

She took him by the hand and told him she had a table.

"I wanted to see you again. I know doctors aren't supposed to date patients, so I asked you to lunch."

"Alright, let's have lunch together," Steven agreed. "What would you like?"

"I have my lunch on the tray, I waited for you."

"Oh, then I'll get lunch."

Christine was wearing black slacks and a white pullover top, both which flattered her figure. She was not as sleek as Gayle, but she was not heavy, either. She looked very good today.

Steven ordered a tuna sandwich, pickle chips on the side, and a Seven-Up.

He sat down across from Christine at the table she found. She reached across and swiped three of the four pickle chips off of his plate.

Their eyes met, Steven did not know what to say, so he said nothing. They both smiled.

Steven heard bells ring once again.

"So tell me," Christine said.

"Tell you what, Christine?" Steven replied.

"Tell me, just tell me. Tell me things," she told him.

"Well, let's see, I'm an intern, I have a mother and father, and I have an older sister who's married. She has two boys, I'm an uncle. Oh, yes, I'm Jewish."

"That part I already guessed," Christine said wrinkling her cute nose.

"Now, you tell me," Steven requested.

"Well, I have two parents and a younger brother. My parents don't have any grandchildren. I'm a substitute elementary school teacher. When I'm not subbing, I work for a hamburger place. I don't like to admit where; you know the place that makes those little square hamburgers."

Steven nodded,

"I'm Catholic."

"I'm not observant," Steven volunteered.

"Neither am I," Christine also volunteered.

"What do your parents do?" he asked.

"My father is an auto mechanic; he owns a garage, but I think he wants to sell and go to work for a car dealership. My mother is a waitress."

My father owns a photography studio; he shoots mostly weddings, Bar Mitzvahs, and portraits."

"Stills or video?" she asked.

"Both, but not at the same time."

"He shoots the affairs himself?"

"Yes," Steven paused, "but not every job; he has some men and a woman who go out and cover jobs for him. He was the first photographer in Greater New York to shoot video coverage. He used to shoot movies, years ago. He is also a partner in a baby photography studio above the store."

"He does well, then."

"He did much better back in the heyday of the industry."

"What does your mother do?"

"She's an account executive at a bank, she was a teller. She has a good head for figures, and she's very good at working with customers. Years ago, she used to help my father with sales at the studio. She does know how to take good picture, too, not professionally, but she takes all the photos on family vacations. She also likes to take pictures of my sister's boys, she's very good.

"What does your sister do?"

"Linda is in the medical field, too. She's an audiologist. Her husband, Mark, is a foreign trade consultant; he travels everywhere. They may be living abroad in the future. What does your brother do, Christine?"

"Call me Chris," she reached across the table, picked up the paper cup of Steven's Seven-Up, and finished it. "He's studying automotives. He wants to be a mechanic, like my father. I'm a mechanic myself, I can fix cars; not like my dad, but I can do an emergency repair."

"I have to get back to work. Can we meet for lunch again?"

"I'd love to, Steven, tomorrow?"

"Fine, here at the cafeteria?"

She nodded.

"Okay, we'll have lunch and work our way up to a dinner date. By the way, what does the A stand for? Your middle initial, I saw it on your chart."

"Alluring."

"What?" Steven chuckled out loud. "No kidding, well you are!"

"Ann, darling, my middle name is Ann."

"Christy," Steven said.

"Huh?" she raised her right eyebrow.

"I will call you Christy."

"I don't like nicknames, Steven," she said with mock testiness.

"I can't help it, it fits. You don't look like a Chris, you look like a Christy, you're adorable."

"That I am, but Christy?"

"You look like a Christy."

"Only you, only you and nobody else may call me that. Let's exchange phone numbers, so you won't stand me up."

"You won't ever have to worry about that."

They exchanged numbers. Steven watched Christy leave. She was adorable from the back, too. He wanted to kiss her, but he knew that was not proper behavior, not on the first date. This was not even the first date, this was just lunch. Tomorrow will be the first date. Still, he had an urge to kiss her. He thought about asking her if he could, but did not. He decided that was best for now.

Steven thought about Christy during the day. He thought about her that night, as well. He had the feeling of being in love. That was truly a wonderful feeling to have. He wondered if Christy was thinking about him. He wondered if she had the same feeling of being in love. He wondered if she heard bells, too. Then Gayle's image flashed in his mind. Steven thought about her briefly, then to dislodge his memory of her, he shook his head vigorously, and returned to thoughts of Christy.

At eleven forty-five Christy was waiting for Steven in the hospital cafeteria. They selected a table at the far end in a corner for privacy. They lunched and laughed.

"What do you want to specialize in, Steven? You didn't tell me."

"Pediatrics."

"That's wonderful, I love children."

"I'm good with them, too, I'm a natural. I wanted hands-on medicine, rather than a passive specialty. I thought about family practice, internal medicine, even obstetrics and gynecology, but I guess I was suited for pediatrics. I guess it's good that you like kids, I mean for your profession."

"Part-time profession," Christy corrected, "yes."

"I bet your students love you."

"Some do, Steven, but remember a substitute doesn't have time to bond with the children."

"I bet your hamburger customers love you."

"Who cares!" she said jovially.

Steven laughed. Christy was wrinkling her little nose again.

"I love your nose."

"Thank you."

"Christy, has anyone ever told you that you have a cute little bunny nose?"

"Bunny nose! No, nobody has ever told me that."

"When my father photographs small children, if they have cute noses, that's what he calls them, bunny nose."

"I have a bunny nose!" Christy exclaimed in mock surprise.

"You do, Christy," Steven told her, "it is one of your best features."

Steven had lunch with his new 'bunny nose.' Her nose wiggled when she giggled, like a little bunny's. She was a joy to be with, to spend time with, and to talk to.

"Tell me a joke," he asked Christy, "I need one today."

"I don't know any," Christy answered.

"I'll tell you one; would you be offended at a joke with Jesus in it?"

"No, not at all, really," Christy shook her head and smiled.

"Well, there was this nail manufacturer, Levy. Business was down," Steven went on, "so he hired this big advertising agency. So, the agency puts up a billboard and, for a week, they have a tarpaulin over it. A week later the tarpaulin comes off, and there's a big picture of Jesus on the cross, and the caption reads, 'Even back then, they used Levy nails!'"

Christy giggled.

"Well, Mr. Levy starts to yell, 'Oh, my God! I'll be ruined, what are you, crazy? Take it down!'"

"So, the advertising agent says, 'Don't worry, I'll fix it!' So, the tarpaulin goes back up and after another week, the agent tells the client, 'I think you'll like this.' He takes the tarpaulin down, now there's a big picture of Jesus falling off the cross, and the caption reads, 'They should have used Levy nails.'"

Christy threw her head back and laughed.

"You weren't offended?"

"No, it was very funny."

"But, you don't know any jokes, Christy?"

"No, darling I really don't."

"Wanna hear a doctor joke?" Steven asked.

Christy shook her head 'yes.'

"This elderly gentleman goes to a doctor and tells him, 'Doc, I think I have a sexual dysfunction, can you see if my equipment works? What I'd like to do, Doc, is come in here with her right now and make love, then you can tell me if everything works.' Well, the doctor is surprised, but he says okay. So, this old couple gets up on the examining table and makes love. The doctor says the man is fine."

"They come back the next day; again, the man begs to let him make love in the office. The doctor agrees, and this goes on for another week. Finally, the doctor says, 'Look, you're both fine, what is going on here?'"

Christy was listening.

"Well, Doc," the old man says, "I'm married, so she can't come to my place; she's married, so I can't go to her place. A motel room costs twenty bucks, you charge us ten, and we get five back from Medicare."

Christy laughed heartily.

"I have another one. This guy goes to a doctor, he says, 'Doc, I have this problem, I fart very loudly. Fortunately, it doesn't smell, but it's embarrassing.' Just then, the guy lets three loud ones rip, PFFT! PFFT! PRFFFT! 'Well, Doc, can you help me?'"

"The doctor says, 'Well, son,' Steven reeled back for emphasis, 'first we're gonna get your nose fixed!'"

"Uh ha ha ha ha!" Christy's throaty laugh.

"An old man and old woman start dating, things get serious, and he goes back to her apartment. She says, 'Before we do anything, I have to tell you, I have acute angina.'"

"The man says, 'I certainly hope so, because you got terrible tits!'"

"You're funny, Steven, you make me laugh."

"Ya wanna laugh, I'll tell you what happened to my father at a wedding I helped him on. Oh, maybe I shouldn't, I don't want to go on."

"Tell me." she insisted, cupping her hands to her chin, and leaning forward on the table.

"Well, when I was younger, sometimes I'd assist my father on jobs. I helped him light. You ever see double lighting at an affair, where the assistant holds the second strobe for the photographer?"

"Yes, I've seen that," Christy answered.

"Alright, so my dad usually doesn't stand on a stepladder for candids, but that night he did. This was a big, lavish Jewish wedding up in Larchmont."

Christy nodded.

"Okay, well he was on the ladder for *Hava Nagila*, you know, it's a *hora* or a fast dance in a circle."

Christy nodded.

"My dad was on the ladder, this big oaf, clowning around, bumped into me, crushing my foot with his big fat foot. I try to pull myself free and when I do, I fly sideways into Dad's ladder, the ladder crashes onto a woman standing next to him, knocking her over, with the ladder falling on top of her."

"So you knocked your father off the ladder?"

"Not quite. He jumped up and grabbed hold of the big chandelier. Can you imagine, with the camera on the bracket held by a strap around his neck."

"That has to hurt," Christy added.

"He had his strobe power pack on his shoulder with a strap, and he's swinging back and forth from that chandelier, like a cowboy actor in a saloon fight scene."

"Did he get down, Steven?"

"I'm coming to that. He saw an opening on the floor below, so he let go; remember he's very high up. The bride moves right under him and he lands on her!"

Christy was laughing, a hard throaty laugh.

"Remember, when you were little, your father gave you a horsey back ride up on his shoulders?"

Christy nodded.

"Same thing! That poor bride, who was not a big girl, gave my dad a wild horsey back ride." Steven got up and spun around to demonstrate, as Christy laughed. "Don't wet yourself," he continued. "One person yelled, 'Get off her, schmuck,' and one lady said, 'Crazy bastard!' Then a Jewish accent yelled, 'Ride 'em, cowboy!'"

"How did he get off?" she asked.

"The bride collapsed, taking him down, too. An old lady said, 'I don't think that was funny!' The bride's mother was crying, she told her husband that she peed in her pants."

"Oh, my God," Christy laughed, "what about the bride, what did she say?"

"Mim, mim, mim, mim!"

"Whaaat?" Christy asked, gasping for breath.

"Mim, mim, mim, mim," that's what she said. "That was all that she was able to say, 'Mim, mim, mim, mim!'"

"Wow! Steven, you're father is not shooting my wedding!"

"Of course not! A father-in-law can't shoot the job."

"Whaaaat?" Christy laughed.

"Never mind."

"Did your father beat the crap out of you?"

"At first he wanted to, I thought he would, but he realized it was an accident. Then the bastard told me that I was an accident, too."

"Tell me one more."

"My grandmother and I had an incident aboard a Brooklyn bus."

"Tell me!"

"I have a Jewish grandmother. Since you didn't have a Jewish grandmother, I'll explain. A Jewish grandmother always goes shopping for you, because she's afraid you'll run out of something important, like Crisco. I was about nine, my mom dropped me off to spend the day in Brooklyn with them, and it was Passover recess. Grandpa drove, but he wasn't home, so she and I went shopping and took a bus. She wanted to get things for my mother. To her, we live in the country, not the suburbs. To her, Hewlett is out in the middle of nowhere. So, she tosses stuff into the cart, saying, 'Look, you can't get this by you,' Steven did a Jewish accent. I said, 'Nana, we can't get Nabisco crackers on Long Island?' She says, 'No out by you, you couldn't get.'"

Christy started laughing. She told him Italian grandmothers are almost the same way.

"So they stuff all the groceries into a bag, which she puts into a clear plastic shopping bag she brought. That is, everything except a bottle of Mazola corn oil. That they put in a small paper bag. So, I have a bag, and she has a bag along with that little bag with the Mazola. We board a bus, everything is fine. As we're coming up on our stop on the corner of Kings Highway, she tells me to pull the string. In those older buses, you pulled a string to let the driver know you wanted to get off."

"Go on, I follow," she said.

"So we're closer to the front door and we get up to move forward, when the bus stops short. We reel forward, I panic because I have a bag in my hand and I don't want to fall. I grab the back of my grandmother's coat, I had to grab something. I yank her back a bit, the small paper bag she's holding rips open, the bottle of Mazola smashes on the floor, and oil goes flying. The bus comes to a stop and the doors open. The bus driver was sitting, turned in his seat, facing the isle, like this. Steven turned in his chair to demonstrate. He's a gray-haired old-timer, and he's probably seen everything, but his mouth is wide open. We turn to get the hell off, and everybody sitting in the front is covered with oil."

"Oh, God!" she laughed.

"There's this old lady, who's about five feet tall, she was very short. She's holding her legs up like this," Steven lifted up his legs to show Christy. "She was mad as hell, the way she looked at us. Globs of oil were draining through her stockings like the way you drain French fries at work. She looks up, and says through clenched teeth,' Jesus Christ, lady, you got oil all over my stockings!'"

"What happened then, Steven?"

"We ran off the bus and down the block to the house; we turned twice and the bus was still there, the third time, it had left. My grandmother said, 'Oy, oy, oy, I can't see where I'm running, I have oil on my glasses.'"

"That's about the funniest story I have ever heard."

"Christy, it's all true. My mother was waiting for us. She opened the door and asked, 'Mother! What happened?' She knew something was wrong. Later when she was telling my grandfather about what had happened, she said,

'Someday I am going to write a book!' Grandpa said, 'You'll write the book in jail, because I think the bus company is going to have you locked up!' My dad tells this story to everyone, because he thinks I'm a schmuck."

"Your grandfather sounds funny, is that who your sense of humor comes from?"

"Part of it, I'll tell you about him sometime. I'll tell you one about him now. I don't care for football, but a game was on the television, and a bone crushing play had just ended. A player was on the field on his hands and knees, crawling about. His helmet was off, and he was just parked there. My mother says, 'Gee, I wonder what he's looking for?' My grandfather says, 'I think he's looking for his eye.'"

She laughed for the millionth time that day.

"Didn't anything funny ever happen to you?"

"Oh sure, once I walked out of my house into the street naked."

"When? When you were twenty?"

"No, you nut! I was two."

"If you did that at two, it was no big deal."

"I once ate my dog's dinner."

"His whole dinner, Christy?"

"Yup, I got on my hands and knees and ate his food out of the dish. It was very tasty."

"Now that was terrible," Steven commented.

"I'll say, the poor baby didn't get any dinner."

"What else? Come on, give."

"Well, if I was angry about being punished, I used to go down to the laundry room and stretch everyone's underwear."

"Your father's?"

"Everybody's, I would stretch the elastic to get even."

"Wow, you're tough."

"I used to be, there was a girl on my block who took drugs; I made fun of her and called her names. One day we had a fight, and she beat me up. I wasn't so tough anymore after that."

"I'll bet not."

"I just don't know jokes like you do," Christy laughed once more.

"You'll learn some," Steven assured Christy.

"I already have, from you."

"You can't have the wedding story or the oil story, those are mine! They're copyrighted."

"Don't worry, darling, I won't use those stories. You should write a book and put those stories in it."

"Oh Christy," Steven sighed, "someday, I'll write my memoires. The trials and tribulations of a young doctor, yeah sure, *uchen vaste*."

"Uckin what?" Christy wrinkled her bunny nose.

"*Uchen vaste.* I'm not quite sure what it means, but my father says it a lot when someone tells him he should do something spectacular."

"I'll bet he's a card like you."

"Even more so, Christy, even more so. Look, let's have a day next weekend; I'll be on my internal medicine rotation, but we'll have a day or two to ourselves, we can go to dinner."

"Next weekend, Steven? Sure, it's a date."

"Thank you!" Steven was on cloud nine. "I'll call you the Thursday before, I can't wait!"

"Neither can I."

"Christy," Steven asked hesitantly, after they both got up from the table, nervously, "may I kiss you."

"Yes," Christy answered, she presented her right cheek to him. "You may."

He kissed her cheek lightly, she kissed his lightly. They did not embrace, and he did not press against her, he sensed that was not what she wanted, as she did not lean over to him. *Good* Steven thought, *keep it platonic for now, it's still just lunch.* It was better to move cautiously early on.

"Until then, Steve," she said.

They bid each other a good day. Steven looked at the back of Christy's dark blue denim skirt as she left. He was aroused. He did not know it at the time, but Christy was aroused, too.

He floated through the corridors of the hospital. He was in love. He felt much differently than he had when he was involved with Gayle. He was in love with Christy, with Gayle it was more like, in lust. He knew that for the first time in his life he was in love.

What a wonderful feeling it was to be in love.

Chapter Forty-Four

Internal medicine was not as wild as psych or emergency, which was not to say it was nonetheless taxing for a young intern not yet dry behind the ears.

An eighty-year-old man came in for treatment. Among his many internal maladies was an enlarged heart.

"My wife told me, that as I got older, my heart got bigger, and my penis got smaller," he told the young interns as he checked in.

On the second day, after a battery of tests, the old man, Mr. Ruben, got out of his bed naked. He paced the room talking to his roommate, the residents and nurses, but talking mostly to himself.

"Here in a hospital," he said, as he stood naked by his roommate's bed, "you have misery, you have dying, people are sick and they come for help, but *gunisht helfen*, they wouldn't recover."

"*Oy oy*, get him away," his frightened roommate cried out. He did not need this.

The staff placed Mr. Ruben in his bed in restraints. Mr. Ruben calmly accepted this and remained quiet.

As Steven walked through the corridor at lunchtime, he heard the theme of the television show, *St. Elsewhere*, coming from a patient's room. *St. Elsewhere*, now syndicated for reruns on a local channel, was the majority of patients' show of choice.

An elderly man with an ulcer condition, whom Steven had seen before his surgery, called out to him in the hallway. Steven went into the man's room. The elderly man, thin with gray hair and a thin grey mustache, sat up in bed.

"Hey, listen, Weitz," he said, "I gotta pee, and no one is doing anything to help. If ya don't mind me sayin' so, this is some fuckin' hospital ya got here!"

"There is a catheter in your penis now, Mr. Fine." Steven pulled back the covers for the patient to see. "Here's the bag on the side of the bed; see, Mr. Fine, you are peeing."

"Oh, I see, okay," the man put his head down on the pillow, "but this is still some fuckin' place!"

"It certainly is," Steven agreed.

Dr. Milton Fromkus, D.O. was the supervising internist. He was short and stout; with his peasant face and thin white hair, he looked like a Jewish version of the late Soviet Premier Nikita S. Khrushchev. He spoke in a Brooklyn sing-song voice.

"Well, Doctor," he greeted Steven, pronouncing doctor as 'docterr,' "how goes the rotation?"

"Very good, sir."

"I am glad you are learning. Come with me now, I asked for a psych consult for Mr. Ruben, and the psychiatrist is finishing up with him now; come, we'll see."

Dr. Blaumauer strode into Dr. Fromkus' office. He playfully rapped Steven in the stomach with the back of his left hand, his right hand clutching Mr. Ruben's chart.

"Hiya, Doctor!" Dr. Blaumauer addressed Steven, then stood in front of Dr. Fromkus' desk, "Fromkus, Fromkus, fuck you Fromkus!" *Yes*, Steven thought, *Blaumauer is the same as my father.*

"Of course, this man is upset, he's past eighty fuckin' years old," Dr. Blaumauer yelled his findings. "Sure as shit, here you have misery and dying, it's a fuckin' hospital! When you're past eighty and in the fuckin' hospital, ain't nothing routine, Fromkus!"

"So, he's alright," Dr. Fromkus confirmed.

"Asshole! By me and my service he's as right as rain; by your service, he's a sick man. Look, call me for something worthwhile, okay, Milt?"

Dr. Fromkus nodded.

"Listen, just treat his ailments and send him on home, if possible," Dr. Blaumauer now spoke in a normal conversational tone, "meanwhile, he's a bit senile, so if he gets agitated, or uncooperative, just place the *altacocker* in restraint, and don't worry about it."

Dr. Fromkus thanked Dr. Blaumauer for the consult. With that concluded, Dr. Blaumauer left.

"You know, Steven, he's a very good psychiatrist, tops in his field, the best in Brooklyn even. But, my mother used to have a saying about people like him," Dr. Fromkus stared at his closed office door.

"What was that?" asked Steven.

"Oooh, common!" replied Dr. Fromkus.

Steven nodded knowingly.

Mr. Ruben was feeling better, his tests and treatments completed, he was to be released in a couple of days. His main problem was that he was old and his body was falling apart. Steve's father often wondered why the period of one's life, when one's body began to fall apart, was called the golden years. The shit and piss stained years, was more like it.

Steven walked in to old Mr. Ruben's room. He was alone, sitting up in bed. He did not need to be on oxygen anymore. Yet, he was concerned about the removal of his oxygen mask.

"Did you see my nozzle?" Mr. Ruben asked Steven.

"You're fine, Mr. Ruben," Steven looked him over, "you don't need oxygen now, you can breathe on your own."

"You didn't see my nozzle?" Mr. Ruben did not appear to hear the young intern. "Maybe you lent it?" Mr. Ruben vigorously nodded his large ancient head, "Maybe you lent it?"

"I think so, well you're doing just fine without it."

"You lent it?"

A senior nurse entered the room.

"What do you think," she asked Steven, "should I put him in restraints? You see, I want to make sure he stays in bed for the next hour, it's time for my soap opera."

"Why not," Steven gestured to the bed, "be my guest."

Steven's friend, a Greek intern named Gregg Boukouris, met him for lunch. Gregg spoke with an accent, and he was not yet familiar with American slang expressions. He always addressed Steven as, "My dear Steven."

"My dear Steven, we have lunch together, yes?"

"Sure, Gregg."

"Aha! I guess new girlfriend not coming today."

"Not today; today, I have a date with you."

"I love this guy!" Gregg shouted to the other doctors, "He is funny, that is why I love him. I love this guy!"

"So, how is everything?" Steven asked.

"Everything, is how you say…sucks."

"That's how you say it."

"Well, I go; before lunch I go smoke my pipe. Pipe relaxes me; my father and grandfather smoke water pipe."

Steven was amazed at how many of the young interns, residents, and older attending physicians thought Gregg Boukaris was very smart, because he was foreign and smoked a pipe.

"Smoking, they say, is not good for you; is not good for you!" Gregg said, "Give cancer! But funny thing is, so many doctors smoke. The old guys here love their cigars; the young doctors puff on cigarettes."

"Go figure," Steven nodded.

Steven and Gregg enjoyed lunch. There was no point in spending time with Christy on such a busy day. He was going to be on an overnight shift anyhow. Being on call was not fun for interns and residents, but it was required. It was a part of training; it was also paying your dues, as a rite of passage in a young person's medical career.

Interns and residents had to call attending physicians at their homes during the night, often waking a doctor out of a sound sleep. Doctors understood that this was part of their job and was to be expected.

There were some doctors who did not want to be bothered in the middle of the night, so they used the hospital as a dumping ground for patients; although deplored by the medical profession, this was common practice.

Then, there were the attendings who thought the interns and residents should be able to handle problems by themselves without disturbing their beauty rest.

Steven had such an encounter this night. He called an attending internist affiliated with the hospital at three A.M. Dr. Nathan Slotkin, M.D. answered his phone.

"Whuh, huh, helluh."

Steven Weitz identified himself, stated the reason why he was calling, in order to find out what course of action the attending wanted taken.

"Get to the point," Dr. Slotkin pressed as Steven stated the patients vital signs, "Get to the point!"

Steven got to the point, and waited for the doctor's prescribed course of treatment.

"SCHMUCK! WHAT DO YOU THINK, I'M A YOUNG MAN!" Dr. Slotkin yelled into his ear.

Steven pulled the phone away. "I realize it's late, sir, but I'm an intern, she's your patient, and you have to make the call."

"You went through medical school, you should know what to do! You can find the course of treatment if you bothered to read this month's medical journal, putz!"

Steven wanted to tell this old fart, it's your call as the attending physician. If you don't want to be woken up, then don't dump your patients on our service, better yet retire! But being reasonable, and knowing very well he was low man on the totem pole, it would not be beneficial to sound off to the attending physicians ala TVs Ben Casey, so he kept his mouth shut. He wondered what his opinionated father would do. Probably call the old bastard a schmuck right back and every other name under the sun.

"Think you can handle it now?" Dr. Slotkin asked.

"Yes, doctor," Steven answered.

"SCHMUCK!" Dr. Slotkin hollered once more and hung up.

During the next day, Gregg Bourkaris stopped Steven in the men's room.

"My dear Steven, tell me what is smuck."

"I see you had to call old man Slotnick, too," Steven said wryly, before explaining schmuck.

Steven had Thursday off; tired and unshaven, he drove out to Hewlett to spend the day. His mother greeted him with a look of astonishment at his appearance. He also had a bag of laundry; he told Norma he would do the laundry here, as he was too tired to go down to the basement in his apartment. Norma told him that would be alright, but he had better get it done before

Dad came home, or else, he would ask for four quarters for the use of his house's washing machine, not to mention four quarters more for the dryer.

"Mom, I met a girl; we've been seeing each other for lunch, and we plan to see each other over the weekend and have dinner."

"That's nice, honey," Norma answered. "What's her name, Steven?"

"Christine, Mom, I call her Christy. She's adorable; I think you'd like her."

"I'm sure I would."

"I was thinking, could I bring her out here for brunch next Sunday?"

"Sure, it's alright with me."

"What about Dad?"

"It'll be fine with him."

"She's a substitute teacher and she works in a hamburger place."

"Is that where you met her?" Norma asked.

"No, I met her in the emergency room, I taped her sprained ankle. She lives by herself in Brooklyn, but she's from Suffolk."

"Oh, well sure, honey, I'd love to have her Sunday!"

"Mom?"

"Yes, Steve?"

"How come you didn't ask if she was Jewish?"

"Steven, I'm a Jewish mother, if I thought your new girlfriend was Jewish, I would have asked. Besides, Christine is not a Jewish name."

"Thank you, Mom. I'll tell Christy Saturday when I see her, that it's on for next week. Will you work on Dad, Mom?"

"Sure, Steve, I promise he'll want to meet your new girl."

"Mom, why lie? He won't want to meet my new Christian girlfriend."

"You're right, he won't, but come with her next Sunday, darling. I'll work on your father."

Chapter Forty-Five

S teven and Christy both clad in jeans and sweatshirts, spent the beginning of Sunday together in Prospect Park, near the Park Slope section. It was a warm early spring day.

They talked about many things; they shared some interests, and had their own separate areas of interest. They both discovered they were non-smokers. Christy's parents quit years ago. Steven's mother quit years ago, he told her, but his father was a chain smoker. Steven admitted that once in a great while he swiped one or two of his father's cigarettes when he was under pressure, but he just puffed without inhaling.

"So, you're a doctor, get him to quit!" Christy scolded him.

"Yeah, I can't tell him anything, nobody can. He listens to my sister. He likes her better than me."

"I do, too, when you talk like that."

"Christy, you haven't met Linda, yet."

"I'm just saying I don't like when you put yourself down. If your father has problems, don't make them yours."

They sat on an old comforter blanket Christy brought. She stretched out, and feeling sure of himself, Steven laid his head in her lap. She felt warm to him.

"My dad shot there a few times," Steven pointed to a restaurant on the park's perimeter.

"Is he a top photographer?" she asked.

"He's a good candid man, not an artist. He won some awards; he never bothered with competitions. He probably could have won more."

"I like to take pictures, Steven."

"That won't impress him."

"Why not?"

"Nothing does. You tell him, 'I like taking pictures,' he'll just shrug and make a face, as if to tell you your conversation is a waste of his time."

"Sounds charming."

"Oh, he is when he needs to be, but when he's not, look out. All you'll get from him is a shrug or a snide remark."

"I'll be careful."

"Try, he isn't going to like the fact you're not Jewish."

Christy shrugged, while making a face.

"Shit!" he exclaimed, "man that was good, you looked just like him and that Semitic gesture of his; it was unnerving."

Christy threw her head back and laughed.

"When I look up, you look like a can opener," Steven said sweetly, "anyone ever tell you that?"

"I know," Christy laughed, "I was supposed to get braces when I was little, but they were expensive, so my parents couldn't go for it. Someday, I'll have my teeth fixed."

"I like you the way you are."

"Do you?"

"I do, you are the most beautiful woman I ever met."

"I believe you, darling. Sean Connery sounded more convincing when he said it, but that's sweet of you."

"That's why I said it, to be sweet, also it's true, you're beautiful. Has anyone ever told you that you have a very nibbleable nose?"

"Whaaaat?"

"A cute nibbleable nose, Christy!"

"I've never heard that one."

"It's true! I want to nibble your nose."

"Oh, really?"

"May I?"

"No, you may not!"

"Awwww!"

"Well, not here anyway."

"I love that bird in your hair."

"Steven! I do not have a bird in my hair, what the hell... Oh, my braid, it is in the shape of a bird."

"I guess you use it to keep you hair off of your ears. You have a cute bunny nose, but you don't have bunny ears."

"Thank God, would you like me to have bunny ears?"

"Only if I didn't have good television antennae! I could marry you for good reception."

Christy leaned over and kissed Steven hard on the lips.

"Ow!" he cried out, "you nicked my gums with your crooked teeth!"

"I know!" she laughed. "I'm sorry, I should have had braces!"

"Oh, I love you, Christy," Steven sighed.

"Oh, I love you, Steven."

"You do?" he asked.

"Yes," she answered. "My parents probably won't like the fact you're Jewish too much. My father is a mechanic, my mother is a waitress. They're probably worlds apart from your parents."

"Not really, Christy, my mom accepts everyone. She could never say a bad thing about anyone, not like my father."

"Sounds like a nice person."

"Oh, she is, Christy, she is. When they were young, my mother helped this newly married wife of another photographer. She taught this young girl how to sew and to cook. Would you believe it?"

"That was nice, Steven, very nice."

"It wasn't so nice years later; my Dad had some sort of argument with this guy. He told my father, pardon my French, "Fuck you where you breathe.""

"I never heard that expression; wow, what did your father say?"

"He probably said, 'Fuck you,' back."

"I can't wait to meet him," she giggled, "he sounds like a pisser!"

"He pisses off everybody. Let's have dinner tonight."

"Alright, we'll find a place."

"Do you really love me, Christy?"

"Yes, darling."

They ate dinner in a small trendy bistro in Park Slope near Christy's apartment. They both had a French-style veal dish and red wine. They split a mousse cake for dessert.

Steven looked at his wristwatch, "After seven, Dad is just getting to work in that temple now."

"Wedding?" she asked.

"Bat Mitzvah, that's for the girls."

Christy nodded that she understood.

"He's shooting up in Great Neck tonight. He's videotaping the job; he says at his age, videotaping the kiddie jobs is easier than shooting the stills."

"I can understand that. Well," Christy raised her wine glass, "here's to your dad."

"You got it, baby!" Steven answered, imitating Sid's voice, his glass raised.

"Is that what he sounds like?"

Steven nodded.

"He sounds like George Burns."

"Kind of a cross between George Burns and Humphrey Bogart, New York accent and all. Sometimes he's as entertaining as old George."

"Would you like to come back to my place, Steven?"

"Yes, I enjoy being with you."

"Let's go back as soon as we finish here," she said softly. Steven, ever the dashing gentleman, paid the check and they left. Steven wanted to stop into an all night drugstore. He told her he wanted to get some lifesavers. She wanted to pick up some items, too. Along with the spearmint flavored life savers, Steven also picked up a small sample bottle of mouthwash and, to be on the safe side, a box of condoms. He played it safe with Gayle; he wanted to be safe with Christy. He thought she probably knew, she could see right through the charade. So what? Just in case this was where the evening was heading, he wanted to be ready.

This was where the evening was heading.

Shortly after entering her apartment, they embraced and kissed. Then they undressed and made love in Christy's bed.

It felt like lovemaking rather than just sex to both of them. They each felt in love and contented.

Steven hungrily kissed Christy's nipples. He noticed her nipples were pink, not ruby red like Gayle's. Christy joked that his penis was not the first circumcised one she had seen.

"MMM," she said later on as she took his penis in her mouth, "a Hebrew National kosher hot dog."

"I bet you say that to all the Jewish boys," Steven moaned.

"You're my first."

"Well, I guess I must be someone very special."

"You're my first Jewish boy, not my first, is what I meant, and, yes, you are very special."

"So are you," he told her. She was different. Earlier when they undressed, he picked up her panties. Christy's scent was different from Gayle's. He wondered if the scent of a Christian woman was different from a Jewish woman.

"I could use one of my father's cigarettes," Steven said as he lay in the dark holding Christy, her naked flesh soft and smooth against his.

"I'm glad you don't have one, darling, I don't want you to get sick ever."

"Eh, I could use one now."

"And burn me to death in bed?"

"Sorry."

"Next time, we'll go to your place. You probably have mirrors over your water bed."

"No," Steven caressed her, "no mirrored ceilings, no water bed."

"I didn't think so," Christy said.

"Blue mirrors," he said softly.

"What was that, blue mirrors? You have blue mirrors?"

"No, I was thinking. When I was small, my father still went out on baby shoots in clients' homes. Remember, I told you he also had a baby studio?"

Christy said that she remembered.

"Well, he used to take blue mirrors out on shoots with him. Especially, when he went to the Bronx, he said it looked good in poor peoples' apartments. But he always took along a canvas background, so what did he use the blue mirrors for? The damndest thing, Christy, was that I never saw any of his photographs with blue mirrors."

"So, ask him."

"One day, I'll have to. I heard a few of his photographer friends talking about his blue mirrors. I think dad used mirrors to work his magic, he can be all smoke and mirrors at times."

"Many true artists are," she said.

"He's not an artist, he's a candid man."

"Being a candid man, Steven, is your father's art." Christy emphasized the word 'is.' Ask him about the blue mirrors, if it's bothering you. Ask him, Steven, or you'll never find out."

They held each other as they faded off to sleep.

Chapter Forty-Six

Next Sunday was here at last. It was time for Christine Copobianco to meet Steven Weitz's parents and sister. She was told that his brother-in-law and two little nephews would also be there. On the way over, they stopped at a kosher style-bakery in Brooklyn so Steven could buy a cake. They picked out a vanilla butter cream. Steven told Christy, he did not know what his mother was serving. Usually in the Jewish faith, you could not serve a dessert with milk as an ingredient following a meat dish. This was to insure that an animal was not cooked in their mother's milk. As Steven's parents were not observant, he explained, it did not really matter.

About a half an hour later, Steven pulled into the driveway of the brown house, number 51 Chesterfield Lane. They pulled alongside Linda's car. Steven commented that his sister was here.

Christy looked at the maroon Lincoln parked in front of them, then at the blue Chevy with rust spots on the rear door.

"This is his car," she stated.

"Good guess," Steven replied, "how could you tell, the rust spots?"

"No, he left a tripod on the back seat."

"Yeah, that's his video tripod; he was probably too tired to carry it in late last night."

Norma opened the door for them; she kissed Steven, and then pecked Christy on her cheek after being introduced. Steven introduced Christy to his sister Linda and her husband Mark, and they exchanged cordial greetings. His young nephews hit it off with Christy; she bent down to hug Peter, and he seemed to like her, which was a good sign. She was also well received by Alec, who was now a toddler.

"Where's Dad?" Steven asked, worried that he cut out because he was not bringing home a Jewish girl.

"In his study, putting away equipment. He had a portrait job today."

"Who?"

"Across the street in number 38. That nice Mrs. Strassberg, the schoolteacher. She wanted a portrait of her three daughters, so Dad shot it this morning."

As if on cue, Sid entered the living room. He was dressed for the occasion, Steven noticed ruefully. Everybody was dressed casual, but Sid was wearing an old pair of jeans, sneakers, and green sweatshirt with San Francisco embroidered on the front, along with a red cable car.

"That's what you wore to your shoot?" Steven asked.

"No, I just changed out of my tuxedo," Sid answered.

"Dad, I'd like you to meet Christy?"

"Would you really? Well I'd like to meet her, too."

"Hello, Mr. Weitz, it's good to meet you."

"Christy, same here."

So far, so good.

Plucky the cat shot by.

"That's Plucky," Peter offered.

"So, Dad, you shaved off the mustache."

"Sorry I didn't call you with the news," Sid shrugged.

Let's sit in the den for awhile, then we'll eat," Norma suggested.

"Mom made her famous brisket," Linda revealed.

"I don't think I've ever had brisket," Christy admitted.

"It's kind of a Jewish London broil," Sid explained. Christy stifled a chuckle when Sid pronounced broil, 'breril.'

They walked to the den. Christy walked alongside of Sid.

"Steven told me that you're a photographer."

"He's right, I am."

"I like to take pictures, too," she told him

Sid looked at her and shrugged.

"I mean, for me, it's sort of an outlet," she said.

"Well, I do more than just take pictures, I record important events, I create cherished keepsakes. It's more than just fun and games for an outlet, Chris." Sid shrugged again, lit a Viceroy, and sat down.

Feeling flustered and crestfallen, Christy sat down along with the rest of Steven's family.

"Christy has a nice 35 mm Olympus," Steven remarked. That got another shrug.

"I've read that a lot of pros use the old Olympus, so it must be a good camera," Christy said.

Sid took the cigarette out of his mouth, shrugged, the spread his arms wide, as if to say either who knows, or who cares?

With that Norma turned to Christy to engage her in conversation to save her from further discomfort.

"So you're an elementary school teacher."

"Well, Mrs. Weitz, I am a substitute or as it is known in the city a temporary per diem teacher. I'm not full time or full fledged, yet. I work part time, flipping hamburgers when I'm not teaching."

"You have a great personality, Christy, I'm sure you get along well with your students, and would you please call me Norma."

Well, Steven thought *it is going much better with Mom, but then again everything did.*

Soon after, they adjourned to the dining room for Sunday dinner. The Weitz family rarely had big Sunday family dinners; due to Sid's occupation, he was seldom home on Sunday afternoons. They enjoyed the rare occasion when they all got together.

They talked about many different things, Sid talking to Christy only when he thought he had to.

They talked about family. Christy talked about her Italian and Irish family, which did not win any points for her from Steven's father. She said that she had so many relatives, that this year she was going to start her Christmas shopping super early.

"In fact," Christy said, "I've already ordered my father's Christmas present, to insure it was in stock. I got him a chrome rear end cover."

"A chrome rear end cover," Sid interjected, "why does your father have a metal ass?"

"Oh, Sidney!" Norma lowered her head and laughed.

Everyone at the table, including Christy, laughed.

"No," Christy explained, "it's for his motorcycle."

"What do I know from motorcycles?" Sid exclaimed. "All I know is they are dangerous and I hate when they cut in front of me when I drive."

"He's into motorcycles, Mr. Weitz."

"You may call me Sid, how old is he?"

"Forty-two."

"Such a young man," Norma said, "he's a mechanic, Sid."

"Good, then he can repair his own motorcycle."

"He's also a truck driver," Christy offered.

"Somehow, I ain't surprised," Sid remarked.

During dessert, Steven took Sid aside in the kitchen. "Well?" he asked Sid.

"Well, what?"

"Well, what do think, Dad?"

"I think I liked Gayle better."

"Forget that! What do think about Christine, who's here now?"

"She looks like a real *shiksa*!"

"She is, Dad, she's a 100 percent, bona-fide card-carrying *shiksa*! Is that all you can say?"

"Well, I think she's a doof, too!"

"You don't like her?"

"She's not Jewish."

"I'm in love with her."

"Steven, there are plenty of fish in the sea."

"So?"

"So, let her finish dessert, then take her home and dump her."

"You want me to dump her?"

"I'd like you to dump her in the Gowanus Canal, but I'll settle for an 'I'll call you sometime.'"

"A *shiksa* and a doof, that's all the positive things you can say, Dad?"

"She needs braces, of that I am positive."

"Shit, Dad."

"Her parents couldn't afford to get the poor kid braces, because they spent the money on motorcycles, and now you want to get involved with such *mishigoyim?*"

Norma told Steven that she liked Christy; she thought she was very nice and adorable.

"Well, what did your parents think about me?" she asked during the ride back to Brooklyn.

"My mother liked you, she told me so. She thinks you're adorable."

"I think she's adorable, too. What about your father?"

"He said you looked like a real *shiksa*."

"*Shiksa? Shiksa?* Your father called me *shiksa?* What is a *shiksa?*"

"It's a Yiddish word for a young woman who isn't Jewish. It can be derogatory or affectionate. I don't think Dad was being affectionate."

"Me neither, is that all he had to say?"

"No, he also called you a doof."

"A doof? Well, I can see that I really went over big with him! I didn't hear him say schmuck."

"An old photographer friend of his told me that sometimes, he uses the word schmuck as a term of affection."

"When he calls you schmuck, he's being affectionate?"

"I doubt it!"

The following week, Sunday dinner at Christy's parents house out in Suffolk County was not any better.

As their relationship and love for each other grew, they knew it was time for both sets of parents to meet. That was a possible volatile situation. Steven's parents reluctantly agreed to drive out for dinner.

As Steven and Christy, along with Norma and Sid sat at the table, the tension was very much in evidence. Christy's father lectured about birds of a feather flocking together.

"If I'm a sparrow," he told them, "then I want to live with a sparrow and not a crow. That isn't anything against the crow, I'm sure he's a very nice bird, but let him live with his own flock."

That lecture aside, Steven and Christy decided to forgo a large interfaith wedding and fly out to Lake Tahoe, Nevada, and were married at a wedding chapel.

Steven called his mother with the news.

"I'm happy for you, darling, I really am for the both of you. It's not going to be without some problems, we both know that, but *mazel tov*, honey."

"Thank you, Mom, can you tell Dad?"

"I'll call him at the studio; he doesn't get much work anymore, so I can talk to him. Besides, I'd rather have him scream over there than over here."

"I hope the grandparents take it better than he does."

"Let's worry about your father first. I love you, honey, I love you both."

"So, do you think your dad will take our wedding picture?" Christy asked him.

"We'll be lucky if he doesn't throw the goddamned camera at us."

Chapter Forty-Seven

S id Weitz did not take the news of his son's marriage well. Norma was not
expecting him to when she called him at the studio.

"So, he married her, he's a schmuck! He's a putz with a medical degree!"
Sid yelled into the phone. "What did he do, get married in the church by a
priest?"

"No, I told you it was a civil ceremony, Nevada-style."

"Oh, so that's supposed to make me feel better?"

"Honey, it was a civil ceremony; our son hasn't converted, and I know he
won't"

"Shit, what about children, how will their kids be raised?"

"Well, Sid, they're going to start with babies, then gradually work their
way up to adults."

"Hah!" Sid let out one of his trademark laughs, which was a gravelly
voiced Hah! You're a real Joan fuckin' Rivers."

"Don't you use the 'F' word with me, Sidney 'C for common' Weitz!"

"Let's have them for dinner; you can make a ham to celebrate!"

"Sidney!"

"I'm disinheriting him!"

"The fuck you will! Yes! That's right! I say fuck! Fuck! Fuck! Fuck! You
disinherit our son, I'll divorce you and take you for everything you have, and
then I'll cut off your balls!"

"What about her family, Norma? I don't think they're exactly dancing the
tarantella over this."

"Sid, everything will be fine, they love each other."

"So, Norma, how do you think our elderly parents will take this? The
good news that their grandson, the doctor, has married a *shiksa*."

"Not well, Sid, but I'll break it to them gently; everything will work out."

I suppose they want me to take a wedding picture."

"Well, now that you mention it, Steven did say something about that. He thought it might be nice if our family and their family came into the studio for some photographs."

"Holy shit! Do whatever you want, Norma, whatever you want! Let me go, I gotta make a living, while I'm still alive." He hung up.

Mona the retoucher came into the studio to pick up her work. She could see that Sid was upset about something.

"What's wrong, Sid?"

"Nothing, I'm celebrating!"

"Celebrating what?"

"My son married a *shiksa*! Sid started to sing, *Mazel tov* and *Siman tov*, and *Siman tov* and *Mazel tov*, *oy Hava Nagila, Hava*....'

"I guess I shouldn't say *Mazel tov*." Mona replied.

"No you should say *Yisgadal v'Yiskadash*!"

"Sid I'm not going to say that!"

"That's my reward for being a good father, a kick in the ass!"

"I didn't know he was engaged."

"Neither did I."

"You didn't mention he was seeing anyone new."

"Mona, what was to mention? You think I wanted the world to know he was involved with a *shiksa*?"

"But now you announce their marriage!"

"That's so somebody like you who knows me can identify me when I drop dead today!"

"You're not going to drop dead."

"Mona, watch the six o'clock news tonight, there is gonna be a murder-suicide at my house!"

"Sid, you could never do anything to Norma."

"Who said anything about me doing it to her? She's gonna get me."

"Shape up, Sid, the kids need you now. Maybe you should call your rabbi."

"My rabbi is a putz! For what I should call him? He's gonna make me feel better spiritually? It ain't his kid. What's he gonna do for me? He'll give me some words of his schmucky wisdom, try to sell me a copy of his book, and ask me if I think Noah was a mediocre man."

"Well, listen, I have other studios to make pickups, I'm going to go. Sid, be well."

"I'll do my best."

Sid and Norma's elderly parents did not take this news very well.

"Listen, you get goddamn grandchildren, you don't know what the hell you get," Norma's father reacted to the news.

"Sure, listen, Norma married such a common bastard, so why not?"

"Sidney?" Aaron answered, "He's not really common, he's just a working man. He's got a big mouth, yeah, but he's good to Norma."

"Good to Norma? *Oy, oy, oyyy!* Common, he curses, and curses. A big shot, with the house on Long Island with the swimming pool, the big Cadillacs, *oy a bruchusmere*, please, he made her miserable."

"The way our daughter lives? Miserable? I should be so miserable!"

"You liked him, I told you not to let her marry him!"

"Sadie, what the hell are you saying, let her? She was a grown woman and it was a good marriage."

"Sure a good marriage. A *shlemiel* she married, I told you."

"Here," said Aaron, gesturing to the window of the apartment they recently moved into, "stand by the window, you'll feel a nice breeze."

"A *shiksa* granddaughter, very nice. Maybe we'll put up a Christmas tree with stockings. I told you if she married him it would be no good. But you, *a shtoomah*, it was alright with you. Everything was alright with you! *Oy, OY!* I'm sick! I'm sick! I'm sick from this!"

"Goddamn it, Sadie!" Aaron bellowed, "Don't make me run out of the house!"

Sid's father, Burton Weitz, was enraged. Sid's mother tried to calm him down. Burton Weitz sat in his recliner in the den of their Brooklyn senior citizens' apartment. Burt was getting ready to watch a boxing match. He was eating a bucket of chicken legs, tossing the bones on the floor. He sat in old work pants and a tee shirt already halfway through his first six-pack of beer.

"Calm down, Burt, what's done is done."

"Shaddap, dummy!" Burt Weitz farted.

Sid's mother quickly opened a window.

"Get the fuck outta here, I'm trying to watch the fights!" He threw an empty beer can at her. She knew not to mess with her husband. Fifty-five years earlier, during an argument, he picked a bunch of bananas off of their dining room table and threw them down the length of the foyer at the back of her head, as she walked away from him.

"Owwww, you take a bunch of bananas and throw them at your wife's head!" she cried. She knew not to mess with him.

"Calm down, Burt."

"Calm down, shit! I wanted our putz son to learn a good trade!"

"He did, Burt!"

"FUCK UP, DUMMY! He wanted to learn to be a photographer, he wanted to learn how to develop and enlarge in a darkroom. I wanted him to learn plumbing, he'd make money!"

"Our son does make money; he makes a lot of money from his business."

"SHUT THE FUCK UP, DUMMY! he roared. He taught the other schmuck photography, that putz couldda been a plumber, too!"

"Saul is a famous highly-paid advertising photographer!"

"Leave me alone, I wanna watch the fights!"

"Just don't start up with Sid and Norma or our grandson."

"I WANNA HEAR THIS!"

"I liked you better when you used to stay out at night and break up saloons and bust heads in pool halls."

"You like taking my hard earned money!"

"Your money? Excuse me, your money?"

"I'M WATCHING!"

"Go take a good look at yourself in the mirror."

Burton Weitz picked up another six-pack of beer that was unopened.

"COCKSUCKER!" He yelled as he threw the six-pack across the room at his wife.

She ran out of the apartment yelling out, "DIE!" as she ran.

Burt got up, walked across the room, picked up the six-pack, and farted again.

"He, heh, heh, now I can watch the fights in peace."

Down in the street, a driver leaned on his car horn.

Burt opened the window and called out, "BLOW IT OUT OF YOUR ASS!"

He then picked up an almost empty flat bottle of Jack Daniels Bourbon, drained it, then flung it out of the window.

"FUCKING IDIOT!" he screamed out.

The day to take pictures of the newlywed couple arrived. The Copobianco and Weitz families assembled in Sid's studio. There were civil handshakes all around. It was the first time that Sid and Christy had kissed.

Norma picked up a small video camera and made a tape of interviews wishing the couple well. Sid took a series of posed portraits and several group photographs.

Lenny Schecter came downstairs from the baby studio to photograph Sid standing in the group picture. Sid was not smiling.

Christy looked cute in the cocktail dress she wore, maybe things will work out.

Linda played a cassette with both a *hora* and a tarantella. Lenny videotaped both families dancing.

Before Steven parted with his lucky bride, Norma gave Steven a check for twenty-five thousand dollars of unreported money they had in a bank vault, with Sid's blessing. She would have given them the money without his blessing. They knew it was much more than what Christy's parents had given them.

Everybody left, Norma stayed to help Sid straighten up and close the studio.

Two married children, grandchildren, and now maybe more grandchildren.

Life was good. Alright, it could have been better.

Chapter Forty-Eight
Winter 1992

S id Weitz was semi-retired. He worked when he worked. He shot jobs mostly for other studios now. He preferred to shoot video instead of stills. Videotaping was less physically demanding for an old cocker like him. He loved photography, but there was too much bending and running involved. With video, you set up your lights and, if needed, the microphones and your set. There isn't any posing or aggravation trying to get everyone to stay still. You have a minimum amount of interaction with the people. Studios also paid more money for videographers than photographers, which struck Sid as odd, because photographers worked harder. Video reminded Sid of the old days when he shot movies.

Their daughter had moved to Boston with her family. They tried to see them when they could. They missed the grandchildren especially. Linda was due with her third child, a daughter, very soon.

Steven and Christy's little girl Angela had already been born. Although she was half Jewish, according to Jewish law, because the mother was not Jewish, their granddaughter was not Jewish at all. Steven and Christy decided not to have a christening, because after all, they were married in a civil ceremony. That did not please her parents. But Sid thought that he could rule out a Bat Mitzvah, too. She was adorable and Sid loved her very much.

Last summer, after Sid closed his studio, he worked less, so they went to the Bronx Zoo with their two grandsons. They had a great day. Peter was laughing as he recounted the day's events for his parents, when they came to pick them up.

"There were a husband and wife gorilla couple sitting together, Sid said they looked like a couple of *shvartzes*."

"Daddy, really!" Linda reproved him.

"I did not say that, did not say that at all! I said that they looked like a nice old *shvartze* couple!"

Mark laughed. Linda told him not to encourage Sid.

"Well, that must have pissed off the gorilla because..." Peter continued.

"Pissed off? Excuse me," Linda interrupted, "where did you pick up that expression? Linda turned to her father, "Oh, never mind, continue."

"Because," Peter continued, "the gorilla got up, picked up a big mound of doody, and threw it at us."

"We ducked," Norma said, "he missed us."

"Yeah, and Sid called the gorilla a putz!" Peter finished the story.

"Tell them about the trip home," Norma prompted him.

"Oh yeah, we went the long way through Manhattan; Sid wanted to take us for a drive through the Bowery to show us the bums. He said this is what will happen to us if we don't do well in school."

"Your grandfather used to do that with us, too."

"And it worked! You became an audiologist, Steven is a doctor, I was right!"

"It woiked!" Peter said. "So we drove through skid row, we saw the flop houses, that's for the men to flop. Sid said they're called flop houses, because that's who stays there, men who were flops in life. We had dinner in Chinatown. Sid lowered the window and called out, 'Hey, Bum! Direct me to Mott Street, Bum!' The bum yelled, 'Rehhh, rehhhh, rehhh, ya bastid,' back at us."

"Your grandpa can be very obnoxious sometimes," Linda informed her son.

"I know, when I told Mrs. Heller, my teacher last year, that my grandfather's a photographer and what studio, she said that he was obnoxious."

"Thanks a lot," mumbled Sid.

"My mother calls him common," Norma volunteered.

Sid liked spending time with little Angela, too. Although she was half Jewish, Sid was relieved she liked her grandpa.

Sid enjoyed photographing her, too.

Everything was going well, except for the fact that Norma had lost a lot of weight.

She claimed that it was her diet and chasing the grandchildren. "What diet?" Sid had asked her. "You're already thin." He reminded her that the only time she was heavy were her two pregnancies. Thin women were always on a diet, she reminded him. There was no need for worry. Still, he worried.

That spring Norma's face appeared gaunt, she was concerned about it, too.

The family doctor referred her to a specialist after seeing her x-rays. The specialist ordered a C.A.T scan and an M.R.I. with a whole lot of other tests.

The news was not good.

"Colon cancer." That was what the specialist told them.

The cancer had spread, it was inoperable, and chemotherapy treatments were her only hope. *Was there any hope? Sid wondered.*

They told the kids, and Norma was upbeat. Their son the doctor was not, he more than anyone knew the whole ugly truth about this disease.

Then Norma's mother, Sadie, suffered a cardiac arrest, and after a brief hospital stay, she died. The funeral services were held in an old Jewish chapel in the Midwood section of Brooklyn, on Coney Island Avenue.

During the eulogy, the rabbi spoke of how family was important to Sadie. To her, the rabbi said, her children by marriage were the same as her own children.

"She always called me common," Sid muttered, not quite under his breath.

"You are!" Norma's sister Marlene said as she turned to him in the pew.

Shortly thereafter, Sid's father had a cerebral hemorrhage. He lived three weeks in a vegetative state in a nursing home. Sid hated that fucking place; it was full of dead, who were not yet dead. As Sid walked through the corridors, there were cries of senile suffering.

"Hymie! Hymie?" An old lady walked past Sid aimlessly, "Vere's Hymie?"

"Vhat time is it? Vhat time is it?" another old lady called out as he walked past her room.

"Half past two," Sid paused and told her.

"Tenk you. Vhat time is it? Vhat time is it?"

An old man sat in a wheelchair brandishing his cane, "Pop vas a bastid! Pop vas a bastid!" he yelled. His daughter pleaded, "Alright, enough about Grandpop please, Dad!" So he began yelling, "Mom vas alvays half nuts!"

An elderly woman beckoned Sid over to her wheelchair.

"You go to school? You go to school?" she queried.

"A long time ago, ma'am," he answered.

"You come to my house? You come to my house?"

"Yeah, sure, why not?" he answered. "We'll have a glass of tea together."

"You got the keys? You got the keys?"

"I'll knock, you'll let me in, *zie gezundt*."

Sid sat with his mother and siblings in his father's room all that day and at five o'clock Burton Weitz opened his eyes; it appeared he was coming out of his coma. He looked around and yelled out, "Fuck you!" and died.

"Dad's last words," Sid's brother Seymour remarked.

"Listen," their mother said, "I think those were his first words, so why shouldn't they be his last?"

After the funeral, the rabbi asked Sid's mother what her plans were.

"Well, Thursday night, I'm going to play bingo."

"I meant what you will do now, for the future, Mrs. Weitz?" She was a woman in her mid-eighties, and the rabbi was concerned.

"Well, I'm going to fix myself up and travel. I have a sister in California, I want to go to Vegas, and maybe Europe again."

Norma was not getting worse, so far. Sid brought her to a medical center on the North Shore of Nassau County once a week for her chemotherapy.

While Norma was in the treatment room, Sid sat and commiserated with a fellow photographer. Sylvia Miesner of Portraits by Sylvia, brought her husband Artie for his treatments at the same time. Sylvia was about Sid's age. She had shot candid events, but was really a portrait specialist. She had developed a crush on Sid many years ago, from observing his demeanor and earthy frank speech.

Linda and Mark's third child and first daughter, Rebecca Brittany Sossin was born. Norma was in remission and well enough to see her new granddaughter.

She looked thinner, and even though she wore a wig to hide her hair loss from the chemo, she looked good. She and Sid enjoyed their four grandchildren. They did not hide in the house; now that Sid was semi-retired they traveled. Sid hoped the remission would last forever or until he was in the ground first.

While Norma was doing well, Sid found the time to do business and shoot some jobs.

On a fall Sunday, Sid videotaped a wedding for a friend's studio. The interfaith ceremony and reception was held at a Nassau County catering facility that first opened during the time of the American Revolution. The bride was Dominican, the groom was a W.A.S.P. The bride was an hour and a half late in arriving from her Brooklyn home. Finally, several Plymouth Furys and Dodge Diplomats from a car service company pulled in front of the reception hall. The bride, the maid of honor, and the bride's parents emerged. Sid had begun the taping of the bride's arrival.

"Wha' hoppen?" a man related to the bride called out.

"De limo broke a down," the bride's father responded.

"DEES EES ALL A DE FAUL' OF MY FUCKIN' FATHER!" the bride tearfully screamed into the video camera as she entered the hall.

The bride's father walked into the hall with his hands raised wiggling his fingers, to indicate that he wanted no part of his daughter's wrath.

Sid wanted to keep a copy of this tape for himself for laughs.

Norma laughed that night when he showed her the raw footage. She also laughed when the frustrated maitre'd commented on the bandleader. A loud Latin band was playing away, ignoring the man's instructions, so the hapless maitre'd looked into Sid's video camera, "I'm trying to work with the man, but he doesn't speak any English," he said with a befuddled shrug.

"You know which tape I like, honey?" Norma asked.

"No. I'm sorry, I don't."

"It's one you shot back in '83; it was the night before Thanksgiving, a Jewish wedding, and the bride was a very heavy girl, remember, Sid?"

"Kind of, baby, but as I recall, the bride wasn't heavy, she was a horse."

"Well, you were doing table interviews, when this very pretty young brunette makes a kiss into the microphone, and she says, 'Mwah! Hello, Sid! I love you!' Remember?"

"No, but what can I tell you, it must be my charm."

"Well, I always said you have a magnetic personality."

Things were getting better. Sid and Norma said that things were looking up, because Norma was getting better. Her hair grew in, but it came in all white. Sid told Norma not to dye it. He thought she looked terrific.

Norma thought she might make Peter's Bar Mitzvah, after all.

The '92 elections were over. The governor of Arkansas was elected president. Sid hoped he would do better than the other democrat, the governor from Georgia, what's his name, Jimmy something or other. The economy might recover. He expected to make some decent money in semi-retirement, he figured now his son the doctor and his son-in-law the foreign trade consultant might make some money. Things were getting better.

Chapter Forty-Nine

Summer 1993

Sunday, a great day to enjoy one's grandchildren. Sid did not have an affair to shoot today, so he and Norma enjoyed their grandchildren, along with their children.

Babies Angela and Rebecca slept in their carriages on the patio while Peter and Alec sat on the grass and played.

Plucky the cat walked past where the two boys played.

"Duckie!" Alec, age four, called out.

"Alec, she is a cat," his dad, Mark, corrected him. "That's not duckie, that's Plucky!"

"She looks like a duckie."

"See, Plucky," Norma called out, "Alec thinks you look like a duckie."

Plucky rubbed her head against Alec and lay down on the grass.

"Poppy looks like a duckie, too," Alec observed.

"You know," Norma looked over at Sid, "you're right! Poppy does look like a duckie!"

Peter decided to annoy his little brother. He kept pulling the fire truck away from Alec.

"Gimmee!" Alec ordered Peter.

Peter handed Alec the fire truck, then took it away again.

"You ass-o!" Alec blurted out, close enough for a kid his age.

"Where did he learn that?" Norma asked her daughter.

"Nursery school, today the kids know the words early on in life."

Alec yanked his fire truck from Peter, who in turn, yanked it back.

"Mmmmuck!" Alec called Peter.

"I think he meant..." Norma said.

"Yes, Mom, that's exactly what he meant!" Linda replied.

"Pete, cut it out!" Sid called from the barbeque, "If you don't stop picking on your little brother, I'm gonna rap you in the teeth!"

"You are?" Peter asked in disbelief.

"Damn right! He's my grandson, too, so if you pick a fight with him, you'll have to fight with me!"

Peter behaved himself after that warning from his granddad.

The gathering was not lighthearted. Norma's cancer had returned and she was to start a more aggressive treatment this week.

Norma gave some of her possessions to her children; she also talked about what if the treatments did not work out. Still, she and the children tried to be upbeat and optimistic.

An industry old-timer called Sid, as Norma worsened. Max Cohn now retired, was one of the founders of the photography association Sid belonged to. He had served as president on both state and local levels. He did not shoot anymore. Now, he just printed photographs and mentored anyone who wanted to learn. Max Cohn had a large studio in his home, near where Sid's studio used to be. He wanted to know if there was anything he could do. Later on, Max told Sid's cronies, "I called him, he didn't want anything from or to do with me."

"You're sure I can't do anything for you. Sid?"

"No, Max, I thank you kindly."

Trying to keep Sid on the line for awhile, Max Cohn tried a different tact. "How's Carl out in Arizona?"

"The fuck do I know? I'm not in touch with him."

"Well, you'll keep us posted?" Max asked.

"Yes, sir, thank you for calling."

At an association meeting, several photographers asked about Norma.

"*Oy*, Sid had a lot of *tzuris*, a Yiddish word for 'trouble' Abe Susskind often used. His wife has cancer, and what can I tell you? She's isn't going to recover. He has to stay home all the time with her. *Oy*, I feel for him."

"He doesn't want to talk to us, his old friends," Max Cohn shook his head sadly.

Norma died the first day of August, she was fifty-seven. Heshy Adomovich and a few photographers showed up for the services. Many men Sid knew in the trade for years did not. He did not keep anybody posted. There was no communication, so they were not there. Still, their absence made Sid very angry.

The funeral was held at a Jewish chapel in Woodmere. Only their grandsons, Peter and Alec attended. Rebecca and Angela, still babies, stayed with a sitter. Mark's sister was kind enough to volunteer to watch them.

The burial was at a Jewish cemetery where both Norma's and Sid's families, along with many of their in-laws had plots. Norma's family was across the walkway from Sid's family. The day before the services, Sid's mother called the cemetery manager and told him to move her daughter in-law and son down a few plots, he complied.

"My daughter-in-law was a wonderful girl, she should rest in peace, she shouldn't have to lie next to my husband. It's already bad enough I'm going to be next to him!"

It was a hot humid day; even so, Sid wore a three-piece black single-breasted suit.

After the burial, many family members visited with other members of their respective families, to either place a stone on their monument, or to go "Hock ptu!" on a detested relation's grave.

Sid sat *shiva* with his children for seven days. During that time, he did not shave in keeping with Jewish tradition, He did change his clothes.

Depressed, Sid could not sleep. He lay awake watching TV, even reruns of old game shows. He started answering the TV back.

While watching an old *What's My Line?* he finished Arlene Francis's introduction for her.

"And now, a man who has a good head on his shoulders..."

"Until, it went through his windshield," Sid cut Miss Francis off, "Larry Blyden!"

He was lonely, the jobs he shot helped to take his mind off his loss, but he was too old to shoot, but not ready to give it up.

At sixty-three, Sid was lucky that he was able to shoot. He occupied his time by shooting stills for his old-timer friend Heshy Adomovich. He shot video jobs for a photography studio in Bensonhurst. The owner was a Jewish fellow who specialized in Italian jobs. Problem was, all the fucking jobs were in Brooklyn.

Shannon, his buxom mail lady came over to say goodbye, she was getting another position with the post office, and it was indoors. That was another familiar face gone.

Dinah Strassman, an accountant who lived across the street, came over. She had already extended her condolences to him when Norma passed away.

"Hi, Sid," she smiled as she approached him getting into his car one Saturday morning, "I see you're still working. I wanted to tell you all my friends love the wall portrait of my daughters that you took."

"I thank you kindly. Yeah, Dinah, still working. I shoot for this guy in Bensonhurst. Today, I have a black wedding to videotape. It's in Flatbush, there's a big hall there, yet, that still does big business. I should be home in the evening."

"Well," she smiled flirtatiously, "maybe you can come to dinner one night."

"Hmm," he closed his left eye and thought about it, "Maybe, maybe I'll take you up on it."

Dinah Strassman, fifty-one, was an attractive, divorced, working mother of three girls. She had light brown hair that she wore short, much like Norma's. She had bright brown eyes. Her nose was average, but to look at her, one could see that she was a Jewish woman. She was five foot four and a bit overweight. Sid found her attractive.

"I'd like to have you over one night. I have your card; I'll call you this week to invite you."

She spoke with a Bronx accent, dropping her Rs, so that dinner, came out 'dinnah,' but Sid's Brooklyn accent, was not offended. When he said first, it came out 'foist.'

"I'd like that, too. Well, I have to go into battle, you take care, Dinah."

The job was an average uneventful job. That was surprising for a black wedding, he thought.

That following Tuesday, he attended his last dinner of the Professional Photographers of Greater New York, before dropping out. He did not want to see his friends grow old; he was well aware of his age, but he did not need to be reminded of it. Besides, he did not know or like any of the young schmucks who were members, with the exception of Jeffery Glassman, his former lighting assistant. Jeffery was now a full-fledged photographer and videographer, working for himself and sometimes for others. He also taught photography in high school. Sid had not seen him since Norma's funeral, and hugged him.

"How have you been, Sid?"

"Winding it down, *bubie*."

"You still work?" Jeff asked.

"When I work," Sid answered.

"But not a hell of a lot."

"Nah, man, I'm retired. Shit, I got rid of the corporation so I could collect Social Security."

Soon after, Sid was approached by a candid man from his generation, Angelo Conforti. Angelo Conforti was the second generation owner of Conforti Studios on Staten Island. His father started it a long time ago. He was from the old school, like Sid. Angelo was about five foot nine, heavy, with thinning black hair.

"Sid, how have you been?"

"Fine, thank God, Angelo. I thank you for the card, how are you?"

"Still shooting; my knee gives me trouble, but I don't want to get rusty. I shot a couple of jobs for Leon Horvitz. I did his Bar Mitzvah, shit it was such a long time ago, Sid."

"I used to work for Leon's father, Harry; he owned this studio that did school portraits, and I worked in his darkroom. He held the paper in the easel down with a vacuum hose; shit Harry was an automated processor back in the days before automation."

"I'm telling you," Angelo continued, "most of these kids in the business today, have never seen the inside of a darkroom. Today, these goddamn kids can't expose, 'cause they never worked in black and white. With black and white, you can tell who knows what they're doing, 'cause you have to know how to expose right. I saw a wedding photo last week taken in black and white. The exposures where awful—they were spics, but they looked like niggers. That Inez Wexler took the pictures, the so-called master photographer."

"Angelo," Sid lit a cigarette and shrugged, "it ain't the same game today."

"Anyway, I shot some jobs for Leon Horvitz, you know, to help him out. But," Angelo shook his head, "he kept sending me out on black jobs. I told him, 'Look Leon, I don't mind helping you out once in awhile, but come on.'"

Sid nodded and puffed his cigarette.

"Even at my studio on Staten Island, we get black weddings, but they are so disorganized, they never go off on time, they run late. I did this job, who knows where the hell they went after the ceremony, but they were late. The caterer was getting steamed, he told me that this wedding ends at five o'clock—on time or not. Well, finally they show up, so now the caterer wants them to be seated, so he can start serving. The DJ starts to play and they all get up and do their jiggaboo dances." Angelo bent his elbows while shifting one foot then the other to accentuate his point.

Sid acknowledged some friends.

"Well, I hope the food isn't salty tonight 'cause I have high blood pressure."

"Angelo, you have high blood pressure from all those *shvartze* jobs you do," Sid said.

Angelo nodded in agreement.

"Shid, Shid, how are you?" Abe Susskind asked, his speech still affected from his stroke. "How are you getting along?"

"Well, Abie, my daughter is in Boston and my son is in Atlanta. I miss them and the grandkids, especially. Soon my daughter is going to Japan with the kids, because my son-in-law is a foreign consultant; how's by you?

"Well, thank God, my wife's kidney transplant worked out, so I'm alright." Abe shrugged.

"At our age," Sid turned to Jeffery, "that's all we can do, just get along, *fashtay?*" *Fashtay* means 'understand' in Yiddish. Jeff nodded, that he understood.

"A long time ago," Abe Susskind continued, "I shot a Chassidic job, I was knocked off of my ladder and ruptured a disc. I had pain for the rest of my life. So, I went to the doctor last year, he says I don't have a ruptured disc anymore. I says, 'I don't?' He says, 'Now you have five ruptured discs!'"

Sid laughed.

"I tell you, Sid, with all that you've been through, your wife, your father…"

"My son's marriage," Sid interrupted.

"Yeah," Abe went on, "I feel for you; *oy* Sidney I give you *the writ of rachmunis!*" Abe handed Sid an imaginary piece of paper.

Sid pantomimed throwing the paper onto the floor. Abe Susskind knew Sid Weitz for over three decades; he knew he was going to do that.

"Well, I'm going to get myself a glass of wine," Sid excused himself.

"Jeff," Abe Susskind leveled his gaze at the young man, "I feel so bad for him…his wife died, he loved her so. His putz son married a *shiksa*, I feel such *rachmunis*; you know what that is, *rachmunis*? It's sorrow you feel for a person—pity, empathy."

"I understand, Abe," Jeff said.

"I feel *rachmunis* for everyone," Abe said, "but, I only worry about my own!"

Jeff nodded.

"Remember that, you can feel sorry for your friends, but you should only care about your own. That, son, is the truth about life and doing business, too!"

At the photography association's dinner, Sid had to endure the new guard of the industry for whom he had contempt.

Those people had contempt for the old guard. The jerks were reckless hotshots, it did not matter to Sid or any of the old-timers how many awards they won. These new guard assholes were now running the association; this is all that mattered to those bastards, power and awards. So many of the new *Goyim* drank like mad, they were always at the bar. Everything at a dinner meeting or board meeting was the bar, the bar, the bar, the bar.

A new officer of the association passed Sid, a short man with a bald spot who had the curious attention-getting name of Tucos Lecher. The phrase *"Tokus lecher"* in Yiddish means 'ass licker.' How this guy could go through life with that name was beyond Sid. Lecher claimed he was Lithuanian; Sid wondered what his name meant in Lithuanian. Several of the members joked Tucos Lecher had a face like a gerbil and a high pitched laugh like a hyena. He was in charge of printing the association newsletter, bilking the association for production costs. Lecher approached association President Jerry Silber, a hooked nose, thirty-something year old who wore his thinning chestnut colored hair in an Art Garfunkel hairstyle. Silber was a rich brat who could afford his studio because the building was his father-in-law's.

Slade Roberts walked over to them. Roberts wore a chain of award medallions around his neck and members of other association sections referred to Roberts as "The Mexican General," because of the awards he wore on his puffed out chest. Tucos Lecher was Slade Roberts' personal *tokus lecher*, carrying out evil acts against other association officers and general members at Roberts' behest. Roberts was the elephant and Lecher was the bird who rode on the elephant's back.

Slade Roberts was a five foot eleven, heavyset man with a fat face. He wore a goatee-style beard. Roberts had medium length brown hair parted on the right. He began as a musician playing trumpet at affairs. He also worked as a disc jockey. After learning photography, he learned videography and won awards in both mediums. To say Slade Roberts, who was born Olaf Lindstrom, was an award hound was an understatement. Roberts was a recovering alcoholic; he could not take a drink so he replaced his addiction by winning awards. His high was how many more blue ribbons to hang on his wall or how much association costume jewelry to wear around his neck. Roberts also satisfied his addictive obsessions by holding every office in both the state and local sections of the photography associations. Industry legend Max Cohn, a past section and state president himself, did all Roberts' custom printing for all of the local, state, and national photographic print competitions he entered. Cohn, also an award-winning photographic craftsman, was disgusted by Roberts' shameless award mongering. Cohn told Roberts flat out, "You have no humility!"

Slade Roberts' nemesis was Larry Kronk. Larry Kronk was also a past state and section president with an ego as big as Roberts'. In Yiddish and German, *Kronk* means 'Sick.' Because of Larry Kronk's paranoia and high voiced tirades about the association's mindless politics, Kronk was dubbed, "The Sick One." Kronk worked as a part-time candid man, before opening his own studio. He was an electrician by trade. One major difference was Slade Roberts had a huge home studio on a sprawling parcel of land. Larry Kronk had a small house with his business name in letters on his living room window. Sid thought that was comical as "The Sick One" lived on a side street where no traffic passed by.

There were stories how Larry Kronk made brides cry and how Bar Mitzvah boys threatened not to attend their own celebration if he was there. One story was passed throughout the industry; a Bar Mitzvah boy told his mother, "If Larry Kronk is at my Bar Mitzvah, I'm not going."

"Now, listen, young man," the boy's mother replied, "Larry Kronk has to be at your Bar Mitzvah, he is your daddy!" Larry Kronk had a son in the business, Irwin Kronk. Larry Kronk was slim, about five foot nine. He had layered medium brown graying hair and a full beard. Irwin Kronk had dark wavy hair and was on the chubby side, and looked nothing like his dad. It was rumored he looked like their mailman.

Irwin Kronk was also a past section president and award-winning photographer like his daddy with an ego to boot. He was engaged to a Mexican girl, then broke it off and married a needle-nosed Jewish girl from his town, which pleased his father. Larry had a designer daughter Fawn, who married an older man. Larry referred to his soon to be ex-son-in-law as an "anti-Semitic drunken alcoholic."

Larry Kronk often engaged unwitting people in acts of malevolence on Slade Roberts and others for the good of the association. He called people, telling them he regarded them as a friend. Most of the dupes he called knew damn well he never came over to speak to them at association meetings. Larry Kronk did not know another association member's name unless he needed that person.

The poor unwitting duped member received Kronk's long winded shrilling phone call, "I don't have an ego, I'm not alcoholic, I don't cheat on my wife, and I don't enter print competitions anymore." This caused the person to giggle, as Kronk already won every print competition there was and to say he did not have an ego, he protested too much. "Now you know, I don't have an ego," he'd shriek, "but Slade Roberts that motherfuckin' cocksucker who used to be an alcoholic..." An educated person would laugh, Larry

Kronk's high school equivalency degree mentality did not understand, as far as alcoholism went, that there was no 'used to be,' an alcoholic was always an alcoholic.

Kronk went on enlisting the help of hapless members in annihilating other association officers. "Biaggio Salvaggio, who I trained, is a raging drunk, cheats on his wife, and is out to destroy me. I want to use this analogy; I had a dog, a Scotty named Hotshot. That dog bit the hand that fed him, he was crazy; he attacked me, but I loved him, and when he died, I cried. Biaggio is just like that. He and his partner Hans Ludwig, whose father is a staunch German anti-Semite who claims the holocaust never happened, want to get their hands on the association's school."

Kronk worried about the workshop, because he and his partner in crime Seth Circlet funneled the money from the workshop into their retirement accounts. Seth Circlet had a reputation for being cheap. He waited to see if his lighting assistant received a tip, he would then add the money from his pocket to make up the balance for the assistant's wages, rather than paying the assistant outright. Circlet was a fat fuck as far as Sid was concerned, the way he double-dipped at cocktail hour was disgusting. Circlet attended a *shiva* call, Sid watched him run out of the room. While expressing his condolences to a widow, when a deli delivery arrived, he left the widow to run to the platter to stuff his face.

Larry Kronk was known for saying, "Sid Weitz, holy shit, that man could offend God." Sid offended Larry Kronk when he was one of his young candid men. Kronk hired a high-priced gay photographer for over ten thousand dollars to photograph his son's wedding to his needle-nosed bride. The photographer who went by one name, 'Arlen,' was Arlen Meizelman of San Francisco, formerly of Brooklyn, New York. Sid knew Arlen when he was a candid man in Brooklyn. He started lecturing, announced he was gay, and left his wife to move to San Francisco to enjoy his alternate lifestyle. Arlen brought his boy toy Ty as a second photographer. Larry Kronk bitterly complained that Ty was as useless as a screen door on a submarine. Sid had no sympathy for Larry, he was happy he blew ten grand on shitty, overpriced photography. There was plenty of local talent to photograph his son Irwin's wedding to 'needle nose.'

Biaggio Salvaggio came over to Sid. He reeked of smoke and booze. He had his head cocked to the side, walking around shaking hands and asking if he could buy anyone a drink. He wanted to be state president one day. Sid thought Biaggio was a lowlife; he was known to drink on his jobs and called the bar where the association met his 'office.' Biaggio got drunk at meetings then walked around in tears hollering, "I want to know why people say I'm a drunk!"

He was with Hortense Blummenritt, a former prostitute, who turned her life around by discovering photography. Larry Kronk told anyone who would listen that Hortense wants only to fuck Biaggio, "She has her head so far up his *tokus*." Sid wanted to puke every time he heard that.

Hortense Blummenritt was also known by her first name. Because of her past she was called 'Whoretense' behind her back. Hortense went drinking after a wedding she photographed and had all of her photographic equipment stolen out of her SUV. Another time, she was arrested for driving while intoxicated after leaving an association dinner. "I sobbed all the way to the precinct," she told Sid. Sid told her bluntly, "Better you should sob in handcuffs to the precinct, than a family member should sob at the morgue identifying a person you killed."

Joyce Van Valen was also with them, she was another drunk. She judged print competitions drunk; Sid thought it was contemptible how she drove drunk with her children in the car.

Sid said hello to portrait photographer Joan Kleinman, owner of Portraits by Yochanna. She was a nice Orthodox Jewish lady and he liked her. Joan Kleinman wore a wig known as a *Shietl,* in keeping with tradition of modesty for an Orthodox married woman. It was beyond Sid why a class act like Joan wanted to be involved with those new guard creeps. She served on the board; when board meetings became heated and tempers along with profanity flew, Joan left the room to lay down in the ladies lounge, after removing her wig and applying a compress to her head. At meetings when those morons screamed, Joan gestured upward and cried out, "I don't know!"

Nacham Shlemmer noticed Sid, who wanted to avoid Nacham Shlemmer like he wanted to avoid the clap. Shlemmer was a short man with greasy black hair and a mustache. He looked like the villain who tied the young girl to the train tracks in those old westerns. Shlemmer made Sid's skin crawl with his appearance and the way he spoke. "Eee, Eee, Eee, for example." He always said, "For example." He'd quote Jewish law and advise colleagues, what his father used to say.

"Eh, Sid," an Italian accent called out. "Give a me five a dollars." The voice belonged to Tosono Tonti of Bensonhurst. He was selling raffle tickets. Tosono Tonti fled Venice when he did not want to continue working as a gondolier. He had a reputation for owing money to everybody he did business with and copying other photographer's works to enter into print competitions. Once while at his studio, Sid saw mouse traps in the basement, and he asked Tosono if he used flour or bread crumbs to make the mouse parmigiana. "You a craze!" Tosono replied. Tosono's wife, Gina Maria, was with him. Gina Maria Tonti was an attractive, tall, heavyset woman almost twenty years younger than he was. Tosono's son Tosono Jr., known as Tony, greeted Sid. Tony hated working for his father because he resented his father's second wife, and the fact his father never paid him for shooting jobs for his studio. Tony was an accomplished photographer and videographer, who occasionally worked for Sid.

"Hey, Sid," he clasped Sid's hand, "I see my old man got you for money. He is pissed at me; his wife started with me at the studio last week, so I tried to stab her."

"You whaaat?" Sid asked in disbelief.

"Yeah, I had enough, man," Tony continued, "so I stuck a knife through the bathroom door at her. I didn't think anything so large could move so fast! She ran down Twentieth Avenue, I ran after her with the knife, and my old man ran after me pulling my hair."

Then Sid said hello to master photographer Inez Wexler and her long suffering husband, Arnie.

"I am not assisting Inez on any more jobs; she had me at an outdoor wedding Sunday, and I ruined my Florsheim shoes," Arnie told Sid. Arnie was as old as Sid. Inez, an attractive auburn-haired woman was of Puerto Rican descent. When she lost her temper, she had the capability to make Rosie Perez blush.

"Sorry about Norma," Inez told Sid. He thanked them for their card. When Sid's son Steven married a *shiksa*, Sid tried to commiserate with Arnie Wexler, who was Jewish. "Good for him," Arnie told Sid. "I was married to a Jewish girl, she took me for everything and my two children with her don't speak to me. It was good your son didn't marry a Jewish girl, they all stink!"

"My God," Inez said, "your son married outside the faith; he isn't going to hell. It should be the worst thing that happened to you. Stop being a Jew!"

Sid looked into his waistband, "That's not possible!" he answered Inez.

They had a daughter they were proud of. Their son was another story, Inez was arguing with the boy on her cellular phone calling him a 'little fucker.'

Tonight there was no talk about marriage.

Sid was offered condolences on his wife's passing. Eva Laurentino, a German married to an Italian, was with the Wexlers. Angelo Conforti hated her because she told a prospective client that his old family-owned studio was filthy. Various members of Angelo's family called Eva in an attempt to find out her prices. Angelo hated Inez Wexler, too; he claimed she and Eva palled around, entered print competitions, and won all the awards. It didn't matter that Angelo never entered anything into a competition.

The association was in need of money as a recently expelled president Spencer Williams, a young black man, embezzled thirty thousand dollars while he was treasurer to have his wife artificially inseminated.

There were a lot of familiar old faces there tonight, Sid noticed. He said hello to Giovanni "Johnny" Romanato, owner of Rome Studios. Giovanni was older than Sid, having served in World War II. After Korea, Sid shot for Giovanni. Giovanni was there with his son "Johnny Jr.". Johnny Jr. now ran the business. Jr. was gay and to his old man's displeasure, started appearing at events with his boyfriend. Once Johnny Sr., who had the same gravelly Brooklyn accent as Sid, told him, "I dunno, the kid didn't turn out right."

Sid nodded at two men who used to work for him and managed his studio in the 1970s, Zachary Kahn and Barnet Weintraub. They were best friends, which Sid found amusing, because they were complete opposites. Zachary Kahn was a hippie who was rumored to be a draft dodger. He never served in the military and attended the Woodstock New York rock concert in 1969. Barnet Weintraub, served in the army, was a conservative republican and he loved Richard M. Nixon. Barnet Weintraub owned Barnet Studios, Zachary Kahn owned The Creative Experience. Weintraub was heavyset and balding, while Kahn was thin, with long graying black hair in a ponytail and a handlebar mustache.

Another man who worked for Sid was there, too, Don Gruber. Gruber was a portly bearded man with bushy brown hair. He fancied himself a comedian, however, not many of his photographer colleagues thought so. He had a huge ego, and when he got angry his nostrils flared. Sid was shooting video at a wedding, where he hired Gruber to shoot the stills. Gruber asked the bartender for a diet seltzer. It was a hectic job and the harried bartender did not need any smart ass cracks from another member of the hired help. He asked Gruber how he would like a knuckle sandwich, with extra elbow. Gruber was now involved with association politics and hell bent on winning awards to wear on his puffed out chest. He was getting involved with Slade Roberts, so much so, he was making a reputation for himself as Roberts' lackey, to the point where people at the associations were calling him "Slade Junior," behind his back.

Jeff sat next to Sid for dinner. A fat German waiter with thin brown hair and a thick mustache came over.

"*Ve heff ser German prgrrime gripp chunight!*" he announced.

"*Vas else?*" Sid inquired.

"*Och ve heff, groast churkey mit cranberry unt ghravy, unt ve heff a filet uff flounder.*"

"I'll have the German prime rib!" Sid said cheerily.

"*Veggry goot sir!*"

After dinner, the only dessert offered was Bavarian apple pie, which Sid did not care for. The owner of the restaurant, who was standing near the bar, recognized Sid from the trade and came over.

"Sir, you're not eating your pie, don't you care for it?" he asked with a smile.

"No, I don't like apple pie."

"Try it, it is real Bavarian apple pie."

"I'll pass."

"But it was baked in an authentic German oven," the owner volunteered.

"So were some of my relatives!" Sid answered. The owner sulked off.

As he pulled in his driveway, Sid felt tired. He had never felt so tired after an association dinner, good thing this was his last, *I'm getting too old for this*, he thought. In fucking life, sooner or later everybody gets too old for something.

The light on the answering machine was flashing. It was Dinah Strassman from across the street, inviting him to dinner Thursday night. He would call her tomorrow and accept.

Sid brought a bottle of Burgundy wine, and remembering that Dinah had two college-age daughters and one in high school, he brought a Black Forrest cake. She appreciated the wine and the cake. He dressed in a gray sports jacket with an open collar white shirt. He was a bit nervous, but he did not consider it a date. This was a nice divorceè inviting a nice widower to dinner.

They had a pleasant evening. Dinah was an accountant for a large firm. Robyn the eldest was in law school, Lauren the middle daughter was in college, studying accounting, and Faith the youngest was still in high school, and not sure of what she wanted to be yet. All three girls were pretty younger versions of their mother, the youngest had dark hair, probably like her father, Sid presumed, who was not part of their life. Sid did not even remember Dinah's ex-husband.

After dinner, they sat and talked for a while. Sid said he had to get up early and do a temple shoot for a Bar Mitzvah. Then he was going to Atlanta to see his son, and then he had a wedding to shoot. Then it was off to Hawaii to shoot a wedding for a friend of a relative, then from there, it was off to Japan to see his daughter and her children, then back home.

Sid and Dinah said goodnight, no kissing or anything romantic, this was just a nice neighborly dinner invitation. He walked home feeling a bit guilty for having dinner with another woman, and a bit upbeat because he did. He promised to call her to take her out for dinner, but that would have to wait until he got back from Japan. He was not in any rush to start dating again after so many years; besides, he had a lot of shit to do, yet.

Chapter Fifty

S id was happy to see Steven, Christy, and Angela, and they were happy to see him. He was happy to see them and Christy was shocked how warmly Sid had reacted to her.

"Listen, Steve, you married a wonderful girl. Of course, I would rather your wife be Jewish, but it's your life, you should be happy, we should all be. I have a beautiful granddaughter, she's healthy, so thank God, that's it."

Steven told his father he appreciated that. That week, he felt closer to his father than ever before.

"Are you going out, Sid?" Christy asked him.

"Dating? No, not really. I had dinner with a nice lady from the neighborhood."

When Steven smiled, Sid told them the lady made an old widower dinner out of pity, not affection.

Sid was allowed to take Angela, car seat, stroller, and all for a walk in downtown Atlanta. He had rented a Ford Taurus, and was looking forward to an outing with his granddaughter.

Angela's vocabulary was still limited, so Sid did all of the talking, but that was the way it was with him, he always did all of the talking.

They walked past the stores, they sat in a park, and Angela loved watching Grandpa feed the birds.

As they passed a large drugstore, Angela lit up with wonder.

"Let's go in, darling; Grandpa has a sore tushie, so he'll get himself some Preparation-H. Gramps also needs some more ciggies, but we'll get something for you, too!"

Sid bought Angela a doll and some safe toys for a baby. She smiled at him on the checkout line.

"Byootiful baby," the lady ahead of him on line drawled. "She yours?"

"My son's."

"Your first?"

"Their first. I have two grandsons and a granddaughter from my daughter."

"Vacationing in ou-uhur faiyah state?"

"Yes, some time off."

"With you-wer wahfe?"

"My wife passed away."

"Oh, ahm terribly sorr-ah. We have grandchildren, we have a lot becauwus, we became grandparents young. We have three boys. Our daughter is the not much older than our eldest grandchildren."

"Well, it was nahyuce talking to you. Jimmy's at his office waiting for me, we're going to have lunch and a reading from the Bible, enjoy your stay with us."

She left with two men in dark suits and sunglasses.

"Dad, I know we didn't always see eye to eye, but I'm glad we're friends now."

"We were always friends, Steve. I'm not so easy to get along with. Your mother, may she rest in peace, could never say a bad thing about anyone, not like me."

"Be happy, Dad, be happy," Steven told his father when he flew back to New York.

"You too, Steve, all three of you."

Sid had a big Jewish wedding to photograph, and a Bar Mitzvah to videotape before flying to Japan.

Sid engaged the services of a light person he did not know. This twenty-year-old fellow was an assistant for another studio. Sid took his name off the bulletin board at his processing lab.

Sid thought he was getting someone who knew how to light. This young man Dave knew how to light, but did not understand Sid's standards. It was big Jewish wedding in a large, plush Great Neck synagogue. Sid was having a bad day to begin with.

Doesn't this kid know how to hold the fucking light properly? he thought.

"You're frustrating me, man! You're frustrating," Sid admonished Dave during a bridal portrait session. "Can't you hold the fuckin' light higher?" he snapped, not giving a shit if the entire bridal party heard him or not. "What, am I giving you to hold a five hundred fuckin' pound pole; it's a couple of pounds—strobe, battery, radio slave, and all! You're frustrating me, man!"

During cocktail hour, the barrage continued.

"Look, Dave, I don't know how the place you work for taught you to light, but you ain't getting it. Maybe they taught you wrong, maybe you're just a putz."

"I'm not a putz."

"Bullshit, I'm gonna teach you. I used to teach people in the old days. Kids who were bigger schmucks than you and they learned. He pointed out a man playing a large white piano. Say you want to light him, how would you hold the light…look at him…. The fuck you lookin' at? Look at me!"

The kid was very confused and upset now.

"To light the bottom of the picture, how would you hold the side light?" Sid asked him.

When the kid held the light at a different angle that was not Sid's idea, he told the kid he was incorrect, then knocked on the kid's forehead, as if to say, is anybody home? The knocking on the forehead was not gentle.

During the *hora* when the bride was lifted up in a chair, the kid did not hold the light high enough.

HIGHER! HIGHER! HOLD THAT FUCKIN' LIGHT HIGHER! Sid screamed on the crowded dance floor. SIX FEET! HOLD THE FUCKIN' LIGHT HIGHER, YOU'RE LIGHTING THE BRIDE'S ASS!"

Dave had never been screamed at like that by a photographer before, and he worked for one of Long Island's top studios.

"Always shoot candids with principals, the most important people of the bridal party," Sid gave Dave a quickie lesson. "If I just shoot anyone, they won't put any of those pictures in the album, so I could just take those proofs and wipe my ass with them."

Dave did not care if this old bastard made any money or not. During the dinner break, Dave got some sympathy from the band members.

"I never worked with this guy before, the man I work for loaned me to him."

"Who the old-timer?" a musician sympathized with him. "Yeah he's been hollering and breakin' your balls all day."

"I've worked with him before," another musician offered, "that guy is a prick, he gives everybody a hard time."

"I knew him from an ice cream store I used to work in," another band member piped up, "he used to come in and hassle us about orders, he was a perfectionist about his takeout ice cream. But, that was a long time ago, when he used to be a somebody in the business."

"LOOK AT HOW YOU'RE HOLDING THE FUCKIN' LIGHT," Sid yelled during a table shoot, "SHIT, HOLD IT LIKE THIS NEAR YOUR GROIN, YOU KNOW WHAT THAT IS? YOUR BALLS, HOLD THE POLE OVER THERE, UNFUCKIN' BELIEVABLE!"

The kid tried to correct it.

"FEATHER THE FUCKIN' LIGHT OUT AT THE LAST PERSON AT THE GODDAMN TABLE, I TOLD YOU; YOU'RE AGGRAVATING ME!"

"I suppose this will make me a better photographer someday," the kid muttered.

"Who gives a fuck what it makes you, I want my pictures to come out. Shit, I'm disappointed in you. I could have gotten myself a light man, you're a fuck up!"

There was a table with exotic coffees during dessert, as they stood by the bandstand. Sid walked over to get one, without asking his assistant if he wanted one, not that Dave expected that old prick to ask.

When they were finishing up, Sid did some hands and rings photographs. Once again, he found cause to yell.

"SHIT, NOW YOU'RE HOLDING THIS POLE LIKE A FUCKIN' GOLD BAR!"

At four-thirty, finally, thank God, the job was over.

They walked to Sid's Chevy. Dave carried Sid's case and the second light, Sid carried his Mamiya 645 on his bracket. Sid opened the trunk, placed the camera on the bracket in, and motioned for Dave to put in the case and second light. Dave noticed another Mamiya 645 body in a plastic bag. *Imagine*, he thought, *leaving a backup camera out in the car, a hell of a lot of good that would do him, this nut must be slipping.*

Sid placed the film in an orange envelop from the lab. Then he took off his bow-tie, put it in his jacket pocket, took off the jacket, folded it, and placed it in the trunk. Then he opened his old Crown Graphic case, took out a pen, and picked up a checkbook that was in the trunk.

"From a light man I usually don't get aggravation; well, I can't cheat you, I have to pay you. How do you spell your last name, David?"

"Kapovsky, K-A-P-O-V-S-K-Y."

"Sounds like a nice Jewish name," Sid remarked as he made out the check.

"Thanks," the kid replied as he took the check, "wait, fifty dollars?"

"Yes, fifty dollars," Sid answered.

"The place I work for pays me seventy-five, I'm sure they told you that. They pay the senior light people between a hundred and a hundred and twenty-five. Fifty dollars, come on."

"No, I pay fifty dollars, that's what you deserve anyway. Come to think of it, you deserve less, but I can't cheat you, I have to give you something, so it's fifty dollars."

The kid looked angry as he folded the check and put it in his tux pocket.

"Go," Sid pointed down the block to where the kid had parked his car.

"I'm sorry I yelled at you." Sid then extended his hand. Dave shook Sid's hand, paused for a moment, said, "Fuck you!" and punched Sid with a right cross hard across his right jaw. Sid fell against the rear of his car onto the grass, his glasses flying off.

Dizzy, Sid saw the kid walk off. He thought, a few years ago, he would have gone after him and killed him. Tomorrow, he would stop the check. Nah! He had to pay the kid, let it go.

Embarrassed, Sid picked himself up. Some guests leaving the wedding saw the event unfold. A young lady in a party dress handed Sid his glasses.

"Thank you," he said.

"Well, you did yell at the poor boy all day. You remind me of the man who shot my wedding, he was arrogant, obnoxious, and had a big mouth; I wanted to kick him."

"This is the guy who shot our wedding," her husband informed her, "he just doesn't have a beard anymore."

"OH!" the lady exclaimed, "Good!"

Sid got into his car, and put on his glasses. He used to wear his glasses only for shooting and distance, now he needed to wear them all the time. He had another pair at home with bifocals on the bottom half of the lenses. They were a pain in the ass for a photographer, because you can't shoot through the bifocals, so he had to take them off to look through the viewfinder.

The night before, he had videotaped a Bar Mitzvah in Brooklyn so he was tired, and he had to pack for his trip to Japan. too.

As he showered before going to bed, he swore he heard Norma telling him he got what he deserved today. He did not argue with her, maybe she was right.

The flight to Hawaii was uneventful. Sid had a few days of rest, relaxation, sunning, swimming, and Island foods and cocktails.

Then he photographed a wedding for friends of his relatives. He called the video company a few days before, and they agreed to lend him an assistant to hold his second light. He brought two cases on the plane, holding his monopod, which he used as his second light and as a walking stick.

The video company loaned him a pretty Island girl to assist. She looked like she could handle herself, so Sid was mindful to praise her often.

"So, you want to be a fashion photographer?" he asked Jeannie.

"I do this for money on the weekends, but I don't have the stamina for weddings and Bar Mitzvahs, we have those here too, you know."

"I know, Bette Midler probably had her Bat Mitzvah here."

"I enjoyed working with you, Sid. I was told you're alone."

"My wife passed away."

"Oh, I'm sorry. If you want, I can show you around Honolulu tomorrow."

"Thanks, I've been here before, been to all the islands, as a matter of fact. Besides, you're way too young for me; I'm a sixty-three year-old grandpa."

"You're not old, Sid, we can have a good time."

"Jeannie, you're gorgeous, but I'm too old for you."

"If you change your mind…"

"You'll be the first to know, here let me pay you." He handed her a hundred dollar bill folded over a fifty dollar bill.

"Wow!" Jeannie gasped, "Wow, I used to assist a still man, he paid fifty dollars. The boss of this video company pays fifty dollars. I guess you pay assistants better on Long Island where you're from."

"I'm from Brooklyn, I live on Long Island, and, yes, we pay better. Fifty dollars? My, my, my! If some cheapskate pays an assistant a paltry fifty dollars, he deserves a crack across the jaw."

"*Mahalo*, Sid, that means 'thank you' in Hawaiian."

"I know, *deñada*."

"But no date, Sid?"

"No date, Jeannie."

"You're sure?"

"Too old."

Jeannie and Sid hugged each other warmly and kissed each other on the cheek.

Sid waved as she left the hotel ballroom. *Too old*, he thought, *not to get laid, just too old to get laid by her.*

Sid finished his job. Before he went to bed, he looked at a wallet-size picture of Norma and wept.

The next morning, Sid visited the hotel men's shop. He wanted to buy some more casual shirts for Japan, even pick up a few more *Aloha* shirts. The Chinese salesman came over.

"I'm looking for some casual pullovers, maybe an Izod," Sid spoke loudly.

"I speak English, what part of Brooklyn ya from?"

"Midwood, near Kings Highway, why?" Sid asked.

"I know the accent; I'm from Flatbush myself, although I was born in Manhattan."

"Chinatown?"

"East Village."

"So, you're here now. I moved to Long Island a million years ago."

"I went back," the salesman went on, "Brooklyn isn't the same, Dubrow's is gone, the Avalon Theater is gone, although I hear Lundy's in coming back."

"They're gonna tear down Brighton Beach Baths, but Senior's is still there, so is Junior's and they both still make cheesecake," Sid informed the salesman.

"But, the goddamn parachute jump in Coney Island still stands."

"Well, listen," Sid shrugged, "a lot of things in Brooklyn still stand, yet. I'm not saying they're not covered with graffiti, but they stand."

Sid bought several pullover and button-down casual shirts, including three Izods. He also picked up some short and long sleeve Hawaiian Aloha shirts.

The flight for Japan was nice; Sid saw a movie with Geena Davis on the way.

Sid was glad to see his daughter, son-in-law, and three grandchildren, growing by the minute.

"My God, Pete! You got so tall, you're gonna be taller than me soon!" Sid exclaimed at the airport.

"Here in Japan, I'm taller than a lot of people," Peter told his grandfather.

"Dad, what happen to your face? Linda asked examining his right jaw. There was a faded welt. Someone hit you?"

"Nah, I was cleanimg out the garage. I've been thinking about selling the house, so I got rid of some junk, and I tripped over an old video dolly and fell, thump! Caught my face on a milk crate, I'm fine."

"Well, please, Dad, be more careful. Still smoking?"

"Not much."

"Daddy, damn it!"

"Don't damn your daddy," Sid shook his finger. "I'm doing the best I can, leave me alone."

Sid loved Japan. It was one of the most beautiful places he had ever been. He had been here before in Tokyo when he was in the Army during the Korean conflict in the fifties. Norma flew over to see him with other military spouses. He did not like traveling as a single; he wished that she was there with him. He loved to travel, but he liked traveling with her better.

Sid visited the factory where his cameras were made, then took a few tours with Peter. Mark was at work, Linda stayed home with Alec and Rebecca, who was now a beautiful, vibrant little girl. Sid felt like the Roslyn Russell character, Mrs. Jacoby in the movie *A Majority of One,* based on Gertrude Berg's play about a Jewish mother from Brooklyn, who goes to Japan with her daughter and son-in-law, who was, oddly enough, a foreign trade executive.

"How's Teddy Sanders?" Linda asked. Teddy Sanders was a photographer, who had a big studio in his home, near where Sid lived. He started out playing trombone with some big bands including Woody Herman and Jimmy Dorsey. Teddy had taken a video course from Sid, and then gave Sid stiff competition. Teddy Sanders also had a career as a professional golfer.

"Dead."

"What?"

"He retired, then he dropped dead."

"Oh, God."

"His wife had a breakdown, I thought she would have had one years ago from their retarded daughter."

"I couldn't stand her," Linda recalled, "I used to hide from her; her mother thought because both fathers were candid men, we should be best friends."

"I remember," Sid shook his head." She'd come to the house every day calling for you. Linduhh! Linduh! She'd say Linduhhh! Beh, beh, behhh!"

"I just couldn't be friends with a retarded girl so I avoided her."

"So did all the kids from the block. Oh, well, *zoy gaytes,* that's how it goes, by the grace of God go we."

Mark took Sid to a synagogue in Tokyo. Membership was American and European Jewish businesspeople and several Jews who lived in Japan permanently.

Long Island was reasonably priced in relationship to Japan. When Sid visited a photography studio, he found out the price of wedding photography and videography and general portraiture. Upon converting the Japanese yen to the American dollar, Sid saw how very high the prices were. Even more than some over-rated New York photography studios.

Sid inquired about cost of living in Japan, and he visited the management office in the building his daughter was subletting; the prices for condominiums and rentals rivaled New York City apartments. Membership for a country club could be as high as one hundred thousand dollars. The Japanese people could afford such luxury; American consumers were paying for it. In fact, members of Sid's photographic profession were largely responsible for the success of the Japanese businesspeople.

Strolling through the park one Sunday, Sid observed a photo session of a Japanese bridal party; the photographer seemed on the ball, the videographer hovered nearby. Later on, he sat at the bar in a large American hotel sipping a sake martini, when he noticed another large Japanese wedding going on in the ballroom. These people were more modern than the last couple he saw. Very Western oriented. Sid wandered over, and looked in through the open doors. He watched the photography and video crew work. The band played American hits. A fiftyish man in a black tuxedo, with a flower in his lapel, walked to where Sid was standing. He assumed he was either the father of the bride or groom.

"*Mazel tov!*" Sid smiled and bowed slightly.

"*Arrigato,*" the man said seeming to understand.

"Beautiful wedding, sir, very good photographer."

"Hai, velly good." The man pulled at the lapels of his jacket, "Botany Fife 100, velly nice."

"Very nice tux!" Sid agreed.

"American suits velly large," the man smiled.

"Not all suits," Sid pointed out.

"Ah so?"

"You see this guy bought a suit, but he wasn't happy with the fit," Sid said feeling the affect of two sake martinis as he continued. "He told the tailor, 'hey, this suit is just like the Grand Central Hotel in New York City.' So the tailor asks, 'Why is that?' The customer says, 'It has no ballroom!'"

"Bah ha, ha, ha!" the Japanese man laughed, "no ball-loom!" The man tugged at his crotch, "No ball-loom, velly funny."

"Please to come meet family," the man invited Sid. "Please to come meet *mishpachah!*" Obviously, this man associated with members of the Jewish faith. Sid wondered if he might be Jewish, but he certainly did not look it.

Sid was impressed with how well mannered the Japanese were. Where he lived, there were many arrogant Chinese people; he thought the Japanese were friendlier and more personable. His grandchildren's Japanese friends were very respectful; upon introduction, they bowed and addressed him as *Weitz sahn*. America was losing her manners. Granted, Sid was not part of the cafe society, he noticed the difference. He knew schoolteachers in his family, including his daughter-in-law Christine, read books on Japanese education and marveled at their advancements in the public school systems.

Sid bid his family a heartbreaking farewell and flew back to New York. He kept to himself for most of the flight, taking a taxi cab home.

He needed a few days to adjust to the time schedule. He spent a few days, passing proofs of the wedding he had shot before leaving, and sending the Hawaiian wedding proofs out to Honolulu.

Something was missing from Sid's life. He felt it as he went about his work. He picked up the piece of paper with Dinah Strassman's phone number written on it.

"Weitz, it's time for a date with a woman your age. You can't sit alone like this, it's time, old buddy."

He picked up the receiver, *this will be a real date* he thought as he dialed her number. She was not in so he left a message on her answering machine. This will not be merely a sympathy dinner, we'll have a date.

Chapter Fifty-One

It had been two days since Sid had phoned Dinah. She said, "When you hear the beep, you know what to do." He knew what to do, he left a message. It has been two days, he was starting to feel rejected.

All afternoon Sid sat at his desk doing busy work. He wanted Dinah to get him, not the machine. He left both his numbers, so he had both house and business phones on the desk. He had a funny message on his home answering machine, as well. "Hi, I'm not in right now, but if you'll leave your name and number with my electronic secretary, I'll get back to you shortly." Still, there was nothing like getting a live human being at the other end, so he waited.

The phone rang; they were the run of the mill asshole cheapskate price shoppers.

All day long Sid's business phone rang.

All day long it was not Dinah.

Unless you were about to retire, in business you have to speak very nicely to people. Sid was about to retire, so he sailed into all the cheapskate *goyim* and occasional Jewish price shopper. He discovered that he liked to occupy his time this way.

"We don't really want to spend a lot of money; in fact, we really didn't need a photographer at our wedding."

"Then why did you call one?"

"What do we get at your studio for a hundred and fifty dollars?"

"Hmmm, well for a hundred and fifty, you get a relative and Fotomat."

"Hello, we need a group portrait; we'd like to see something cheap."

"If you want to see something cheap, look in a mirror."

"I'm getting married, we don't want to spend a lot of money on pictures, ya know what I'm sayin'?"

"No."

"I mean we don't need a lot of pictures, we want something very cheap. Ya know what I mean?"

"No."

"We're paying for this ourselves and we think lots of pictures are redundant, we don't need a lot of pictures."

"I see, well thank you for calling."

"Hello, sir," a young boy's voice spoke, "do you shoot brides?"

"Yes, we do."

"Then you should be in jail!"

"Good one, kid!"

"Montclair, good afternoon."

"Hi, Sid?"

"Yes."

"Dinah, how are you?"

"Dinah, I'm alright," Sid lit up, "how are you, dear?"

"I'm fine, Sid. I'm sorry I couldn't call you back sooner, but I was busy with my bean counting and all. I'm glad you called."

"Well, I was visiting my son in Atlanta and my daughter in Japan. I had a couple of jobs to do before I left, so I was tied up myself. I thought I would ask you to dinner Saturday night. I don't have any jobs, and I really want to see you again."

"That would be fine, Sid. I'd love to; it would be great seeing you again."

They went out to dinner on Saturday night. Then, they went out for lunch, breakfast, brunch, and coffee. They enjoyed each other's company. Dinah thought Sid was fun to be around, he was very charming, entertaining, and she loved his gravelly sounding, Brooklyn accented voice.

Sid loved Dinah's kind gentle demeanor and sweet personality. He liked women who were the ying to his yang. His late wife, Norma, even his former partner Carl served as the ying to his yang. Dinah had the right ying, and Sid felt it was time in their relationship to show her his yang.

One evening, when they were alone in her house, he got to do just that. They were kissing passionately on Dinah's living room sofa. Sid moved his hands towards her chubby bosom, "Can I touch?" he asked. She nodded 'yes.' Shortly they were in her bedroom naked.

It had been a long time since Sid had engaged in lovemaking, not since before Norma's illness. After her death, he jerked off every once in a while. He was happy, there was some life left in the old dog. He could still get it up, and he could still shoot straight, even though it took him a little longer to reload.

Sid and Dinah fucked harder than people their age were expected to. They fucked again and again.

Sid took off the condom. His dick popped up again ready to go as he stroked Dinah's voluptuous lower abdomen.

"Can I cum on your tummy?" he asked.

"Yes," she whispered breathlessly.

He lay on top of her, his hard dick on her tummy. He masturbated while kissing her, until he ejaculated. His semen came out warm on her tummy, soon cooling off as the fluid ran down her sides. Her breathing slowed as he rolled off of her. Side by side they drifted off to sleep as one.

Sid spent more and more time at Dinah's house, in her bed. He realized he no longer needed his house. His children where living elsewhere, and for an old fart like him, the house was becoming too much of a burden to carry. So, he called a realtor and put the house up for sale.

Steven and Linda came over to retrieve the remainder of their belongings. They were happy Dad had found someone; they were not all that happy he was moving in with a woman who had three daughters of her own. He did not give a shit about their happiness; he was entitled to some happiness of his own. He moved his possessions and equipment over to her place. He hired a handyman to move his office furniture to her house. He set his office up in one of the daughter's former bedrooms. He answered his business phone and edited videotapes from there. Dinah had a huge den that was part of a finished basement. He met with clients there at a large round wooden table. Although the den was large enough to accommodate studio props, Sid did not do portrait work anymore.

Dinah had a beautiful split level house, but it was in need of refurbishing. He wanted to help her do that, now that he was living there. Her creep bastard ex-husband gave her nothing, nothing but heartache, that is. He was not even a factor in his daughters' lives, and they turned out quite well without him.

Dinah's house needed new siding, a new roof, and a new front door. Sid undertook that project as the new man of the house. The interior also needed a complete overhaul; the grand piano in the living room was the only feature that added class. The interior would be Dinah and Sid's next project after the exterior.

Dinah's three daughters took to Sid very well. To the girls, who were really young women, Sid became a father figure. He wished that he had known the girls when they were younger, as he had fallen in love with them. He would have liked to have been there for them when they were in their younger years. He did not share this thought with his two children, however.

Within two months, a young affluent Jewish couple with two small boys bought Sid's house. The real estate agent did a good job; after commission, Sid netted two hundred fifty thousand, five hundred dollars for the old homestead. He paid less than thirty thousand for it.

Sid enjoyed sleeping with a woman once again; he liked being part of a steady family unit. Between his new lady, her three daughters, his two children, and four grandchildren, he felt contented.

When Sid went to his video association's meeting, he bubbled about his lady friend to his former lighting assistant Jeffery Glassman.

"Jeffery, Jeffery! Fuck you, Jeffery!" Sid greeted his young friend in the lobby of a large hotel in Uniondale, Long Island, where the video association meetings were held.

Jeffery Glassman was so embarrassed by his mentor's greeting, he wanted to crawl into a hole and die. But, that was Sid.

"Hi, Sid, we had my grandfather's unveiling yesterday."

"You told me, I'm sorry I couldn't make it, *bubie*."

"The family is getting smaller, and we didn't even have ten people at the cemetery, so the rabbi couldn't recite the Kaddish."

"But he did El Moleh Rachamin," Sid responded.

"That's what he did."

"My lady friend is gonna be pissed at me because I didn't call to tell her I'd be busy tonight. So now, I'm gonna call her and tell her I'll take her out for ice cream tomorrow. See, Jeff, if a lady gets angry at you, take her out for ice cream."

"That always work, Sid?"

"Most of the time, if you didn't do something too terrible to piss her off. You can always try the old standby flowers and candy, but for me it was always ice cream."

"You're smooth, Sid," Jeff replied in awe of his old mentor.

I'll tell you something else, pussycat, women like it when men cook for them. Last night I made Dinah my special brisket."

"What is the recipe, Sid?"

Sid shrugged, "The secret is a can of beer and a half a cup of ketchup, and either a packet of instant onion soup or the can type. You see, young Jeffery, the way to a woman's heart is through her stomach."

"Just don't put too much onion soup into her stomach, or she'll fart in your face during coitus."

"Dinah would never fart in my face."

The video association had an interesting meeting—everything you wanted to know about editing, but were afraid to ask—or, as Jeff thought, *afraid to ask Sid, because he would call me a schmuck for not knowing something*. They talked during the break, Sid and Jeff really missed each other. At ten P.M., Sid excused him to call a client.

"I gotta call this bride, I'm doing a black wedding on Friday in Brooklyn, and I have to ask her something."

"Isn't it a little late to call a client, Sid?"

"Eh, I don't give a shit," Sid shrugged.

Driving home, Sid was happy that he got to see his young friend again, but he really wanted to put the business behind him and wind it down. He knew that he would have to dissolve his corporation to collect Social Security anyway.

That night after they finished their lovemaking, Dinah asked Sid if he remembered how they first met.

"You called at the studio to take pictures of your daughters, being neighbors, sometimes we'd chat on the street or in the shopping center or at *shul*."

"No, that isn't it."

"It isn't?" He lit a cigarette.

"Oh no, not in my bed you don't," she yanked the cigarette out of his mouth. You really don't remember?"

"No."

"You were shooting the wedding of our neighbors Irma and Fred Shransky's daughter Melanie, remember?"

"I remember I did their job, that's about it."

"Well, I was a guest, and you were shooting something when you said something mean to me."

"I said something mean to you?"

"I was wearing a very seductive dress; you came over and said something suggestive."

"What did I say?" he asked.

"Something really rotten," Dinah answered, squeezing Sid's testicles. You were very cute, though."

"Ayyiee! Don't squeeze the family jewels."

"Well, after your wife passed away, I took pity on a lonely old man, who was very attractive, so here we are. Besides, I love your voice."

"Well, whatever I said to you couldn't have been all that mean, because we've spent a lot of time together fucking our brains out."

Sid enjoyed sleeping with Dinah, so he bought her a ring; they were an item, that was for sure, and they started going away together. That was the part of retirement he loved, the vacations; sometimes he traveled to Boston and Atlanta to see the grandchildren without Dinah when she had to work. He boasted that he had a younger lady in his life that had a good job, so he could live comfortably, vacationing while she supported him.

The phone rang one cold winter afternoon and it was Jeffery Glassman.

"I'm fine, *bubie*, enjoying my retirement. My brother passed away, Seymour, the lawyer."

"I'm sorry, Sid, gee."

"I thank you. He had emergency heart surgery, and after they were through, while he was in intensive care he wasn't feeling well, so they opened him up again, but they saw nothing wrong. He passed away that night."

"I'm getting married, Sid, will you shoot it?"

"Is she Jewish?"

"Yes."

"Then I'll shoot it. I'll just do the video, but I'll see if I can get Gary Nagel to shoot the stills. This will be my last."

"For sure?"

"For sure and period, baby. I wanna get out; I put down the equipment, and haven't touched it, that's it. I shot this job upstate, but I'm too fuckin' old, so it wasn't that great. I need three days to rest up from a fuckin' job, so now I don't even dabble."

"So you want out?"

"I'm not doing any work, and I don't want to do anymore work. Somebody called for a portrait, I put them off. They asked for me, I disguised my voice, 'He's not here!' I say, fuck it! So, next week I'm going over to shoot and that's it! I just bought a new car."

"Another Chevy?"

"Fuck no, a Ford Taurus. I always drove a big car because of all the shit I had to carry, but I don't need a big car now. Fuck, I could get a convertible with two seats and no trunk. I was gonna get a car coming off a lease, but the price was not all that great. What with the daughter up in Boston, I figured I'd get a new car already, so I bought the Ford."

"You have another car, don't you?"

"Dinah has this small Honda. I've used it on jobs, I've driven it around, but it's not too big."

"So you're traveling, then."

"I'm going to Atlanta to see my son; I found this low-price, no frills airline."

"No frills?" Jeffery interjected, "Low price? They always go down, I'd be careful."

"They all stay up, unless the plane that you're on goes down."

"Well, if you save money…"

"Also, I get a good parking deal at Kennedy Airport. I leave the car, when I get it back, they wash it, and in the winter, they turn the heater on for me, so I get into a nice warm car."

"When am I going to see you, Sid, before the wedding, I mean?"

"The fuck knows. I got a fax machine, so fax me the information about your wedding. After I come back, I gotta drive to Boston to help my daughter move to San Francisco."

"Your cat will like it out there."

"That's right, my cat lives with them now. After Norma passed away, we decided we had enough of one another, so Plucky moved in with my daughter."

"You're a good father, Sid, to help her move."

"Well logistically it's a bad move, especially with all the packing involved."

"Well, Sid, packing and shit is always involved with a move," Jeffery answered.

"True, but this is really something. They wanted me to drive up to Boston, because the kids ask my advice about packing. Dad, what should we do with this? How should we pack that? I'm a good father."

"Yes, you are, Sid."

"I'm a good father. I told them to hire a kid to help you throw out what you don't want. Let him tie up the books my son-in-law doesn't need and take them to the curb. His office is upstairs, so we gotta run upstairs and downstairs to the basement. I'm too fuckin' old for that."

"You're a good father."

"I'm the best. Now my daughter has another problem. You see, fuckin' Boston is crazy."

"How?" Jeffery asked.

"Well, all the shit that has to be placed out at the fuckin' curb can't be picked up. They tell Linda, you can't put your special pick up garbage out on Thursday if your special pick up day is on Friday. She says, 'But we have to put the shit out because we're moving on Friday.' They tell her, 'So, we'll give you a ticket.' She says, 'Where ya gonna send it?'"

Jeffery laughed.

"Yeah," Sid continued, "see what I mean? She should have hired a dumpster to put all the shit into. So anyway, the man who bought the house is pissed, because he's moving in on Monday, and the truck won't be able to pull up to the curb."

"Well, Sid, I take it you enjoy retirement; it sounds like it agrees with you."

"Retirement is wonderful, that is, if you're amongst the retired folks who have the money to play with, so's you don't need a retirement job to make ends meet."

"I see."

"Yeah, Jeffery, my boy, which is why I want to talk to you."

"About what?"

"I'm getting out. I shot a job a couple of weeks ago, it was shitty. I'm too fuckin' old to run around."

"Shitty pictures from you, Sid? I don't fuckin' believe it," Jeffery sounded surprised.

"Nah, not shitty, but not my best. I'm not at the top of my game anymore. It takes me two days to recover from a job."

"So that's it then, boss."

"That's it. Come take all the video shit; I got camcorders, microphones, headphones, decks, monitors, tripods and dollies, camera lights, room lights, batteries cases, hand trucks, hardware, whatever you need, plus the editing system. Shit, I even have an old tube video camera from the early '80s. It's good for a surveillance camera in your toilet."

"Wow."

"Yeah, I put the shit down and never touched it again. You can pick it up, walk outta here, and shoot the job. Are you interested in stills, too?"

"What?"

"I got a bunch of Mamiya 645s with lenses, cassettes, and prisms. I also have the square format Mamiya C330s because my partner Carl liked them; they're all with complete gear. Also, I have the old 6x7 Koni-Omega Rangefinder cameras with lenses and backs, and I have a couple of my old Crown Graphics, two of which I converted to passport cameras, with image splitters on the lens."

"Everything is in working order?"

"What the hell kind of question is that?" Sid sounded hurt, "Of course, I take care of my stuff. I dunno, I always see guys who have to take their equipment in for repairs. They just toss it in their trunk. Some guys are prone to it, I guess, but my stuff works."

"I'm sorry, Sid."

"Don't be. Also, I have strobe units, radio slaves, photocell slaves for backup, tripods, different tripod heads, power winders, light stands, background stands, portable backgrounds, studio strobes, a mono-light, umbrellas, posing tables, posing stools, effects filters, and matte box sync cords; just pack it up and you're in business."

"Any 35 mm?"

"No, never really used it. I had some Nikon bodies and lenses that I sold years ago, to a fashion photographer, because he was looking to pay for it. Also, I got rid of the twelve hundred watt second studio strobes when I closed the studio. I also sold the large studio backgrounds and the prop furniture, the chairs, the benches, but I still have a baby poser, you can have that."

"Nice stuff."

"You bet your ass, *bubie*," Sid replied. "I also have an airbrush and retouching pencils and my oil paints for heavy oil portraits. You know, in the old days I did retouching, you had to in those days. Fuck, I did my own developing, proofing, and custom printing back then, too."

"No compressor for the air brush?"

"No, I sold that years ago. I think I have an old movieola for editing, and I have a few old floodlights from the old days, too. You can have my sample albums, videos, and what is left of my frames in the garage."

"You don't want anything?"

"I'm not doing anymore work, I don't wanna do anymore work. I just bought for a hundred bucks a point and shoot 35 mm camera, and for six hundred I picked up a small camcorder to shoot the grandchildren, that's it."

"How much do you want, Sid?"

"The fuck do I know? As much as I can get!"

"What's that?"

"For you, Jeff, a good price. I tell you when you come; don't worry, I ain't gonna screw ya."

When Jeffery visited Sid, Sid spent two hours bullshitting about his war stories, which Jeffery loved to hear; an hour showing him the still and video equipment; an hour taking apart his video editing equipment; then an hour helping Jeffery to load it into his mother's car. Sid had told Jeffery to borrow his mother's Oldsmobile station wagon.

After everything was loaded, Jeffery wanted to know how much.

"Hmmm," Sid closed one eye, "how much can I rob from you? Let's see, you can have all my equipment for twelve dollars."

"Really?" Jeffery asked in shock.

"ARE YOU NORMAL? How can I give it to you for twelve dollars? How can I? Give me thirteen dollars."

"Thirteen dollars?"

"One ten and three singles; reach into your pocket and take it out."

Jeffery handed the thirteen dollars to Sid, and he pocketed it with a courtly, "I thank you, sir. You may also have the prop bouquet for communion, the assorted prop prayer books, and the prop tails." There was a box of imprinted yarmulkes on the floor, which Sid had collected over his years of shooting. "I'll keep the skullcaps."

As Jeff was about to leave, Sid transferred the corporation over to him.

"With your teaching photography, all the stuff, and my corporation, you'll do well. You better remember I taught you!"

"I'll remember, now I'm a full service video and photographic organization."

"Yeah, right!" Sid exclaimed. "They're all going away; the old guys are selling due to old age. Why are the young fellows selling? All the young guys are becoming camera salesmen, photo lab sales reps, or sales reps for album binderies; the smart ones went into digital and electronic imaging. I wish young people starting out lotsa luck. You don't quit the day job."

"I won't, Sid."

"Good boy. Alright, you're a big candid man now, go, get out of here go build your studio."

After Jeffery pulled away from the curb, Sid said out loud, "Go work hard today for an unappreciative ball-breaking public and go break your ass."

Chapter Fifty-Two

Retirement was wonderful, for Sid Weitz, anyway. Dinah still worked for the accounting firm. They took trips back and forth to San Francisco and Atlanta to see his children and grandchildren. Sid's youngest grandchildren were told by their parents to call Grandpa's 'lady friend' Dinah, not Gramma, as Sid requested. This time Sid and Dinah represented themselves to both their families as common-law husband and wife. Both families accepted this, but his children did not want Dinah addressed as 'Gramma.' Norma was their grandmother.

That summer, they took a flight to England, then a cruise along the French and Italian Riviera. Sid could afford himself that luxury, what the hell, he was not a candid man anymore. He and Norma took vacations in the summer, but business weighed on his mind. It was refreshing to just have the events of the trip on his mind.

Sid had quit smoking cigarettes altogether, he wanted to be around, life was good.

Life was good up until Sid went for his annual physical examination in January and was diagnosed with lung cancer. Now life was not so good. In fact, now life was a question mark.

Jeffery Glassman felt guilty, he had not called his mentor in two months, as he was doing well teaching photography and shooting affairs. He wanted Sid to know all was well.

Sid did not sound like all was well.

"Hello ho ho," Sid sound as if he had just been woken up.

"Sid, did I wake you?"

"No oh, oh, I was just doin' some work hererrr," he sounded asleep and terrible. Jeff knew it was not unusual for a retiree to snooze during the day, but not Sid. He said good morning to Jeff, which caused Jeff to think he had just got up. He was concerned.

"How are you, Sid?"

"Fine, listen, I gotta go make some deposits, I'll call you back."

Jeffery was not convinced that Sid was alright. He called Sid two weeks later when Sid did not return his call.

"I ended up in the doctor's office Jeff, but now I'm fine." He sounded strong. "I'm coming off chemo."

"What the hell happened to you?"

"Well that's when I kept putting you off, I well…"

"What the fuck did you do to yourself?" Jeffery asked, fearing the worst.

"Small cell carcinoma in the right lung," Sid said matter-of-factly.

"Shit," Jeffery's worst fear was realized.

"Well, it isn't operable, but the chemo can slow it down, for how long and whether it comes back, this they cannot tell you."

"Gee, Sid, I'm sorry to bother you."

"No, no, no, I'm glad you called. I need to take my mind off of things. I'm glad I gave you all my stuff 'cause I'm not gonna need it."

"Sid, don't talk like that. The only reason you don't need your stuff is because you're retired."

"Well, anyway, I go back on chemo Monday, so we'll see. So far, it hasn't spread."

It went this way for months; Sid endured chemotherapy and radiation treatments. The only consolation was his children and grandchildren, a new woman in his life, and her three daughters. This would not change the outcome, but at least he did not have to suffer by himself.

Steven and Linda were strong for their father. Steven, a doctor, did not kid himself, he knew lung cancer had a one in twenty recovery rate, but he tried not to dwell on that. His father did not dwell on that either.

"Dad, are you taking care of yourself?" Linda called everyday to ask Sid.

"Don't worry, I have good days and bad days, but I try to stay upbeat, and I'm hanging in there."

"Please, let me come up and help you, Daddy."

"Linda, I'm not an invalid; the chemo is shrinking the tumor, it isn't like it's inoperable, and goodbye."

"I'd like to come up."

"You take care of your family; don't make me sicker than I am."

"Well, you take it easy."

"I will, honey, and in between chemo sessions I can come out." Sid was able to attend his grandson Peter's Bar Mitzvah. He made a terrible pain in the ass of himself, supervising the photography and video crew. Members of the family were shocked at Sid's weight loss and thinning white hair. Even the lenses of the eyeglasses he now wore all the time, looked thicker.

Sid arranged for Jeffery Glassman to come see him in the spring; he wanted to see the kid again.

"I'll try to be good looking for you, Jeff, but I lost a lot of weight. My hair was falling out, so I shaved my head, and now I look like Kojak. Funny thing is, when Telly Savalas went through treatments for the prostate cancer that killed him, he probably looked normal," Sid chuckled.

"I'll bring you some Tootsie Roll lollipops."

Jeff kissed Dinah, and shook hands with Sid. Sid wore beige shorts and a white tee shirt. Yes, he was now totally bald and very thin, although not gaunt. This man was sick, but he was not an invalid, not yet.

Jeffery was ushered downstairs into the large family room. The first thing that caught Jeffery's attention was Sid's stereo unit. On a large shelved wall unit, sat a turntable, hooked up to an AM/FM radio console, with a cassette deck. A CD player was also hooked up to the speakers. There was a separate eight-track unit on another shelf, next to a large reel to reel tape recorder.

"Don't let anyone shit you," Sid spoke, "these eight-track players were great. Here, did I ever show you my reel to reel machine? I don't think I ever did."

Sid pressed his remote switch and turned on his cassette player. A *hora* started to play loudly. He gestured to the cabinets next to the wall unit, full of cassettes, vinyl records, reels of tapes, and eight-track cassettes.

"Quite a collection, eh?" Sid smiled. Upstairs I have an old four-track cassette player and an old mono record player. I used to have the speakers wired throughout my old house, remember? I had a speaker out back by the pool."

"I remember," Jeffery said.

"Years ago, I wanted to wire the studio for sound, so my partner Carl and I went to this appliance store to get a stereo. I needed a new one for the house, too. So this goddamned salesman comes over, tells me the unit I want is no good, and he tries to sell me a piece of shit. Now I know that fuckin' unit is tops, okay? So I tell him, I need to buy two of these, one for my place of business and one for my house. The salesman says, 'I can see you're very discerning, I'll go get my order book.'"

Sid turned off the music, and took the cassette out of the deck.

"You like spirituals, Jeff?" He flipped over the cassette, "See, I got Jews on one side and niggers on the other."

"Oooh, Sidney!" Dinah called out from upstairs.

"I'll play this," Sid turned on the unit again, it was hard rock. "I like rock, I love jazz, jazz rock fusion, rhythm and blues. I'm not really into that dentist office shit I used to play in the studio."

Sid and Jeffery sat down at a round wooden table together.

"Hairpiece tape?" Jeffery picked up the box.

"Well, I use it when I'm invited to an affair; it keeps the yarmulke on my bald head. I'm just a guest at these fuckin' parties now, son. I don't shoot anymore. I don't even take a picture anymore. Last week I went to Atlanta, I took my point and shoot autofocus, 35 mm camera with me. I took pictures of the grandchildren, they came out looking like shit."

"Aw, come on, Sid."

"*Emmis!* I loved photography, now I don't even dabble."

"How did the Bar Mitzvah go?" Jeffery asked.

"The whole day was beautiful. Harry Lowenstein didn't shoot it for me. Harry and I used to be close, but he couldn't make it to my wife's funeral, so fuck him."

"Who did you use?"

"I used this old candid man, Barney Godell; he used to shoot for me all the time. My daughter got this video man up in Boston. I told you they had the Bar Mitzvah in Boston, not in San Francisco. Now Barney is pissed at me, because they stole Barney's equipment out of the hotel ballroom where we had the reception. He cursed me," Sid laughed, "so I gave him one old Mamiya 645 body I kept for myself, just in case. That shut him up for about five seconds. He says it's my fault his equipment was stolen," Sid laughed again.

Jeffery saw Sid later that year in December. It was right after Christmas, and Sid and Dinah had just married.

"I'm sorry I didn't tell you," Sid apologized to Jeffery. "We got married at six in the morning in a rabbi's study. The rabbi was Orthodox, he wanted a *minyan*. It was just us and the kids. I've been living with her for a few years now; I figured it was time to make an honest woman out of her."

Sid's hair was thin and darker; his beard was growing in, too. He looked thin, but not gaunt; he also looked at peace with himself.

Dinah's daughter had just gotten married down in Florida, and she found a studio in Fort Lauderdale that offered both video and stills. Dinah spoke to someone there, she had mentioned to the receptionist, her husband was Sid Weitz, owner of Montclair Studios, but she did not know him. Within five minutes, the kitchen phone rang; the studio owner, Tony Montaforti, was calling to tell Dinah he knew her husband when he lived on Long island as a kid, and that he had shot for her husband when he was just starting out.

"But how are you?" Jeffery asked.

"I'm fine, baby, not getting radiation anymore, but still on chemo with a lot of fuckin' needles."

"Veins still good?"

"Nah," Sid shook his head, "they inserted ports in my chest; my veins are shrinking with the rest of me, and they don't want the veins to collapse. I have to tell you this, cancer is a disease that tires you out. Hair loss, then I'm constipated, if not constipated, I have diarrhea. If you get diarrhea, they tell you at the oncologist, you can't do it here. Look, look, these ain't my real teeth. I was having problems with my teeth due to age, but the chemo kills your teeth. So they pulled my teeth, and now I wear dentures."

"But you're making progress, Sid."

"I know the reality of lung cancer, Jeff, I try to stay upbeat. I'm still here."

"You're not going anywhere, Sid. How are your treatments coming along?"

"Well, they started me on a new chemotherapy, and supposedly this chemo has no major side effects, it's easier to endure. The sheet they gave me read,

'If you experience dizziness, nose bleeds, insomnia, chest pains, nausea, constipation, or diarrhea, call the office at once.' So I ask, 'What is the side effect? Is my dick going to fall off?'"

Jeffery laughed at Sid's irreverence.

"Jeff, you know how it is with doctors…God bless my son, may he only make millions. Doctors, well, eh, what can I say? I went to the oncologist after my radiation treatments. I told him my throat was sore, and it was hard to swallow. He felt my neck." Sid reached over and felt Jeffery's neck. "Hmmm," the doctor said, "yes, it's sore."

"Enough illness, Sid, tell me, how did your stepdaughter's wedding pictures come out?"

"Everything was beautiful."

"You said the photographer knew you in New York?"

"Yeah, Tony something or other."

"I assume he didn't use a 645."

"No, he used a square negative. He shot with a Bronica."

"Satisfied?"

"Yes, but some things could have been better. It's not easy to be in this trade today. You see, Jeff, today, people take your proofs to a place that has a color copier, bam! They copy 'em, and piss away the profits for you!"

"There is a copyright on my proof, which is supposed to be honored."

"So what? You can't prevent copying? I know some of the new photographic papers have anti-copy technology. So what? Big shit! Someone will find a way around that, too!"

"Yep, you can scan everything on a computer; it rivals a photo studio's work."

"You know unfortunately, Jeff, the business today, you really can't count on additional orders making up a vast part of your business. I don't imagine that people are adding much to their order. People aren't gonna take a fifty picture book and make it ninety. A studio wants twenty-five dollars in eight by tens, or in that category, people say, 'I'm not gonna spend seven hundred dollars to add pictures. I'm not gonna put pictures in my album if I got the proofs.'"

"Absolutely right, Sid," Jeffery agreed.

"And you know, look," Sid went on, "I'm a customer today. You know, I'm not the seller. My stepdaughter just got married; I don't remember what the price was, it was about twenty-six hundred dollars, the video was thirteen hundred dollars. The boss did me a favor, he lowered his prices a little bit for me, I said, 'Fine, thank you very much, I do appreciate it.' So, I believe her album has fifty in it, ours has thirty-six. When she came up to visit us, she brought the proofs with her, she had them out about two months, but we hadn't seen them. The truth of the matter is, they came out beautiful, but there was a lot of redundancy. They had four hundred and fifty pictures, but they didn't have four hundred and fifty poses. He took every picture two or three times. If you do that, you end up with the same hundred and seventy-five pictures."

"I don't repeat pictures with same poses unless I'm sure that somebody blinked, flinched or whatever," Jeffery replied, "the way you taught me."

"So, in any event, she asks, how should we pick them out? We like, we like, we like, I says, very simple, you bring 'em here. 'I don't know if we can leave them here a few weeks for you to pick 'em out,' she says. I says, 'We can pick 'em out in ten minutes.' I lied, it took twenty. You just divide them into groups—portraits, ceremony, reception, you got pictures of the bride, and you got six. Put six pictures down, pick the two that you like, pick four that you like. After you finish picking count 'em up. You got fifty-six, you don't want to buy twenty more, it's easier to delete twenty. But, thirty-six pictures are more than enough for us. There were some additions; her sister wanted to order pictures, so they ordered pictures not knowing how much they're gonna cost. He wanted, I believe it was, fifteen dollars a 5x7, twelve dollars under that, and uh, twenty-three dollars for an 8x10. So her sister says, just a minute, that comes to a hundred and ninety dollars. I says fine, you don't need it, take the proofs from your sister, and then you go through the same bit. The bride says, 'They're my proofs!' What? You don't have enough pictures with the four hundred for the album, you can't give any to your sister?"

"That's right."

"And that thirteen hundred dollars for that videotape, was for three videotapes. They sent us out a tape, we looked at it one time, fast forwarded it, posted it, and that was it! Could the job have been better? Absolutely! Do I know what I'm talking about? Absolutely! Could the stills have been better? Absolutely!"

"Of course, you know what you're talking about! Fifty years experience!"

"But, the kids liked them, they liked him, his parents thought they were nice, that's the end of the story, what am I gonna do? I'm gonna point out what could have been better? Ya gotta be an idiot!"

"You didn't!" Jeffery said in mock astonishment.

"No, sir! No reason to do it. Look, his folks have a restaurant, am I gonna come there for dinner and say, 'Oh, I've eaten better food than this? You didn't cook it properly! You should have put more ketchup in!' Not nice! So, it was the same thing with the pictures. If they came out badly, if they say shit! Not good! We were disappointed! But they're saying they liked them. And the truth, really, is that they came out fine. For the portraits, he hung a background and they were multi-lit, you could pick out the portraits where the kids look good. A lot of the reception was single light, his light man disappeared."

"For the most part, studios in Florida are not too big on double lighting," Jeffery said.

"Unless you come from New York." Sid added, "I say New York, then you're interested in that type of an affair, and the coverage you're familiar with. If you live in Florida, and you're not exposed to anything, single light is fine. But, if your folks just moved down from New York, then they're exposed to everything up here. When they get used to going to dinner at three o'clock in the afternoon, they become Floridians. 'Oh, we'll make early bird, yeah; oh, what am I gonna do until eight o'clock at night?' Go to sleep." Sid laughed, "Shit, Jeff, I like an active retirement."

Sid coughed uncontrollably, which was disturbing to Jeffery, but he soon stopped and caught his breath.

"All these things that I said, the photography business today, is not a great business, Jeff."

"Oh, you're telling me!"

"You run big numbers, you think you're doing great, you got a twenty-six hundred job...you're not making that much money on twenty-six hundred dollars. I talked to my friend Heshy the other day; he was telling me the prices candid men get today. No more two hundred dollar candid men, now they want five hundred! They come in with backgrounds and room lights, and they're schlepping a lot of shit around, so they want to get paid for it. You may find a two hundred dollar candid man, but they're the ones who desperately need the work."

The visit came to an end. Jeffery wanted to see Sid again, but he did not know when that would be. He had a busy schedule teaching and shooting. Sid had a busy schedule, with chemotherapy treatments and visiting his grandchildren.

Sid was not an invalid, Jeffery wanted Sid to beat the cancer, or at least have a long remission. But Sid was upbeat, so Jeffery tried to be.

Chapter Fifty-Three

Jeffery and Sid spoke by phone during that year. At the end of May, Sid told Jeffery he was going to start a new aggressive chemotherapy. He told Jeffery the tumors had shrunk for a while, then it was status quo.

"I did a Bar Mitzvah for your former clients, Carol and Keith Smollen. Remember them?"

"The name sounds very familiar," Sid sounded hoarse and weak from his new chemotherapy treatments.

"You knew his parents from your town," Jeffery continued, "you shot their wedding the night before Thanksgiving at a hall up in Woodbury. You did the video, Sal did the stills."

"Sal Esposito!" Sid remembered.

"She said it was an early video job for your studio."

"I remember Carol, she was a big horse! It took five men to lift her up in the chair for the *hora*. Is she still heavy?"

"Fatter than ever! She had four kids."

"No shit!" Sid laughed, "I'm very happy you're doing well with my business name." He coughed; his coughing had a "REH REH RRREEHHH" sound

"I shot that job with my old Newvicon tube video camera; shit, we had so many fuckin' video cameras over the years."

"Yes, Sid, it was always changing."

"It's an expensive industry. That was for sure, this was an expensive industry, not just the capital equipment, but the cost of doing business, the cost of surviving."

"I'm gonna go eat, Jeff. I'm glad you called, you always get me in."

"It's the old George Burns joke, Sid."

"What old George Burns joke, Jeff?"

"He said, 'Bob Hope calls my house once a month, if I answer, he knows I'm still around.'"

"Hah!" Sid laughed, "Well, I'm still around, and he's not! I'll speak to you shortly, Jeff, be well."

"You too, Sid, take care."

Six weeks later in mid-July, Jeffery picked up the phone in the small Long Beach, Long Island apartment he shared with his wife.

"Hello, Jeffery, please." It was a young woman's voice, it sounded familiar.

"Speaking."

"Jeffery, I tried to reach you at your studio, but you had already left, so I thought I'd try you at home instead of leaving a message."

Jeffery wondered who this could be, as his clients did not have his home telephone number.

"Jeffery, this is Linda Sossin, Sid's daughter, remember me?"

"Yes, I do, Linda, how are you?" Uh, oh! A voice in Jeffery's head said something is wrong. "Is anything wrong?"

"Jeffery, my father, er uh, Sid passed away this afternoon."

"Oh, God! I'm so sorry. I wish I had called him, I spoke to him a few weeks ago."

"If you had called him, he wouldn't have known who you were. He was very bad toward the end. The funeral is Friday morning at ten, at Shapiro's on Broadway in Hewlett. Burial is in Elmont."

"I'll, er, we'll be there."

It was a hot humid morning, not an ideal day for outdoor picture taking, worse for a funeral. Shapiro's funeral chapel was not overly crowded. Nobody from the industry was there. Sid's oldest friend in the photography business, Heshy Adomovich was there with his wife, and former baby photography partner Lenny Schecter was there with his wife, Sherry. Old candid men Barney Godell, Freddie Chertoff, Sal Eposito, and Mel Lander were there. Barney, Freddie, and Sal shot for Sid years ago; they still shot, but were not as active. Mel Lander was once a partner in a North Shore Studio. In later years, he shot stills and video for Sid. He sometimes filled in as a light man, when needed. Jeffery remembered a video association meeting, after Mel became a grandfather; it was right after Mel had a hernia operation. "Mel," Jeffery remembered Sid warmly congratulating Mel, "*Mazel tov* on your granddaughter and *Mazel tov* on your balls!"

But, more candid men should have been there. Jeffery and Heshy both mentioned that to Dinah, before the start of the service.

"A lot of people in the trade liked him," Jeffery told her.

"Yeah, well, a lot of people didn't like him," Dinah said, drying her eyes. This was true, Jeffery recalled long ago a former association president who was a top photographic craftsman, admonished Jeffery, "He is not to be emulated!"

It is funny how you remember so many things about a person, when a person dies. Jeffery recalled the man who had admonished him, had also told a story about a group trip to Italy that Sid was on. Sid's friend (also deceased) Vito D'Andrea, who was born in Italy, told the waiter in Italian to give Sid the group's dinner check. He told Jeffery Sid turned red, boy was he angry!

Linda told Jeffery, along with a talis and shroud, Sid was wearing a new two-piece black suit he bought when he lost weight. He also had his wallet with some cash, an inexpensive wristwatch, and one of his 'lucky' costume jewelry rings. They wanted their dad to be accessorized. Linda told him he had socks and shoes on. He was given his black overcoat and a black Cavanagh snap brim fedora. Sid liked to look good when he dressed. Jeffery told Steven he could not recall Sid wearing a fedora. Steven had told him that Sid had not worn one since the '60s, when all the men on the block wore them to work.

Jeffery went into the chapel. Sid's casket was on the trestle table. It was so final. When you see a closed casket in a funeral chapel, you are aware of the sense of finality. The person is inside, the lid is closed, that's it, that's all there is.

The casket was a dark wooden box with a Star of David on the lid. Jeffery touched the casket solemnly. It was cold. He heard a voice call out from the casket, "Jeffery! Jeffery! Fuck you, Jeffery!" Jeffery patted the lid and sat down in the pew.

Sid's grandchildren were there. Did the younger ones really understand what was going on? Members of Sid's first wife, Norma's family were there, too. Sid's ninety-three year-old mother was escorted into the chapel by her son Saul, a retired commercial photographer, and daughter Helen. This was the second son the elder Mrs. Weitz lost.

The service was the standard Jewish funeral service. Rabbi Jordan Lasher eulogized Sid as a man of the community, whatever the hell that meant. Sid could not stand the man; he thought he talked too much.

After the prayers and the information about *shiva*, the rabbi concluded by saying, "Life, especially Jewish life is an ongoing learning process, because we believe in the sweet fruit from the tree of knowledge. Our friend Sid Weitz graduates today with full honors, from the university of life, all too soon at the age of sixty-nine."

Heshy Adomovich leaned over to tell Jeffery that it was arranged for Sid's Jewish friends to wheel the casket to the hearse at the end of the ceremony.

"Will everyone please rise and remain standing until the oron has passed," requested the rabbi. Jeffery, Heshy, and Sid's other friends pushed the trestle over to the rear door of the chapel. A shiny new black Cadillac hearse was backed up to the door, its rear door open. They slid Sid in, the driver secured the casket, and Heshy closed the door.

There was another almost identical hearse parked next to Sid's, which was loaded and waiting. That hearse had black windows in the back, which obstructed the public's view of the dearly departed. Sid's hearse had clear windows with curtains, which afforded everyone a view of the casket bouncing on its way to the cemetery.

"He was a good man, he was a nice man," one man who knew Sid said to another man, as they walked across the parking lot to their car. "But to tell you the truth, now that he's gone, he was garbage."

"You ain't kidding," the other man said. "Sid was for Sid, he worried only about himself. Shit, I'm surprised he didn't get divorced by the second wife."

"The second one?" the first man replied, "I'm surprised the first one, may she rest in peace, stayed with him."

Jeffery thought a funeral is the time to acknowledge your true feelings for a person. It is too bad a eulogy cannot be the real truth about the departed.

The procession got off the parkway on the way to the cemetery; they passed by the processing lab Sid had used for most of his career. Then, they stopped at the site of his former studio. Sid had spent about a third of his adult life there.

Sid was laid to rest next to his first wife, Norma. Jeffery was amazed at the size of the Weitz family plot. To think Sid was now lying among family members he could not stand. Linda told some people that her mother's family had a plot across the road. She said loudly enough for Dinah to hear, that she was happy her parents were together again. Dinah wondered who she was going to be buried next to. She thought maybe after she would ask if she could be on the other side of Sid, or somewhere near him.

Sid's relative's placed stones on relative's monuments. Some went, "Hock ptu," and spit on Sid's father's grave. A charming man his father was.

"The worms," Sid's mother said, "the worms, my husband should only lay with the worms." She then looked at Seymour's grave, then at Sid's casket, "Oh, my two good boys, both my poor darlings."

After Sid was lowered into the ground, everyone took a turn shoveling dirt onto his casket. Jeffery wondered how many people who told Sid in Yiddish, "*Gay en draid*," which means 'go into the dirt' would have liked to have been there.

"Sidney Weitz is returning to the earth," the Rabbi said, "ashes to ashes, dust to dust."

"Kiss my ass and make it bust," Barney Godell muttered. His wife elbowed him in the ribs.

"A cemetery in the Jewish faith," the rabbi continued, "is called the house of life; we believe the soul is eternal. Here our loved ones will live on forever in our hearts as it says on Norma's monument."

Everyone took a moment of reflection.

"You have photocopy sheets of the Mourner's Kaddish, for those who would like to read along; it is both in Hebrew and transliterated in English, and there is also an English text on the sheet."

Kaddish was said and the remains of Sid Weitz were committed to the earth.

"Well, that's the end of Grandpa," Sid's youngest grandson Gary, his son's son, called out jovially as he turned from the gravesite.

"What?" Christy asked her little boy, "Are you happy about it?"

"No," the little boy answered his mother.

"Why did they have to put Grandpa Sid in a box?" his sister Angela cried.

"Cause they couldn't fit him in an envelope!" Lenny Schecter answered her.

"What my husband means, dear," Sherry cut him off, "is that is how we send somebody we love up to heaven and to God in a special crate. It's sort of like a UPS delivery to paradise."

Back at the house Dinah cried, it was a sad day. She told friends that their project for the summer was to refinish their floors; Sid planned to be around for awhile.

"We thought we were going to grow old together," she told Jeffery.

"I'm sorry I didn't call him; last time we spoke he was holding his own."

"Jeffery, don't feel guilty, he was fine until two weeks ago when it spread to his brain," she sobbed.

Heshy told Jeffery, "She called me, Dinah said, 'If you want to see him, come and see him.' But I had so many things, my daughter and her kids were coming in from Israel. The truth is, I'm seventy years old, who knows how long I have left, and I didn't really want to see him."

Jeffery was shocked to see what a whiner Dinah was. Linda told her that she had just spoken to Sid's former partner Carl and his wife, Cynthia, out in Arizona. They knew Sid was sick.

"They didn't talk to me," Dinah complained bitterly, "I know Carl was great as a photographer and I know Carl and Sid didn't talk, but they could have spoken to me!"

"They were very sorry," Linda said.

"Well, I don't think Carl is too nice! Even your father's friend Louie came up from Boca Raton for the funeral, and he's been retired from photography how long? Carl should have talked to me!"

"Yeah, well they didn't," Linda retorted.

Jeffery wanted to leave; he extended his condolences once again. Dinah walked him to the door.

"Will his mother be alright?" Jeffery asked concerned. "It's her second boy."

"Sid's mother is ninety-three and she's in better shape than you!" Dinah said, "Don't worry about her, *cock a mun!*"

"I'll miss him, Dinah."

"Yeah, he was a good guy; I loved his voice."

"He was an original."

"I liked him," she said.

"He loved you dearly, Dinah." They stood together in the doorway and sighed.

"Do you use double-sided tape in your yarmulkes?" she asked Jeffery as she looked at the table by the front door that had some skull caps from the funeral on it.

"No, it would get my hair sticky, I use a bobby pin; why do you ask?"

"When Sid lost his hair after those chemo and radiation treatments, that was what he did when we went to affairs. He'd use double sided tape to keep the yarmulke on his little bald head," she sobbed.

Jeffery stifled a laugh; his bald head wasn't so little,

"I met him at a wedding, Jeff. I knew him as a neighbor, but he was shooting a friend's wedding, and he came over and said something mean to me."

"You must have annoyed him, did you get in his way?"

"No, Jeff, I was wearing a seductive dress and Sid said something, well it was suggestive, to me. The *chutzpah* of the man!"

"So you pursued him."

"No, Jeff, he was married to Norma at the time; I pursued him after she passed away. She was stunning, but I loved him and I guess he was attracted to me."

"You made him happy once again, Dinah."

"And he me, I wonder who he's shooting up in heaven now? You know, Jeff, the women at affairs Sid shot, thought he was a very sexy man. Really, Jeff, don't laugh, he was!"

"I'm going to miss his voice," Jeff said.

"Oh, I will, too. I kept a tape of him, his mother took one of our tapes from the answering machine, I really loved his voice!" she cried again.

They said goodbye and Jeffery started toward his car.

That was the end of a legend, but will Sid Weitz be remembered? Many of his past brides, Bar Mitzvah boys, and portrait subjects will not remember him. Some might remember the obnoxious guy who shot their wedding, but they'll concentrate on those dear to them in front of the camera, instead of thinking about the man behind the camera. Jeffery saw a wedding video when a beautiful young brunette took the microphone during a table interview, and made a loud kiss into the mic, "MMWWAAHH, Hello Siiid! I love you!" That certainly helps to close a sale if that is a demo tape. If you met Sid at some time or another in your life, you would remember him...you may not have liked him, but you would remember him.

The truth is there were photographers before Sid Weitz, there will be photographers after Sid Weitz. People get married whether you're their photographer or not. Life goes on with or without you. People marry, boys get bar mitzvahed, people graduate, husbands murder wives, people commit suicide, and photographers die. They don't merely fade away, old photographers get cancer and die.

Sid's son asked Jeffery if his father ever mentioned blue mirrors to him. He told Jeffery, when his father was a young in-home baby photographer, he brought blue mirrors along when he worked up in the Bronx and did not explain why. Jeffery did not know either. Now they would never know.

As Jeffery was about to enter his car, a man walked past, heading for the house to pay a *shiva* call.

"I liked him, young man, I liked Sid. I used to play cards with him, he was my friend. I had a store near his years ago. He was a beautiful man! The cancer was terrible, he should not have had to go like that. I feel so terrible for him. I feel bad about anybody who is sick like that!"

Jeffery remembered something, old master photographer Abe Susskind once said, "I feel *rachmunis* for everyone, but, I only worry about my own."